Of Power and Pain

A Detectives Daniels and Remalla Mystery Thriller

J. T. Bishop

Eudoran Press LLC

Eudoran Press LLC

6009 W. Parker Rd. Su. 149-193

Dallas, TX 75093

www.jtbishopauthor.com

Publisher's Note: This is a work of fiction. Names, characters, places, and incidents are a product of the author's imagination. Locales and public names are sometimes used for atmospheric purposes. Any resemblance to actual people, living or dead, or to businesses, companies, events, institutions, or locales is completely coincidental.

Author Photos by Nick Bishop and Mayza Clark Photography

Book Editing by P. Creeden and G. Enstam, C. Marquis and C. McGuire.

Cover Design by J.T. Bishop

Of Power and Pain/ J.T. Bishop -- 1st ed.

ISBN 978-1-955370-18-9

Dedication

To my remarkable niece, Alex. You're a tough chica and an amazing woman. You're brave, smart, compassionate, and fearless. I hope you know how rare that is and how special you are. I'm blessed to be your aunt.

Other Books by J. T. Bishop

Of Breath and Blood
Of Body and Bone
Of Mind and Madness
Of Power and Pain
Of Love and Loss

The Redstone Chronicles

Lost Souls
Lost Dreams
Lost Chances
Lost Hope

Chapter One

Oswald Fry slowly lowered the woman's limp body to the floor. Moving carefully, he supported her head and gently laid it against the tile of the kitchen then smoothed her hair and clothes and straightened her limbs. When he was done, he thought she looked like a sleeping doll, much like the one he'd seen in the window of a toy store he'd walked past a few days earlier.

Smiling at his efforts, he looked around, content that nothing seemed out of place. Although she'd fought him, he'd worn adequate clothing and gloves, so he had no scratches or bruises on his skin. Everything had gone just as he'd expected. Recalling his lack of academic and social skills from his youth, he was happy to note that he could do something well. It gave him a small sense of pride. In his mind's eye, he gave a middle finger to his old schoolteachers. He doubted any of them could have done what he'd just accomplished.

Feeling energized, he took a moment to walk through the house, noting the family photos, the minimal furniture, the strange art on the walls, and the small room where the woman saw her clients. Pleased, he returned to the kitchen and sat on the floor beside his victim and closed his eyes. He sensed the energy of her and felt it mingle with his own. The moment she'd left, he'd felt her spirit join his, and it had been so gratifying. Breathing deeply, he absorbed the essence of her, and when he felt fulfillment, he opened his eyes, and knew it was time to leave. Although he wanted to stay, he had to go before her lack of life force began to deplete his own, and he couldn't risk that.

He stood, took a last look around, then reached into his pocket and with his gloved hands, pulled out a black marker. After uncapping it, he squatted beside the woman and drew the symbol on her upper arm. Satisfied with the result, he stood and set the marker down on the counter. Then he took a plastic bag from another pocket, opened it, and removed a blank piece of white paper. He set it on the kitchen counter, took out the black bow tie and rested it beside the paper.

Using the marker once more, he wrote on the paper, recapped the marker, and returned it to his pocket. Adjusting the paper and tie to sit beside each other, he smiled and sighed. Today was a good day.

Taking one last look at the body, he spied a silver bracelet on the woman's wrist. Seeing it sparkle, he walked over, removed it, and slipped it into his pocket. Then, pleased with his handiwork and ready to go home and eat, he checked his reflection in the mirror. He raised his hood, put on his sunglasses, and walked out the back door.

Chapter Two

DETECTIVE AARON REMALLA SAT on a bench in the cemetery, under a large shade tree. A row of tombstones stretched out in front of him, and Jennie's lay at the end. The marble stone had an angel and the name Jennifer Carson etched into it, along with the years of her birth and death and the words *Gone too soon, but forever loved*. A single yellow rose lay in front of it.

Rem eyed the flowers in his hand. He'd brought her some lilies, which she'd always liked, but had yet to place them on her grave. He wondered about the rose and who had brought it. Her family would have contacted him if they'd been visiting, but they hadn't been in touch, and his partner, Daniels, would have told him if he'd swung by and left it. It could have been a friend, but in the various times he'd visited, he'd never seen flowers on her stone before, unless it was from family.

Shaking his head, he stopped staring at the yellow rose and sat his flowers beside him on the bench. Trying not to think, but failing, he reflected on the last several months.

He reluctantly recalled his encounters with Victor D'Mato and Allison Albright, and his near death at their hands. His struggles with the PTSD, preparing for Allison's upcoming trial and her revelation that the child she carried was his. Then, when he'd thought he'd survived the worst of it, Margaret Redstone, a psychopathic follower of Victor, whose crazy blue eyes, wild cackle, and demented attraction to Rem made him fear her more, had escaped the psychiatric facility where she was being held.

Three months later, there was still no sign of her. He'd been doing his best to cope but there were times when he needed to escape, and he often found himself here, with Jennie. Although he knew Margaret could get to him no matter where he went, it was one of the few places he felt safe. Maybe because he figured if he died next to Jennie, he would be okay with that.

Sighing, he realized there was one bright spot in the hell of the last few months—Mikey Redstone, Margaret's sister. She was the only person who could relate to his trauma, and she was a good friend. She'd survived her own horrific experiences with Victor, and she'd helped him through his recovery with an acceptance that he appreciated. He knew Daniels would stand behind him no matter what, but he never expected to find that same loyalty with anyone else.

Eyeing Jennie's tombstone, he wondered if Mikey could become more than a friend. Did he love her? Maybe. He didn't know. So much had happened recently that it was hard to keep his thoughts straight. Mikey had begun seeing Kyle, but she'd informed Rem that she had restricted their relationship to business-only while her brother Mason was in drug rehab and Kyle had stepped in to help with Mason's business. But Mason had since returned home, and Rem wondered if Kyle hoped to resume his relationship with Mikey, and if Mikey did, too.

Rem wouldn't blame her if she did. From what he knew of Kyle and after their brief meeting, he could see why Mikey would like him. And with Margaret still at large, any potential relationship between Rem and Mikey was out of the question. If it meant attracting Margaret's interest or anger, Rem wouldn't risk it. Mikey's safety was more important than whatever feelings he had for her. And he still hadn't found the courage to tell her about Allison's pregnancy. That alone would likely have Mikey running for the hills. Daniels disagreed about Rem keeping his distance, but Rem couldn't help how he felt. He'd already lost one great woman in his life, and he couldn't imagine losing another. And Mikey sure as hell hadn't signed up to help Rem co-parent, nor would Rem expect it of her.

Rubbing his temples, he sighed again, wondering what to expect next. His mantra was to take it one day at a time, but there were moments when he desperately needed a reprieve. That's when he would come here and talk to Jennie. Sometimes it helped, but other times, he'd descend further down the rabbit hole, and he'd go home and get drunk. Luckily, those moments were few, but when it happened, it would take him a day or two to resurface. Thankfully, he had a partner and a captain who understood, but he couldn't expect them to take care of him every time, so he did his best to stay positive or hide when the going got rough. In the past, Mikey had been a strong source of support, but with the two of them seeing less of each other, he'd kept his struggles to himself.

Trying to relax, Rem closed his eyes and listened to a bird sing in the tree above him. Several minutes passed, and feeling a little more centered, he opened his eyes and, blowing out a breath, he stood and picked up his lilies. He walked to the tombstone and squatted in front of it. He slid the rose back and set the lilies beside it and again wondered who'd placed the rose.

"Hey, Jen," he said. "I brought you some flowers." He swiped some leaves away. "But it looks like someone beat me to it." He smoothed a petal on a lily. "I guess I'm glad someone else is thinking of you, though."

Rem sat cross-legged on the ground. "I'm feeling a little sorry for myself again, so I stopped by. You always help me feel better." The wind blew his long hair, and he tucked a strand behind his ear. "Not much has changed since I last visited. Maybe one of these days, I'll have some good news for you."

A cool breeze prickled his skin, and he rubbed his arms. "You here with me?" He smiled softly. "Sorry. Dumb question."

He sat for a minute, enjoying her presence, letting his mind quiet, and wondered what he'd do with the rest of his day off. In the past, he'd call Mikey and they'd go to a movie, but he couldn't do that now.

Feeling more at ease, he was about to say his goodbyes, when his phone rang. He pulled it out of his pocket, and saw it was Daniels. Shaking his head, he wondered how his partner always knew when he was at the cemetery. He answered. "Hey."

"Hey," said Daniels. "How's Jennie?"

Rem smirked. "Quiet, as usual. But still present."

"Good. How are you?"

"Taking a moment but hanging in there. You?"

"I'm hanging with J.P. while Marjorie runs some errands. She's on her way back, though, because I've got to go. And so do you."

"I do? Where are we going?"

"Lozano called. I hate to interrupt your moment but there's been a murder. He wants us on it."

"Us? Why us? It's our day off."

"He didn't elaborate, but said we'd understand when we got there. I'll text you the address and meet you there."

Rem sighed, not anxious to go to a crime scene, but figured the distraction might be a good thing. "Okay. I'll head out."

"I'll be right behind you. See you soon."

"See you."

Rem hung up. He eyed Jennie's grave a second longer and stood. "Duty calls, Babe, but I'll be back soon. Enjoy your flowers."

A strange tingle ran up his spine, and he had the odd feeling that he wasn't alone. His skin breaking out in chills, he scanned the area, but didn't see anyone. Only tombstones stared back. He walked down a few rows and eyed the surrounding trees, but it was quiet. Figuring he was paranoid, he shrugged it off, but stayed aware just in case Margaret popped up from behind a gravestone and rushed at him, her blue eyes blazing. With a last glance around, he returned to Jennie's grave, and his heart thumping, he whispered a goodbye and left the cemetery.

Daniels hung up the phone, and texted the address to Rem. His eighteen-month-old son, J.P., ran into the kitchen holding his toy truck. "Hey, little man," said Daniels, ruffling J.P.'s hair. He put his phone in his pocket. "About ready for some lunch?"

J.P. knelt and immediately ran his truck across the floor. Daniels squatted next to him. "Mommy will be home soon. You want some yogurt or some fruit?"

J.P. looked up at him with his bright blue eyes and messy hair. "Pay, dada." Daniels smiled and eyed the time. "We've got about fifteen minutes before Mommy gets back. Do you want to play or eat something?"

"Pay. Pay cars." J.P. jumped up and ran back into the other room.

"I guess that was a stupid question," Daniels muttered to himself. He eyed a darkening banana on the kitchen counter. "How about I get you something to snack on while we play?" Wanting some orange juice, he grabbed the handle to the refrigerator door. "That way we'll kill two birds with one stone," he said to himself.

J.P. squealed from the other room, and Daniels shook his head, hoping he'd get J.P. to eat before his wife, Marjorie, returned. Before opening the door, he paused, surveying the pictures on the refrigerator. Not long after J.P. had been born, Marjorie had begun to add photos to the outside of the fridge with magnets. As J.P. grew older, she'd switch them out, adding the older ones to photo albums and replacing them with new ones.

Daniels noticed one was missing. At J.P.'s first birthday party, Rem had snapped a photo of Daniels, Marjorie, and J.P. in front of J.P.'s birthday cake. J.P. had grabbed the side of the chocolate cake and had smeared it all over his face. Daniels and Marjorie had laughed just as Rem took the photo. It was one of Daniels' favorites and Marjorie had printed it and placed it on the refrigerator just beside the door handle.

Not seeing it, Daniels frowned. He scanned the array of other photos and wondered if Marjorie had moved it. After a few seconds of searching, he found the photo at the bottom right corner of the fridge. He leaned over, pulled it and the magnet off, and wondering how it had ended up at the bottom of the door, he returned it to its original spot. Smiling, he studied it—J.P.'s blond hair, blue eyes, and the dimple in his cheek, and noted how much his son looked like him.

J.P. squealed again, yelling for daddy. "I'm coming, big guy," said Daniels. "Just a second." Daniels opened the refrigerator and pulled out the orange juice. He set in on the counter and grabbed the banana. Peeling and slicing it, he wondered about his captain's phone call. If Lozano was sending him and Rem to a crime scene on their day off, it had to be something pretty interesting. With Allison Albright's trial nearing, her pregnancy progressing, and Margaret Redstone's escape, Lozano knew Rem had a lot on his mind. He'd assigned them the simpler cases since he and Rem had returned from Merrimac, but Daniels realized at some point they'd get something bigger.

After cutting the banana and dumping the slices into a bowl, he poured himself some orange juice and brought his glass and the banana to J.P. He sat on the floor with his son, picked up a truck to play, and waited for Marjorie's return.

Chapter Three

REM PULLED UP AND parked at the curb, seeing several police cars parked in front of a small one-story house with two large trees in the front yard. He turned off the ignition and sat in the car thinking. Anticipating the crime scene, he wondered what he was about to walk into. He glanced at his watch and noted that Daniels would probably be another few minutes. Tapping his fingers on the steering wheel, he took a deep breath to prepare himself before he opened the door.

He slid out of the car and stared at the house. A patrolman stood outside the front entry, and a crime scene van was parked in the driveway. He closed his door, stepped onto the curb, and ducked beneath the crime scene tape. An officer approached him, he flashed his badge, and the officer nodded. Rem walked across the grass and jogged up the steps to the concrete patio.

He recognized the patrolman. "Hey, Smithers. How's it going today?"

Smithers, a younger officer who'd been on the job a few years and had a wife and kid that Rem had met at the annual picnic, nodded. "Afternoon, Detective. Sorry you had to come in on your day off."

"Lozano said he wanted us on this. I'll be curious to find out why." The front door was ajar, and Rem peeked inside the house. He spotted a crime scene technician taking photos. "Have they been in there long?"

Smithers shook his head. "No. Not very."

"Ibrahim on this one?" asked Rem.

"Yeah, he is." He glanced inside. "I think he's checking the body now."

"Daniels will be here soon. I'll wait while they finish." He noted Smithers' pale features. "Who called it in?"

"The mother contacted nine-one-one asking for a welfare check. Apparently, a friend was supposed to meet the victim for lunch. When she didn't show or respond to messages, the friend called the vic's mom, and the mom called us, demanding someone check on her daughter." He tipped his head toward a patrolman on the sidewalk. Rem spotted Smithers' partner, Hendrix, who was talking to a man in a jogging suit. "I think that's the neighbor."

"What was your reason for going in?"

"We almost left when she didn't answer. But Hendrix wanted to check the back and we looked through the window."

"What did you see?" asked Rem.

"A woman lying on the floor in the kitchen. We'd hoped she was unconscious, but when we got inside, we realized she wasn't."

Recalling his own days as a young officer, Rem could empathize. "Was it bad?"

"From what I can tell, she'd been strangled." Smithers looked like he'd eaten food way past its expiration date.

"I wish I could tell you it gets easier," said Rem, "but it doesn't."

Smithers ran a shaky hand through his hair. "She looks like my wife, you know? It just kinda hit me."

Rem swallowed, thinking of Jennie. "It happens. It's hard not to think of our own loved ones when you see something like this."

A man stepped out of the house wearing a blue jacket with identification around his neck. His wire-rimmed glasses rested on his forehead, and he slid them down to his nose. "Hello, Detective. Where's your better half?"

"Hey, Ibrahim." Rem checked the time again. "He should be here any minute. What have we got?"

"Female. Probably around thirty years old. Strangled. Been dead about twenty-four hours." He glanced back inside the house. "My guys should be done in a few minutes."

Rem nodded. "That's fine. I'm waiting for Daniels anyway." He crossed his arms. "That way we can both be horrified together."

Ibrahim pulled off his glasses and cleaned them with the hem of his shirt. "It never gets easier, does it, Detective?"

Rem eyed Smithers. "No. It never does." He wondered why Lozano had sent them to the scene. "Lozano told Daniels he wanted us on this one. Any reason why?"

Ibrahim put his glasses back on. "I have an idea. But I'll let you and Daniels decide for yourselves when you get inside."

His interest piqued, Rem was about to ask about Ibrahim's cryptic comment when he spotted Daniels pull up to the curb and park behind Rem's car. Rem watched as his partner left his vehicle, approached the crime scene tape, flashed his badge to an officer, and jogged across the grass up to the patio.

Daniels tucked his badge into his pocket. "I didn't expect a welcoming committee."

"We just couldn't wait to see you," said Rem.

"Marjorie tells me that all the time," said Daniels, with a smile.

Rem smirked. "Even when you forget to bring dinner home? Like the other night?"

Daniels' face fell. "I'll admit. She told me something different then." He held up his index finger. "But in my defense, I was helping you finish a report."

Rem scoffed. "Don't blame me, sport. I suggested you stop and get some Taco del Fuegos when you left. Remember?"

Daniels scowled. "That's probably why I forgot. You made me lose my appetite."

Rem tipped his head toward the house. "Speaking of losing appetites, we've got a body inside. I was waiting for Crime Scene to finish." He gestured at Ibrahim. "The Doc here won't tell me what's got Lozano all worked up."

Ibrahim shrugged. "I told him you two could sort that out for yourselves. Check the kitchen counter, though. I think you'll find it interesting." He peered inside the house. "I think you guys can go in now. I'm going to grab something from the van. I'll be back in a second." He pulled coverings out of his pocket and held them out to Rem. "Make sure you wear these."

"Thanks," said Rem, taking the shoe protectors and gloves. He handed a set to Daniels. "You ready?"

Daniels took them. "As I'll ever be."

They slid the protectors over their shoes, put on the gloves and entered the house.

Rem followed a narrow hall down to a modest living room with a small worn couch and end table. A TV hung on the wall and a wooden coffee table sported a large pink crystal in the middle of it. Rem saw the legs of the victim extending into a square dining area beyond the kitchen tile. A technician had left the kitchen and was taking photos of the rest of the house. Rem walked to the body, seeing a pretty lady in a yellow sleeveless dress lying on her back on the kitchen floor. Her dress had been smoothed to lie flat and her limbs had been straightened. The only thing that marred her appearance was her bruised neck. On her right bicep was a symbol written in black marker. Rem determined it was either the number eight or the infinity sign. Daniels walked up beside Rem. "She looks posed," said Daniels.

"She does," said Rem." It almost looks like she's sleeping." He squatted next to her. "Look at her hair and clothes. They've been intentionally arranged."

Daniels nodded. "There's no way she fell backward like that. It's almost like the killer wanted her to be comfortable." He squinted. "What's that mark on her arm?"

Rem looked closer at the strange symbol. "Looks like the killer is telling us something."

Daniels turned toward the circular glass dining table. "That must be her purse," He spoke to a technician who walked through the room. "You guys get a picture of this?"

The technician nodded. "Yes. Feel free to look through whatever you want."

Daniels walked over and went through the purse. He pulled out a wallet. Rem entered the kitchen.

Daniels read from a driver's license. "Her name's Stella de la Rosa. Age thirty-two."

Rem opened some kitchen cabinets and drawers. "Anything else that will tell us a little more about her?"

Daniels opened a pocket. He pulled out what looked like business cards and read from one of them. His eyes widened. "Interesting."

Rem walked back and looked over Daniels' shoulder. "What is it?"

"Guess what Stella does for a living?" He read from the card. "She's a psychic masseuse."

Rem tried to imagine what that was. "What the hell is a psychic masseuse?"

Daniels pursed his lips. "My guess? She gives massages and psychic readings. Possibly at the same time."

"Seriously?"

"Guess what her motto is? Rest, recoup, and get the scoop." He lowered the card. "Catchy."

Rem found it hard to believe. "How is it that we always catch these cases?"

Daniels returned the license and put the wallet and cards back in Stella's purse. "Maybe that's why Lozano asked us to investigate. Maybe he knew something we didn't."

"How would he know that she's a psychic masseuse? You think he was a client?"

"I doubt it," said Daniels with a chuckle. "But Lozano has surprised us before."

Ibrahim returned. "You guys see what you need to?" He gestured toward the counter. "Did you note the items the killer left behind?"

Rem glanced toward the far counter. "Haven't gotten that far yet. We're learning about Stella's occupation. She was a psychic masseuse. Ever heard of that?"

Ibrahim shook his head. "Can't say that I have. But I think you two will be far more interested by what's been left on the counter."

Rem walked to the far corner of the kitchen and Daniels followed. Eyeing the countertop, he saw a piece of lined notebook paper with words written in black marker lying beside a black bow tie. Rem read the note and felt a chill run up his spine. "Hell," he whispered.

Daniels read it out loud. "Four more days." Beneath that was written *For Margaret*. Next to that was the infinity sign.

Rem almost grabbed the counter for support. "You don't think...?"

Daniels studied the note again. "That our killer is referring to Margaret Redstone?" He eyed Rem. "Now I think we know why Lozano sent us."

"Maybe it's a different Margaret," said Rem, hoping and praying it was.

Daniels frowned. "What's your gut tell you?"

Ibrahim nodded toward the body. "You notice the same symbol was on her arm?"

"We did." Rem's gaze returned to the note. "I wonder what that means." Imagining Margaret Redstone's frenetic blue eyes and loud cackle, Rem's heart skipped. "You think Margaret Redstone has something to do with this?"

Ibrahim raised a brow. "She's the lady who escaped the psychiatric ward, right?"

"Yeah. Three months ago," said Rem, feeling as if it had been three years. "There's been no trace of her, and no indication of what she might be up to, until now."

"The question is, what's Stella's connection to Margaret?" asked Daniels. "Why was Stella a target?"

"Maybe Stella didn't have a connection," said Rem. "But obviously the killer does."

Daniels sighed. "We need to learn more about our victim. Maybe she can give us a few clues as to why she was murdered."

Ibrahim pointed toward the back of the house. "There's a bedroom, plus an office and massage room down the hall. If I were to guess, she saw clients in her house."

Daniels glanced in that direction. "If that's true, then maybe one of Stella's clients killed her." He shot a look at Rem. "Maybe this has nothing to do with Margaret Redstone at all."

Something told Rem that was wishful thinking. "Let's go find out."

"I'll bag these," said Ibrahim, pointing toward the items. "We'll check them for fingerprints and DNA. Once I have my initial report, I'll send it to Lozano."

"Thanks," said Rem. He followed Daniels through the living room and into the hall. Daniels peered into a doorway on his left and Rem poked his head into another on his right. Rem saw an open massage table with a towel folded on it, and various shelves cluttered with crystals, candles, and pictures. It smelled of incense, and Rem stepped inside. "I got the massage room."

"This is the office," said Daniels. "I'll check it out."

Rem studied the walls around Stella's massage table. There was a business license displayed and two framed diplomas. One was a certificate for a completed massage therapy course from three years earlier. Next to it was a diploma from a local community college for a Bachelor's degree in Kinesiology. He moved to the shelves and eyed the various colored crystals and rocks amid bottles of oils. A shelf above held books about meditation, stress relief, massage techniques, essential oils, and general well-being.

"I've got a laptop in here," said Daniels from the other room. "We'll have to get our tech guys to look at it."

Rem glanced at another shelf, seeing an array of framed photos. Some were of Stella in a group, everyone sitting cross-legged with their eyes closed. In another photo, Stella was lying on the ground with two people sitting near her head with their hands on her temples. Other photos showed Stella with friends or maybe family. They were all framed except for one loose picture that was propped against a framed photo of Stella in front of the Grand Canyon. Rem studied it. It was Stella with a smiling man on either side of her, her arms around each of them. Recognizing one of the men, Rem froze. Shock rippled through him, and he stepped back. The blood rushed through his ears and his vision briefly swum. Trying to keep his balance, he bumped up against the massage table and sat back against it.

Daniels entered the room. "I asked Ibrahim to grab the laptop. He said he'd bag it and bring it with him."

Rem took a steadying breath. His vision cleared and he blinked.

"What's wrong?" Daniels stopped beside him. "You don't look so hot."

Rem held his stomach. "The photo...."

Daniels frowned. "What photo?"

Rem's belly churned and he wished he'd skipped his breakfast. "On the shelf. Above the rocks and books."

Daniels eyed Rem for a second. "You okay?"

Rem centered himself. "I'm fine. The urge to puke is easing."

"I hope. Ibrahim won't be too happy if you mess up his crime scene."

"I'm well aware." Rem swiped at his brow.

Daniels watched him a second more and turned toward the shelf. His gaze traveled over the pictures, and he stopped at the unframed one. His breath caught. "Is that who I think it is?"

His shock abating, Rem stood and approached the shelves. He eyed the one that had set his teeth on edge. "If you're thinking Victor D'Mato, you're right. Stella knew him." Rem closed his eyes, trying to shut out the swirling memories of his abduction and near death. He recalled the note on the counter and opened his eyes. "Which means Margaret Redstone hasn't gone anywhere, and whatever she's up to, it's just getting started."

Chapter Four

MASON REDSTONE OPENED THE door to his linen closet and spotted his mother's blanket on the shelf. He pulled it down with a sigh, closed the door and headed to his bedroom, where he returned the blanket to the foot of his bed.

He left his room and entered his living area, where his sister Mikey sat on the couch with her laptop open. Her smooth, purple-tipped brown hair rested against her shoulders and the diamond stud in her nostril sparkled in the light from the window. She'd been living with Mason since he'd left drug rehab two weeks ago. Mason had no intention of letting Mikey stay in her apartment while their sister Margaret remained on the loose. She'd almost killed Mikey, and Mason had no desire for her to try again, so until she was captured, Mikey would remain with Mason. "You know," said Mason, "if you want to borrow Mom's blanket, that's fine. Just return it to my bed when you're done."

Mikey looked up. "I didn't borrow Mom's blanket."

"Then why was it in the linen closet?"

"I don't know. I didn't put it there." Mikey typed something on her laptop. "Maybe Trick did."

"Why would Trick mess with Mom's blanket?"

Mikey sighed. "Because he slept on the couch the other night after he had too many beers and didn't want to drive home."

Mason recalled the other evening. Trick had picked up hamburgers after a busy day at SCOPE, Mason's paranormal PI agency, and had brought them to Mason's for dinner. Since Mason's return home from Windhaven's drug treatment center where he'd uncovered a major conspiracy and exposed the Montes Pharmaceutical company's deceit, business at SCOPE had been brisk. So much so that Mason had asked Kyle Willow, the man who'd helped cover for him while Mason was out of the office, to continue to help. Kyle had joined them for the hamburgers but had left early to help his grandmother Lena with a case of her own. Trick had stayed, watched a basketball game on the small TV Mikey had finally bugged Mason enough to purchase, and then claimed it would be better if he stayed the night because of his drinking. Mason had offered Trick the couch, a pillow, and his mother's blanket.

"I swear Trick had returned it to my bed before he left." Mason thought back. "But maybe I'm wrong."

"It wouldn't be the first time."

Mason narrowed his eyes. "You really want to bring up each other's mistakes?"

Mikey's expression fell. "No. Not really." She went back to her laptop.

"Let me ask you something," said Mason, thinking back. "Do you really think Trick had too much to drink that night?"

Mikey typed something else. "He'd had a few beers but by the time the game was over, he was fine. I think he just likes knowing we're safe." Her phone beeped and she picked it up. "So he comes up with excuses as to why he can spend time here."

Mason nodded, sensing Mikey was right. "He thinks by staying close that he'll keep Margaret away?"

"Or he thinks there's safety in numbers. If she shows, it's better to have three against one instead of two."

Mason sat on the sofa with a sigh. "I wonder if we'll ever be free of our sister."

"I'm not counting on it." Mikey punched buttons on her phone. "Rem and Daniels are here. They're asking if we're free to talk to them."

"Here?" Mason frowned. "Isn't it their day off?"

"It is." Mikey stood. "Which is why I'm curious." She walked to the door and opened it.

Mason could see Detectives Remalla and Daniels approaching. He stood, too, as Mikey waved them in. "Rem. Daniels." Mason put his hands in his pockets. "You two enjoying this pretty day?"

"I wish," said Rem. "I'd planned to crash on the couch, eat a couple of dogs, and catch some old movies."

"And I was supposed to take Marjorie and J.P. to the park," said Daniels. "But that didn't happen."

Mikey spoke to Rem. "Too bad. *Wait until Dark* comes on in an hour." She glanced at Mason. "I plan on watching it. I'm sure Mason can't wait, either." She closed the door behind them. "You two are free to join us if you want. I'll make some popcorn."

"Since when am I joining you?" asked Mason. "I'm going to finish planting those flowers you bought the other day that are still sitting in their pots."

"I started planting them yesterday," said Mikey. "In fact, I went out there this morning, and two of them were trampled. You need to pay more attention to where you're stepping."

Mason didn't know what she was talking about. "I didn't step on any flowers, Mikey. I haven't even been outside this morning."

Mikey returned to the couch and sat. "Then it must be that damned neighbor's dog. The Golstons swear they patched that fence, but obviously they didn't." She shook her head. "I'll have to go out there and check it." She eyed Rem and Daniels. "You guys have a seat." She moved her laptop and set it on the coffee table. "You want something to drink? Coffee or water?"

"I'm good right now," said Rem.

"Me, too," said Daniels.

Mason noted their tense expressions and posture. Neither of them sat. Obviously, they weren't here for small talk. "What did you two want to talk about?"

Mikey raised an eyebrow. "If you don't want coffee, Rem, then it must be serious."

Rem and Daniels glanced at each other. "We got called to a crime scene," said Rem. "A woman was strangled in her home."

"Lozano wanted us to take it," said Daniels. "There was something there he wanted us to see."

"What was it?" asked Mikey.

Daniels pulled out his cell phone, hit a button and swiped a few times. "The killer left this note at the scene. Near the body." He held out the phone.

Mason walked over and looked at the picture. He saw a piece of notebook paper with writing on it next to a black bow tie. Mikey walked up next to him. They both read the note. Mason's heart thumped.

"Oh my God," said Mikey. "Is that a reference to our sister?" She stared at Mason who didn't know what to say. "Did Margaret have something to do with the murder?" she asked.

"We weren't sure at first," said Rem. "The victim's name is Stella de la Rosa. She's a psychic masseuse. We didn't want to assume anything, but then I walked into her massage room." His expression paled and Mason thought he looked like he'd had green vegetables for lunch. "That's when I saw this." He nodded toward the phone.

Daniels swiped again and a new photo appeared. Mason and Mikey looked. Mikey gasped, and Mason's blood ran cold. He recognized Victor D'Mato, his former friend turned cult leader who'd abused Mikey and abducted Remalla. "Son of a...," said Mason.

"My thoughts exactly," said Rem.

Mikey turned away and sat on the couch. She leaned over and held her head.

"You okay, Mikey?" asked Mason. He walked over and sat beside her.

Rem and Daniels took a seat in the chairs opposite the couch. "It took me a second, too," said Rem. "I didn't expect to see his face."

Mikey looked up. "It's amazing how seeing him brings it all back."

Rem held his stomach. "I almost lost my breakfast."

Daniels put his phone in his pocket. "We needed to let you know about the note. And ask if either of you recognize the other man in the photo with Stella."

"I don't recognize him, or Stella," said Mason. He put a hand on Mikey's back. "Do you, Mikey?"

Mikey gripped her temples for a second, then raised her head. "I don't recognize them either."

"You never saw either of them at one of Victor's parties?" asked Daniels.

"No," said Mikey. "Not that I recall." She blew out a shaky breath. "But it's been a few years since I've been around that scene." She paused. "Do you think Margaret targeted Stella?"

Rem leaned back in his chair. "I don't know. It's hard to tell from the note whether Margaret is involved in the killing, or if the killer is trying to get Margaret's attention. But either way, Margaret seems to have some connection to this murder. We just don't know what."

Mason recalled the symbol on the letter. "Was that the infinity sign on the note?"

Daniels nodded. "We assume so. The same symbol was drawn on the victim's bicep with a black marker. We don't know what its significance is, either. Nor do we know what the four days refers to. Or the bow tie."

Mason thought about it. "The infinity sign suggests something never ending, or eternal. That has to have something to do with why Stella was killed."

"It's possible," said Daniels. "Victor and his cult had an interest in prolonging life. Maybe this guy was a follower."

"If Stella had psychic abilities," said Rem, "it would explain her connection to Victor since he attracted those types. Maybe she knew something that got her killed."

"Victor's been dead almost six months," said Mikey. "Why would the killer go after Stella now?"

"It must have something to do with Margaret," said Mason. "It's the only thing that makes sense."

Daniels put his elbows on his knees. "So, Margaret is either manipulating a killer, or a killer is possibly targeting Margaret." He rubbed his jaw. "You two know Margaret best. Which one do you think it is?"

Mason almost chuckled. "Either way, it isn't going to end well."

"Stella's photos were all framed, but the one with Victor wasn't," said Rem. "You think that means something?"

"Maybe she'd just received the picture," said Daniels. "I found a ripped envelope with Stella's address on it in the trash in her office. Maybe somebody sent it to her in the mail."

"You think it was a warning?" asked Mason.

"Could be." Rem scratched his knee. "But Stella didn't see it that way. She displayed the photo."

"Her memories with Victor are obviously better than ours," said Mikey.

"Seems so," said Rem. "But if we can find somebody who knew Stella, or the other man who was with her and Victor in the photo, then maybe that will help." He looked at Mikey. "Any ideas of where to start?"

"I have a couple," said Mikey, looking weary. "But you're not going to like them."

Daniels pulled out a notepad and a pen from his pocket. "What are they?"

Mikey sighed heavily. "Gina Rodriguez. My friend, or who I thought was a friend, from Victor's cult." She eyed Rem. "She's the woman I told you about who threatened me. She said she knew what Margaret was up to, remember? Trick and I were investigating her sister Lenora's death before Mason got out of rehab. Gina and I had that huge fight, and I haven't seen her since." Mikey studied her hands. "She might have some knowledge of Stella or that man in the photo."

Daniels scribbled in his notepad. "I recall that. We had a patrol watch her but never saw anything suspicious. We'll follow up. Anybody else?"

Mikey peered at Mason, her expression somber, and then glanced at Rem. "The obvious."

Rem sunk in his seat. "You're not serious."

Daniels looked between them, and his eyes widened. "You don't mean...?"

Mason, finally understanding, frowned. "You're not referring to Allison, are you?"

Rem groaned.

Mikey nibbled her lip. "Unfortunately, I am. She's Victor's former girl-friend and accomplice. If you want to know about Victor and his associates, she's the one to ask."

Chapter Five

Remalla jolted awake on the couch. Sweaty, he blinked his eyes, trying to get his bearings. The images flashed in his mind. Cursing, he pushed himself up into a sitting position and tried to slow his breathing. It had been a couple of weeks since he'd had a bad nightmare, and this one had made up for it.

He'd been back on the slab, the torches and followers surrounding him, and Allison on top of him holding the knife. He'd been tied down, and she'd touched the tip of the knife to his chest. Terrified, he'd begged her to stop. She'd laughed, and then her face had morphed into Margaret's. Rem had whimpered and squirmed hard against his bindings, but he couldn't move. Margaret's blue eyes sparkled in the torchlight and her laugh had transformed into its standard cackle. "You're all mine," she'd said. "You will be mine forever."

Rem tried to scream, but his throat had locked up. Margaret leaned low and put her lips to his ear. "I wish to savor you right here, right now."

Still holding the knife, she'd slid her hand down his chest, past his waist, and moving even lower, Rem's throat had unlocked, and he'd finally screamed. That's when he'd come awake.

Taking a breath, Rem leaned over and put his face in his hands. He figured his new case had triggered the nightmare. Now that there appeared to be activity regarding Margaret, he had to assume his subconscious would not let him off the hook.

After meeting with Mikey and Mason, he and Daniels had stopped by the station to review what they knew and determine what to do next. They'd planned to talk to as many of Stella's family, friends, neighbors, and clients as they could, hoping someone might have information regarding Stella's personal or business life, and who might want her dead. And if any of them had information about Victor, that would be a plus. The police had done a canvas of the area around Stella's house that afternoon, but no one had seen anything.

After they'd organized their thoughts and contacted Lozano to give him an update, they'd arranged to meet with their captain in the morning and had gone home. Daniels had still hoped to have dinner with Marjorie and J.P., and Rem planned to catch a movie at home and eat a hot dog. He'd done both and had ended up falling asleep on the couch.

Trying to shake off the nightmare, thoughts of Allison swirled in Rem's head. Both he and Daniels realized that Mikey was right. Allison would be a good source of information about Victor's cohorts. After Margaret's escape, they'd considered questioning her about Margaret but had decided against it. They'd doubted Allison would know anything, and even if she did, she'd likely lie or use whatever information she had for her own benefit.

But with a murder on their hands, Rem realized someone needed to talk to her. He and Daniels had discussed it and decided they'd ask Mel and Garcia to visit Allison. Neither Rem or Daniels could do it, considering the upcoming trial and their roles in it.

His heart rate slowing, Rem sat up. He eyed his warm, half-filled glass of beer and decided to open another can. He hoped it would settle his nerves before he went to bed.

Standing, he shook out his hands, and headed toward the kitchen when someone knocked on his door. He startled, recalling the dream.

Get a hold of yourself, Remalla. It's probably a neighbor. But always vigilant, he went to his front closet and removed his service weapon from his safe. Tucking it into the back of his jeans, he walked over to peer out the peephole. A man was standing on his porch. He seemed familiar, but Rem couldn't place him. "Who is it?"

"Sorry to bother you. I'm your neighbor from across the street." The man pointed behind him. "I think my cat ran into your backyard."

Rem studied him for a second and realized he'd seen him before. A few weeks earlier, a moving truck had pulled up. Rem had observed a man out front directing the movers as they carried furniture into the home. He'd waved as Rem had backed out of his driveway and driven off.

The house across from Rem's had been vacant since its previous occupant had been murdered in the backyard. At the time, Rem and Daniels had been pursuing a kidnapper and the kidnapper's accomplice, Ginger, had been watching Rem from the neighbor's yard. The neighbor had likely surprised her and had died because of it.

The house had been quiet until recently. A few days before, Rem had been watering his grass when a woman had left the house. Her hair had been pulled back into a low ponytail and she'd worn big sunglasses, an oversized jacket, and a fancy hat. She'd tossed a suitcase in her trunk, gotten into her car, and driven off without giving Rem a second glance. He wondered if the man on his doorstep was her husband.

Rem stared through the peephole for another second before disengaging the alarm and opening the door. The man on his porch had an angular face and shaggy brown short hair. He wore baggy jeans and a sweatshirt with a bulldog on it.

"I'm so sorry to bother you," he said. "My cat got out and I chased her over here. She slid under your fence. Do you mind if I take a look?"

Rem studied him, looking for any signs of dishonesty or deception, but the man seemed genuinely anxious and friendly.

"I'm Kevin Chapman, by the way. Your new neighbor." The man offered his hand.

Rem told himself to relax. Not everyone was a bad guy. He shook the man's hand. "Aaron Remalla. Nice to meet you." He shot out a thumb. "Why don't you go around to the gate. I'll meet you there."

"Thank you," said Kevin. "I appreciate it."

Rem shut the door and locked it. He walked through his kitchen to the back door which led to the yard. He flipped on the outside lights, opened the door, and walked out to his porch, down the steps and into the grass. He undid the lock at the gate, and Kevin entered the yard.

"What's your cat's name?" asked Rem.

Kevin's gaze traveled. "Chester."

Rem smirked. "Didn't you say it was a she?"

"It is a she. My niece named her. My wife insisted we keep it. With gender issues being what they are, I didn't argue." He leaned low. "Here, Chester. Here kitty, kitty." He made a smooching sound with his lips.

Rem eyed his brown grass and thin shrubs but didn't see any cat. "Does Chester usually come when you call her?"

"No. Not usually. Which is why I brought my secret weapon." He reached into his pocket and pulled something out. "Here, Chester. Want a treat?" He held out his hand.

Rem saw several brown squares in his palm. "Where do you think Chester would go? Does she climb?" He hoped Chester wouldn't require a fire truck to rescue her from one of Rem's tall trees.

Kevin walked towards the porch, holding out the treats. "I don't think so. She tends to frequent hidden, dark areas." He squatted and looked beneath Rem's porch. "My guess is she's under here."

Rem imagined the murky space beneath his patio and immediately re-called the lightless room he'd been held in after his abduction. "That's not where I would hide."

"Me, either." Kevin called Chester again. "But what do I know. I'm not a cat."

Rem watched Kevin crawl through his grass. "This is why I don't have a pet. Too much work."

Kevin smiled. "I agree, but my wife loves Chester. Plus, it's a good way to meet the neighbors."

"Ever heard of a potluck picnic?" asked Rem. "The neighborhood has one in the park every summer. It's a lot easier on the knees."

Kevin clicked his tongue. "Here, kitty." A short-haired, black and white cat popped its head out from beneath the wooden deck. "There you are," said Kevin. He held out his hand. "You want a treat?"

Rem watched the cat tentatively step out and approach Kevin's hand. Kevin swooped it up into his arms. "Gotcha," said Kevin. He held Chester in his grasp and offered the cat a treat. "Bad kitty. But let's not tell Mommy, okay? This is just between you and me." He petted the cat's head and spoke to Rem. "Thankfully, Nancy is out of town."

"I saw the movers unloading a couple of weeks ago," said Rem. "You guys settling in?"

Kevin nodded. "We are. Most of the boxes are emptied. Now it's just the little stuff."

"I wondered if anybody would rent that house," said Rem. "It's been empty a while." He didn't know whether to mention the murder or not.

"I heard what happened there. Our realtor disclosed it. But the price was hard to beat, and the location is perfect, so we went for it." He adjusted his hold on Chester who was eagerly trying to eat the rest of the treats. "Besides, I grew up in a house where a murder-suicide took place, so this didn't seem that big of a deal."

Rem raised his eyebrow. "Really? I guess that puts things in perspective."

"It does. When I was a kid, my parents purchased a home where a man shot his wife and then himself. Nobody would live in it, but my dad couldn't pass up the price. After we moved in, I would see shadows, and hear things, and so would they, but we managed anyway. You get used to it after a while."

"What does your wife think about what happened? Does it bother her?" asked Rem.

Kevin shook his head. "She travels a lot, so she's not home most of the time. I work from home, so if anyone has to deal with it, it's going to be me."

"Any shadows or weird sounds at the new place?" Rem shivered at the thought.

"Not so far," said Kevin. "Except for Chester here." He patted the cat. "She can be a handful."

"I can see that."

Kevin adjusted his hold on Chester. "I'll get out of your hair. I'm sure you'd like to get some sleep."

Rem sighed. "Sleep and I don't always agree. I tend to toss and turn, then get up and watch an old movie to pass the time." Rem paused, thinking of his nightmare. "I think I sleep more on the couch then in the bed."

Kevin started walking toward the gate. "I've been having the same issue since moving in. It takes a while to get used to a new place. I was up until three a.m. the other night watching a *Star Trek* marathon."

"I watched the same thing," said Rem, following Kevin. "I still love the original shows the best."

"You can't beat William Shatner and Leonard Nimoy."

"No, you can't."

Kevin reached the gate and opened it. "I met your next-door neighbor the other day. She brought me muffins."

"That's Mrs. Wilson. Nice lady, but a little nosy. She makes a great muffin, though. Her blueberry ones are my favorite."

"I got banana nut," said Kevin. "They were delicious. But you're right about the nosiness. She wanted to know all about me and Nancy. She also told me you were a detective. But not to bother you even if there was an emergency. She said to call nine-one-one instead."

Rem chuckled. "Yeah, that's what I had to tell her. She kept phoning me every time she heard a strange noise in her house. I was about to move, until she found out she had squirrels in her attic."

Kevin smiled. "I guess everyone has a neighbor like Mrs. Wilson."

"At least she knows how to bake," said Rem. "When they found out they had squirrels, she made me an entire cheesecake."

Kevin's eyes widened. "That's definitely a perk." The treats gone, the cat squirmed in Kevin's arms. "I better get Chester back before she gets away again."

Pleased that his new neighbor seemed normal, Rem held the door to the gate. "And contrary to what Mrs. Wilson says, if you do have an emergency, don't hesitate to contact me. My hours aren't great, though, so you'll probably end up calling the cops anyway."

"This neighborhood seems pretty safe, so I don't anticipate any problems. You ever need a cup of sugar, though, or six-pack of beer, feel free to stop by." He gripped Chester when she squirmed. "I owe you after tonight."

"I'll remember that," said Rem. "You do the same."

"Thanks. I appreciate it and your help with Chester. If she'd disappeared, I'd be a divorced man." He walked through the gate. "Have a good night."

"You, too. And nice meeting you." Rem waved. Kevin waved back and Rem closed the gate.

As he walked through his yard, his phone rang. He pulled it out of his pocket and saw it was Daniels. Returning to his house, he answered. "Hey."

"Hey," said Daniels. "You got a sec?"

Rem closed the door behind him and locked it. "I just met my new neighbor from across the street. I think he's actually normal. Although he's got a trans-gender cat."

"Good for the cat," said Daniels. "Has Mrs. Wilson given him muffins yet?"

"Banana nut."

"The lady works fast," said Daniels. "I just got off the phone with Lozano. He let me know he's stopping at the D.A.'s with Kate on his way into work tomorrow, so we'll meet with him after he gets in. He's guessing the D.A. wants to talk about Allison's possible plea bargain. He asked me to give you a heads up."

Rem's chest tightened at the thought. He'd been going back and forth about how to handle the plea bargain. Kate had left it up to him whether or not to offer it, but every time he thought he'd decided, he changed his mind. "I guess they want an answer." He stopped at his refrigerator and grabbed a beer.

"Probably. Our two followers are still planning to testify, though, if that helps."

Rem recalled the meeting with Kate Schultz, the prosecuting attorney in the case against Allison, after one of the two witnesses who'd planned to testify had threatened to back out. Worried, Kate had suggested offering a plea bargain, which would avoid a trial altogether. The offer would be for twenty years with a chance for parole after fifteen. Daniels had been incensed and Rem hadn't been too thrilled, either. But he understood Kate's reasoning behind it. If they went to trial without one or both followers' testimony, Allison could be acquitted. On the flip side, even without the witnesses, if a jury believed Rem, Allison could be sent away for the rest of her life. The thought of testifying made Rem sick to his stomach, but he wanted people to know what Allison had done to him and how dangerous she was.

Allison's pregnancy also had to be considered. She was almost six months along with Rem's supposed child. He didn't know what was worse – no trial and dealing with Allison's release after a mere fifteen years or taking her to trial in hopes of throwing away the key, only to have her serve no jail time at all. If the child was his, he had to consider what was best for his kid. Unfortunately, he didn't have an answer. Kate had requested a paternity test more than once, but Allison had refused it. Daniels believed that meant Allison was lying but Rem felt it was more than that. Allison wanted to keep Rem unsettled and vulnerable. It was the game she enjoyed playing.

Rem closed the refrigerator and popped his beer open. "Guess I have a decision to make." He drank from his beer. "Which means I won't get much sleep. Shocking."

"If you want to talk about it, let me know. But there's no pressure from me, whatever you decide."

"Thanks, partner."

"But try to get some sleep, anyway. Maybe if you stop thinking about it, you'll get an answer. Mason swears by meditation after his rehab stay."

"You think I should meditate?"

"Can't hurt." He paused. "I bet you know what you want to do, you're just second-guessing yourself. Maybe quieting your mind will make it crystal clear."

"I suppose. Nothing else seems to be working." He took another sip of his beer.

"Then give it a shot. It worked for Jill, remember?"

"Don't remind me." Rem thought back on his and Daniels' pursuit of the serial killer dubbed The Makeup Artist. Jill Jacobs had been stalked by the Artist and had assisted with the investigation. Rem had dated her afterward. "It almost got her killed."

"Hell." Daniels paused. "You're right. Bad example, then. It's working for Mason, though."

Rem leaned a hip against the kitchen counter. "I'll think about it."

"Good. We can talk more tomorrow. Right now, just enjoy your beer, get some rest, and I'll see you in the morning."

"Yeah. See you." Rem hung up and took a gulp of his beer. On his way back to the couch, he returned his gun to the safe and reset his alarm. He double-checked the lock on his door and returned to his couch. A news anchor relayed the events of the day and Rem frowned. Wondering when he'd switched to a news station, he grabbed the remote and flipped it back to his movie channel, then settled back to finish his beer.

Walking up his stairs, Daniels said goodbye to Rem and hung up. He stopped at J.P.'s room and peeked inside. Happy to see his son was fast asleep, he left and went into his own room. Marjorie was in their bed. Her bedside lamp was on, and she was reading.

She lowered her book. "All done?"

"I am now. Just needed to call Rem after I spoke to Lozano."

"Come to bed. You look tired."

"I am." Daniels set his phone on the end table next to his side of the bed. He pulled off his shirt and tossed it in the laundry basket. "Be right there." He entered the bathroom and eyed himself in the mirror. After the brutal investigation of Victor D'Mato and his cult which had almost resulted in Daniels' near mental breakdown and Rem's death, he'd committed himself to hitting the gym regularly. It helped to clear his mind and relieve his stress, which there had been plenty of recently. Plus, he secretly wanted to recapture his arm-wrestling trophy from the annual policeman's picnic. He'd missed the picnic last year, but he had every intention of winning again and regaining his status as the force's strongest man. He smiled at the memory of winning it the first time. Rem had hooted and hollered so much that Daniels had almost given him the trophy.

After washing his face and brushing his teeth, he raked his blond hair off his face with his fingers and flipped off the light. He returned to the bed, pulled off the rest of his clothes, tossed them into the laundry pile, and slid into the sheets. Leaning his head against the pillows, he blew out a relieved sigh.

"Better?" asked Marjorie.

He rested an arm on his forehead. "It feels good to lie down."

She put her book down, rolled toward him, and snuggled into his shoulder. "It sucks you had to work today."

He lowered his arm and put it around her. "It was bound to happen. Lozano's been taking it easy on us since we got back from Merrimac. Plus, this case might have a connection to Margaret Redstone, so it makes sense he'd want us on it."

"You think Rem can handle it?"

"He can handle it. In fact, I think it's exactly what he needs. This not knowing or hearing anything is worse. We've both been on pins and needles waiting for something to happen."

"I think that's what scares me. If this does have something to do with her, what's she planning?"

Daniels wondered about that himself. "I don't know. This could just be someone who wants to get Margaret's attention."

"That's scary, too. What if whoever it is kills again?"

Daniels had to assume the killer likely wasn't done. "Let's hope we catch him before he does."

She sighed and laid her arm over his waist. "I hate this. I worry about you two. If this person wants to get Margaret's attention, they could come after you or Rem."

Daniels had considered that himself. "I know, but we can't think like that. Every case brings its own set of concerns, but most of it never pans out."

She raised her head. "It did with Victor D'Mato."

Daniels eyed the ceiling. He recalled the creepy statue that had been sent to him, hating the memories of what it had done to his psyche. "That won't happen again. We're more prepared now, and we know what Margaret's capable of." Marjorie went quiet, and he sensed her doubt. "Try not to worry. We'll be okay." He stroked her back. "Can we talk about something else? What about you? Were you talking to Moira earlier?"

She narrowed her eyes at him. "Nice deflection, Detective."

"It's why I'm good at what I do."

Marjorie snuggled back into his shoulder. "She's doing great. Bryan brought her and the baby home from the hospital today. Plus, the school found a sub to take her classes while she's on maternity leave."

"That's great. I bet she's happy to be home."

"I'm going to go over there this week to see her and the baby. You want to come? You and Bryan can share newborn war stories."

Daniels groaned, remembering the late-night feedings and lack of sleep. "I don't miss those days." He pulled her close. "I doubt with this new case, though, that I'll be able to join you."

She traced a finger over his ribs. "You thought any more about having another one?"

Daniels did his best not to react. "I thought we were going to give it six months and then discuss it once J.P.'s a little older."

"I know. I just wondered if you'd had any change of heart."

"To be honest, I told myself not to think about it because I know you want one thing and I want another. In six months, when J.P. turns two, we'll decide what to do. But until then, I just want to enjoy my son and beautiful wife." He kissed her head. "And our happy life."

She ran her fingers up his sternum and his body tingled. "All right," she said. "I won't push you. But if you want to go with me to Moira's and hold sweet little Nathan, you let me know."

He chuckled. "Sweet little Nathan, huh?"

"With his soft skin and tiny fingers and toes."

Daniels rolled to his side to face her. "What if I'd rather hold my sweet little wife?" He ran his hand under the covers and down her hip and thigh.

Her breath caught and she smiled. "You're deflecting again."

He lowered his face to hers and kissed her. Marjorie wrapped her arms around him and pulled her body against his. He slid his lips down her cheek to her neck where he nibbled her. "Told you I was good at what I do."

She giggled and gasped when his hand slid lower. "I knew I married you for a reason." Wrapping her leg over his, she rolled him onto his back, straddled him, and he moaned when she covered his lips with her own in a passionate kiss.

Chapter Six

REM PARKED OUTSIDE THE station in his usual spot. Once he'd turned off his car, he sat, thinking. After tossing and turning for two hours the previous night, he'd finally sat up, frustrated. Thinking of Daniels' advice, he'd leaned against the headboard, crossed his legs, and closed his eyes. It had taken several minutes, but he'd finally managed to quiet his mind. Doing his best to think of nothing, he'd focused on the hum of the air conditioner. Several more minutes passed, and as he'd relaxed more and more, the tension had eased from his shoulders and neck. Tired, he'd slid down in the bed, pulled the sheets up, and had fallen asleep.

That morning, he'd opened his eyes and known exactly what he wanted to do. Feeling better than he had in a while, he'd showered, had some breakfast and coffee, and had headed to the station, the whole time feeling confident. But now, sitting in his car, realizing he'd be meeting with Kate Schultz soon, he needed to talk to someone. Checking the time, he saw he had a few minutes. He picked up his phone and dialed a number.

"Hello?" asked Mikey. "Rem?"

"Hey, Mikey." Rem paused, considering what to say. "You got a minute?"

"I just walked into SCOPE." Rem could hear a door close and what sounded like keys on a desk. "Is something wrong? Is this about your new case?"

"No. It isn't. It's something else." Rem gripped the steering wheel. "It's about Allison." Rem thought about Allison's pregnancy. He debated telling Mikey, but his anxiety rose, and he held back. "It's the plea bargain. I made a decision."

"You did? What did you decide?"

Rem imagined her putting her purse down and sitting on the couch in SCOPE's office. He could see her in her typical black skinny jeans and black T-shirt. "I don't want Kate to offer the plea bargain. We'll go to trial."

He heard her soft intake of breath. "That's a gutsy call," she said.

"I don't know how gutsy it is. I doubt Measy, Allison's attorney, would have advised her to take any deal. But at least I made the call and not her."

"You don't know what would have happened. Allison may have gone for it. I know she talks a good game, but I'm not sure she's willing to risk life in prison." She paused. "What made you decide on a trial?"

"I remembered what you said to me when I first told you about the plea bargain. You said I had a right to tell my truth, and that's what I want to do. I want to face her in court and tell the jury what she did to me and others. Then I'll let the chips fall and see what a jury decides." He exhaled. "She may still get acquitted, but I know if I don't do this, I'll regret it for the rest of my life."

"I'm proud of you. You're standing up for yourself and I'm glad. Personally, I think it's the right decision. You can't let your fear stop you from doing what you think is best."

Rem dropped his head, happy to hear her say that. He didn't know why it was so important for him to tell Mikey, but he'd been thinking of her all morning. He thought again of Allison's pregnancy. "Thank you. It means a lot to hear you say that." Feeling wistful, he realized he wanted to see her. "Listen. I know my week is going to be crazy, but if I get a few minutes, you want to go get a coffee?"

"I'd love that. It's been a while."

"I know. We need to make up for lost time and we need to talk."

"You just let me know when you're free. I can always meet you somewhere."

"I'll call you." If anybody deserved to know what was going on with Allison, it was Mikey. If he had enough guts to go to trial, then he could certainly handle telling Mikey the truth, no matter how uncomfortable it might be.

"Great," she said. "You need anything, you know where to find me. You and Daniels be careful."

"You be careful, too." Feeling good about his decision, Rem relaxed against his seat. "See you soon."

"See you."

Rem hung up and put his phone in his pocket. Pleased he'd called, he grabbed his keys, got out of his car, and headed into the station. Walking into the squad room, he saw Daniels at his desk. "Good morning."

"Morning," said Daniels. "Did you get some sleep?"

"Got more than I thought. I tried your meditation suggestion, and it worked."

Daniels raised his brow. "Really? Did you decide?"

Rem slid off his jacket and hung it around the back of his chair. He opened his mouth to speak when the squad doors opened, and Lozano and Kate Schultz entered. Rem saw his captain's face and frowned. "Morning, Cap." His captain approached their desks. "Everything okay?" asked Rem.

The captain barely broke stride. "I need to see you two in my office." Kate followed Lozano, and Rem and Daniels shared a look.

Daniels stood. "He doesn't look happy."

"I didn't even have time to get a cup of coffee." Rem followed Daniels into Lozano's office, and Daniels closed the door behind them.

"What's up?" asked Daniels.

Kate set her briefcase and purse on the floor beside Lozano's desk. "I want to talk to you two about Allison's plea bargain."

Lozano sat in his chair. "We talked to the DA."

Rem raised a hand. "Before you say anything, and I change my mind, I've decided I don't want to offer the plea bargain to Allison. I want to go to trial."

Daniels walked up beside him. "Good for you."

Kate crossed her arms. "I made the offer last night. Measy is taking it to Allison." Her expression remained flat. "I expect to hear something soon."

Rem dropped his jaw. Lozano opened a drawer, threw something in it, and slammed it shut. Daniels glared. "What the hell is going on here?" asked Daniels. "I thought you told Rem it was up to him."

"The DA changed his mind," said Kate. "He told me to offer it."

Rem didn't know what to say. "Why?"

"Says it's too risky." Kate rubbed her forehead. "Said it's better to plead it out. He doesn't want egg on our faces if we lose."

Daniels put his hands on his hips. "You mean he's up for reelection and he doesn't want to look bad." He shot out a hand toward Rem. "Did he forget that this woman tortured and almost killed a police officer?"

"Believe me," said Lozano. "I told him exactly what I thought." He shot a dirty look at Kate. "I'm sure the chief will hear about it. I'm not expecting a promotion anytime soon."

"You all know how this works," said Kate. "This is the way it goes sometimes. It surprised me as much as you."

Weary, Rem sat in one of the chairs. "I've been losing sleep over this decision for weeks and you end up making it for me." He sighed deeply. "It would've been nice to have known that sooner."

"I don't believe this," said Daniels.

"Just because we offered it, doesn't mean they'll take it," said Kate. "This may still go to trial."

Rem's mixed emotions swirled. All his confidence and certainty from the morning had evaporated. Indecision tormented him. What if Allison took the deal? Would he feel happy or sad? Part of him felt the familiar pang of relief at the thought of not testifying, but another part of him felt anger that the decision had been taken from him. "I just don't understand why the sudden change?" asked Rem. "I thought the DA would at least have enough guts to let me make the decision."

"To be honest," said Kate, "I was surprised when he left it to me in the first place. I guess I shouldn't be shocked that he went back on his promise. He is a politician after all."

"But we still have the two followers' testimony," said Daniels. "We have a rock-solid case."

"Said he had to look at the bigger picture," said Lozano, leaning forward with his elbows on his desk. "Said if we could get her to take twenty years, it would be the better option." He scowled. "I reminded him that my detective had a right to offer an opinion. Rem's life was on the line, and he should have had a say in what happens to Allison."

"Obviously, he didn't agree," said Daniels.

"Said that wasn't Rem's job. He's too emotionally involved." Kate began to pace. "I asked him to reconsider, but he wouldn't."

Frustrated, Rem sat up. "Too emotionally involved? You're damn straight I'm emotionally involved. All the more reason for me to be included." Angry, he stood and walked to the window. People walked down the street without a care in the world and he envied and wished he could join them.

The office went quiet, and Rem raked his hand through his hair. The control he'd thought he'd had was gone and now he was left to wait for Allison's decision. He wondered how long it would take. He eyed the cars driving by and told himself to relax. What was done, was done, and there was nothing he could do about it.

A phone rang, and Kate dug her cell out of her purse. "It's Measy." She eyed the three men in the room. "Give me a second." She left the office and closed the door.

Rem stared at the busy street, wondering what the verdict would be. "I guess we're about to hear her decision."

"Whatever it is," said Daniels, "we'll handle it."

Lozano swiveled in his seat and faced Rem. "So, you wanted to take it to trial. Why?"

Rem put his hands in his pockets. "I wanted to face her in court. To look at her and tell the world what she did. I wanted her to know I'm not scared of her anymore." He didn't know if that was true, but he wanted to say it.

"You might still get that chance," said Daniels. "But if you don't, at least she'll be put away for fifteen to twenty."

"Are you trying to convince me there's a silver lining in all of this?" asked Rem.

Daniels shrugged. "Mr. Positivity makes a comeback." He offered Rem a somber look. "How am I doing?"

"Don't quit your day job," said Rem.

"Cut me some slack. I don't have a lot to work with, especially with an idiot DA," said Daniels.

Rem held his head and squeezed his temples. "It doesn't matter. Either option sucks in its own way. I don't know why I'm complaining."

Daniels approached Lozano's desk. "You have every right to complain. Every time you think you're headed in one direction, the rug gets ripped out and you're turned in another. Not to mention Allison's pregnancy and the possible return of Margaret. I don't know how you're doing it, but you're dealing with a hell of a lot. So, bitch all you want. Lozano and I can be your sounding board."

Lozano turned on his monitor. "I'd give you the day, but with this new case, that's not an option. As soon as Kate leaves, that's our next topic."

"I don't want the day off," said Rem. "I just want some sanity in my life." He looked out the window again. "And to be able to walk down the street without thinking about Allison, Margaret, or potential fatherhood." He huffed. "Or to get a damn cup of coffee with Mikey without having to worry about her dying because she's with me."

"Rem—" said Daniels.

The door opened, and Rem turned to see Kate enter. She held her phone in her hand and closed the door behind her. His heart thumped. "Well?" asked Rem.

"They turned it down," said Kate, tossing her phone back in her purse. She smiled softly. "I hope you're ready, Detective, because we're going to trial."

Chapter Seven

DANIELS FOLLOWED REM OUT of Lozano's office. Rem sat heavily into his chair and Daniels sat across from him at his desk. Daniels eyed his partner warily. "You okay?"

Rem sighed heavily and stared at the ceiling. "I feel like it's already been an eight-hour day." He raised his head. "I need some coffee."

Daniels pointed. "Looks like it's your lucky day."

Rem narrowed his eyes. "Are you trying to be funny? Because it's not working."

"No. I'm not kidding. Look behind you."

Rem swiveled in his seat. His eyes widened when he saw a freshly made pot of coffee on the counter behind him. The pot had been empty when Rem had arrived. "At least somebody loves me." He stood and grabbed his mug. Looking around the squad room, he raised his voice. "Whoever made the coffee, I owe you for life."

Detective Mellenbuehl walked by. "That would be me. And I'd love tickets to the Padres game."

Rem grabbed the pot and poured some coffee into his mug. "How about the zoo? My cousin works there. He can get you in for free." He returned the pot to the machine. "I may even be able to get you behind the scenes at the reptile exhibit. You can hold a snake."

Daniels shook his head. "Don't do it, Mel. He told me the same thing. I ended up shoveling elephant dung into the back of a truck."

"I told you," said Rem. "The snakes were sleeping that day."

"What does that have to do with anything?" asked Daniels. "I smelled like elephant shit all the way home."

"Marjorie loved the visit, though," said Rem.

"That's because she got to hold the baby monkeys." Daniels eyed Mel. "You've been warned."

"I think I'd prefer the Padres tickets." Mel returned to his desk and sat.

Rem added sugar and creamer to his coffee and stirred. "Well, I don't have any cousins that work for the Padres but if that changes, I'll let you know."

"What about your cousin Tito?" asked Daniels. "Doesn't he do something in sports?"

"He scalps tickets," said Rem. "If I got you some of those, Mel, I'd have to arrest you."

Mel looked up. "I'll pass. Just enjoy your coffee. Based on what I could see in Lozano's office, I think you need it."

"You have no idea." Rem sipped his drink and groaned in satisfaction. "That's good."

Daniels leaned back in his chair and spoke to Mel. "You and Garcia good with going to chat with Allison Albright? Lozano told us he'd asked you to visit her today."

Mel nodded. "No problem. We're looking forward to it."

Rem returned to his seat. "Don't get your hopes up. She probably doesn't know anything, and even if she does, she probably won't tell you."

"It's worth talking to her, though," said Daniels. "If she has information about Stella's murder, or Margaret's involvement, we need to at least try to get it out of her."

Mel wrote something on a piece of paper and put it in a folder. "We'll do our best. We'll go after lunch and let you know how it goes."

"And if her attorney is there, try not to kill him, although you'll be tempted." Rem sipped some more of his coffee.

"He's lucky we'll have to check our guns at the front," said Mel. He stood and grabbed his jacket. "I'll talk to you guys as soon as we know something."

"Thanks. See you, Mel." Daniels spoke to Rem, whose mug was already half empty. "Where do you want to start, partner?"

Rem set his drink down. "Well, we've got Mel and Garcia questioning Allison. Titus and Georgios are talking to Stella's family members. Which leaves us the client list."

"Don't forget Gina Rodriguez."

Rem's face fell. "That's right. Her, too. Something tells me that she'll be as helpful as Allison."

"Only one way to find out."

"Yeah. I guess."

Daniels tapped on his keyboard and his laptop screen lit up. "Tech found the list of Stella's clients. Thankfully, she kept good records." He opened his email and pulled up the names. "Unfortunately, she's got a lot of them." He rubbed his jaw. "What do you say we talk to her latest clients first, and work our way down?"

"Sounds good to me," said Rem. "Maybe we'll get lucky, and somebody will give us a lead."

"Let's hope," Daniels hit the print button. The printer whirred to life and began to spit out the list. Eyeing his desk, he spotted his snow globe, which sported a hot dog and bun with yellow flakes inside it, beside the printer. Normally, it sat on the left corner of his desk. The snow globe had once belonged to Jennie, Rem's girlfriend who'd died almost three years earlier. Daniels had given it to her as a joke, and after she'd died, Daniels had asked if he could keep it. It had sat on his desk ever since. "Did you move my snow globe?"

Rem glanced at Daniel's desk. "No."

Daniels stood. He went to the printer and picked up the globe. He shook it and the delicate yellow flakes swirled and settled around the hot dog and bun. "Huh." He set it back on the corner of his desk.

Rem gestured toward the globe. "Maybe the cleaning staff moved it."

Daniels grabbed the papers from the printer. "What cleaning staff?"

"The one that theoretically comes in here every night."

Daniels picked up a piece of trash from the floor. "Along with the magical fairies?" He tossed the trash in the waste basket.

"Yeah. Them, too." Rem leaned back in his chair. "How long is the list?"

Daniels ran his finger down the names. "She's got thirty-six clients." He eyed the dates. "She saw two clients the day before she died. And three clients two days before she died." He looked up at Rem. "I say we start there."

"We have addresses?"

Daniels nodded. "And phone numbers."

"Okay," said Rem. "Let me finish this coffee. And we'll get started."

Daniels returned to his desk. "Take your time. It's going to be a long day." Thinking of their meeting with Kate and Lozano, he leaned forward. "You want to talk about Allison rejecting the deal?"

Rem looked up from his coffee. "I'm not sure how to feel about it. Despite how we got there, I guess I should be happy we're going to trial." He set his cup down. "Although 'happy' is a relative term."

"You mentioned Mikey. Are you planning to see her?"

"I called her this morning. Told her I wanted to take her to coffee."

Curious, Daniels lifted an eyebrow. Ever since Margaret's escape, Rem had been reluctant to spend any time with Mikey. Daniels had tried to convince him otherwise, but Rem had held his ground. He'd been convinced that being around her would somehow attract Margaret's attention. After what had happened to Jennie, Daniels knew Rem feared the same tragedy repeating itself. "What changed your mind?"

Rem ran his fingers through his long hair, pulled it into a low ponytail and wrapped a band around it. "I want to see her. I need to tell her about Allison."

Daniels almost sighed in relief. "I'm glad. I hope this leads to you two hanging out more often."

Rem shrugged. "We'll see. I guess it depends on what happens with this case."

"Well, you already know how I feel." Daniels, along with Mason and Trick, Mason's partner, could see the attraction between Rem and Mikey, but the timing had never been right. Daniels had finally convinced Rem to tell Mikey how he felt about her, but Margaret's escape had changed everything. And to complicate matters, Mikey had been working with Kyle Willow, who'd also expressed interest in dating Mikey. Based on what Mason had told Daniels, Mikey and Kyle were keeping it friendly for now, but Mason sensed that may not last for long.

"Yes," said Rem. "I'm well aware of your opinion. But you know why I've been hesitant."

"I do and I get it. But you can't wait forever." Daniels paused. "I know Margaret and Allison have thrown a wrench into things, but don't let them dictate your happiness."

Rem picked up his coffee. He stared into his mug. "Easier said than done. But I hear you."

Pleased his partner was at least open to discussing it, Daniels smiled. "Good." He pulled his jacket from the back of the chair and stood. "You ready to go talk to some clients?"

Rem finished his coffee, grabbed a paper towel from a roll beside the coffee machine and wiped down his mug. "You mind if we stop for a cup of coffee on the way?"

Daniels spied Rem's desk. "Where's your travel mug?"

"I can't find it. I thought I'd left it in my desk, but I haven't seen it." Rem opened the tall drawers and dug through them. "Maybe the theoretical cleaning crew took it." He closed the drawers and gestured toward the snow globe. "And left that behind."

Daniels snorted. "I can't imagine why." He glanced at Rem's messy desk and the surrounding area but didn't see the insulated mug. Thinking it was odd since Rem had had that mug for as long as he could remember, Daniels lifted the list and shook the papers. "Let's go crack this case wide open, and then we'll buy you a new thermos. Sound like a plan?"

Rem put on his jacket and waved a hand toward the door. "After you, Kemosabe."

A few hours later, they'd made little progress. They'd visited Stella's last three clients but none of them had known anything about Stella's connection to Victor or Margaret. They'd stopped by Gina's apartment, but no one had answered the door. After talking to a neighbor, they'd learned that Gina was out of town and would be returning the following day, so they made plans to return to Gina's tomorrow.

Rem eyed the list in his hand as they approached a small house on a wooded lot. They were here to talk to Thomas Lenore, who'd received a massage from Stella two days prior to her death. Rem and Daniels walked to the front door and Daniels knocked.

Rem folded the list and tucked it into his pocket. "Let's hope Thomas knows something."

"We have to consider," said Daniels, "that her clients won't know anything."

"Or that one of them could be the killer."

Daniels put his hands in his jacket pockets. "That, too."

The door opened and a man with curly blonde hair, a strong jaw, and what looked like peanut butter smeared on his face, opened the door. He held a small child with wispy blonde hair that Rem guessed was around six to eight months of age. "Yes?" asked the man. "How can I help you?" The child screeched and smacked a chubby hand on the man's cheek.

Rem and Daniels held out their badges. "Sorry to bother you, sir," said Daniels. "I'm Detective Daniels and this is my partner Detective Remalla. Are you Thomas Lenore?"

The man looked between them, and the child screeched again. "No. That's my husband." He bounced the little girl in his arms. "What's this about?"

"We'd like to ask him about Stella de la Rosa," said Rem. "We understand he had an appointment with her for a massage a few days ago."

The man rolled his eyes. "Stella? What did she do? Did she look inside her crystal ball, sniff some essential oils, howl at the moon, and tell somebody they're going to find their Prince Charming and win a million bucks?" The child shrieked again and smacked again at the man's cheeks. The man took her hand and held it. "Take it easy, little Violet. Daddy's going to make you lunch." He eyed Rem and Daniels. "Thomas ran to the store but he should be back any minute. You want to come in and wait?" He stepped back and widened the door. "I need to feed Violet and Paul."

Rem and Daniels exchanged a look and Daniels nodded. "If you don't mind, we would like to talk with him."

Rem heard another child yell from inside. "Daddy. I'm hungry."

"I'm coming, Paulie. Be right there." The man bounced Violet to keep her from crying. "My name is Jeremy, by the way. Welcome to the zoo."

"Thank you, Jeremy." Rem walked inside and Daniels followed. "We'll try not to get in your way," said Rem.

Jeremy closed the door behind them. "In my way? I've got two hungry kids to feed. As long as you guys don't expect lunch, we should be fine." He walked through a living room littered with toys. "Don't mind the mess." He entered a kitchen.

Rem stepped over a toy, and Daniels inadvertently kicked a ball which rolled across the carpet. They walked into the kitchen and Rem saw a little boy sitting at a dining table. He had an electronic toy with flashing lights in his hand, and he was sipping from a sippy cup. He looked to be around three years of age.

Jeremy went to the kitchen counter where two pieces of bread were on a plate, with a jar of peanut butter and a jar of jelly sitting beside it.

"Who are you?" asked Paul, who bobbed his feet up and down and played with his toy. He pressed a button and lights swirled and music played.

"Don't mind them, Paulie. They need to ask Dad some questions when he comes home. I'm getting your sandwich now." Jeremy opened a drawer and pulled out a knife. Violet squirmed in his arms and Jeremy sighed. He eyed Rem. "Would you mind?" He set the knife down and held Violet out to Rem.

Rem froze for a moment and glanced at Daniels who shrugged at him.

"I promise," said Jeremy. "She's harmless." He paused. "Usually." He held Violet and waited for Rem to take her.

"Uh, sure." Rem reluctantly took Violet and settled her on his hip. She immediately began to play with his jacket pocket and grabbed at a strand of his hair that had fallen from his ponytail.

"Don't worry, partner." Daniels looked amused. "It's not any different than holding J.P."

"It's been a while since J.P.'s been this little." Violet squirmed and Rem adjusted his hold.

"It's like riding a bike," said Daniels.

Jeremy slathered peanut butter and jelly on the two pieces of bread. "Sorry to have to put you to work, but I'm going to take the help when I can get it. I told Thomas two kids would be a handful, but did he listen to me? Paulie was hard enough, and I love Violet, but man, I just need some sleep." He finished making the sandwich and cut it in half. "You guys have kids?"

"I have an eighteen-month-old," said Daniels.

Rem couldn't help but think of Allison. "None." He nodded toward Daniels. "But I think you're helping my partner here make a big decision."

Jeremy grabbed a napkin and the plate and brought them over to Paul. "Let me guess. Your significant other wants another kid."

Daniels shifted on his feet. "She's mentioned it."

Jeremy grabbed Paul's sippy cup and brought it to the kitchen. "You want my advice? Don't do it. Or at least give yourself plenty of time in between. I love my kiddos, don't get me wrong. But damn." The toy flashed again, and another song played. Jeremy opened the refrigerator and poured some apple juice into the sippy cup. "Thomas and I haven't had a date night in six months. But we finally decided to splurge. Thomas got a massage, and I'm getting a facial tomorrow. I can't wait. We've got a babysitter coming this weekend and we're finally going to dinner all by ourselves."

Violet squirmed some more and tugged on Rem's hair. He brought her to a sliding glass door where she could see outside. He pointed toward the trees and a bird on a branch. "See the birdie?" His mind drifted, and he couldn't help but wonder if he'd be holding his own daughter six months from now.

"You're good with her. She doesn't usually like strangers." Jeremy brought the filled sippy cup to Paul. "Here you go, buddy. Eat up."

Violet patted the glass and tried to lick it. "No licking the glass," said Rem. He stepped back, and she squealed. He spoke to Daniels. "You want to hold her?"

Daniels grinned. "You're doing just fine." He took Violet's hand, and she squeezed his finger. "I think you're a natural."

"Isn't that what everyone says when they're holding somebody else's child?" asked Rem. He moved Violet to his other hip.

Jeremy returned to the refrigerator. "Let me just get her food ready and I'll take her."

"No rush," said Daniels. "Violet's in good hands."

Rem made a face at Daniels which Rem hoped translated appropriately. Daniels chuckled. "You said Thomas would be here soon?" asked Daniels.

"Yes." Jeremy grabbed some baby food jars and set them on the counter. "He ran out to get some diapers. Violet's already moved into the next size. It's amazing how fast they grow."

"That's true," said Daniels. He eyed Paul and Violet. "It's kind of why I want to enjoy my first one before I consider another child."

Rem held Violet's arm to keep her from yanking the hair out of his head. "Oh, I don't know. If you're going to have a second one, you might as well have it now. Get all of the diaper changes and sleepless nights out of the way."

"That's what they all say," said Jeremy. "But if I had to do it again, I'd wait." He spooned out some baby food into a bowl. "The house is a mess, and Thomas and I are exhausted; we haven't slept in on the weekend in three years. Childrearing is rewarding, but it's also tough." He stirred the food. "Sorry if I'm talking too much. Thomas would kill me if he knew I was spilling my guts to you. He loves all the chaos." He stirred the food. "So, what's up with Stella?"

Daniels righted Paul's sippy cup when Paul knocked it sideways. "You said Thomas had a massage with her. Had he been to see Stella before?"

Jeremy rolled his eyes again. "Yes. He and Stella are friends. They met at some sort of mystical, spirit, love and peace festival. You know the type. She's been trying to get him to do a reading and massage. I think she's flaky, but he likes her. So, he finally made an appointment."

"How did it go?" asked Rem. "Was her reading accurate?"

Jeremy warmed the food in the microwave. "She told him he would be successful and happy this year. But also tired. Said this year would be challenging, and to take care of himself. She also told him there would be conflicts in his relationship and to be patient with his partner." He rinsed the spoon in the sink. "Can you believe that?"

"I hope the massage was good, even if the reading wasn't." Rem brought Violet back toward the glass and pointed toward the bird to distract her.

Jeremy shook his head. "Conflicts." He rolled his eyes. "Everybody has conflicts, don't they?" He glanced toward Rem and Daniels. "I bet you two have had your arguments."

Daniels met Rem's gaze. "We've had one or two," said Daniels.

"But nothing worth losing our friendship over." Rem turned back toward Jeremy, waiting for the food to be ready.

"How long have you been partners?" asked Jeremy.

"A long time," said Daniels.

"You're obviously good friends." The microwave dinged, and Jeremy took out the food. "You'd make a cute couple."

Rem shot a look at Daniels. "He should be so lucky."

Daniels snorted. "I think you've got that the wrong way around."

Violet saw her food and squirmed even more. Rem struggled to hold onto her. "She's a strong kid."

"When it comes to food," said Jeremy, "she'll crawl through a brick wall." He smiled. "She takes after me." He set the bowl of food on the table, walked to Rem, and held his hands out. "Come here, sweetheart. Time to eat."

Violet reached for him, and Jeremy took her from Rem. Rem eyed his jacket for any unexpected stains but was happy to see he'd escaped unscathed. Jeremy sat at the table and slid Violet into a highchair. He put a bib around her neck and began to feed her. "I didn't even ask why you wanted to question Thomas about Stella." Jeremy wiped Violet's face when food dribbled down her chin. "Is everything okay?"

"Well," said Daniels, "we—"

The back door opened, and a man entered. He had dark skin, a lean frame, and short hair cut close to his scalp. He held a plastic bag and stopped when he saw Rem and Daniels. "Were we expecting company?" he asked Jeremy.

Jeremy fed Violet another bite. "These are two detectives, Thomas. They want to ask you about Stella. You can tell them all about your so-so reading and fab massage."

Thomas set the bag on the kitchen counter. "I'm telling you, Jer, you should try it. It would do wonders for your mood."

"Sleep would do wonders for my mood," said Jeremy. "And it doesn't cost anything."

Thomas shook his head and eyed Rem and Daniels. "Sorry. He's a little cranky. How can I help you?"

"We need to ask you about Stella de la Rosa," said Daniels. "How well did you know her?"

"We're friends," said Thomas. "I've known her a couple of years." His face fell and his eyes narrowed. "Is she okay? Why would two detectives want to ask me about her?"

Daniels sighed. "I'm sorry to have to tell you, but Stella was murdered. Her body was found in her home, and you were one of her last clients."

Thomas dropped his jaw.

"You're kidding." Jeremy lowered the spoon. "Stella's dead?"

"Unfortunately," said Rem. "She is. We're investigating her death and talking to anybody who knew her."

"I don't believe it," said Thomas, holding his chest. "Who would want to kill her?"

"We're hoping you can help us with that," said Rem.

Daniels held out his phone. "There was a picture found in her massage room." He raised the phone. "We're wondering if you recognize either of the men in the photo?"

Still looking shocked, Thomas leaned in and studied the picture. "I don't know either one of them." He put his hand over his mouth. "I'm just in shock."

"The killer also left a note," said Rem. "He mentioned a woman named Margaret. And there was a bow tie left at the scene." He crossed his arms. "Does any of that mean anything to you?"

"A woman named Margaret, and a bow tie?" asked Thomas. "I have no idea."

"Can you think of any reason why anyone would want Stella dead?" asked Daniels.

"No," said Thomas. "I can't." He dabbed at watery eyes. "I wish I could help you."

Rem made eye contact with Daniels, sensing his partner's disappointment, and feeling his own. He pulled out one of his cards. "If something comes to mind, or you remember something of importance, please call us."

Thomas took the card. "I remember when I showed up for my appointment, Stella was arguing with someone. Could that be important?"

Daniels frowned. "Arguing? With who? Did you see them?"

Thomas stammered. "I... I don't know. I heard voices when I got to the door, but I knocked, and the arguing stopped. I waited and Stella opened the door. She seemed fine, and another woman walked out. She said goodbye, got in her car and drove away."

"Can you describe her?" asked Rem. "Or the car?" Hopeful they had a lead, his heart began to race.

Thomas put a hand on his head. "I didn't pay much attention to the car, but I got a decent look at her. She had long, straight, dark hair, and was average height, but on the thin side." He snapped his fingers. "I remember she had striking blue eyes."

Rem's heart raced faster. "Blue eyes?" His skin prickled.

Daniels swiped through some photos on his phone and held it out. "Is this the woman you saw?"

Thomas leaned over, and Jeremy stood and peeked at the picture. Rem got close and saw a mug shot of Margaret. Thomas's eyes widened. "Yes, that's her. That's the woman I saw leaving Stella's house." He straightened and put a hand to his mouth. "Did she kill Stella?"

Chapter Eight

REYNALDO BELMAR SLID THE jacket onto his customer. He smoothed the sleek material and adjusted the fit. The customer admired himself in the mirror. He turned to see the back and side views. "I like this," he said.

Reynaldo smiled. "You can't do much better than this designer. It's wonderful on you." He stepped back and circled the small pedestal. "I like it better than the Armani." He paused. "What do you think of the color?"

The customer buttoned the jacket. "I like the chocolate, but I think I'm leaning toward the navy. What do you think?"

Reynaldo debated between the two. "You do both of them well, but I do agree, if I were to pick one it would be the navy."

The customer nodded and pulled on the waistband of the pants. "I think the pants could be taken in slightly."

Reynaldo approached and checked. "It could be, a touch. It would be an easy fix." He stepped back again and held his jaw. "Of course, if you want to go top-of-the-line, there's nothing better than a custom-made suit. I recommend it to all my high-end clients."

The customer ticked up a brow. "Really? Even more so than Gucci or Armani?"

"A custom-made suit would fit you perfectly. And it would be designed to emphasize your broad shoulders and long frame and minimize any perceived flaws. You can choose the fabric, the color, the cut. I have my own team. As I'm sure you've heard, there is nothing better than a custom suit made at Reynaldo's." He swiped at a speck of dust on his customer's sleeve. "If you need some examples of my work, I can certainly provide references."

"There's no need for that," said the customer. "The whole reason I'm here is because of all the praise I've heard about you. One of my friends actually recommended your shop. His style was unparalleled. He told me before he died, if I ever want a beautiful suit, go see Reynaldo."

Reynaldo grinned, happy to hear the praise. He glanced at himself in the mirror and adjusted his bow tie. "I'm curious. Who is it that spoke so highly of me?"

"Victor D'Mato."

A sliver of anxiety traveled up Reynaldo's spine. "Victor? I haven't heard his name in quite a while." He shook his head. "Terrible thing what happened to him. He was a good friend and customer."

"I heard you two were close."

Reynaldo forced the smile to remain on his face. "We were, for a time. When I first met him, he had an abysmal taste in clothes. He invested in my shop. One of the main reasons you're standing here today is because of Victor."

The man adjusted one of his sleeves. "It must've been a shock when he died."

"Indeed, it was. We'd had a bit of a falling out and I hadn't seen him, but I'd always anticipated we would repair our friendship." He sighed, remembering the relief he'd felt at the news of Victor's death. "Unfortunately, that never happened."

"I can understand," said the customer. "In the end, Victor kept some unusual company. It made some people uncomfortable."

"I'm sorry to say that's what we argued over," said Reynaldo. "I disagreed with the direction he was going in. I should have kept business and personal relationships separate, but I failed. So, when Victor left, so did his business."

"He still recommended you, though. For a time, I wanted to be just like him." He stared off. "I emulated him and did whatever he asked of me." The look on his face hardened.

Reynaldo recalled his contentious relationship with Victor. "You weren't the only one. He attracted a lot of people who wanted to be around him. He was easy to like. Until..." Reynaldo chose not to say more and changed the subject. "So what do you think? Stick with this beauty?" He touched the sleeve of the suit. "Or let's take it up a notch and go custom? Either way, you can't go wrong."

Eyeing himself in the mirror, the customer tipped his head. "If Victor was a fan of the custom-made, then so am I." He unbuttoned the jacket and slid it off. "How long does it take for you to create a tailor-made suit?"

Reynaldo took the jacket, smoothed it, and draped it over his arm. "We'll need some additional measurements, and I can show you the fabrics to choose from. We could do that today or make an appointment. Once I have all the information, it will take around two weeks and then you can come in for a fitting."

"Excellent. Let me change and we can discuss my options."

Reynaldo watched his customer step into the dressing room. "That's perfect. I'll be out here when you're ready." He rehung the jacket and set it aside to be returned to the back. He walked to the front of his private shop and pulled out his book. He flipped to the appropriate page and saw that his next customer would arrive in thirty minutes. He set the book aside and straightened the area around him.

Reynaldo liked to keep a clean store. It's what his customers expected of him. He'd loved fashion and design for as long as he could remember, and one of his first well-paying clients was Victor D'Mato. Reynaldo had revamped Victor's wardrobe and his style had shifted with Reynaldo's flashy, but sexy, touch. They'd been friends until Victor had begun to change. The people around him became almost driven to serve him, and Victor had adored their attention and expected almost complete obedience.

Reynaldo could recall a tense exchange when he'd disagreed with Victor regarding a particular suit. Victor had become outraged that Reynaldo had questioned his taste. Although he'd taken Reynaldo's advice, he'd left the store and Reynaldo hadn't seen him for months. One day, though, Victor had unexpectedly walked in, smiling as if they'd never argued, and proclaiming how he was on the brink of an amazing discovery. One that would change his life forever, and Reynaldo's, too, if he was willing to pledge his loyalty to Victor and honor his secrets at the risk of death. By then, Reynaldo had heard the whispered rumors of Victor's ties to drugs and other illegal activities and how he'd gathered unique people around him willing to do his bidding. Reynaldo had gathered his courage and politely declined the offer. The look Victor had given him had made his blood run cold, but Reynaldo had held firm. Victor had grinned, expressed his disappointment, wished him well and had walked out. Months later, Reynaldo had heard of Victor's death. Some part of him had not been surprised.

The curtains opened, and his customer reappeared wearing his comfortable slacks and long sleeve shirt. He smoothed back his ruffled hair, smiled, and adjusted his collar. "So, when do we take these measurements?"

"I have twenty minutes right now, but to be honest I'd like more time." Reynaldo returned to his book and flipped open a page. "Can you come in tomorrow?"

"Tomorrow?" The customer paused. "Actually, how about the day after? What times do you have?"

Reynaldo flipped to the next page. "How about four p.m.? I think it will take about thirty minutes."

The customer smiled. "That's fine."

Reynaldo picked up a pen. "The name is Oswald Fry, correct?"

The man nodded. "Good memory. Yes. Oswald Fry."

Reynaldo scribbled in his book. "Perfect, Mr. Fry. I look forward to seeing you in two days. I think you'll be very happy with your custom suit."

"I believe so, too," said Mr. Fry. "Maybe if I'm lucky, you'll throw in one of those bow ties."

Reynaldo touched his collar. "I've always been known for my bow ties. You might look quite dapper in one."

Fry grinned. "I just might." He held out his hand. "I'll look forward to my custom suit."

Reynaldo shook his hand. "As will I." Fry gripped his palm for a moment and when Reynaldo tried to let go, Fry held on. For a moment, Reynaldo felt a strange tingle run up his arm, but then Fry let him go.

Fry took a step toward the door. "You have a nice day."

Reynaldo rubbed his fingers together, curious about the strange sensation. "You, too." Shaking out his hand, and feeling strangely tired, he watched Oswald Fry leave his shop.

Rem closed the car door, stepped onto the sidewalk, and leaned against the hood while Daniels sat in the driver's seat and spoke to Lozano on the phone. He eyed the apartment building where Gina Rodriguez lived and wondered how this questioning would go. He recalled Mikey's description of her last conversation with Gina. It hadn't ended well. Mikey and Gina had known each other during their time as members of Victor's cult. According to Mikey, Gina had the rare ability of PK, or psychokinesis. When she got mad, she could throw you into a wall. Her gift had attracted Victor and he'd lured Gina in as a follower, as he did with many others who'd demonstrated unique abilities.

After both had left the cult, Mikey had assumed she and Gina had remained friends, but after reconnecting with Gina recently, Mikey had learned that Gina did not feel the same. Gina had accused Mikey of using her close bond to Victor to protect herself at the cost of others and blamed Mikey for her mistreatment. They'd argued and Gina had stomped out of SCOPE, threatening Mikey with knowledge of Margaret and her intentions. Despite Rem and Daniels checking into Gina's background and assigning a patrol car to watch her, there had never been any indication of Gina's involvement with Margaret.

Mikey had assumed that Gina had only used Margaret as a threat, since Gina and Margaret had hated each other. Mikey had reminded Rem not to take Gina lightly, though. She could still be dangerous.

Waiting for Daniels, Rem debated again how best to approach Gina. As far as Rem knew, Gina was not aware of Rem's connection to Mikey, or his assault at the hands of Allison. Gina had left the cult prior to then, but she'd obviously heard of Allison's incarceration and Margaret's escape. He and Daniels had discussed the best approach and had decided it was better not to mention their connection to Victor D'Mato or Mikey.

Rem glanced at Daniels through the windshield and saw him hang up. Daniels got out of the car and closed the door.

"Well?" asked Rem.

"We got Ibrahim's initial report back. Stella was strangled. There are no fingerprints or DNA on the items left on the counter. The only fingerprints in the house appear to be Stella's other than the ones in her massage room, and those are going to take time to sort out."

"So our guy is smart. He didn't leave anything behind."

"They found fibers on her. They're likely from sweatshirt material or possibly a hoodie. So nothing concrete that will lead us to him. And since Mel and Garcia struck out with Allison yesterday, all we have is Thomas Lenore seeing Margaret leave Stella's on the day of his massage. That's the first sighting of her since her escape and our only confirmation that she's involved."

"Yeah," Rem sighed with fatigue, recalling the people they'd talked to the previous day. "Unfortunately, none of Stella's other clients helped," said Rem, "so I'm doubtful any of the remaining ones will either."

"Maybe, but maybe not. We still have about sixteen more to go. One of them could have a connection to Margaret or may have had a reason to kill Stella."

"I doubt whoever did this was Stella's client. Margaret's got somebody on a leash and he or she is doing exactly what Margaret wants them to do. The question is why target Stella?" Rem pushed off the car. "She obviously had a connection to Victor. But why would Margaret kill her?"

"And is Stella the only one? Or is somebody else next?" asked Daniels.

Rem thought about Victor and his women. "If Stella was close to Victor, could Margaret have been jealous?"

"We could toss theories around for days," said Daniels. "But until we figure out Stella's exact relationship to Victor, we won't know for sure." He scratched his head. "Lozano thinks we should talk to Bartolo and Fallon."

Rem narrowed his eyes. "The two witnesses testifying against Allison?"

Daniels nodded. "It's possible they know something."

"It's also possible that if we tell them Margaret's responsible for Stella's death, they'll worry they'll be next. Which may sway them not to testify."

"I mentioned that," said Daniels. "But Lozano says it's still worth trying. He'll send Mel and Garcia."

"Not us?"

"Since we're also testifying, Lozano figured it would be better for someone else to do it."

Anxious, Rem groaned. "I hope Mel and Garcia don't scare them off."

"They know what they're doing and what's at stake. They'll be careful."

Rem took a deep breath and eyed the apartment building. "I guess there's not much we can do about it." He raised a hand. "You ready?"

"Let's hope Gina's home." Daniels followed the sidewalk and headed toward the building.

"Remember," said Rem, following Daniels. "Don't make her mad."

"I don't intend to." Daniels glanced back at Rem. "Don't you make her mad, either."

"I'll do my best, but you know me."

"That's exactly why I'm worried."

They approached the apartments, found Gina's door, and knocked. They waited a few seconds and heard someone yell, "One second." The door opened, and Rem saw a tall woman with thick, dark, wavy hair, wide brown eyes, and full eyebrows. She wore dark jeans and a white silk blouse with silver jewelry. "Can I help you?" she asked.

"Gina Rodriguez?" asked Daniels.

"Yes," she said.

Rem and Daniels held out their badges and introduced themselves. "We'd like to ask you a few questions if you have a minute?" asked Daniels.

Gina put a hand on the doorframe. "What's this about?"

"We understand you're an acquaintance of Victor D'Mato. We're investigating the murder of a woman who also had a connection to him." Rem slid his badge in his pocket. "We're wondering if you can help us."

Gina paused for a second. "Victor? I haven't seen him in a long time. Isn't he dead?"

"He is, ma'am," said Daniels. "But we have reason to believe someone who knows him may have killed our victim."

"What makes you think I know this person?" asked Gina.

"You may not," said Rem. "But we still have to ask." He gestured. "Can we come in?"

Gina stood at the door, her expression flat. Rem half expected her to tell them to leave, but then she stepped back. "Sure. Come in."

"Thank you," said Daniels. "We appreciate it."

Rem followed Daniels inside. "This shouldn't take long," said Rem.

"I hope not." Gina eyed her watch. "I've got to head out in a few minutes." She closed the door behind them.

"The woman who died is Stella de la Rosa." Daniels pulled out his phone, accessed her picture, and showed it to Gina. "Do you know her?"

Gina studied the picture. "No, I don't. How do you know she was friends with Victor?"

Rem looked around Gina's apartment. It was sparse but clean, and there were various colorful paintings on the wall. He walked to a bookshelf and studied the titles that filled the shelves. Gina appeared to be a fan of Dan Brown, Nora Roberts, and Dean Koontz. She also appeared to collect arrowheads. There were several of various sizes in front of the books. A bottom shelf contained numerous board games. "We found a picture of her with Victor and another man." Rem picked up a pink arrowhead and studied it.

"This is the picture, said Daniels. "We know that's Victor, but do you know who the other man is?"

Rem put the arrowhead down.

Gina eyed the second picture. "No, I don't. He isn't familiar." She straightened. "I'm sorry I can't be of much help." She crossed her arms. "What happened to Stella?"

Rem turned from the bookshelf. "She was strangled. Does the infinity sign have any significance to you or someone you know?"

Gina frowned. "That's an odd question, but no. It doesn't. What makes you think this has something to do with Victor D'Mato?" she asked. "Just because there was a picture of him at the scene?"

"There are a few reasons," said Daniels. "There was a note left behind. Along with a bow tie. The note mentioned the name Margaret."

A quiet moment passed, and Rem wondered what Gina was thinking. Gina spoke. "You mean Margaret Redstone?"

"You know her?" said Daniels.

"I sure as hell do." Gina raised the side of her lip. "I know she's escaped, and this has her scent all over it." She tipped her head. "How did you two know to question me? Who told you I knew Victor?"

"We are aware of some of Victor's other acquaintances," said Rem.

Gina chuckled. "Did you talk to Mikey Redstone? Did she direct you to me?"

"We can't divulge where we get our information," said Daniels.

Gina's smile fell. "Did you ask her about Stella? And her own connection to Victor? She's Margaret's sister, after all. If anybody knows anything, it's going to be her."

"Were talking to everybody," said Rem. "If someone had any involvement with Victor or Margaret, we want to know." He inwardly chastised himself for sounding annoyed.

Gina smirked. "So, you're looking for Margaret. I knew it."

"What was your relationship to Margaret?" asked Daniels.

"My relationship to that witch? I think you can guess." Gina narrowed her eyes. "She and her sister are both experts at looking out for themselves. Victor took care of them, and they returned the favor. They had his attention, and more, if you know what I mean."

Rem's aggravation rose. "Just because Mikey is Margaret's sister doesn't put her in the same boat as Margaret. Margaret's a psychopath."

Gina raised a brow, and Rem cursed himself again. Gina took a step toward him. "You know Mikey?" Her eyes glittered and Rem broke out in chills. "I'm beginning to understand." She tipped her head. "You like her?"

Rem recalled Mikey telling him that Gina had similar empathic abilities to Mikey's. She could easily sense things, and Rem realized he'd given himself away.

"Watch out, Detective," said Gina, holding Rem's gaze. "I wouldn't trust Margaret or Mikey as far as I can throw them."

Rem's irritation notched up some more. "From what I hear, you could throw them pretty far. Especially when you're in a mood."

Gina's face tensed. "Mikey's got a big mouth, but she's not wrong." She set her jaw. "Would you like me to demonstrate?"

Rem debated telling her to bring it when Daniels stepped in front of Gina, breaking the eye contact between Gina and Rem. "We're familiar with Mikey and Margaret Redstone," said Daniels. "But what we came here to ask about is Margaret's connection to Stella. And if you know why a bow tie was left at the scene."

Gina glared at Daniels instead. "I don't know about any bow tie or infinity sign, or what Margaret's connection is to Stella, but if Margaret wanted her dead, then she didn't stand a chance." She peered around Daniels at Rem. "And if you think Mikey's innocent, you might want to reconsider. She threw me to the wolves, and if she had something against Stella, then she threw her to the wolves too." She scoffed. "She and Margaret are probably working together."

Rem forced himself to keep his mouth shut, knowing whatever he had to say would not benefit the conversation.

"If you have evidence to support that," said Daniels, "then we'd like to see it. Otherwise, if you're just pissed at some perceived slight from Mikey or the Redstones, then that doesn't help us."

"You came here for information. I'm telling you what I know. Take it or leave it." Gina put a hand on her hip. "I knew Margaret and Mikey. I saw what they were capable of. Victor's dead, and now Allison's awaiting trial. I have no doubt Margaret's waiting in the wings, ready to pick up what's left behind. If you think Mikey has nothing to do with that, then maybe you should think twice. She put herself first when we were with Victor. And if you think she wouldn't protect her sister, you're in for a shock." She eyed Rem. "She's hurt others to protect herself, and she'll do the same to you."

Rem didn't want to hear another word. "I think we're done here." He headed for the door. "You have any more questions?" he asked Daniels.

"No. Not at the moment." Daniels followed Rem to the door and pulled out a card. He handed it to Gina. "Should you recall any useful information, then please get in touch." He paused. "And if Margaret contacts you, we need to know."

Gina took the card but laughed. "Margaret get in touch with me? That's funny. You just tell Mikey to leave me out of it. I want nothing to do with her or the Redstone family."

Rem opened the door, anxious to leave. He and Daniels walked out, but Gina wasn't finished. "Let me give you a word of advice," she said to Rem. "Stay away from Mikey, Detective. She'll only hurt you."

Rem began to tell her what she could do with her advice, but Daniels took him by the arm and pulled him down the sidewalk. Rem reluctantly remained silent and let himself be led. Daniels glanced back. "Thank you for your time, Gina. We'll be in touch if we have any more questions."

"Can't wait," said Gina.

Angry and wishing he could tell her exactly what he thought, Rem heard Gina slam the door shut behind them.

Mikey walked through SCOPE, holding a dust wand, and cleaning the office. She, Trick, and Mason took turns with the cleaning duties, and Mikey was two weeks overdue. She'd vacuumed but hating dusting, so she'd put it off. After Rem and Daniels' visit the other day though, she needed something to keep her busy. Mason was currently at a therapy appointment, Trick was working a case of his own, and Kyle had finished his own a few days earlier and wouldn't start another until next week.

Thinking about Rem's phone call, Margaret's supposed reappearance, and Kyle's frequent presence, Mikey needed to distract herself. She'd followed up on her checklist, had finished her other business items, and figured she might as well clean.

She'd sorted through the papers on her and Mason's shared desk, put them in their proper places, and dusted the desktop and computer monitor. Feeling satisfied, she walked to Trick's desk and did the same. Then she moved to the shelves against the far wall. There wasn't much on them other than the wooden box Mason refused to get rid of, and the two freaky statues in their plexiglass containers. Mason had since added a few family photos, but not much else. Mikey had added some books, but it still looked bare. Trick had suggested starting a shot glass collection, but Mason had shot him a *you're about to die* look. Mikey didn't know if Trick had been serious or not, but she'd chuckled.

She wiped the dusty shelves from top to bottom, moving down to the lower shelf with the box and containers. She dusted the Plexiglas, trying not to pay any attention to the weird statues. They still freaked her out. Even though Mason said he'd cleared them of any negative energy, Mikey recalled what one of them had done to Detective Daniels, and she didn't want to take any chances. After finishing with the statues, she moved to the wooden box. She stopped when she noted how the box did not line up with the dust lines beneath it. There was a narrow section of clean shelf beside it as if the box had been moved. Mikey wondered why, since the box was rarely touched. Figuring Trick may have bumped into the shelf, she finished dusting, and put the dust wand away. Thinking they needed a few more supplies, she returned to the desk, and made a list of items to purchase.

Sitting back, she looked around the office, and wondered what to do next. Her thoughts wandered, and she thought of Rem and his phone call. She couldn't help but admit she'd felt a tingle of happiness that he'd wanted to share with her his decision regarding the plea bargain. Knowing the choice had been tough, and that he'd valued her opinion, she smiled. Missing their talks, she hoped they'd be able to get their coffee soon.

At the same time, she thought of Kyle. Since Mason's return from drug rehab, Kyle had taken a smaller role at SCOPE, but due to the uptick in business, and Mason's reduced schedule because of his outpatient therapy, Kyle remained involved. Realizing that Margaret was still a danger, and understanding Mikey's need to wait, he hadn't pushed for a date, but Mikey knew that was temporary.

Leaning back in the chair, she considered her future. It was indeed possible that Margaret may never be caught. What would that mean? Was she supposed to be alone forever, waiting for Margaret to reappear? If Rem eventually told her he liked her, would she date him? Kyle was no doubt the safer option, but Mikey wasn't sure she wanted to play it safe. Something about Rem made her heart race. Not that her heart didn't thump around Kyle, but her shared trauma with Rem and their experiences with Victor had created a bond between them that was difficult to ignore. Rem had trusted her enough to discuss his darkest fears, and she'd done the same with him. And she'd be lying if she didn't admit there was something enticing about that. There was a trust factor with Rem she didn't yet have with Kyle.

Lost in her thoughts, she heard the door open and checked the monitors. She saw Mason walk through the outer office. Mikey sat up as he entered SCOPE and closed the door behind him.

"Hey. How's your day going?" he asked. He wore dark jeans, a long-sleeved red shirt, and his usual boots. Smoothing his handlebar mustache with his fingers, he tossed his hat on a chair and sat on the couch. "Did you get through your checklist?"

Mikey stood and walked to the couch. "That and more. I finally dusted this place and started a list of supplies we need." She sat beside him. "How was your appointment? Everything go okay?"

Mason nodded. "Yes. Tarina and I talked about me and Dad. My favorite subject."

Mikey recalled the last family session with Tarina Phelps, Mason's psychotherapist. "She doesn't want you to reconnect with him, does she?"

"I don't think so. Not that it matters, because I won't."

"We're all in agreement with that. It's better he's out of our lives for all our sakes. All we ever do is argue."

"That's what I told her. I don't think she expects us to reconnect, but rather talk about his influence on my life and how it could have led to my addiction."

"Sounds deep."

"It was. Tarina's a tough cookie."

Mikey recalled their session when it had just been her and Mason. "I'm well aware."

Mason settled back on the couch. "Have you seen Trick?"

"No, but I expect him soon."

"So do I," said Mason. "I spoke to him earlier. He's picking up some supplies for me."

"What supplies? Did we need something, other than cleaning stuff?" asked Mikey.

"Not for SCOPE, but for the house."

Mikey tried to think of what they might need at Mason's. "What is he buying?"

"Don't worry," said Mason. "I'll fill you in when we're done."

The outer door opened again. "That must be Trick," said Mikey.

"Probably."

A second later, Trick entered. He saw Mikey and Mason. "I got what you wanted, Red. It's in the truck."

Mason stood. "Great. Let's get to it."

Mikey looked between the two of them. "Let's get to what?"

Mason grabbed his hat from the chair. "Trick and I have a project. We're heading to the house. You hang here and finish the day."

Mikey frowned. "What are you two up to?"

"You'll know soon enough," said Trick.

Mikey joined them at the door. "Why are you being so secretive?"

Mason put a hand on her shoulder. "Because I know when I tell you, you're going to have a lot of questions. And I don't want to delay. I need to get this done, preferably this afternoon."

Trick smiled. "You'll get the scoop tonight. I think you'll like it."

Mikey didn't know what to think. "This better not be some weird project that I'm going to have to convince you two to stop doing." She paused. "Does Val know you're doing this? Would your girlfriend approve?"

"Absolutely," said Mason. "She's the one who suggested it. I can't believe I didn't think of it myself." He patted Trick's elbow. "Let's go." He glanced back. "We'll see you at the house later."

"Why can't I go with you?" asked Mikey.

"Because I want you to stay at SCOPE. Kyle said he might stop by. He's got a potential case he wanted to run by us. You can talk to him and let him know whether we can take it."

Mikey crossed her arms. "And once I talk to Kyle, I'm leaving. So whatever secret project you've got going, it better be done by the time I get there."

Mason pointed. "Ask Kyle to take you home. I don't want you going by yourself. I can drive us in tomorrow."

Mikey groaned. "Mason, I am perfectly—"

Mason shot her a look. "We agreed. It's one thing to be alone at home or at SCOPE, but when we're out, we need to be with someone whenever possible."

"You just drove to therapy by yourself," said Mikey.

"I said whenever possible," said Mason. "There will be times when we don't have a choice, but Kyle will be here, and I know he values your safety as much as I do. So, humor me and ask him to get you home safely." He paused. "Please."

Mikey knew she'd lost the argument. "Fine. I'll ask."

"Thank you," said Mason.

Trick lifted his hat and smoothed his hair. "I grabbed some food while I was out. Once our project is complete, I'll throw some enchiladas in the oven. We'll all have a beer and appreciate our hard work. Tell Kyle he's welcome to join us."

Mikey pointed. "You better hope I appreciate whatever it is you're up to."

"You will," said Mason. "I promise. I know what I'm doing." He walked out the door behind Trick. "See you at the house."

Chapter Nine

DANIELS AND REM ENTERED the squad room. Tired after a long day, Rem fell into his chair. Daniels did the same and sat at his desk. "Well, Lozano will be thrilled to hear we can scratch the other clients," said Daniels. He stifled a yawn.

Rem rubbed his neck and shoulders. "It was a long shot to begin with." He glanced behind him at the coffee machine. "My luck's run out. Looks like a cold, half-filled pot of coffee."

The squad doors opened, and Rem looked to see Mel and Garcia enter the squad room. They each held two cups of coffee. Rem's hope blossomed. "Please tell me one of those is for me."

Mel approached their desks and sat one of his cups in front of Rem. Garcia set one of his in front of Daniels. "We figured you two might need a pick-me-up," said Garcia. "We had a busy day ourselves."

Rem picked up his cup. "You really do want those Padres tickets, don't you?"

Mel chuckled. "This one's on the house. Nothing expected in return."

Daniels opened his lid. "Don't worry," said Garcia to Daniels. "We got yours black."

Mel spoke to Rem. "I put as much cream and sugar as I could into yours."

Rem sipped his and sighed. "Something ever happens to Daniels or Garcia, Mel, you're my new partner."

"You're so easily bought," said Daniels. He put the lid back on his drink and took a sip.

Feeling the coffee hit his system, Rem relaxed. "The whole reason we're partners is because you bought me a coffee during my first stakeout."

"And I haven't been able to get rid of you since," said Daniels. He sat back in his seat. Studying Mel and Garcia, he narrowed his eyes. "What's the real reason for the coffees? We've had long days before without so much as a glance from you two."

Mel and Garcia made eye contact. "That's true," said Mel, "but today's different. Lozano wants to talk about our meeting with Allison yesterday."

Rem straightened. "You said you struck out."

"We did," said Mel. "She didn't give us anything useful, but she did say a few things. Things we told Lozano, and you two should be aware of them. You were too busy earlier to go over it, but Lozano said when you returned, we'd talk."

"Obviously, it was interesting enough for you to provide coffee." Daniels slid off his jacket and threw it on the back of his chair.

"What did she say?" asked Rem. A prickle of anxiety ran up his spine.

"Lozano asked us to wait." Mel glanced toward the captain's office. Lozano was on the phone, but seeing his detectives, he raised a hand and waved. "Guess he's ready," said Mel.

"We also talked to your two followers who are testifying," said Garcia. "We can discuss that, too."

Daniels stood. "Maybe you should have brought us some booze."

Holding his coffee, Rem stood. "You should have added it to the coffee."

"We considered it," said Garcia. "Especially when it comes to Allison Albright. We figured, though, if you're up for it afterward, we can stop and get a drink somewhere."

Mel headed toward Lozano's office. "I think we're all going to need one."

Uncomfortable about what he might hear but telling himself it couldn't be any worse than what he'd already experienced, Rem entered Lozano's office and took a seat. Daniels sat beside him, and Mel and Garcia grabbed two foldout chairs, unfolded them, and sat. Lozano ended his phone call and hung up.

Lozano spoke to Mel and Garcia. "Did you tell them what this is about?"

Mel nodded. "Yes."

"We're wondering what's so interesting that we all have to meet together," said Daniels.

"What happened when you spoke to Allison?" asked Rem.

Mel sat back in his chair. "When we got there, she was already in the room behind a pane of glass, so we spoke with her through a phone. Her attorney, Measy, wasn't present and when we asked if she wanted him there, she just shrugged at us, so we proceeded with the questioning. We asked her about Stella and showed her the picture. She didn't say anything, and we wondered if she'd even speak."

Garcia set his coffee on Lozano's desk. "She's got a way about her."

"Tell me about it." Rem held his coffee cup.

"All she did was smile," said Mel. "Then she told us Stella and Victor were friends, but she didn't know much more than that. She thinks Stella may have given Victor a few massages and readings."

"Anything else she might have given him?" asked Daniels.

"Allison wouldn't elaborate," said Garcia. "All she would confirm is that Victor and Stella knew each other. She didn't know the man in the picture or why the bow tie was left behind. And when we mentioned Margaret, she just laughed."

Rem almost shivered, recalling Allison's glee after she'd drugged his wine when he'd had dinner at her apartment while undercover, and he'd given in to her sexual aggression. "What did you say about Margaret?"

"We asked her if she knew that Margaret had escaped." Mel tipped his chair and leaned back on two legs. "She said she'd heard."

"That's it?" asked Daniels.

"That's it," said Garcia.

"Her attorney, Measy, must have told her," said Rem.

"So we asked her if Margaret, or anyone close to her, would have any reason to go after Stella." Mel's chair creaked as he rocked back in it. "She just smiled again and said Margaret didn't need a reason to do anything."

"I can see why you said you didn't get anything out of her," said Rem. "Even if she knows something, I doubt she'd tell us."

Garcia scratched his jaw. "I decided to get a little more direct with her and see if I could get a reaction."

"What did you do?" asked Daniels.

"I came out and asked her if she and Margaret were working together and if she knew what Margaret was up to. And would there be any more victims?"

Rem tightened his hold on his coffee. "How did she respond?" More memories flashed of Allison straddling him on the stone slab.

Mel crossed his arms. "She grinned and said that was none of my business."

Daniels rubbed his forehead. "She basically told you nothing. So why are we having this pow-wow?"

Lozano picked up a pencil and tapped it on his desk. "Tell them what she said next."

Garcia glanced at Mel. "We figured at that point we weren't going to get anything out of her," said Garcia. "She was just having fun with us. We told her thank you and got up to leave."

Mel set his chair back on all fours. "That's when she stood, and we could see she was visibly pregnant. She spoke through the phone and told us if we want her to talk then she wants to speak to Remalla and Daniels." Mel paused. "Then she rubbed her stomach, and said Rem's daughter's life might depend on it, and maybe a few others."

The room went quiet, and Garcia and Mel eyed Rem, whose stomach twisted.

Lozano pointed with his pen. "You can see now why I thought we should all be in the same room."

His face furrowed, Daniels stood and paced. "She's using us. She doesn't know a damn thing." He gestured toward Rem. "She's trying to mess with your head before trial."

Lozano loosened his tie and pulled it off. "Obviously, with the trial approaching, you two can't speak with her. Kate wouldn't go for it."

"On the other hand," said Rem, "what if she does know something? What if she knows what Margaret is up to? Is it worth finding out?"

"You are not doing anything," said Daniels. "If anybody goes to see her, it's going to be me."

"As of right now," said Lozano, "nobody is seeing anybody. I'll run it by Kate and see what she thinks. I just wanted you two to know what was going on."

"Can I ask the obvious, Cap?" said Mel. He looked at Rem. "Is she carrying your kid?"

The twists in Rem's belly turned into knots. "That's the million-dollar question. I don't know, but she sure as hell is telling everyone she is."

Garcia cursed. "That must be messing with your head."

Rem held his stomach. "It's been a rough few months."

"Then you've got more at stake here," said Mel. "If Allison was just one woman spouting nothing but threats and innuendo, that's one thing. But we're talking about a child." He glanced at Rem. "Maybe your child."

Daniels paced some more. "I think I should go." He stood in front of Lozano's desk. "If Kate and Measy are present to ensure the subject stays on Margaret only, and not the trial, it should be fine. But Mel's got a point. It's worth talking to her."

Rem gathered his courage. "I should go, too."

Lozano and Daniels spoke at the same time. "No."

Rem slumped in his seat but didn't have the energy to argue. Although he wished he had the nerve to confront her, he knew his emotional state wasn't strong enough, and he'd need every piece of mental fortitude to confront her at trial. "This whole meeting will be pointless if you go in there and she clams up because I didn't show."

"Rem," said Daniels, "the whole reason she wants you there is to screw with you. I'll do it. I can handle her. And if she's really worried about her daughter's life, she won't hesitate to tell me whatever it is she might know."

"What would Margaret want with Allison's daughter?" asked Garcia.

"Probably nothing," said Lozano.

"But it could be my daughter, too," said Rem. The thought of Margaret going after his child was scarier than anything he'd encountered. "You think Margaret believes that?" The shock of the possibility made him break out in a cold sweat.

Daniels returned to his seat. "Don't get ahead of yourself and think the worst. Nobody knows who the baby's father is, and that includes Margaret. I doubt Margaret cares either way, but it is an effective way to get into Allison's head. Maybe that's what Margaret wants. The same way Allison wants to mess with you."

Lozano rolled up one of his shirt cuffs. "Margaret and Allison are not friends. With Allison looking at life in prison, I expect Margaret would be very happy to leave her behind bars but give her something to worry about at the same time."

"Exactly," said Daniels. "Margaret's probably thrilled about Allison's situation. Allison realizes that, but also knows you're out here scrambling, trying to deal with both Margaret and the pregnancy. She's bluffing. She just wants us both ruffled before we testify. And if I know Measy, he'll turn this into a conversation about Allison. He'll use whatever he can to get an edge at trial."

"Which is why I think nobody should visit her," said Lozano. "Let Allison sit and stew. Maybe when she realizes nobody's coming, then she might talk."

Rem sucked in a big gulp of air and blew it out. "Allison doesn't care about Margaret, Stella, me or anybody else. The only person she wants to help is herself." Trying not to envision the worst, he swallowed. "I bet she's terrified of being incarcerated as her little girl grows up while Margaret's free. I can see Margaret using that against her." He hesitated. "And maybe me, too."

"Before we all think the worst, let's talk to Kate," said Daniels. "If she's up for seeing Allison, then so am I." He pointed toward Rem. "But not you."

Rem stared at his coffee and nodded. "I'm not going to argue with you."

Daniels patted Rem's arm and settled back in his chair. "There's a first time for everything."

Some of the heaviness lifted from Rem's shoulders, but his fatigue remained. "Guess it's your lucky day."

"It's way overdue." Daniels offered Rem a comforting glance and Rem nodded back at him. "Trust me on this one, okay?" asked Daniels. "You've got enough to think about. Let me handle this."

Rem realized there was more to say on the subject, but for now, he needed to acquiesce. "It's all yours."

Daniels offered a soft smile. "I need to mark this day in history. That's two times you're not arguing with me."

"Maybe you should buy a lottery ticket." Feeling a little calmer, Rem sipped his coffee.

"Let's discuss the witnesses," said Lozano. "Penny Bartolo and Dexter Fallon. What happened with them?"

"Bartolo went fine," said Mel. "We asked her about Stella and her connection to Victor. She didn't know anything about Stella, or what the bow tie meant. You could tell though that she's scared of Margaret. Said she's crazy and Penny tried to keep her distance from her. But she was cool when we left and is still eager to testify." Mel paused. "Fallon, though, was another story."

"Hell," said Rem. "I was afraid of that."

"We asked the same questions," added Mel, "and he immediately thought the worst. He's wondering if Margaret is targeting Victor's enemies."

"Fallon isn't Victor's enemy. He's Allison's," said Daniels.

"He's scared either way," said Garcia. "Thinks his testimony could still be construed as breaking his oath to Victor and the cult. Margaret was devoted to Victor. He's convinced he could be next on the list. We had to pull him off the ledge."

"How'd you manage that?" asked Daniels.

Garcia shifted in his seat. "Told him we still don't know why Stella died or if Margaret is even involved. We were just asking questions."

"And even if he chose not to testify, it didn't make him any safer," said Mel. "First of all, his reduced sentence in exchange for his testimony would be rescinded, and second, it's possible his testimony might protect him. If Margaret hates Allison, she might be pleased he's testifying. That seemed to help."

"When we left, he was back on board," said Garcia. "But you ought to be prepared in case he bails." He picked up his drink. "We left him our card in case he wanted to get in touch."

"Disaster averted again," said Rem. "Until something else spooks him."

"That's just it," said Mel. He sat forward and put his elbows on his thighs. "He called an hour ago. Said he wanted to tell us something."

Daniels frowned. "What did he say?"

Mel glanced at Garcia, and back at Rem and Daniels. "Said he'd heard Allison was pregnant."

Rem's head started to pound. He didn't know what else to expect. "How'd he know that?"

"Maybe Kate told him?" asked Lozano. "She's been talking to him and Bartolo."

"Fallon didn't mention how he knew, and we didn't ask. It was Allison he warned us about." Garcia sighed. "He told us that in the months before that final ceremony where Allison was arrested, Victor had spoken to Dexter about fathering a child."

Rem tensed.

"But Victor had had a vasectomy," said Daniels.

Mel shook his head. "Not Victor as the father, but Dexter. Dexter has three kids with three different women, two of which thought they couldn't get pregnant. I guess Vic thought that was Dexter's superpower. He suggested Dexter sleep with Allison."

Rem felt the color drain from his face. "What? Why?"

"Dexter was scared to tell us when we'd spoken earlier," said Garcia, "but our conversation got to him. And with the trial nearing, his conscience is eating at him."

"About what?" asked Daniels.

Mel hesitated. "Victor was obsessed with youth and living forever, as was Allison. Allison believed drinking the blood of others would provide it, but, according to Fallon, Victor was considering taking it one step further. According to Dexter, at least at the time, Victor was interested in child's blood."

Rem gripped his coffee, the cup crumpled, and coffee spilled all over the floor.

Chapter Ten

DANIELS OPENED THE DOOR to his house and heard J.P. cry. He closed the door and tossed his keys on the front table. J.P. wailed again from upstairs. "Babe?" he called. "I'm home." Tired, he removed his jacket and tossed it on the stair railing. The two beers he'd had at the bar had helped relax him, but the effect was wearing off.

Marjorie poked her head over the banister above. "There you are." She glowered. "Where the hell have you been?"

Daniels looked up. "I told you. We stopped to get a drink on the way home."

Her face tightened. "Glad you could enjoy yourself. Meanwhile, I've got a crying kid who won't go to sleep because his blanket is missing, I'm exhausted after a crappy day, the house is a mess, I've barely had time to eat and shower, and while I'm dealing with that, my husband has been socializing with his friends."

Daniels raised his hand and softened his tone. "I'm sorry. I didn't realize you were having a hard night. I would have come home sooner if I'd known. Rem was just having a rough time—"

"Rem?" she yelled. J.P. wailed again. "How about your wife?" She barked out a laugh. "Sometimes I wonder who comes first. Me or him." She left the railing and Daniels heard her stomp away. He put his hand on the banister, wondering why she was so angry. They'd had fights before over his long hours, but she'd never spoken a harsh word toward his partner. He jogged up the stairs and into J.P.'s room, where his son stood in his crib, crying. "Hey, little man."

"Dada," said J.P. Tears streaked down his face. "Bankie."

Daniels picked him up. "We'll find it." He held J.P. who dropped his head against his shoulder as Daniels headed into his and Marjorie's bedroom. Marjorie was going through a drawer.

"I've looked everywhere," she said. "It was in his crib earlier. How could it just walk away?"

"You check downstairs?"

She glared at him. "I said everywhere, didn't I?" She slammed a drawer closed.

Daniels told himself to shut up and start looking. "I'll go check."

Marjorie went into their closet. "Whatever." She started rifling through clothes.

Holding J.P., Daniels returned to the first floor and looked around the living and dining area but didn't see the blanket. He'd recalled seeing it in J.P.'s room that morning and wondered if Marjorie had picked it up without realizing it and had left it in her car. He headed toward the garage, but passing the laundry room, he stopped and peered inside. J.P.'s folded blanket was lying on top of the washing machine.

He walked in and picked it up. Had Marjorie washed and forgotten it?

Seeing his blanket, J.P. reached for it. "Bankie."

"There you go, buddy." Daniels unfolded it and handed it to him. J.P. held it, stuck his thumb in his mouth and laid his head back on Daniels' shoulder, halfway asleep. Obviously, everyone was tired in the Daniels household.

Daniels returned upstairs and placed J.P. in his crib, where he rolled to his side, cradling his blanket, and closed his eyes. Daniels patted his back for a second, and satisfied J.P. was asleep or close to it, he left the room and entered his own.

"Found it," said Daniels. "J.P.'s happy now. He's already asleep."

Marjorie was holding a pile of clothes. Her face fell and she tossed the clothes back on a shelf. "Figures. Mom's a mess and can't get it together, but Dad comes home and saves the day. I'm an idiot while you're the hero."

Daniels straightened. "Whoa. That's not true."

She left the closet. "Where was the blanket?"

"In the laundry room. On top of the washing machine."

"What the hell was it doing there?"

"I don't know." Marjorie was in no mood for him to ask if she'd put it there and had forgotten after a busy day. "But it's found. Crisis averted. J.P.'s down for the night."

She walked through the bedroom, gathering clothes from the bed and oversized chair. "Guess I should run a load and accomplish something today. Did you have a nice time at the bar? I hope someone around here had a chance to unwind."

Daniels walked over to her and took the clothes out of her hand. "Leave them." He tossed them in a pile on the floor. "I'll take care of it. Why don't you sit for a second?"

She dropped her jaw. "Because this house doesn't run itself, you know? While you've been out, I've been running around, trying to get J.P. cleaned and fed, then attempting and failing to get some work done, plus dealing with this messy house. I'm just wiped." She rubbed her forehead. "I've had a headache since lunch."

"Why didn't you tell me when I texted you earlier? I would have come home."

Her expression darkened. "Because I want you to know what's wrong without me having to spell it out for you. Is that so hard?"

He sighed. "Sorry, Babe. My intuitive superpower is on the fritz. My day wasn't much better than yours." She narrowed her eyes and he backtracked. "I'm not comparing our awful days. And yes. I've had a couple of beers, so your day was much worse."

She grabbed a shirt from the bed. "I'm guessing you haven't found your bow tie killer."

"No. Not even close." He took her elbow and guided her toward the chair. "Sit."

Marjorie hesitated, but then she followed his guidance and sat in the chair. He took the shirt from her, tossed it in the pile, walked behind her and started to massage her neck. "Tell me about your day," he said, kneading her tight muscles.

Groaning, she sighed. "God, that feels good."

"You want some aspirin?"

"I took some already."

"Good. So...?" He focused in on a knot in her shoulder.

She groaned again. "It was just non-stop. I had a teenager shout expletives at his teacher. I had to call the parents and get them involved. Then another kid stopped by to talk about why he wanted to drop out of school. It didn't help that we had two teachers call in sick, along with Moira being out. That's three subs and kids always act out when they have a sub. I usually have lunch with Moira, who's my sounding board, but since she's not there, I ended up having lunch with the gossip girls. Moira's sub got stuck with them, too. That poor man will be a trooper if he makes it for the full six weeks."

"You like him?" asked Daniels. He felt Marjorie start to relax and he focused on her upper neck. "What's your opinion as the high school's counselor?

"He's very nice." Marjorie moaned and tipped her head. "He's adjusting quickly, and he's good with the kids."

"Then maybe you and he can be each other's sounding board while Moira's out."

She sighed. "Maybe once I get to know him a little better." Wincing, she sucked in a breath. "Right there. It's super tight."

He kneaded the knot.

"After lunch, it didn't let up. I had two kids get in a fight during gym, and that's when the headache kicked in and the fatigue hit. I've just wanted to crawl into bed all day. And then you texted, and I got pissed." She tipped her head in the other direction. "I wanted to tell you I was having a lousy day, but I knew you were on this case, so I didn't bitch. But, hell, it was hard. You get to have a beer and I had to handle J.P. and everything else."

Daniels pressed against another tight spot. "You've had days where you've gone to have drinks with your work buds."

"I know. I guess I just needed today to be one of those days."

"You should have said something."

"I didn't want to be *that* wife."

"What wife is that?"

"The kind I was when you came home."

Daniels smiled. "Honey, that's got nothing to do with being a wife. That's got everything to do with life. You had a crappy day."

"I'm sorry I snapped at you."

"No need to apologize. You were right. I should have come home."

She shook her head. "No. You've got a murder case and I know what that does to you. You need some decompression time."

Daniels recalled his meeting with Lozano, Mel, and Garcia. "Yeah, we kinda did. Normally, I'd have declined, but we all needed a drink."

"You mentioned Rem. Is he okay?"

Daniels wasn't sure how to answer. "He's better. I'll admit, he's the main reason I went. I didn't want him to go home until he could have some time away from work."

"I didn't mean what I said earlier about you and Rem. I was just angry."

"I know."

"I realize you put Rem first."

Daniels gripped her shoulders. "Wait a—"

She chuckled. "I'm kidding. I'm just giving you a hard time. I know where I rank, and I know you'd walk through fire for me if I asked you."

"Without a flame retardant suit and with no water hose in sight."

"And you'd do the same for Rem. I knew that when I married you. It's why I love you. You're a good man, friend, and husband."

"Thank you." He moved his hands back to her shoulders.

"Is it Allison and the baby? Is he struggling?"

"It's more than that. Mel and Garcia talked to one of Victor's followers. He mentioned that Victor had suggested getting Allison pregnant, presumably to get access to child's blood for their rituals." The mere act of saying it made him want to gag.

Marjorie went still. "What? Are you kidding?" She glanced back at him.

"I wish I was." He ran his fingers into her hair. "Rem's freaked that Allison may have used him to get pregnant so they could have a child of the light that they'd sacrifice the way they almost did him. And he can't help but think that could still be their plan."

"My God. No wonder he's upset."

"The beers helped a little. Mel, Garcia, and I reminded him that this came from a follower whose talk with Victor happened months before Rem and I ever got involved in the case. Everything he said is pure conjecture, and Allison doesn't strike me as a woman who has any intention of hurting her child."

"She's much more interested in using her baby to manipulate Rem. It will be hard to do that if the baby is sacrificed. Plus, her followers are scattered." She paused. "You think Margaret would do such a heinous thing?"

Margaret was the only part of the equation Daniels couldn't predict. "I think Margaret's capable of some awful things, but I doubt this is one of them. Margaret uses fear to intimidate, so maybe she would threaten it, but acting on it is altogether different." Daniels thought about it. "She was close to Victor, so maybe he told her his plans." He shook his head in frustration. "I don't know. There are so many moving parts to this puzzle, it's hard to think straight. I just need to get Rem through the trial, but Margaret and Allison aren't making it easy." He massaged her scalp.

"He's lucky to have you. Just like me."

Daniels smiled. "Feel better?"

"I do. Thank you."

He leaned over, kissed her neck, and whispered in her ear. "Stay right there."

She reached for him, and he took her hand. "Where are you going?" she asked.

He kissed her palm. "You'll see." He let her go and walked into the bathroom, where he started the tub. He waited for the water to warm, plugged the drain, and tossed in some bubble bath. After finding some matches, he lighted a candle.

Marjorie entered the bathroom. "What are you doing?"

"Starting you a bath." He stood and walked over to her. "Then you are going to get in and enjoy some alone time. I'll start a load of laundry and clean up."

Her gaze softened. "That sounds wonderful."

He moved closer and put his arms around her. "Relish it, because God knows when you'll get it again."

She hugged him and pulled back. "You sure you don't want to join me?"

Daniels kissed her nose. "Tempting, but no. It's all yours, my love." He gave her a squeeze and walked her to the tub. "I want you to wind down. You'll sleep better if you do."

The tub slowly filled, and she ran her hands through her hair. "You're the best."

"Remember that next time you're mad at me." He found a washcloth and set it, along with some flowery soap, on the edge of the bath.

"No promises." She pulled off her shirt and Daniels admired her ruffled hair, weary eyes, and the curve of her shoulders.

"And hey...," he said.

Pausing as she unbuttoned her jeans, she met his gaze. "What?"

He reached up and touched her cheek. "You always come first with me."

Smiling, she gave him a quick kiss. "I love you," she said.

"I love you, too."

—ell—

The next morning, Daniels sat at his desk, reviewing what they'd learned so far. It wasn't much. They still didn't know who the man in the photo was with Stella, why the bow tie or infinity sign had been added, and what the four days meant. The only client of Stella's who could confirm Margaret's presence at Stella's home two days before she died was Thomas. No fingerprints or DNA of consequence had been left behind, and no one in the neighborhood had seen anything suspicious. There'd been no forced entry into the home, so they assumed Stella had known her attacker. Could he have been a previous client or a follower of Victor's? They still didn't know.

Frustrated, he sat back in his seat and eyed the time. Rem had still not arrived. Daniels resisted the urge to call because he didn't want to hover. He suspected Rem had not slept well after a difficult previous day, but he knew his captain would be in soon and wouldn't be happy with Rem's lateness. He reached for the phone when the squad doors opened, and Lozano walked in.

Daniels sighed. "Morning." He glanced at Rem's desk. "Before you say anything, I was about to call him."

"No need." The captain stopped at Daniels' desk. "I told him to take a couple of hours this morning. After yesterday, he needs it. Plus, Kate is stopping by to discuss a possible visit with Allison. I didn't think Rem should be around." He checked his watch. "She should be here soon."

Daniels sat up. "That's good. I'm glad you called him. He could use the rest. If Kate agrees, maybe we can see Allison this afternoon." He waved toward the papers on his desk. "So far, we've got nothing useful. So if she knows something, we need to hear it."

Lozano nodded. "That note left at the scene said four days. Assuming it means four days since Stella's death, that makes today the fourth day, so if something's going to happen, it will be soon."

"I considered the same thing," said Daniels. "We'll have to see what today brings, but hopefully it's not another body."

"Let's hope." Lozano headed toward his office. "When Kate gets here, just come on in."

"Will do." Daniels returned to his paperwork.

Chapter Eleven

REM SAT IN THE coffee shop, observing the other patrons. About half the tables were taken and there were two people in line. Nothing odd stood out among them, and he kept an eye on the door and windows to ensure his and Mikey's safety. After Lozano had called and told him to come in later, Rem had decided to contact Mikey and set up their coffee date. She'd happily agreed to meet him and an hour later, he'd grabbed a couple of coffees and was sitting at a table. While waiting, he couldn't help but reflect on the previous day. He wondered again if Allison would consider harming her child. Had that been her intention all along? Could she really do something so horrific? And Victor asked her to do it? Just thinking about it made Rem ill. Plagued with nightmares, he hadn't slept well. The detour to the bar after work had helped to take his mind off of things, but the minute he'd returned home, his thoughts had returned to Allison and the baby. Once the child was born, would she be safe? Would some crazy follower want to follow through? He couldn't imagine. It was the one thing that gave him hope; nobody would be sick enough to do something so vile.

The bell over the door rang, and Rem spotted Mikey. He waved and she headed toward his table.

"Hey," she said. She wore her usual black jeans and shirt and put her small purse in the empty chair beside her. "Good to see you."

Rem slid Mikey's coffee cup over to her. "Good to see you, too. I got your usual."

"Thank you." Mikey picked up the cup and took a sip. "It's good." She settled back in her seat. "I was glad when you called. It's been a while since we've shared a coffee."

"I know." Rem considered everything he needed to tell her. "Lozano gave me the morning, so I figured now was as good a time as any." He took a sip of his drink.

Mikey raised a brow. "Since when does your captain give you the morning off, especially in the middle of a murder case?" She paused. "Did you do something you shouldn't have?"

Rem smirked. "That's a logical assumption, but it's not the case this time. I got some unsettling information yesterday and Lozano is taking pity on me."

"What kind of information?"

Rem sat up and put his elbows on the table. "It's about Allison. And I wanted to ask you about it."

She frowned. "Ask me about what?"

Rem debated where to begin. He'd been trying for weeks to tell Mikey about Allison's pregnancy and the possibility that the child could be his. But every time he'd come close, he'd backed out. Still uncomfortable, he cleared his throat. "I've been putting off telling you something."

Mikey studied him. "I know you've had something on your mind. What is it?" When he didn't answer, she set her cup down and leaned in. "You can tell me."

Rem bounced his knee under the table. He wondered why he struggled but had to assume it was because he feared once she knew, she'd reconsider any future with him, no matter how unreasonable that seemed. "This murder we're investigating that has ties to Victor and Margaret..."

"What about it? Have you got any new leads?"

Rem shook his head. "No. Not anything helpful. We talked to Gina, and she didn't know much. And you're right to stay away from her. She didn't have anything positive to say about you."

Mikey widened her eyes. "She mentioned me? How did I come up in the conversation?"

Rem shrugged. "She asked why we contacted her and assumed it was because of you. It didn't take her long to figure out I knew you. Especially when I got defensive when she started insinuating that you shouldn't be trusted."

Mikey traced a finger along the lid of her cup. "Gina is very intuitive, probably more so than me. I should have warned you about that."

"It's fine. She didn't know anything about Stella or her connection to Victor. She didn't hide her contempt for Margaret, though. Or you."

"I can imagine."

"Just keep your distance from her."

"That shouldn't be a problem." Mikey interlaced her fingers around her cup. "What happened after Gina?"

Rem groaned, exhausted just thinking about it. "A lot of legwork but with few results. One of Stella's clients believes he saw Margaret leave Stella's house but other than that we didn't get much."

Mikey tightened her grip around her cup. "So Margaret knew Stella?"

"Seems so, but what it has to do with Stella's murder is still unclear. Between the note left behind and your sister's visit, it's got to mean something." Rem sipped more coffee. "Anyway, seeing as how we weren't getting anywhere, Lozano thought somebody should talk to the two followers who've agreed to testify at Allison's trial. He suggested they might know something. I was nervous about it because I didn't want to scare them off, but I could see his point."

"I suppose it's possible they could know something. But I doubt either one of them got that close to either Margaret or Victor."

Dreading his revelation, Rem shifted in his seat. "One of them got a little close. Dexter Fallon." He set his jaw, uncertain of what to say.

"Dexter knows something? About Stella?"

"No, not Stella. About Victor." Rem hesitated. "And Allison."

Mikey narrowed her eyes. "What are you trying to tell me?"

Rem sucked in a breath, held it for a second, and blew it out. "Allison's pregnant." He waited for her reaction. "Almost six months."

Mikey didn't move or say anything, but then she dropped her jaw. "Are you kidding?"

"No, I'm not kidding." Anxious, he tapped his finger on the table.

"How long have you known that?"

Rem recalled his conversation with Allison at the jail. "She told me when I visited her. That's when I took off to Merrimac."

Mikey furrowed her brow. "What does this have to do with Dexter Fallon and Victor?"

Rem clenched his fingers together. "Dexter told the two detectives who questioned him that Victor had asked him to consider impregnating Allison. Dexter said Victor wanted child's blood for a ceremony to extend his youth and live forever."

Mikey went still, and Rem noted the tension in her neck and shoulders. "Is Dexter the father?" she asked.

Rem shook his head. "Dexter declined the invitation." He glanced at a patron who walked by the table. "He just thought we should know since he'd learned Allison was expecting." He squirmed. "Did Victor ever talk to you about having a child? Or using child's blood during a ceremony?"

Mikey gasped. "Never. He never mentioned anything like that to me. I honestly can't believe he even considered such a thing. Margaret never said anything about it either. She's depraved toward others, but when it comes to animals or children, she's always been weirdly protective."

Rem hoped Mikey was right. "We're thinking Victor was just messing with Dexter. He tends to be a little paranoid. He's threatened more than once not to testify. We're just not sure how serious to take this information."

"I can't believe for one second that Allison would ever allow harm to come to her baby. She may be crazy but she's still a mother." She went quiet. "Who is the father? Maybe he can help you figure this out."

Unable to look her in the eye, Rem stared out the window. "We don't know for sure, because Allison may be lying."

"Lying about what? Who is she saying is the father?"

Nervous, and his heart thumping, Rem released a drawn-out sigh. "Me." He met her gaze.

Mikey's mouth went slack, and she stared back. "You?"

Rem looked away, his heart heavy. Although what had happened wasn't his fault, he hated speaking the words. "I didn't know how to tell you."

"You've known all this time?" She stammered. "How could you not have told me?"

Flustered, Rem struggled with how to respond. "Mikey, I..." Trying to find the words, his gaze flicked to the window, and he caught sight of a woman on the sidewalk peering inside. Their eyes met through the glass and their blue color sent shockwaves down his spine. Her long dark hair blew in the wind, and she smiled. Spikes of fear raised on his skin, and he jumped up. "Oh my God."

The woman grinned and he imagined the cackle in his head, then she turned and walked past the window, disappearing from view.

Mikey straightened. "Rem, what is it?" She glanced behind her.

Rem's heart rate zoomed. "Margaret. It was her."

Mikey twisted in her seat. "What? Where?"

Forcing himself to act, Rem leaned over Mikey, who turned back, and he pointed. "You stay here. Don't leave this shop. Call Daniels and Mason." He sprinted away from the table and, ignoring her pleas to wait, Rem ran out of the shop.

Kate sat in the chair beside Daniels and crossed her legs. "You really think this is a good idea?"

Daniels shifted in his seat to face her. "I say it's worth a shot. Allison's not going to talk to any other detectives. She asked for me and Rem."

"Rem can't go," she said.

"He's not," said Lozano, who sat at his desk. "We already made that very clear. Which is why I didn't invite him to this meeting."

"We're getting nowhere on this case, and Allison has insinuated she has information." Daniels rested his elbow on the armrest of the chair. "Add to that Dexter Fallon's news about Victor's intentions to get Allison pregnant."

"That has nothing to do with the Stella de la Rosa case," said Kate. "If we're doing this, we stick to the facts about Stella's murder. We're not there to talk about anything else." She swiped at something on her skirt. "You know she's going to use this to mess with you."

Daniels understood her point. "Believe me, I'm aware. And when she realizes it's just me, she may clam up. But if she really has information, I might be able to convince her to talk. And maybe, if she fears for her baby's life, she'll be willing to do something about it."

Lozano nodded. "For all we know, whoever killed Stella could go after Allison and the child. Maybe that's why Allison might be willing to talk to us."

Kate paused, appearing to think about it. "If Allison was worried about that, she would've talked to your other detectives. She asked for you and Rem because of the trial. She's got something up her sleeve. And there's no way we're doing this without her attorney present."

"Absolutely," said Daniels. "This has to be by the book. We'll make it very clear upfront that we are only there to ask questions about a murder case." Daniels debated again whether this was a smart thing to do, but his gut told him he had to try. "If she or Measy doesn't play by the rules, we leave."

"And what if she requests Rem's presence?" asked Kate.

"The interview ends right there," said Lozano. "She's not running the show, we are."

"My hope is her worry for her baby will get her to talk," said Daniels. "That's what she implied when she spoke with Mel and Garcia."

"Allison didn't say 'her baby.'" Kate shook her head. "She used the words 'Rem's daughter.' She's playing with his emotions. And if he's not present," she said eyeing Daniels, "she'll mess with you, hoping it will get back to your partner."

Daniels straightened. "I'm aware of her tactics. I'll be ready."

Kate narrowed her eyes at him. "Can you ever be ready for Allison?"

Lozano grunted. "He's a cop. He knows what he's doing. And besides, that's why you're there. You can shut it down if you have to."

Kate looked between the two of them. A moment passed, and she nodded. "Okay. I'll see what I can set up." She stood and straightened her jacket. "I'll contact Measy."

Daniels stood, also. "The sooner, the better. See if we can meet with Allison this afternoon. Stella's killer is still out there, and he might strike again."

"I'll see what I can do." Kate picked up her briefcase. "I'll call you, Captain, as soon as I hear something." She headed toward the door.

"Thanks, Kate," said Lozano. "We appreciate your help."

"Don't thank me, yet," said Kate. "I just hope we don't come to regret this." She eyed Daniels.

"And I don't want to regret not talking to her," said Daniels. He thought about Rem and the trial. "We trust you to handle this, Kate. I wouldn't do this without you there."

Kate put her hand on the knob and opened the door. She glanced at Lozano. "Your detectives are good liars." She smiled softly and walked out, closing the door behind her.

Lozano settled back into his seat. "Don't I know it," he mumbled. He shot a look at Daniels. "You sure about this?"

Daniel sat again. "I don't think we have a choice. If this child does turn out to be Rem's, we have an obligation to protect his daughter." He paused. "And if it means going into the lion's den to do that, then it's worth it."

Lozano pointed. "You just be sure to follow Kate's lead. Don't let Allison get to you." He lowered his hand. "You lose your temper, and Measy will be all over you at trial."

"I know," said Daniels. "As Rem says, I'll be as cool as a beer in the fridge." His phone rang.

Lozano chuckled. "Your partner has a way with words."

Daniels saw Mikey's name on his cell's display. "That he does." He answered the phone.

Rem raced down the sidewalk, looking for Margaret. The coffee shop was in an older section of town where unused warehouses were being converted into retail shops and condominiums. The building next door was one of a few under construction, and scanning the sidewalk, he didn't see Margaret, but for one second, he thought he saw someone with long hair dart inside the building. He deduced that she'd gone inside to hide. He ran up to the door, pulled his weapon, and entered an open space filled mainly with scaffolding. The interior had been gutted and was being completely rebuilt. Tall wooden beams that supported and framed the interior obstructed his view. Dirty windows allowed in the murky light and the farther he walked in, the murkier it became. He aimed his gun out in front of him.

His heart thumping fast against his ribs, he carefully stepped through the construction around him. "Margaret," he yelled. "I know you're in here." Breathing hard, he took slow steps toward the back of the building. He could still see her face at the window, and his skin prickled at the memory.

Not seeing or hearing anything, he walked farther and saw a staircase leading to a second floor. He approached it and peered up the stairs. "Margaret," he yelled again, but there was no response.

Eyeing the space above him, he took the stairs, his gun raised. He started to sweat and told himself to stay focused. His mind whirled with what he would do if he found her. He could hear Daniels' voice in his head, telling him to wait for backup, but he knew Margaret wouldn't stick around for long. He had to find her.

Trying to slow his breathing, he reached the top of the stairs. The second floor was similar to the first floor, but with fewer windows. It was darker, with more spaces to hide behind. Swallowing, Rem moved toward the center of the space, looking in every corner, but didn't see anything. He moved toward the back where the light became dimmer and hesitated. He still didn't like dark spaces, but he told himself to keep moving.

Nearing the back, he slowed his steps. The space toward the rear of the building had one window and two sections where the beams ended, and the drywall had been completed. If anybody wanted to hide, this would be the place to do it. He approached one wall, and with his back to it, he slid down toward the edge, listening for any noise. All he could hear was the distant sounds from the street. He expected to hear police sirens soon.

Approaching the edge, he gathered his courage, and swiveled quickly to face what was behind it. It was another dusty space with a concrete floor with various building supplies stacked up. He moved farther in to get a better look but saw no one. Relieved, but at the same time frustrated, he lowered his weapon, but jumped when he heard something clatter behind him. Startled, he turned and raised his gun. "Who's there?"

There was a moment of quiet, then a squeak from below. Rem looked down just as a rat ran over his foot and scampered across the floor. His body went rigid, and he clenched his eyes shut as the memories raced back. The rats, scurrying in the dark, and him hearing, but not seeing them. He put a hand against the wall to balance himself and sucked in a hard-fought breath, His brain registered footsteps behind him, but before he could react, something went over his head, and he was plunged into darkness. His mind went blank. He touched the fabric around his face and realized it was a hood.

Instantly, he was transported back to the day he'd been abducted, where he'd been put in a car, a hood had been placed over his head, and his next stop had been a tiny, lightless room with a dirty mattress, a bucket, and the rats for company.

Flashing back, Rem's legs buckled, and he dropped to his knees. He couldn't move. His muscles locked up and his throat closed in. Someone took the gun from his hand, and he plastered himself against the wall, terrified he would be taken again. Some part of his mind told him to remove the hood, but he feared if he did, he would be back in that room.

His breathing came in sharp gasps, and he fought to control his fear, but it ran rampant. More footsteps neared, and he froze. Someone touched his shoulder and he jerked.

A whispered voice spoke in his ear. "Bring back memories?" It was a woman.

Thinking he heard another rat scamper across the floor, he huddled down and gripped his knees. "Get away from me." He'd tried to shout it, but it was only a strangled whimper.

A hand ran down his arm and the whispered voice returned. "You are still the light."

The words triggered his anger, and Rem found the courage to push up although he was still on his knees. He swung out an arm. "Don't touch me."

He heard a muffled cackle and a distant siren. Shaking and trying to get his bearings, he struggled to confront the darkness and flailed when the hood was yanked off his head. Terrified to open his eyes, he told himself he was okay, and scooted away. Hearing more footsteps, he forced himself to open his eyes, and blinking, he saw only murky light. His gun lay on the ground. He reached for it and stood on shaky legs, holding his weapon out, but his hands were trembling so hard, he couldn't have aimed at anyone. Forcing himself to move, he slid back to the edge of the wall, and after taking a second to collect himself, he swiveled to face the interior, but no one was there. He was alone.

Daniels pulled up and screeched to a halt in front of the coffee shop. Two police cars were already present and two more joined him as he ran up to the door. Mikey opened it and she and Mason ran out. Daniels took her arm and pulled her to the side. "What happened?"

Mikey's eyes were wide. "We met here for coffee. We were just talking, and then Rem stood and said he saw Margaret. He told me to stay put and call you and Mason."

Daniels looked around the area. "Which way did he go?"

Mikey pointed down the sidewalk. "That way. He had to have gone into one of those buildings."

Daniels eyed the street. Beyond the coffee shop were some brick buildings under renovation. If Rem had stayed on the street, Daniels figured he would've turned around by now. But if Margaret was trying to lure him, the buildings would be a good choice. Hoping his partner was okay, he directed two officers to watch the street, two to go into the farthest building, two to go into the middle one, and two to follow him into the one next door. He pulled out his weapon. "Mason, stay with Mikey."

Mason nodded. "I intend to." He took Mikey's arm. "We'll be in the shop until we hear from you. Be careful."

Mikey, her face pale, touched Daniels' arm. "I'm scared."

Daniels glanced at her. He didn't want to admit that he was, too. "He'll be okay. I'll find him." He stepped away from her and headed down the sidewalk. The two officers with him followed. They approached the entrance of the first building, and moving slowly, they entered. The interior was only partially constructed walls, scaffolding, and a cement floor. Bricks, beams of wood, and other materials were strewn along the ground. Daniels and the other officers checked the first floor but didn't find anything. Daniels spotted a staircase and one of the officers noticed a door that likely led to an alley. Daniels directed the officers to check the rear of the structure and he approached the stairs.

Nodding, the officers headed toward the back as Daniels slowly stepped up to the second floor. It was quiet, and as he neared the top, he swung his gun from the front to the back of the building. "Rem?" he called. The area was darker and harder to see. Moving carefully, he approached the rear. He saw two completed walls and he approached with his gun raised. He stopped at the edge of one and swiveled around it. There was nothing there, and he turned to look behind the other wall. Daniels spotted only a partially opened dirty window at the side of the building. It was the last place to look, so he walked up and peered through it. The window led to a fire escape. Daniels leaned out, followed the stairs to the ground below, and saw his partner sitting in the dirt with his back against the brick wall.

Rem sat on the hard ground, his hands on his knees, taking deep breaths and telling himself to relax. He'd heard the sirens and figured Daniels was looking for him. He'd wanted to call out, but his voice wouldn't work. It was as if his fear had sucked the strength out of him. And if he was being honest, he didn't want his partner to find him like this. He needed to stand up and get moving, but his muscles didn't want to engage.

"Rem?" Footsteps sounded on the stairwell.

Recognizing his partner's voice, Rem cursed. Looking up, he squinted against the light.

"Rem? Are you okay?" The clanging footsteps grew louder, and Rem saw Daniels slide down the fire escape and jump to the ground.

Gathering his fortitude, Rem forced himself up. His balance wobbled, though, and he grabbed the wall for support.

Daniels ran up to him. "What happened?" He put a hand on Rem's shoulder, and he hesitated. "You're as white as a sheet."

Rem put his forehead on the brick. "I'm okay."

Daniels holstered his gun. "Mikey said you saw Margaret."

Rem held his stomach, grateful he hadn't upchucked his coffee and breakfast. "I did. She was here."

Daniels took his elbow. "You look like you're about to faint. You need to sit down."

Rem bit his lip when all the anger he'd failed to project earlier suddenly erupted. "I don't want to sit down. Stop talking to me like I'm a school kid." He pushed off the wall and started to pace, surprised that his legs were holding him up. He ran his hands through his hair. "I... I'm okay. She just wanted to scare me." His pace picked up and, recalling the hood, he broke out in a cold sweat.

Daniels softened his voice. "It was her? You saw her?"

Rem stopped. He clenched his eyes shut and opened them. "I saw her at the window of the coffee shop. I chased her into the building. I... I couldn't find her. I thought she'd gotten away. But then... then..."

"Then what?"

Rem did his best to hold it together. "Someone threw a hood over my head, and everything went dark." He set his jaw, mad at himself. "And I froze."

"Rem..." Daniels reached for him. "Just settle down."

Rem stepped away. "I couldn't do anything. I was back in that room. I told myself I wasn't, but it didn't matter." He paused, trying to take Daniels' advice. "She touched my shoulder and whispered in my ear. She asked me if it brought back memories. And told me I was still the light." Clutching his elbows, he shivered, recalling the fear. "Then the hood was yanked off. It took me a second to gather my courage, and when I opened my eyes, she was gone." He went back to the wall, put his hand on it and dropped his head. "She was right there, and I let her get away." The anger he'd felt so abruptly vanished, and he was left with an aching hole of regret. He lifted his head and eyed Daniels. "And if she hurts anyone after today, it will be my fault."

Daniels' face tightened. "That's ridiculous."

Rem wearily pushed off the wall. "No, it isn't. I'm a cop and I froze. I couldn't do shit." Feeling helpless, he looked up and studied the clouds.

"She knew exactly what she was doing."

"If I'd fought back, she would be in custody right now."

"You don't know that. She probably wasn't alone." Daniels approached him. "If you'd fought back, you could be dead."

Rem put his hands on his hips and stared off, imagining various scenarios, his fury with himself rising. Eyeing the street, he started walking.

"Rem...wait..."

But Rem ignored him.

Chapter Twelve

DANIELS STOOD IN LOZANO'S office, his back against the file cabinet. Crossing his arms, he stared out the glass, seeing Rem sitting at his desk. His computer monitor was on, but he stared blankly at the screen. He was bouncing his knee and every few seconds, he would close his eyes and rub his forehead. After leaving Daniels, Rem had returned to his car, had barely spoken to Mikey other than to tell her he was okay, and had left. Daniels had stayed long enough to calm Mikey and direct the officers to canvas the area. They needed to find the hood and corroborate Margaret's appearance. So far, they'd been unable to do either.

Lozano followed his gaze. "He won't go home?"

"No." Daniels rubbed his own forehead. "Not that I can blame him. He'd just sit there and replay this in his head, over and over again."

Lozano made a grunt and leaned back. "Nobody saw anything?"

Daniels pushed off the cabinet. "No. They're still canvasing, but nothing so far. Mikey didn't even see Margaret." He walked to the glass, then turned and faced Lozano.

Lozano expelled a long breath. "I have to ask the obvious. You think it happened or did he imagine it?"

Daniels' anger bubbled up. "Imagine it? What the hell kind of question is that?"

Lozano sat up. "You said he told Mikey about Allison and the baby, and that's when he saw Margaret. He chases her into a dark building, someone throws a hood over his head, and he freezes. The hood hasn't been located and no one else saw Margaret. You and I both know he's been plagued by PTSD and flashbacks. What if this was one of them?"

Daniels glared. "He may have had flashbacks but once he's past them, Rem has never had an issue telling the difference between reality and fantasy. Besides, Margaret spoke to him. That part wasn't a flashback." Frustrated, he started to pace. "This was intentional."

"It's a hell of a plan. She'd need the perfect set up."

"It's been three months. She's been waiting for Rem and Mikey to relax, and the minute they do, this happens." Daniels shook his head. "Hell. He finally opens up and Margaret screws with him."

"You realize I won't be the only one questioning his story?"

Daniels threw out a hand. "And that's exactly what she wants." He put his hands on his hips. "Damn it."

Lozano slumped into his seat. "As much as I'd like to dispatch the force to find her, I can't. We've got nothing to go on, and we still have a murderer to catch." He tipped his head toward the glass. "You think he can handle continuing the investigation?"

Daniels glanced back at Rem. "He'll handle it. It's what he does. Buries himself in his work when he needs to stay distracted." He watched Rem grab his shoulder and stretch his neck. He looked tired and anxious. His phone rang and he jumped slightly, but then answered. Daniels turned toward Lozano. "The bigger issue is when he goes home and is alone with his thoughts. After this, he'll hunker down even more." He approached the desk and kicked at a chair. "We've got to catch this woman before Rem ends up in his own psychiatric ward."

"All I can tell you is to hang in there. She'll make a mistake eventually."

Tired himself, Daniels pinched the bridge of his nose. He sighed and looked up. "You sure about that?"

Lozano didn't answer and tapped on his desk. "You think we need to request another patrol to watch him and Mikey? The chief may not go for it, but I can ask."

Daniels offered a sad chuckle. "If I thought it would help, I'd say yes. But it won't."

Lozano's gaze traveled to behind Daniels. Daniels heard a knock and turned as Rem opened Lozano's door and stuck his head in.

"You two done talking about me?" he asked.

Daniels frowned and eyed Lozano, who shrugged. "Seems so," said Daniels.

"Good." Rem waved a paper. "Because we've got another body. Our bow tie killer has struck again."

Daniels deflated. "Shit."

Rem spoke to Lozano. "Am I still working?"

Lozano knitted his brow. "Any reason you shouldn't be?"

Rem looked between Lozano and Daniels. "None that I can think of."

Lozano nodded. "Good. Then take your partner and go. And keep me appraised."

Rem paused with his hand on the knob. "Thanks, Cap."

Daniels headed toward the door and patted Rem on the shoulder. "Let's go, partner."

Daniels pulled into a small parking lot. He parked in front of a narrow storefront with the name *Reynaldo's* on a white sign above the door. Rem got out of the car and Daniels joined him. His partner hadn't said much on the way over, and Daniels had let him be, figuring he didn't want to talk yet. Two police cars and a crime scene van were also in the lot, and

Daniels and Rem approached the entrance. A tech handed them gloves and shoe protectors and they put them on and entered. Other than a few mannequins dressed in fancy suits, the shop was sparse. Daniels saw a wall of mirrors beside a couple of dressing rooms, plus a counter with a register. The body lay beside the counter, and Ibrahim was squatting next to it.

Daniels approached and noted that the body had been positioned similar to Stella de la Rosa's. The man was flat on his back with his legs straight and his arms stretched out beside him. He wore a black suit with a navy bow tie, and he had a thick mustache and short black hair. His collar had been undone and the infinity symbol was drawn on his neck. "Same MO?" asked Daniels.

Ibrahim looked up. "Hey, guys." He pushed up and stood. "Appears so. Strangled, but only been dead about an hour."

Rem approached the counter. "That soon? Who called it in?"

"A customer," said Ibrahim. "Walked in and found Mr. Reynaldo here on the ground."

Daniels eyed the victim. "Maybe our killer was his previous customer."

"That would be a logical conclusion," said Ibrahim.

Rem scanned the shop. "Any cameras?" He stopped and pointed. "Over there."

Daniels looked to see a camera situated in the corner of the shop facing the counter. "If that works, we may have our killer on video."

"Let's hope," said Rem. He gestured toward the back were there was a closed door. "Maybe that's an office where we can check the footage."

Daniels gestured toward the body. "At least now we understand the bow tie reference."

"Yeah." Rem glanced around. "But he's not the guy in the photo with Stella."

"No, he isn't." Daniels looked around the shop. Everything looked neat and tidy and there were no signs of a struggle. Seeing pictures on a wall, he walked over and saw the victim in the photos. In each one he wore a nice suit with a bow tie, and he was with various other men also wearing nice suits. "Looks like our victim is definitely Reynaldo." He scanned the rest of the photos but didn't see any that roused suspicion. "I'm guessing this is him with his happy customers."

"Any crazy notes left behind?" asked Rem.

Ibrahim scribbled something in a notepad. "Check behind the counter." He resumed his scribbling.

Rem glanced at Daniels, who returned to the counter. They walked behind it and Daniels spotted a lined piece of paper lying beside the register. The words on it were written in black marker, the same as Stella's. He leaned over and read it.

Two more days. For Margaret.

An infinity symbol was drawn below it and beside it was a piece of a puzzle. Looking closer, Daniels thought it looked like a section of sky. It was light blue with a white edge. "It's definitely our guy."

"Only this time it's not a bow tie," said Rem. "It's a puzzle piece."

"And now it's two days instead of four." He glanced at Rem. "I guess that means we have two days before he strikes again?"

Rem sighed. "That's the assumption I would make." He walked closer to the register. "What's that?"

Daniels turned to look and saw a torn white envelope. The edge of a photograph stuck out from the top. Daniels pointed. "Ibrahim? Did you guys see this?"

Ibrahim tucked his note pad away and glanced over. He nodded. "Yes, we caught it. Took some photos but haven't opened it yet. It's all yours."

With his gloved hands, Rem picked up the envelope and slid the picture out. Inside was a photo of Reynaldo, similar to the pictures on the wall, only the man standing beside him was Victor, dressed in a fancy suit.

Daniels stiffened. "Definitely the same guy." He glanced at the body as technicians arrived to take it away. "Victor must've been his customer."

Rem returned the photo to the envelope. Some color had returned to his face after the morning's events, but after seeing the picture it faded again. "The question is, was Reynaldo more than just a customer? Why would the killer target a man who Victor bought his suits from?"

Daniels stepped away from the register, wondering the same thing. The technicians pulled out a body bag. "So our killer is targeting acquaintances of Victor. He sends them a photo of themselves with Victor just before they're murdered." He thought about the photo at Stella's. "The other guy in Stella's photo was just a random person. He was never a target. The only reason Stella got the picture was because Victor was in it."

Rem nodded. "The killer mentions Margaret in his notes, so he either knows her and she's orchestrating this, or he's doing this for her without her knowledge." He glanced back at the note. "And he's giving us a timeframe. Four days until this murder, and now two days until the next. And the puzzle piece is our clue." He paused. "The infinity sign is just his signature."

"It's a line that never ends. You think that means he'll keep going until we catch him?"

"Maybe," said Rem. "Let's hope Victor didn't have many friends."

Daniels eyed the camera in the corner. "How much you want to bet we won't find a thing from the camera?"

Rem leaned his hip on the edge of the counter. "If he was a customer, then he knew that camera was there. My guess? It either doesn't work, or our killer took care of any recordings before he left." He frowned at something beside him and turned. "Look at this."

Daniels walked to the front desk. He spotted a heavy notebook with the word *Appointments* across the front. "Looks like Reynaldo is old school."

Rem opened the book and carefully flipped through the pages. "Definitely old-school. No online calendar for this guy." He arrived at three days prior and saw that Reynaldo had three appointments. Rem flipped to the next page and saw the ragged edge of a torn-out sheet in the crease of the notebook.

"Hell," said Daniels. "Appointments for the last few days were removed."

"Yup." Rem closed the book. "Which means he was definitely a customer."

"A recent customer," said Daniels. "Somebody who was here just over an hour ago." He waved at an officer near the front door. The officer jogged over, and Daniels directed him to start a canvas of the neighboring shops to see if anyone saw anything within the last twenty-four hours. The officer nodded and walked away. Daniels returned to the counter and spoke to Rem. "If we're lucky, maybe somebody saw him."

Rem told Ibrahim about the appointment book and Ibrahim confirmed they would bag and fingerprint it along with the note and the envelope. They'd fingerprint the rest of the shop, as well.

Rem groaned out a long breath. "Well, where do you want to start?"

Daniels gestured toward the office. "Let's check the back. If he's got a computer, maybe there's something on it that will explain his link to Victor. And we can look for video footage." He paused. "If that doesn't help, we'll have to go through his clients like we did with Stella. Let's just hope we get a lead somewhere because our time is short."

Rem stretched his neck, looking tired. Daniels suspected he was exhausted but knew his partner would be in no hurry to go home. "We've got two days," said Rem. "With nothing but a puzzle piece to go on, and that Victor likely bought his suits from this guy. That's not much."

"At least now we know Victor's the connection," said Daniels. "You should talk to Mikey. See if she knows Reynaldo. And once Kate sets up that meeting with Allison, I can ask her about Reynaldo, too."

Rem grimaced and looked away. "Maybe you should talk to Mikey."

"What for?" Daniels narrowed his eyes at Rem. "Have you spoken to her since this morning?"

"No. She called but I haven't called her back." He hesitated. "And I'm not sure if I'm going to."

Daniels studied Rem. "You can't ignore her. You finally told her about Allison."

"After this morning, that's the last thing I want to discuss. I wish I hadn't said anything."

Daniels reminded himself to be patient. "On the contrary, it was way overdue. Mikey needed to know."

The technicians began to move the body into the bag. "You should've seen her face," said Rem. "I felt as low as the bottom of my shoe. I didn't know what to say, which didn't matter because that's when Margaret showed."

Daniels debated his response, knowing the morning was still fresh on his partner's mind. "Mikey will understand. I can ask her about Reynaldo if you want me to, but it's just putting off the inevitable."

"It may be inevitable, but it doesn't have to be today." Rem paused and gestured toward the back. "I'm going to check the office." He took a step and looked back. "And I'll pay you a million dollars to stop for a large coffee and a Taco del Fuego on the way back to the station."

Worried, but willing to change the subject, Daniels smiled softly. "How about half a mil? I'm in a good mood today."

Some of the fatigue lifted from Rem's face and he smiled back. "You got it. I'll write you a check."

He turned back toward the office, stepped around the body bag, and Daniels followed.

Chapter Thirteen

REM OPENED THE DOOR to his home and closed it behind him. Feeling like he'd been sprinting all day through hilly terrain, he tossed his keys on the table in front of him and blinked his weary eyes. After leaving the crime scene at Reynaldo's, they'd grabbed tacos and coffee and had returned to the station where they'd spent the rest of the day learning everything they could about Reynaldo. Their assumptions about the camera had proved correct. The camera worked, but any footage from the previous three days had been erased. They'd gone through the appointment book but all they had were names and phone numbers. Reynaldo didn't keep records as well as Stella. They'd spent the afternoon and evening calling everyone in the book without any luck. The canvas had turned up nothing. Realizing the killer had covered his tracks, they were right back where they'd started, which was nowhere. Daniels had called Mikey and Gina. He'd left a message with Gina, but Mikey had had a vague recollection of accompanying Victor for a suit fitting. She believed the tailor had been Reynaldo. He'd been a nice man who'd worn a bow tie and had been chummy with Victor, but she could think of no reason why someone would want to kill him. Then she'd asked Daniels to tell Rem to call her when he was ready to talk. Daniels had conveyed the message.

His muscles tight with fatigue, Rem again recalled his morning and his stomach churned. He was almost glad another body had turned up because it had kept him busy the rest of the day. After leaving the warehouse, all he could think about when he closed his eyes was the hood over his head and hearing Margaret's voice in his ear. His heart would race, and he'd break out in a sweat. He could barely speak to Mikey much less anyone else when he'd left the scene that morning.

Standing in his foyer, he looked around his house, noting the quiet. He debated sitting on the couch and watching TV but knew the ugly thoughts would return. He needed sleep but almost laughed at the thought. Groaning, he put his hands in his pockets and turned toward the front. Glancing out the window, he gazed at his sad-looking front yard. A neighbor kid mowed his grass for him, but he had a patch of dirt with flowers planted on either side of the porch steps. The weeds had almost overtaken the space. Despite his fatigue, he decided he needed to do something before attempting to sleep. Rem went to the kitchen and opened the fridge. He grabbed a beer and headed toward his bedroom to change into some old sweats. In his bedroom, he stopped beside the bureau against the wall across from his bed. After he'd done laundry a few days earlier, he'd stacked the clean clothes on top of the bureau. With their recent workload, he'd been too lazy to put them away. Beside the stack of clothes stood a lamp which Rem would leave on at night since he didn't do well in the dark. Flicking the lamp on, he saw the framed picture of himself and Jennie taken by Daniels during a visit to an art fair. It was one of his favorites. Rem stopped. The picture normally sat to the left of the lamp but now it was on the right. He stepped closer and picked up the photo, noting his smile and Jennie's grin. It had definitely been taken during happier times.

Feeling sadness bubble up and knowing he was too tired to be reminiscing, he returned the photo to the left side of the lamp, assuming he'd moved it when he'd placed his laundry beside it. That's all his exhausted brain could imagine.

Telling himself not to think about Jennie, Mikey, or Margaret, he went into his garage, found his gloves and a trowel, and walked out the front door. After going down his porch steps, he squatted beside his neglected flowers, dug his trowel into the dirt and began to remove weeds. One by one, he pulled them from the ground and dumped them beside him. Recalling his beer, he was about to go inside to retrieve it when he heard voices. He turned to see his neighbor's house across the street. The front lights were off, but the interior lights illuminated the outside enough for Rem to see a woman step down the porch and walk across the grass. She wore a long jacket and a baseball cap on her head. Kevin, his neighbor, stood at his open front door, yelling. Rem couldn't hear all of it, but he could make out a few sentences.

"Basically, you're walking out on our marriage," yelled Kevin.

The woman walked to her car. She opened the door and yelled back. "It's long overdue. I should have done it two years ago." She got in, slammed the door shut, started up the engine and drove off.

Rem eyed Kevin, who stood at the door for a moment. He stared in Rem's direction, then went inside and closed the door. Rem sat back in the dirt, realizing he wasn't the only one with problems. He removed his gloves and stood. After running back into the house and grabbing his beer, he kneeled in the grass again and reached for his gloves when something darted past him. Startled, he almost yelped, when he recognized Chester the cat walking through his weeds.

Holding his chest, Rem cursed. "Chester. You scared the shit out of me."

The cat meowed, walked up to Rem's leg, and nuzzled Rem's knee. Rem figured the cat must have escaped while Kevin had stood with his door open. Rem scratched the cat's ears. "You probably should go home. Your dad is going to be looking for you." Although Kevin had told him his wife would be pissed if the cat escaped, Rem guessed Kevin wouldn't be too happy either. Rem didn't savor returning the cat right after the fight, but Rem didn't plan on keeping the animal overnight, so he stood and picked it up. "C'mon, Chester." The cat began to purr, and Rem held it against his chest. He walked across the street, up the porch steps, and knocked on the door.

The porch light came on, and Kevin opened the front door. He looked almost as tired and weary as Rem felt. He eyed Chester and rolled his eyes. "Damn cat."

"He walked through my flower bed while I was weeding," said Rem. "I figured you'd notice he'd escaped eventually."

"He must have run out when I had the door open." He paused and sighed. "Sorry about our public altercation. I didn't mean to broadcast our fight to the neighborhood." He took the cat from Rem. "She...my wife...just pissed me off."

Rem nodded. "No judgment from me. We've all been there."

Kevin held the cat in his arms. "I guess so, but when it happens, it feels like you're the only one."

Rem recalled his morning. "I know how that goes." He wiped some cat hair from his shirt. "I had a rough day myself."

Kevin scratched Chester's head. "I was wondering about your sudden desire for a clean flower bed at this time of night."

Rem chuckled sheepishly. "Yeah, well, I needed a distraction."

Chester squirmed. Kevin dropped her onto the floor, and she ran off into the house. "I was about to have a beer. Care to join me? Sounds like we could both use one."

Rem glanced back toward his yard, debating. He could either resume his weeding or get to know his neighbor. He shrugged. "Sure. That sounds great." He swiped at his pants to knock off any loose dirt. Kevin stepped back and Rem entered. "Sorry about the messy clothes."

"Don't worry about it." Kevin closed the door. "This house could use a little dirt. My wife likes it obsessively clean." He gestured toward the living room which was on the left. "Have a seat on the couch. I'll grab us a couple of beers."

Rem nodded as Kevin headed into the kitchen. Rem noticed the house wasn't much different than his except it was bigger. He walked into a cozy living room and sat on a big leather couch. The TV was on, and a nature program was playing. A lioness was stalking an antelope, and Rem couldn't help but think that after his day, he felt like an antelope, too.

Kevin returned holding two beers. He handed one to Rem and sat in a chair across from the couch. "We can change the channel. Nancy likes her nature shows." He picked up the remote and flipped to another program. Rod Serling appeared and the familiar theme music from *The Twilight Zone* played. "That's much better." Kevin lowered the volume and set the remote down.

"Don't change it on my account," said Rem.

"I didn't." Kevin took a sip of his beer. "The last thing I want to think about right now is her."

Rem sipped his own drink, wondering how much Kevin wanted to discuss. "How long have you two been married?"

"Three years." He sighed and watched the TV. "The first year was decent."

Rem picked at the label on his bottle. "Ever try counseling? And it's fine to tell me to mind my own business."

Kevin waved a hand. "No, it's fine. We did do counseling for a while. But then she started this job and then came the traveling, and that was the end of that." He held his beer and massaged a temple. "That's what we argued over. She just got home and now she's leaving again."

Rem nodded. "Then let me ask the obvious. Why not separate?"

Kevin settled back in his chair and put his foot on the coffee table. "Believe me, I've thought about it. But sometimes I think it's easier being married."

"Why do you say that? Especially if you're miserable."

Kevin raised the side of his lip. "Because the world is geared toward couples. Have you noticed?"

Rem almost chuckled. "Yeah, I have."

Kevin smirked. "You can't get an invitation without a plus one added, tables are either for two or four, and don't get me started on engagement

parties, wedding showers, anniversaries, and, of course, Valentine's Day."
He snorted. "Name one day that celebrates singles."

"Birthdays," said Rem.

"Doesn't count. Couples get birthdays, too."

Rem understood. He'd been on both sides, and the couple one was far
easier in terms of a social life. "Doesn't mean you should stay married. It's
not worth being miserable just because you don't want to be alone." He
sipped his beer and thought about it. "There is something to being on your
own that you don't find when you're with someone else. I've learned that
these last few years."

"You're not dating anybody?" He paused. "Never been married?"

Rem gripped his bottle. "I came close once." He looked up. "She died,
though."

Kevin was quiet. "I'm sorry. And here I am bitching about my marriage."

"It's fine. Everyone has their challenges. Comparisons are a lousy barom-
eter for how you're supposed to feel."

"You mentioned it's been a few years. Has there been any one since?"

Rem thought of Mikey. "Maybe. But my life is complicated. Plus, it's
hard to open that door again."

"I can imagine." He ran a thumb over the condensation on his bottle. "I
guess it's just a question of whether you prefer your own company or hers."
He met Rem's look. "As long as she's the right one."

"She could be." Rem set his jaw. It was the first time he'd admitted to
himself that Mikey could be more than just a girlfriend.

"Then I guess the only question is, is she worth risking another broken
heart? That's what it comes down to, isn't it? Eventually."

Rem couldn't imagine suffering through the pain of losing someone
again. "I barely survived the first time."

Kevin shifted in his seat, and he set his elbow on the arm rest. "Are we
talking about death or a breakup?"

"I worry about both. In my line of work, I have to expect the unexpected." Rem shook his head. "My partner keeps telling me that I need to stop thinking so much. He's happily married with a kid, so maybe he's right. Maybe there isn't a dark cloud hovering over my head, although it sometimes feels like there is."

"You should listen to your partner. I suspect he knows what he's talking about." He sighed and stared at the ceiling. "I wonder what he would tell me?"

"He'd tell you to be happy. And to do whatever it took to get there, whether it's as a single person or not."

Kevin glanced over. "It's sound advice." His gaze returned to the TV. "This is a good episode. Have you seen it?"

"Yeah. It's the one with the lady and the hitchhiker. One of my favorites."

"You do know your TV. I bet you are great at trivia."

Rem smiled. "Only when it comes to entertainment. I'll crucify my partner every time. But he kills me in all the other categories."

"You two are obviously close."

"Like brothers. I've got a ton of family, but nobody knows me better than him."

"I guess that's what partners are for." He scratched at his jeans. "Especially doing what you do every day."

"In our job, you have to rely on your partner, or you could wind up dead, or with a huge shrink bill."

"I bet you've seen some things."

Rem recalled Reynaldo's body. "We have. We're currently looking for someone who's killed two people and is threatening to kill more. It's why I was weeding the front yard. I needed to decompress before going to bed."

"I'd expect your flowerbeds to be immaculate then."

"You'd think, but usually I just crash in front of the TV. This time, though," he thought of the hood over his head, "I needed something stronger, and since chugging down vodka wouldn't be smart, I thought I'd be productive."

"What could be worse than a killer on the loose?"

"You'd be surprised." His heart raced again at the thought of Margaret being close enough to whisper in his ear and his failure at stopping her.

"Sorry. I didn't mean to pry."

Rem sat up. "No. It's okay." He eyed the TV episode, but his mind was elsewhere. He'd left the house without setting the alarm. Or even locking the door. "Listen, I should go. It's late and I'm sure you'd like to get to bed. I should do the same." He stood. "Thanks for the beer, though." He paused. "It helped, and it was nice to sit and talk. Even if it was about your crappy marriage and my lousy past."

Kevin stood, too. "You're welcome anytime. I'm usually here by myself, so feel free to knock if you want to share a beer again. It's stupid for us to drink alone."

Holding his bottle, Rem headed toward the front door. "It's not often, but occasionally I host a poker game with my partner and people from work. Next time, you're welcome to join us."

"Thank you," said Kevin. "I appreciate that. And thank you for returning Chester. My wife and I are in your debt." He opened the door. "I think that cat is the only thing keeping us together."

Rem stepped outside. "Then we better keep Chester safe."

"Chester has nine lives. I think she's in the clear." He hesitated. "Maybe we should focus on ourselves. And take your partner's advice."

Rem thought of Daniels. "You're probably right. But I'm not going to tell my partner that."

Kevin smiled softly. "Good night, Detective."

"Call me Rem. I think we're on a first name basis now after saving Chester twice."

Kevin laughed. "Chester is good for something."

Rem raised his half-filled beer. "Good night, Kevin."

"Night, Rem."

Chapter Fourteen

STIFLING A YAWN, DANIELS stood in line at the register in the downstairs cafeteria. He held a black coffee for himself, a cream and sugar-filled coffee for Rem plus a cinnamon roll and a granola bar. He approached the register.

"Hey, Detective," said Tony. "How are you today?"

"I'm trying to stay awake," said Daniels.

"Sorry to hear that." He rang up the items. "But I see you're keeping your partner fed. That's a good thing."

"You're not kidding. He gets moody when he's tired and hungry. I figured I better get him a huge coffee and a roll."

Tony chuckled. "I saw him yesterday afternoon. He definitely looked like he had something on his mind."

Daniels nodded. "It's definitely been a tough couple of days." He offered his card and Tony took it. "Hopefully, this will cheer him up."

Tony swiped the card and handed it back. "You keep feeding him to cheer him up and he's going to gain twenty pounds."

Daniels put his card away. "He could stand to gain a few." He raised the bag with the roll in it. "This will help."

Tony tore the receipt off and handed it to Daniels. "You tell him next time he comes down here, the coffee is on me. That goes for you too, Detective."

Daniels smiled. "Thanks. I appreciate it but be prepared because Rem might kiss you." He grabbed his drinks and slipped his granola bar into his jacket pocket.

Tony chuckled again. "It wouldn't be the first time."

Daniels raised a brow at him, paused, and shook his head. "I'm not even going to ask."

"You wouldn't believe it if I told you."

"I'll take your word for it. You have a good day."

"You too, Detective."

Daniels turned, left the cafeteria, and headed up the stairs. He and Rem had spent the last couple of hours reviewing everything they'd done the previous day regarding Reynaldo and Stella's murders. Ibrahim's initial report from Reynaldo's crime scene had revealed little. They'd dusted and discovered various fingerprints at the shop, but none had triggered suspicion. Reynaldo had died from strangulation, but no DNA had been found on the body other than Reynaldo's. The tech guys had the computer and were attempting to recover the deleted files from the camera but so far, they'd had no luck.

Rem had seemed better that morning and had even beaten Daniels to the station. Daniels had overslept after a difficult night of his own. He took the stairs to the second floor and entered the squad room.

Rem was staring at his computer monitor and looked over when Daniels approached. He eyed the bag and coffee. "You're a lifesaver."

Daniels set the bag and cup on Rem's desk. "Next one is on you."

Rem reached for the bag and peeked inside. "You got it." He picked up his coffee and sipped it, then closed his eyes and sighed.

Daniels sat at his desk. He set his own coffee down and dropped his granola bar beside it. Tired, he rubbed his eyes and yawned. "You learn anything while I was gone?"

Rem shook his head. "I wish. Any startling revelations while you were in the cafeteria?" Holding his coffee, he leaned back and rested his head against the top of the chair.

"As a matter of fact, yes. When did you kiss Tony?"

Rem raised his head and smirked. "That's between me and Tony."

Daniels squinted, but Rem didn't say more. "I'm sorry I asked," said Daniels.

Rem chuckled.

Daniels noted his partner's calmer demeanor. "You look better today. Did you get some sleep?"

Rem nodded. "A decent amount. I went home and did some weeding last night."

"Weeding? As in pulling weeds?"

"I needed a distraction after yesterday. TV wasn't going to cut it and I knew I wouldn't sleep, so I decided to clean up my flowerbeds. Then I talked to the neighbor for little bit, went home and hit the hay."

"Talked to the neighbor? It seems like an odd time for a chat."

Rem shrugged. "I saved Chester the cat, and Kevin offered me a beer. We didn't talk long, but it was enough to realize his marriage sucks."

"Sounds like a deep conversation."

"While I was weeding, he and his wife had an argument on their front lawn and then she drove off. I think he was a little embarrassed."

Daniels recalled his own night. "Marriage is tough...for everyone." He slumped back against his chair.

Rem raised an eyebrow at him. "What's up with you?

Daniels waved a hand. "It's nothing."

Rem studied him. "You've been yawning your way through this morning. I understand we're tired, but you usually sleep like a rock through the worst of cases." He paused. "Everything okay between you and Marj?"

Fatigued, Daniels held his temples. "We argued last night."

"About what?"

Daniels raised his head. "She was tired, and I was tired. J.P. is teething. She was mad because I came home late again, and I got mad because I'm working this case and she knows it." He shook his head and snorted. "It's just one of those weeks. Her best friend is out on maternity leave, and I think Marjorie feels a little lost. She can't vent to her friend when she needs to. Work's been tough, and she comes home to an empty house with a child to take care of. I get it that it's hard. I understand why she's upset, but at the same time I have to find a murderer before he kills somebody else."

Rem fiddled with the lid on his cup. "You two are both busy and tired. It's not surprising you take out your frustrations on each other. It won't last, though. We'll find this guy and Marjorie's friend will come back to work. You'll get back on track."

Daniels sat up and put his elbows on his desk. "This is why I'm reluctant to have a second child. It's hard enough with just one. You saw how Jeremy was with his two kids and he was even at home with them. I can't imagine doing this with J.P. and a baby in the house. I think Marjorie would have shot me last night."

"I thought you two decided to table that discussion for now until J.P. was older."

"We did." Daniels scratched his jaw. "But with Moira, Marjorie's friend, having a new baby, it's brought the whole subject back up again. I think that was part of the issue. Marjorie stopped by Moira's on the way home. She held the baby. It made her wistful and when I got home, she mentioned it. But I guess I didn't have the reaction she expected. Combine that with me being late, missing dinner and J.P.'s bedtime, well, it all hit the fan."

Rem straightened. He reached for his bag and pulled out his cinnamon roll. "Don't worry. You guys will be fine. You have your moments and then make up, which is the fun part." He licked icing off his fingers. "How about we make sure you get home on time tonight?"

Daniels snickered. "In case you've forgotten, there's a killer on the loose who will likely kill again tomorrow. Now is not the time to leave early."

"I hate to tell you this, but we've got nothing to go on. Unless that puzzle piece somehow illuminates our killer's next steps, until this guy screws up, we're not going to find him. And you getting out of here on time to have dinner with your wife and see your kid is not going to change that." He picked up his cinnamon roll. "Your marriage is more important than spending another few hours on this case and getting nowhere." He took a bite of his roll.

Daniels considered that. "Well, I appreciate the thought. Why don't we see where we are tonight and then decide?"

Rem chewed and swallowed. "Suit yourself. But if there's not a breakthrough, you might as well spend some time with your family. I can stay here and finish up. Plus, Mel and Garcia are helping too. Nobody is going to hold it against you."

Daniels reached for his granola bar. "Thanks, partner."

Rem licked more icing off his thumb. "Cheer up. I didn't even tell you the good news yet."

Daniels perked up. "Good news? Is it about the case?"

"It is. Although whether or not it actually helps remains to be seen." He leaned forward. "Kate called while you were downstairs. Measy agreed to a meeting between you and Allison." He eyed his watch. "Kate will be here soon to go with you to the jail."

Daniels nodded, happy to potentially make some progress. "That's something, at least." Although he understood the need to talk to Allison, he still felt uncomfortable with it. He wouldn't admit that to Rem, though.

"I'll say it again. I doubt she'll tell you anything." Rem set his roll down on a napkin and wiped his fingers on the edge of his shirt. "You still sure I should stay here?"

Daniels pointed a finger. "No way you're going. She got you there once, but she's not going to do it again. I'll talk to her. If she won't say anything, then so be it."

Rem picked up his coffee. "Just be careful with her."

"She's in jail. What's she going to do?"

"Between her and Measy, there's no telling. She won't offer anything without wanting something in return." He paused. "And that something will probably have to do with me."

Daniels interlaced his fingers. "That's where Kate comes in. I'll let her handle that. But we're not going to let Allison use you as a bargaining chip."

"Then you might as well stay here. It will be more productive."

"Unfortunately, considering how little we know, we have to try. I agree Allison is unpredictable, but she's also facing life in prison. That might sway her decision-making."

Rem studied his coffee. "Maybe. I still think we'd get more out of her if I went."

"Feel free to think about it all you want, but it's not happening. Besides, you got something else you need to do." Daniels picked up his bar and opened the wrapper.

Rem pursed his lips. "I do? You mean other than search for Stella and Reynaldo's killer?"

Daniels checked his watch and figured the timing was right. "Yes." He braced himself for the reaction. "I talked to Mikey on the way to the cafeteria."

Rem's face fell. "Mikey? About what?"

"She wanted to be sure you were okay. You haven't called her back." He paused. "I told her to come by the station."

"You did what?"

"You heard me."

Rem widened his eyes. "We're in the middle of an investigation."

"I believe you just told me that leaving early wasn't going to change anything. I think you can spare twenty minutes for Mikey."

Rem sputtered. "Here? You want me to talk to her here?"

"Why not? I believe interrogation room one is open."

Rem glared. "That is not the point."

Daniels held his gaze. "What is the point then? You dropped a major bomb on her yesterday then disappeared in pursuit of Margaret. Don't you think that warrants a conversation?"

"Yes. I agree we need to talk. But it's not up to you when that happens."

Daniels steeled himself. "I admit, I may have overstepped my bounds. But you can't leave her hanging like this. I know you. You'll bury your head in this case and avoid her. That's not fair to Mikey or you. You may be pissed, but I'd rather ask for your forgiveness than your permission."

Rem gripped the edge of his desk. "I could kill you right now."

"You could, but then you'd be arrested. Lozano will have tons of paperwork, J.P. will be fatherless, and your mother and numerous cousins will have to visit you in prison next Christmas. You want that on your shoulders?"

Rem put his coffee down and stood, his face stony. "When is she supposed to be here?"

"Uhm...," Daniels eyed the clock on the wall. "Right about—"

The squad doors opened, and Mikey strode in. She saw Rem, stopped, and put her hands on her hips. "Why the hell haven't you called me back?"

Rem walked into the interrogation room behind Mikey and closed the door. He shut the blinds to the two-way mirror and leaned his back against the wall. "Have a seat." He gestured to the two chairs in the room, but Mikey paced.

"I think better when I move," she said. "You know that."

Rem prepared himself and crossed his arms. "I'm sorry I didn't call you back."

She stopped and stared. "How could you leave me hanging like that? After what happened yesterday?"

He hung his head. "I didn't know what to say."

She faced him. "How about starting with why you waited so long to tell me about Allison?"

Rem inwardly cringed but he had to be honest. "Because I was embarrassed." His frustration bubbled up. "This woman, who I'm testifying against and hoping will be thrown into prison for the rest of her life, could be the mother of my child. I don't know how to deal with that, and I hated telling anyone. Ask Daniels. Why do you think I disappeared to Merrimac?"

"I get it that it shocked you. But you've had three months to absorb the news. What was your plan? Wait to tell me once the baby was born?"

Agitated, Rem pushed off the wall. "I didn't have a plan. I tried more than once to say something. I just...couldn't do it."

Her face tightened. "Did you think I'd blame you?"

Rem ran his hands through his hair. "Maybe. I don't know."

"That's ridiculous. How could I possibly fault you? That woman drugged and assaulted you."

"Then maybe I blame myself." Feeling a little shaky, Rem pulled out a chair and sat.

"You shouldn't." She pulled out the other chair and sat across from him. "You need to work on that."

"I am, but I have my moments." He blew out a breath. "Listen. I guess I just didn't want to lay this on you. You and I...we're close...and I didn't know how you'd handle hanging around someone who's raising a child with Allison."

She straightened. "Is that what you've decided to do?"

Rem hesitated, still uncertain himself. "I may not have a choice. If it's my child, I have a responsibility. I can't hand her over to foster care, or let Allison raise her if, God forbid, Allison's acquitted."

"Her?" asked Mikey.

"It's a girl."

"What about a DNA test? Don't you think you should find out if she's yours?"

Rem scoffed. "We've tried. Allison won't go for it." He raised a hand. "And that doesn't mean anything. She's using this because the not knowing is what kills me, and she likes that." He paused. "But I have to assume the baby is mine."

Her face pale, Mikey studied her hands. "So, if Allison is sent to prison, you'll raise your daughter, and if Allison's acquitted, you intend to fight for custody."

Rem stood and stared out a narrow window overlooking the parking lot. "I don't know, Mikey."

"I think you do."

He swallowed. "If the child's mine, then I guess yes. I'll raise her, whether Allison's in prison or not." He looked back at her. "Which means I'd have to leave the force. I can't be a single dad, doing what I do."

"Does Daniels know that?"

"We've talked about it. He gets it."

She huffed. "Well, at least you told him."

"I'm sorry." He faced her. "I know I should have said something."

"Did you'd honestly think I'd run for the hills? Abandon you?" She stood. "Rem. We've told each other things that would make other people cower. Why would you think I couldn't handle this?"

"Because I was scared, okay?" He stepped away from the window. "I can't expect you to want any part of this. We've talked about a lot of things, but this goes way beyond any of that." Conflicted, he turned away. "When I went to Merrimac, I was falling apart. My mental state was a mess. If Daniels hadn't showed, well..." he recalled being falsely accused of murder after spending four days in an alcoholic haze while visiting his aunt, "...I don't know where I'd be right now. And then, I pulled it together and

I planned to tell you everything when I got home. And then Margaret happened, Mason went into rehab, and then Kyle..."

Her face furrowed. "Kyle? What does Kyle have to do with this?"

"You went out with him."

Her jaw dropped. "We went for coffee."

"And if Mason hadn't gone into rehab and Margaret hadn't escaped, would you have done more?"

"I don't know what I would have done," she yelled. "And what does that have to do with anything?"

"Because I like you, Mikey," he yelled back. He softened his tone. "I was going to tell you that after I got back from Merrimac. Despite Allison."

She didn't speak for a moment. "Why didn't you?" she finally asked.

"Because of what I just mentioned. Everything hit at once, and I couldn't pursue anything with you. You were dealing with Mason, and we both had to worry about Margaret. Add Allison and the baby, and I retreated." He took a second to gather himself. "And then you introduced me to Kyle."

She frowned. "So?"

"He's a nice guy. And he likes you. I can see that."

"We work together. He's a friend."

"It's more than that and you know it."

Mikey shook her head. "I know he likes me that way, but I haven't pursued it."

Rem studied the floor. "Maybe you should." He closed his eyes for a second and then lifted his head and opened them. "He'd be better for you than me. You wouldn't have to worry about your crazy sister going after him, or raising his child with a sociopath, or getting killed while on the job. And I—" His throat closed.

"You what?" she whispered.

He composed himself. "I wouldn't have to worry about losing someone again." He set his jaw.

"You're not going to lose me."

He scoffed. "You know as well as I do that with Margaret loose, you're a target. Even more so if we pursued a relationship. I'd be jumping at every sound and looking around every corner. It's bad enough as it is. I mean, look what happened yesterday."

"Yesterday?" she asked. "You saw Margaret. You went after her."

His anger surfaced. "And what did I do? I froze when she got close. She put a damn hood on my head, and spoke to me, and I lost it. She was right there. I had a gun. And I didn't do shit."

"Rem, she was messing with you. She wanted to intimidate you—"

"And she succeeded." He threw out a hand. "Which only reinforced the fact that I can't protect you. I only put you in more danger." He groaned at the painful realization that he and Mikey could never be together. "And I can't live with that. I can't be responsible for putting you in harm's way. You mean too much to me." He hesitated when his throat tightened again. "You're better off, and safer, with Kyle."

"Rem, listen..."

Feeling the weight of his decision and its impact on Mikey, he pushed through it. "I'm not saying we can't be friends. I hope we can, but I'll understand if you'd rather not. It would be easier for Kyle, I guess."

"Would you shut up?" She walked up to him. "You've said your piece. Now let me say mine."

Rem looked away. "There's nothing to say."

"The hell there isn't." She poked him in the shoulder. "How about we start with how you've coupled me up with Kyle without having the slightest interest in how I feel about him."

"You like him."

"I do like him, but that doesn't mean we're getting married. Yes. He's a nice guy, and yes, if I were to give him the green light, he'd be thrilled. He's told me as much."

Rem sighed. "There you go."

"But I haven't given him the green light, or anything else."

"Because you're working with him, and because Mason's in therapy."

"Mason is out of Windhaven and back at work, in case you haven't noticed, and Kyle's presence in the office is vastly reduced."

"You're worried about Margaret, too."

"I'd be stupid not to be. Anybody hanging out with me is also at risk. I have to consider that."

"I understand. But he's still a safer bet than me."

She took a step closer and glared. "I don't want to be with someone because they're safer. That's stupid."

"It's not stupid. I know that for a fact. If Jennie hadn't been with me—" He had to stop and clear his throat. "She'd still be alive. I wish to God every day she'd picked someone safer."

Her eyes rounded. "Rem. What happened to her isn't your fault."

"That's an easy thing for you and Daniels to say, but not so easy for me."

Mikey put her hand on his arm. "She didn't want anyone else. She wanted you. She loved you."

"And look where it got her."

"Rem—"

Emotional, Rem swiped at his eye. "Listen. I need to get back." He tried to change the subject. "Did you hear Daniels is going to talk to Allison at the jail about our case?" He sniffed and stepped back. "He's hoping she knows something about whoever is targeting Victor's friends. I told him it was pointless, but he's trying anyway."

"Rem, listen—"

"Daniels talked to you about Reynaldo, didn't he? I guess he sold Victor some suits and got killed for it. Our killer left a puzzle piece behind this time. It was blue with a patch of white. Daniels thinks it could be from a puzzle with a sky in it. Strange."

She raised her voice. "I don't want to talk about Reynaldo."

He backed up toward the door, needing to get out of the room. "Mikey, listen. I'm sorry, but let's be honest. I'm not good for you. I wish to hell

I was because I'd sweep you off your feet, but I'm not. I can't protect you and I'm not safe. Kyle is, though. He's kind and he adores you. He'd be good for you. So go to him and tell him, okay? Give him a chance. I want to see you happy."

"Would you listen to yourself?" Mikey's eyes swirled with tears. "I don't care about Allison or the baby. I don't care about Margaret." She wiped away a tear that spilled down her cheek. "I care about you."

He smiled softly and fought back his own tears. "I care about you, too." Resisting the urge to wipe her fallen tear away with his finger, he held strong. "Which is why you and I can never be together."

Her face fell. "Don't say that."

He bit the inside of his lip, determined to tell her the truth. "I have to. My sanity teeters on the edge most of the time, and if I had to add you to the mix, I'd never be able to do my job. I'd want to hide you away. But I can't do that. You're not a hider. You'd risk yourself to protect me and anyone you loved. I admire that so much about you, but I won't let you sacrifice yourself for me." He chuckled sadly. "Daniels may have signed up for that, but you didn't."

She sniffed. "Margaret won't be out there forever."

"Neither of us knows that. And whether it's months or years, you shouldn't wait. I want you to have a life."

"How about you let me decide what kind of life I want to have?"

He sighed and allowed himself to raise his hand and touch her cheek, which was damp with her tears. "I know I can't stop you from doing whatever you want. But what I can do is stop you from being with me." He trailed a finger along her jaw. "And if that's what it takes to keep you alive, then I'll do it."

She lifted her hand and put it over his. "You're not thinking this through."

"I am. I've done nothing else but think." He stroked her skin, wishing he could tell her other things. "Go be with Kyle, Mikey. Be happy."

More tears fell, and she bit her lip.

He took her hand and squeezed her fingers. "I've got to go." He released her and stepped away, hating to see her cry. "I'll...uh...see you."

Mikey swiped at her face. "Rem. Please."

Struggling to breathe, his mind whirling, and unable to stay any longer, Rem walked out of the interrogation room.

Chapter Fifteen

DANIELS SIGNED IN AT the jail and relinquished his weapon. The woman behind the desk told him and Kate to have a seat and someone would arrive to take them back. He thanked her, and he and Kate sat in some plastic chairs to wait.

Thinking about what he would say when he saw Allison, Daniels fidgeted in his seat.

Kate set her purse in the empty chair beside her. "Nervous?" she asked.

Daniels didn't see the point in lying. "Yes. I haven't spoken to this woman since I yanked her off Rem and that stone slab." The memory still gave him chills.

"If it's any comfort, I'm nervous, too." She crossed her legs. "Don't tell anyone, but she gives me the willies."

"You?" he asked. "You always seem calm and focused, but intense. Sometimes, you scare me."

She smiled. "I have to project strong energy, or this job would eat me up. I show weakness, and I might as well be a seal in shark-infested waters."

"I understand that. Being a detective requires the same."

"You can be a little intense yourself. Which is why I want you to follow my lead in there. Don't let her get to you."

Daniels gripped the armrest. "I'll do my best."

"You'll do it, period. If this turns into some yelling match, or you lose your cool, Measy will use it against you."

Tired, Daniels leaned his head against the wall behind him. "I know." He looked over. "Rem still thinks he should have come with us."

"I admire his courage, but I would have said no."

"Me, too." He paused. "But I see his point. She may not talk without him."

"Then so be it." She shifted to face him. "We give her what she wants, and she'll continue to play games with us."

Daniels nodded. "It's hard though. How do you balance your own safety when someone else might die tomorrow? What if she has information that could save somebody's life?"

"Then her holding back lays the blame at her feet, not yours. It's not your fault if someone dies. You're here, doing your job. If she refuses to help, that's not on you." She glanced up as a buzzer rang and a door opened. A visitor stepped out, signed the form, and left. "But she'll do her damnedest to make it feel like it's your fault. That's what you need to be ready for." She straightened her jacket. "Allison's good at mind games. Victor taught her well."

"I guess he did. He was a pro at it. It's probably where Margaret learned it, too."

"Something tells me Margaret taught Victor a few things."

Daniels bounced his knee, wondering how much longer they'd have to wait. He wondered how Rem had done with Mikey. He'd left before Rem had returned and Daniels hoped the two were on better terms after hashing it out. "You're probably right."

She smiled at him.

"What?" he asked.

"Did you ever think we would be sitting here like this, all those years ago when you and I were kids, riding our bikes around town?"

Daniels chuckled, recalling the past. Growing up, during the summers, Kate would visit her aunt and uncle who lived down the street from his parents. She and Daniels had become fast friends and they'd ride their bikes to the small-town square, where they'd buy sodas or candy, and then hang out in the park until it was time to go home. They'd done it every year until Daniels had turned sixteen and Kate's aunt and uncle had moved away. They'd stayed in touch for a while, but had gradually drifted apart, until one day, Daniels had bumped into her at the courthouse. They'd grabbed a coffee and had caught up on lost time. She'd gone to law school and had become a prosecuting attorney, and he'd told her about his journey to become a detective. "Are you kidding?" he asked her. "The only thing I thought about during those days was food, cars, girls and getting out of that town as soon as I was old enough."

"You never did like that place."

"No. I didn't. Much to my father's disappointment."

"I'm sorry to hear that. How are your parents?"

Daniels thought of his last phone call home. It had been over two months ago. "They're the same." He smirked.

"Apparently." She sat back against the seat. "What about Marjorie and J.P.?"

The previous night's fight flashed in his mind. "They're great. It's been a rough week, though, for all of us."

"Yeah. Murder cases will do that. Add to that this visit, the impending trial, and Margaret's escapades, and I wonder how you stay married."

Daniels raised his eyebrow and her face fell.

"Sorry." She raised a hand. "That wasn't an opinion or expectation. Just ignore me." She sighed. "To be honest, I'm jealous of you and Marjorie. You two seem very happy."

"We have our moments, but usually stressful times bring us together. This time around, though, well, it may be getting to us."

"This stuff we do, it can wear anyone down after a while." She stared off.

He frowned. "What about you and Allen? Weren't you expecting him to pop the question?"

She studied her fingernails. "He moved out last month." Looking up, she ran her fingers through her hair. "Apparently, he was auditing a lot more than tax returns."

Daniels dropped his jaw. "Oh, hell. I'm sorry, Kate."

She shrugged. "It's just as well. He snored and always burned the pancakes, so I think it worked out for the best."

"I'd love to give you the 'hang in there' speech, but it's so cliché."

"Thank you for sparing me. I've already heard it from my mother."

"It's his loss, though. I can tell you that much."

She smiled. "Thanks. That means something, coming from you."

"It means something no matter who says it."

Another person entered the waiting area and signed in at the desk.

She narrowed her eyes and tilted her head. "Did you really not know that I had a serious crush on you when we were kids?"

Daniels sat up. "Seriously?"

"Seriously. Remember that last summer, when we went to the baseball diamond and sat at the top of the bleachers?"

Daniels recalled them going to see a baseball game between a local and a visiting town's team. The local team had lost miserably, and Daniels and Kate had stayed after and hung out by the bleachers. "I remember."

"I recall it vividly. I wanted to tell you how I felt, and I imagined once I did, you'd kiss me. Right there on the bleachers. But I chickened out, and that was that."

"Really?" asked Daniels.

"Really," she answered.

Daniels laughed to himself. "You're not going to believe this, but I had a crush on you, too. But Johnny Weymuller told me you liked some guy back home, so I didn't act on it."

She widened her eyes. "Johnny Weymuller? That creepy kid who worked at the drug store? Why'd you believe him?"

Daniels scoffed. "He said you told him."

She stared off. "That asshole. He grabbed my rear end one day in the store, and I shoved him away. Told him if he did it again, I'd kick him in the balls." She sighed. "He just told you that so you'd stay away from me."

Daniels had always wondered why Kate had confided in Johnny. "I should have known. Johnny always was a troublemaker."

"Unbelievable." Kate rubbed a temple. She was quiet before she looked back. "Makes you think, though, doesn't it? About what if?"

Daniels scratched at the armrest, wondering that very thing. "I've always been a firm believer that things work out for the best."

"I suppose." She paused. "I guess we just weren't meant to be," she said, "which is a shame, because you're one of the good guys." She put a hand on his forearm.

He met her gaze. They didn't say anything and for a second, Daniels' face warmed, but then the door buzzed and opened. Daniels startled and turned when a man stepped out. "Allison Albright?"

"That's us." Kate grabbed her purse and stood.

Glad to be moving, Daniels joined her, and they walked through the door.

Oswald Fry stared at himself in the bathroom mirror. His eyes were bright, and his cheeks had color, but he could already feel the slight drag on his body. His muscles, although strong with use, felt heavy and the skin below his eyes was shadowed. He closed his eyes and took a full breath, held it for a second, and blew it slowly out. He wished he had fifteen minutes to meditate but he had to get back before he was missed. He thought again of his hands around Reynaldo's neck and relished the memory. The minute he'd shook the man's hand the day before his death, he'd known

Reynaldo's life force, while strong, was not that of Stella's. He was pleased he'd shortened the time to two days instead of three.

Thinking of Stella, he recalled her vibrant energy, which he'd attributed to her healthy lifestyle and habits. He'd felt her power the moment he'd stopped her in the park to ask for directions. Reynaldo, though, suffered from the common issues that came with running a business, the main one being stress. It had affected his energy levels, and Oswald had not borne it well.

Thinking of his current situation, he was thankful he had a wealth of resources to carry him over. It was easy for him to glean some extra energy from those around him. He'd become skilled enough that the mere presence of another person allowed him the ability to draw from them. In the past, it had required a touch, a brush against skin, or shaking a hand. And while that was still the most effective way, it was by no means the only way. Merely standing near someone was all he required. And his current situation provided a wealth of opportunity.

Taking another deep breath and blowing it out, he opened his eyes. He thought about his next victim and played out his plans in his head. Smiling, he reached into his pocket and pulled out a puzzle piece. It was similar to the one he'd left behind at Reynaldo's shop. He studied it, noting its blue color with dabs of white and again savored the opportunity to continue his game. He'd studied his victims, knew their habits, schedules, strengths, and weaknesses. Their connection to Victor had revealed many things, but not everything. And while his unfolding plans had a higher purpose, he reveled in the ability to draw his victim's life force from them and into him. It was the most satisfying and revelatory action he'd ever taken. He looked forward to his next transfer and all that would come with it. His next target had a magnetic energy and abilities that had attracted Victor, among others. He relished the thought of that energy joining his. There were other reasons why this death had been requested, but he cared little about those. All he sought was the thrilling feeling of one's dying breath becoming his fulfilling one.

He took a few more seconds to center himself, smoothed his hair with his fingers and smiled into the mirror, admiring his reflection. Then he stepped back, straightened his shirt, and left the bathroom.

Entering the hall, he saw a few students at their lockers, and others walked down the corridor toward their classrooms. Oswald went down to the end, turned left, and was about to enter his classroom.

"Oswald, hold up."

Turning, he smiled when he spotted his new friend, Marjorie Daniels, the high school counselor, approach. "Hi, Marjorie," he said. "I'm about to start class. You need something?" Marjorie was good friends with the woman he was substituting for. When the opportunity had arrived to take her place, Oswald had immediately applied for it. It was the perfect opportunity to get close to Mrs. Daniels.

Marjorie held out a clipboard to him. "I'll be quick. Can you just sign this incident report? I have to have it by the end of the day."

Oswald took the clipboard from her. "Is this necessary? Everything's fine now." He thought of Tommy, one of his students. Tommy had argued with him over a grade on a quiz Oswald had given the previous day. Oswald had explained the reason behind the grade, but Tommy continued to argue. He'd told Oswald that his previous teacher, Mrs. Garber, would have graded it differently. Oswald, never being the patient sort, had explained as much as he was going to, and when Tommy hadn't backed down, he'd reached across the desk and touched his hand. Tommy had immediately turned pale and pulled his hand back. His eyes had widened, and he'd stepped forward and shoved Oswald. The other kids in the class had gasped but Oswald had smiled. The surge of energy he'd felt when he'd touched the boy's hand filled him with tingles.

Reactions from people after Oswald made contact were varied. Most just stepped away and left him alone, but on occasion, he'd get the aggressive response. It was if they sensed what Oswald was doing and didn't like it. Tommy had been one of those people. Oswald had sent him to the office and resumed his class. When he'd seen Tommy later, Tommy had apologized. He'd returned to class the next day with no issues whatsoever, although he was far less animated. Oswald knew it was from the aftereffects of the interaction. Most people who were around him for very long found themselves lacking energy, suffering headaches, and feeling generally agitated and on edge.

Eyeing Marjorie Daniels, he could see his proximity to her was having its effects.

"Unfortunately, yes," she said. "Everything has to be documented. It will go in his file, but it won't have any long-term effects unless he does it again."

Oswald quickly signed the document. "Okay. Whatever you say." He handed the clipboard back to her. "You want to have lunch in the cafeteria today?"

She smiled, but rubbed her forehead, looking weary. "That would be great. Maybe this headache will ease up by then."

"I hope so." He gestured toward his classroom door. "I better get going. I'll see you at lunch."

Marjorie nodded. "Okay. See you." She turned and walked down the hall.

Oswald watched her, smiled, and entered his classroom.

Chapter Sixteen

THE GUARD LED KATE and Daniels down a long corridor where he stopped at a door and opened it. Inside was a table with four chairs and Measy was sitting in one of them. Kate leaned close and whispered. "Remember, calm and composed."

Daniels braced himself and walked in. Kate followed and they took the two chairs opposite Measy and sat.

"No visit through plexiglass and phones?" asked Daniels.

"We requested a room," said Kate. "Figured it would be easier for all of us to talk."

His dark eyes stoic, Measy stared at Daniels. He wore a silky gray pin-striped suit, and his thinning hair was slicked back. "Detective."

Daniels recalled the last time he'd seen Allison's sleazy attorney. Measy had confronted Daniels in the cafeteria of the station, telling him how Rem's testimony was full of holes and how Measy was eager for trial to expose his partner's lies. It had taken all the strength Daniels could summon not to punch the man in the face.

"Counselor," said Daniels. He hoped Allison would arrive soon so he wouldn't be forced to make small talk.

"Obviously, your partner isn't joining us," said Measy. "How is he?"

"That's none of your business," said Daniels.

"We're not here to discuss Detective Remalla," said Kate. "How about we skip the chatter until your client arrives."

Measy smirked. "Suit yourself."

Daniels hated that smirk and wondered why he'd been so worried about Allison when Measy made his skin crawl. He glared at the man and then looked away.

They sat in uncomfortable silence for about thirty seconds when a side door opened. Allison, wearing an orange jumpsuit tight around the middle from her growing belly, walked in with a guard. He undid her handcuffs and led her to the chair, then he walked out and shut the door.

His heart thudding, Daniels studied the woman who'd almost killed his partner. Her hair was still long and thick and trailed down her back. Her eyes were dark and piercing and she met his gaze. Exuding confidence, she leaned forward and put her elbows on the table. "How are you, Detective Daniels?"

Daniels didn't speak, but Kate did. "Allison, I assume your attorney has told you why we requested this meeting."

Allison glanced at Measy, who nodded at her. "He told me. I told those other detectives that I wanted to see Detective Remalla, too."

"Remalla couldn't make it." Daniels told himself to relax. "You'll just have to talk to me."

She smiled and her eyes twinkled in the light of the room. "I recall our last meeting, Detective. That was quite a day."

"We are not here to talk about that," said Kate. "We are here only to discuss the murders of Stella De la Rosa and Reynaldo Tovar." She paused. "We need to understand their connection to Victor and why they were targets."

Allison ticked up a brow. "Reynaldo? Is he dead?"

"You know him?" asked Daniels.

"Sure, I know him. You'd think he made suits of gold if you asked Victor. Victor wouldn't buy from anybody else." She sat back, her face flat. "I never understood the appeal."

"What about Stella?" asked Daniels. "What was her relationship to Victor?"

Allison shrugged. "I didn't really know her too well. At least, that's what I told those other two detectives, which was mostly true."

"Mostly true?" asked Daniels. "What does that mean?"

"It means I didn't want to talk to them. I wanted to talk to you and Rem. You two are much more interesting and it's boring in here."

"So, you know more?" asked Daniels.

Allison raised the side of her lip. "Stella was a masseuse. She gave Victor massages, and maybe more. I didn't ask and I didn't care. He did his thing...and I did mine." She grinned. "Ask your partner."

Daniels told himself not to take the bait. "Stella also did psychic readings. Did Victor get readings from her?"

"Probably, knowing Victor." She made an ugly smile. "Maybe she told him something he didn't like. Or what somebody else didn't like." Her eyes widened. "Maybe she predicted his death."

"Then she should have been given an award," said Daniels.

"Apparently," said Allison, "someone out there does not share your views."

"What does Margaret have to do with all of this?" Daniels crossed his arms. "Is she involved in these murders?"

"How should I know?" Allison pulled on her jumpsuit. "Margaret and I," she paused, "weren't exactly friends."

"How close was Margaret to Victor?" asked Daniels.

"Close enough. She and her sister both." She put her elbows on the armrests and touched her fingertips together. "Those women were two peas in a pod."

"Margaret's sister had left the cult before you arrived," he said.

She grinned. "Let's just say I've heard a few things."

Daniels chose to sidestep the subject of Mikey. "What about Gina Rodriguez? How well did you know her?" He took a long slow breath as his heart rate slowly returned to normal.

Allison scoffed. "Gina?" She snorted. "She'd left, too, but she visited a few times. Total pain in the ass. A drama queen. Wanted Victor's attention and got pissed when she didn't get it. Thank God she took off with some loser. Good riddance if you ask me."

Daniels figured that was a fair assessment of Gina. He considered his next question, but based on what he was hearing, Allison wouldn't be of much help. "Do you know of any reason why Margaret would want Stella or Reynaldo dead?"

Her body language shifted, and Daniels sensed she was agitated. "Margaret lives by her own rules. I think that's what Victor liked about her. She admired him, but never catered to him." She tipped her head. "Victor liked to pit women against each other because it amused him."

"So you don't know why Margaret, or anyone else, would target Stella or Reynaldo?" asked Daniels.

She chuckled softly. "Margaret's mood shifted with the time of day. Drama and pain made her laugh and quiet days made her angry. Maybe she was jealous, or Victor told her something about Stella or Reynaldo that pissed her off. Who knows?"

Daniels went quiet, wondering if he should continue his questions. Allison had said remarkably little about Rem or the baby and Daniels didn't want to push any buttons. He thought of the clues left behind. "Does a puzzle piece mean anything to you? It's blue with a bit of white, like a piece of sky."

Allison studied a nail. "I've never been much for puzzles."

"What about the infinity sign?"

She glanced at him. "What about it?"

"Any significance? To Margaret or anyone else?"

She studied the ceiling. "My math teacher in high school thought it was cool." She squinted. "Or was it the physics teacher?"

Daniels didn't push, figuring even if he did, she'd keep wasting his time.

"Anything else?" asked Measy.

Kate glanced at Daniels.

Thinking of one more thing, Daniels sat up. "Do you have any reason to fear for your own life, or your child's?"

Her expression clouded and she straightened her shoulders. "I have no illusions. Considering who I am and what I've done, I'll always be a potential target." She touched her stomach. "And so will my daughter."

Daniels hesitated to ask his next question but did anyway. "Did you ever have any discussion with Victor about getting pregnant in order to use child's blood in your ceremonies?"

Allison dropped her jaw. "What?" Her eyes darkened. "Who told you that?"

"Did you, or didn't you?" asked Daniels, holding her gaze.

Her body rigid, she interlaced her fingers. "You've just accomplished what few can. You've shocked me."

Daniels studied her for any dishonesty. "You haven't denied it."

She put a hand on the table and gripped the edge. "I may not be the motherly type, but I was just as shocked about this baby as your partner was. To think I would intentionally get pregnant to do something like that is insane. I would never allow my child to be harmed. If Victor considered, or even mentioned such an atrocity, then I'm glad he's dead."

Measy cleared his throat, and Allison shot a look at him.

"What about Margaret?" asked Daniels. "Would she consider something like that?"

Allison allowed a rare laugh. "Margaret wouldn't think twice about harming adults. She was particularly good at mental torture, as I believe you're well aware."

Recalling the cursed statue sent to him, Daniels shifted uncomfortably in his seat.

"But mess with children or animals, and you'd be her next target. Victor knew that, so he'd never have suggested it to her, unless he was pushing her buttons. The whole idea is ludicrous."

Relieved to hear that, Daniels nodded. "At least there's some sense of sanity left in you."

Kate cleared her throat, and Daniels shot her a look.

Allison rubbed her round stomach. "I'm quite comfortable with who I am and what I've done. I'm guilty of nothing. I intend to raise my child in a healthy and happy environment...with her father's help." She smiled. "I'm looking forward to co-parenting."

Daniels grit his teeth.

Allison appeared to relish his discomfort. "I think your partner will be, too, once he adjusts. Who knows?" she asked. "Maybe we can resume our relationship once he sees I'm not the bad guy."

Kate put a hand on Daniels' forearm and spoke. "We are not here to discuss Detective Remalla or anyone's future." She eyed Measy. "Please instruct your client to refrain from making unnecessary and inflammatory comments."

Measy raised a brow. "Please don't make inflammatory comments, Allison." He glanced toward Daniels. "You might upset the detective."

Daniels fought the urge to tell Allison exactly where she'd be in the future. He made a serious effort not to react. "I think we're done here."

Kate reached for her purse. "Then let's go."

Allison watched them. "You sure you don't want to ask me anything else?"

Daniels stood. "No. Enjoy your jail time because you're going to be behind bars for a long time."

Allison rested her hands on her stomach. "What about other followers?"

Daniels stopped. "What other followers?"

"You asked about Margaret, Victor, and Gina, but there were others."

Daniels thought of Dexter Fallon and Penny Bartolo. Was this Allison's way of accusing them?"

She waved a hand and rolled her eyes. "And this is not about your pathetic witnesses."

Daniels faced her. "There was someone else?"

Allison returned her elbows to the armrests and smiled. "Oh, most definitely. Margaret cultivated her own set of devotees, much to Victor's annoyance. They were all ultimately led by him, but Margaret brought them in and developed them in her own special way."

A cold twist of fear ran up Daniels' back. "Anybody in particular you'd like to mention?"

She reached up and twirled a piece of her hair through her fingers. "There was a man. Very unique. He had an odd attachment to Margaret and an almost obsessive devotion to Victor. He was extremely protective of them. It wouldn't surprise me if someone had slighted either Victor or Margaret, that this follower might...react in a negative way."

"You mean murder?" asked Daniels.

"If he's under Margaret's influence," she added, "there's no telling."

"Wouldn't that make you a target?" asked Daniels. "You killed Victor."

"Don't answer that," said Measy. He glared at Kate. "Please ask your pit bull to refrain from making inflammatory comments."

"I think he heard you," said Kate.

Allison smirked. "I'm not worried. My pregnancy protects me, in more ways than you know."

Daniels wondered what that meant. "Who is he? You know his name?"

She ran a hand down her thigh. "I do."

Hopeful, Daniels waited, but she didn't say anything. "Well?" he asked.

She grinned. "I'm not going to tell you, but I'll tell Detective Remalla."

Daniels did his best not to curse. "He's not coming here."

"Then I guess the name stays with me." She glanced at Measy. "You ready?"

Measy grabbed his briefcase. "I was ready fifteen minutes ago."

Daniels glanced at Kate, who shot him a warning look. "Somebody is going to die, Allison," he said. "Probably tomorrow. You could save them."

Allison tucked a strand of hair behind her ear. "Keep something in mind, Detective. This man is targeting people he feels betrayed Victor or Margaret, or both." She pointed toward Daniels. "You would fall under that category as much as anyone else." She slid her chair back and stood. "And it's not up to me to save you, your lovely wife, or anybody else." She paused. "It's up to your partner."

Measy went to the side door and knocked.

Thrown, Daniels felt the color drain from his face. "What does my wife have to do with this?"

The guard returned, took Allison by the elbow and led her to the door, where she turned back. "Tell Rem I look forward to seeing him soon."

Speechless, Daniels watched the guard lead Allison away.

Chapter Seventeen

M IKEY SAT ON M ASON'S couch, holding a tissue, and staring off into space, replaying her conversation with Rem in her head over and over again. She sniffed and dabbed at her nose.

Hearing keys in the lock, she cleared her throat and composed herself when Mason entered, saw her, and closed the door. "I have been waiting for you at SCOPE and wondering where you were. Why did you come here after leaving the police station?"

"I texted you," said Mikey, her voice rough. "I told you I was safe and not to worry."

Mason sat beside her on the couch. "We're supposed to tell each other where we are. I was scared something was wrong." He paused and studied her. "Are you okay?"

She fiddled with the tissue.

"Mikey?" he asked, putting his hand on her elbow. "What's wrong? Did you talk to Rem?"

She nodded and got mad at herself when fresh tears surfaced. She'd hoped after some time passed, she would pull it together, but she couldn't seem to do it. The last thing she'd wanted was her brother to worry about her and her stupid relationship issues.

"I'm fine." She cleared her throat again and dabbed at her eyes.

"You've been crying."

"Still am, although I'm trying not to."

"What happened?"

Mikey nibbled her lip. "Rem and I talked."

"Is this about Allison?"

"It's about a lot of things."

Mason shifted to face her. "What did he say?"

Mikey closed her eyes, wishing she could forget the conversation. "I, uh, asked about Allison and the baby." She opened her eyes. "She's saying it's Rem's child, and if it is, Rem intends to raise her. It's a girl."

Mason was silent for a moment. "That's a big step."

"It's messing with his head, which is why he disappeared to Merrimac when you went into rehab. I'll admit, it threw me, but I understand his decision. He's not the kind of guy to abandon his child."

"No, he isn't. Is that why you're upset?"

Mikey shook her head. "No."

"Then what is it?"

She sniffed again. "He...uhm...was going to tell me how he felt about me, despite Allison, when he returned from Merrimac, but that's when Margaret escaped, and he changed his mind. And then he met Kyle..."

Mason frowned. "Mikey, I'm trying to keep up here. What does Kyle have to do with this?"

Mikey shot a look at him. "That's what I said." She stammered to try and explain. "Rem's convinced himself that I'm not safe around him, but I am with Kyle. He knows Kyle likes me and will take care of me. I told him I hadn't pursued anything with Kyle, and he said I should. That no matter how much he might want me, he can't risk it. He's scared of losing me like he did Jennie. He blames himself for her death and he can't stomach the thought of hurting anyone again. I told him it wasn't his fault, and shouldn't I decide what's best for me? But he wouldn't listen and said he could never be with me, but that I still deserved happiness. Kyle could give that to me, but he couldn't. Then he...he left...and I don't..." Her lip trembled and more tears rose and fell from her eyes. "...I don't know what to do."

"Oh, Mikey." Mason put his arm around her and pulled her close.

She gulped in some air and wiped at her eyes.

"Listen," said Mason. "Rem is going through some things. He just needs time to sort it all out."

"He said with Margaret loose, he could never be with me. No matter how much time it took to find her, I shouldn't wait for him." She wiped her nose with the tissue.

"Just try to take some breaths." He rubbed her arm. "Think about all he's been through, and then what happened yesterday. He's reeling."

"Yesterday just made it worse. He's mad at himself because he let Margaret get away. It just solidified his belief that he's helpless to protect me and that I'm in danger around him."

Mason sighed. "I think you just need to give him some space. He'll come around."

"I'm not so sure."

"If he really cares for you, he's not going to want to see you with Kyle."

"That's not what he said. He told me to pursue Kyle."

Mason paused. "Well, if you think about it, he's helped you make a big decision."

Mikey sat up and reached for another tissue. "What decision?" She blew her nose.

Mason smiled softly. "Mikey, you've been going back and forth between Rem and Kyle for a while now. Every time anyone's asked you about what you've wanted, you've never been able to answer. Now you and Rem finally talk, and he tells you, point blank, to forget him and go to Kyle, which paves the way for you to pursue a relationship with Kyle, but you're sitting here in tears. I'd say you know what you want now."

Mikey hiccupped and tried to breathe evenly. "Great. So the man I want doesn't want me, and the man who does want me is about to get bad news." She pressed the tissue against her cheeks. "My life sucks."

Mason patted her knee. "Your life doesn't suck. You've just been given powerful information."

"How so?"

"You know now how Rem feels about you and you know Kyle's not the one. You can let Kyle down easy, but then you pull up your bootstraps and prepare."

She lowered her tissue. "Prepare for what?"

Mason reached for another tissue and gave it to Mikey. "For getting past Rem's defenses and convincing him that you are exactly what he needs. He's telling himself he's doing this to protect you, but he needs you just as much as you need him."

"I don't understand."

"In many ways, you've been where he is. Maybe not in the exact way, but you've both endured traumatic situations. It took you a long time to get back on your feet. If you recall, you were worried about me for a time, and that followers might retaliate against you for leaving the group. That never happened."

"But he's got a point about Margaret."

"He does, but whether you're with him or not doesn't make you any less of a target."

"Not in his mind."

"We could say the same thing about us. You and I staying together could be dangerous. I worry about you every day, but it doesn't stop me from working with you. We just have to make the best of a dangerous situation."

Mikey held her head. "How do I get him to understand that? Especially with what happened with Jennie?"

"It's called time. And that magnificent Mikey charm."

She lifted her head. "I have charm?"

"Loads of it. And when used properly, it can be quite disarming, especially around a man who's doing his damnedest to act like he doesn't care."

"But how do I do that?"

"Simple. You keep doing what you're doing. You're still his friend, right?"

Mikey nodded. "Yes. I guess."

"Then be there for him. Keep up the friendship. This is where you can help because you understand what he's going through. Tell him you're not pursuing Kyle, so he knows you're free. But continue your conversations as best you can. Don't pressure him but let him come to you when he's ready. Maybe that will happen before Margaret's caught, or maybe after, but if you're willing to wait him out, I suspect Detective Remalla will fall hard and fast."

Mikey crumpled a tissue in her hand. "You think that will work?"

"How much do you want to be with him? Have you thought that through? Because this won't happen overnight."

Mikey stared off, thinking, and her heart hammered against her chest. Fresh tears emerged. "I think I'm in love with him."

Mason nodded. "Well, then, he's worth the wait."

Mikey swiped at her falling tears. "He is."

"And one of these days, it's going to hit him between the eyes that he feels the same way, and regardless of Jennie or Margaret, he'll knock Daniels flat on his ass to get to you."

Mikey made a sad attempt at a chuckle. "You think?"

"You're good for him, Mikey, and eventually he'll see that." Mason grinned. "Besides, I know these things. You're not the only empathic person around here."

Mikey slumped, feeling a small measure of relief. "What if..."

"What if what?"

She picked at her tissue. "What if he doesn't love me?"

Mason was quiet. "This man told you to pursue another man to keep you safe. He could have easily said nothing, or not cared at all. He's mad because he can't protect you and he compared you to Jennie, the love of his life. I'd say, Mikey, that he's been in love with you for a while but doesn't know or can't admit it, and if Margaret hadn't screwed it up, you two would already be together."

Mikey set her jaw.

"Hang in there, Mikey. You've got him right where you want him." He took her hand. "Like Mom always said, everything happens for a reason."

Feeling encouraged, she squeezed Mason's fingers. "Those therapy sessions are working wonders for you."

"They should. I'm paying enough for them." He took her elbow. "Come here." He pulled her close and gave her a big hug.

Mikey buried her face in his shoulder. "Thanks, big brother. I appreciate your advice."

"What are big brothers for?"

Thinking of Rem, and hoping Mason was right, she wrapped her arms around his waist and hugged him back.

Anxious and angry, Daniels paced in Lozano's office. Allison's words were like a turning carousel in his mind.

"Sit down, Daniels. You're going to wear a hole in my floor," said Lozano.

"I don't want to sit." He gripped his temples.

"Where's Kate? Did she come back with you?"

"She had a phone call. She's in the hall."

Lozano loosened his tie and pulled it off. "Try not to overreact. Remember who you're dealing with."

Daniels stopped. "She mentioned my wife," he said tersely.

"Of course, she did. She's not stupid. Allison knows what strings to pull, and she pulled them. She wants Rem there and she's using you to do it."

Daniels ran a shaky hand through his hair. "I don't believe this."

"You knew this was risky going in. Rem said she'd have something up her sleeve and she did."

"Damn it." Daniels wondered what in the hell he was supposed to do.

A soft knock on the door made him turn as Kate popped her head into the office.

"Come in, Kate," said Lozano. "I'm trying to calm Daniels down."

Kate entered and closed the door. She dropped her purse in the chair. "Good luck. I tried and failed on the way back." She looked through the glass. "I didn't see Remalla."

"He's out with Mel working a few new leads," said Lozano. "Garcia's bad knee is flaring up, and Rem offered to go instead. He said he needed to get out of here for a while."

Kate nodded. "That's good. He shouldn't be here for this conversation."

Daniels picked up his pacing again. "He's going to ask about it."

"And what are you going to tell him?" asked Lozano.

Daniels ran his hands behind his neck and interlaced his fingers. "God. I don't know."

Kate crossed her arms. "You're not going to tell him anything."

"I can't do that," said Daniels. "He won't buy it."

"You can tell him what Allison said, and even mention this possible follower," said Lozano. "Just don't mention the deal she made. Keep that to yourself."

Daniels dropped his arms. "Allison suggested that I or my wife could be targets. What am I supposed to do about that? Nothing?"

"You tell Remalla and the first thing he'll do is head to the jail," said Kate. "It's what Allison is expecting. She's playing you. If Rem goes to see her, it not only risks him, but the entire case against Allison. I may not be able to protect him."

Daniels squeezed his head between his palms. "I'm screwed either way."

"Marjorie is not involved whatsoever with either Margaret or Victor. There's no reason for her to be a target," said Lozano.

"She's my wife," said Daniels, his voice raising. "That's reason enough."

Lozano raised his voice, too. "Has there been any indication that she's in danger? Has she seen anyone suspicious? Anyone watching her or the house? Anything strange at work?"

Daniels shook his head. "No. Not that I know of. But that doesn't mean there isn't a threat."

"Then tell her to stick close to home the next few days. Even better, maybe she can go stay with someone until we catch this guy." Lozano pointed. "Rem mentioned you needed to leave early today. That's a good idea. I want you to go and spend some time with your family. Ask Marjorie if anything odd or strange has happened and then talk about what you want to do next. If there are no red flags, then we hold off on telling Remalla anything."

"I don't like this," said Daniels. "Rem needs to know. I don't like lying to him." He blew out a deep breath.

Kate took a step toward Daniels. "Then tell him that Allison said she had a name but won't share it with anyone but Rem. He already told us he was expecting that. I'll reiterate that we aren't bargaining with her. For all we know, she'd tell him it's George Washington or Billy the Kid. That would be just like her. I think he'll understand and stay away."

"I agree," said Lozano. "Until we actually know that Allison's information has some merit, we don't respond."

Realizing that was true, some of Daniels' fears eased. Allison was likely bluffing and using Daniels' family to scare him enough to convince Rem to visit her. Daniels was on the verge of doing exactly that. He closed his eyes and told himself to relax. "Okay. I can do that." Tense, he put his hands on his hips and opened his eyes. "But if I get a hint that Marjorie could be in trouble..."

"Then we'll reevaluate," said Lozano. "But until then, for Rem's sake, keep Marjorie out of it." He sat back and rolled up the cuff of his sleeve. "If we need to, I'll put her in protective custody."

"You're not going to keep that from Rem," said Daniels. "And Marjorie wouldn't be too thrilled, either." He imagined what Marjorie would say once he told her about his visit with Allison. She'd been mad enough with him this week and this would be another stone to throw on a growing pile.

"I don't think it's going to be an issue," said Kate. "Allison is messing with us, and she knows where to point her arrows."

"I underestimated her," said Daniels. "I should have known better." His body ached and he was weary from worry.

"Go see your wife and kid," said Lozano. "I'll tell your partner when he gets back that I sent you home and I'll tell him what we agreed on regarding Allison. That way, you don't have to do it. If he finds out later, he can blame me. Not you." He leaned back and rocked in his seat.

Daniels felt the pang of an oncoming headache and stretched his neck. "Somehow I don't think he'll see it that way."

"He'll understand," said Lozano. "Once you tell him the reason behind it, if he even has to know at all."

Daniels knew Rem would be pissed if he discovered the truth but had to agree with Kate and Lozano. Rem would rush in and risk everything to protect Daniels and his family.

"You good for now?" asked Lozano.

Daniels' thoughts traveled back to his recent conversation with Marjorie about whether she or Rem came first. The situation was forcing him to reconsider his answer. Was he doing the right thing? Should he risk his partner's sanity and future for his wife's safety? Based on what he knew about Allison, he understood she couldn't be trusted. She'd played him and he was on the verge of letting her succeed. "I'm good for now." He paused. "But I reserve the right to change my mind."

"Just consider the repercussions of any decision you make," said Kate.

He smirked. "That's not going to be an issue, but thanks for the advice." He headed for the door and strode out of the office.

Chapter Eighteen

DANIELS SPOTTED MARJORIE'S CAR as he pulled into his driveway. Eyeing the time, he guessed she must have left work early as well. After leaving the station, he'd stopped by the grocery store and had picked up some food. His intention was to let his wife rest while he took care of dinner and J.P.

Still thinking about his meeting with Allison, he grabbed the grocery bags and headed up the walkway. He opened the door and not seeing Marjorie, he called her name.

She didn't answer, and Daniels was about to call again, assuming she was upstairs, when he heard J.P. laugh from the kitchen. "Dada," he heard his son say. He turned and stopped cold when he saw J.P. standing on the kitchen counter. A pot, with billows of steam rising from it, was on the burner. A distinct smell filled the air and Daniels dropped the bags and rushed to his son, who was perilously close to the burners and the boiling pot.

"J.P." he yelled. "Stop." He ran over and grabbed J.P. and held him close. His heart thudded when he realized how close his son had come to getting burned. A chair had been pulled up to the side of the counter and the cookie jar was close to falling off the edge. J.P. had apparently decided to help himself to some cookies and had figured out how to do it. He definitely took after his Uncle Rem.

Still holding J.P., Daniels turned off the burner, grabbed an oven mitt and moved the pot to the stove. A minuscule layer of water remained in the bottom and the pot had begun to burn. Daniels set it in the sink. He hugged J.P., wondering what would have happened if he'd come home late.

He moved the chair in the kitchen back to the table. "Marjorie?" he called. He was caught between anger and worry. Where was his wife? He immediately thought of Allison. Was the threat against Marjorie legitimate? "Marjorie?" he called again, walking back into the foyer.

J.P. smacked his shoulder. "Mommy seep."

"What?" asked Daniels. "Mommy's asleep? Upstairs?"

J.P. pointed toward the living room.

Daniels walked toward it and saw Marjorie lying on the couch.

J.P. squirmed. "'Pane."

Daniels set him down. "Go get your airplane. Daddy's going to wake Mommy."

J.P. ran off to find his toy, and Daniels squatted next to Marjorie. He shook her shoulder. "Marjorie?"

Her eyes twitched and she moaned, then sucked in a breath and opened her eyes. She squinted at him. "Gordon?" Blinking, she looked around. "What time is it?"

"Are you okay?" He studied his wife for any sign of illness or injury but didn't see anything wrong other than her fatigue. "You were sound asleep on the couch."

She started to sit up when her eyes widened. "Oh my God. The water." She sat straight. "J.P."

Daniels put a hand on her knee. "I got the water. The pot's slightly burned. And J.P.'s okay, although he was about to help himself to some cookies."

She wiped at her eyes. "Cookies? But they're on the counter."

"I know. He's got some skills." He chose not to tell her how close J.P. had come to getting injured. He knew how awful she'd feel.

Her jaw fell. "He got up on the counter?"

"He pulled the chair over."

She put a hand to her mouth. "He could have been hurt. And I was asleep."

Daniels pushed up and sat beside her. "He's okay."

"I can't believe it. I've never done that. And I've been plenty tired before."

"Did you leave work early? You're not usually home yet."

She nodded. "I did. I brought some work with me and left. I could barely keep my eyes open. I picked up J.P. and I was going to make him some soup, but I wanted to lie down for a few minutes."

"Do you feel all right? Are you sick?"

"No. I'm not sick. Just tired. And I had a headache earlier."

Daniels observed his wife. "Anything happen at school? Any reason you'd be this worn out? Any issues or problems?"

She looked over at him, her eyes puffy. "I'm a high school counselor. When don't I have problems?" She shook her head. "It's just one of those weeks. I slept okay last night, but I guess it wasn't enough."

He took her hand. "How about you go upstairs and lie down? I stopped and got groceries and I'll make dinner. I'll call you when it's ready."

She frowned at him. "What are you doing here? I didn't expect you until late."

"I left early, too. I figured you needed a break."

"What about your murder case?"

"Rem's staying late tonight, but to be honest, we're out of leads. We both figured I'd be more useful here."

She rested her head in her palm. "I'm not useless, you know? Don't let a killer go free because you think I'm falling apart."

Daniels told himself to be patient. "I didn't say that. You're not falling apart. But I know you've been worn out and figured you could use a break."

She snorted. "You're looking at me like you're worried."

Daniels debated what to say. "I'll admit. You haven't been yourself."

She pulled back. "I'm just tired. I'm allowed to be tired, aren't I?"

"Of course. That's why I'm here." He decided to table any more discussion for later. "Go upstairs and rest. I'll get J.P. fed and bathed, and then get dinner going."

"I really screwed up, didn't I?"

"You didn't screw up."

"I'm a terrible mother." She put her face in her hands.

"Don't be ridiculous. You're a great mother." He rubbed her back. "J.P.'s a lucky little boy and I'm a lucky husband."

She groaned. "You don't have to be so nice. I appreciate you coming home early but I know it's just to placate me. I suspect you'll be late tomorrow. Again."

Daniels wasn't sure how to respond. Everything seemed to irritate her. "I don't know what will happen tomorrow."

She huffed. "Well, I do."

Daniels' frustration rose. "Marjorie, what do you want me to say?"

Standing, she stared down at him. "I don't know." She stepped around him. "Just ignore me. I'm in a pissy mood. Thanks for coming home early. I'm going upstairs."

J.P. ran up to her and showed her his airplane and she caressed his cheek and gave him a kiss.

Daniels stood. "I'll let you know when dinner is ready."

"Fine." She didn't even glance back as she headed up the stairs.

Frustrated, he wondered if something else was going on that she was keeping to herself, but he couldn't imagine what it might be. Marjorie was either at school or their house, and other then her visit to Moira and picking up J.P. at daycare, she hadn't been anywhere else. Telling himself not to overthink it, he got busy. He put the groceries away, fed J.P. a snack and gave him a bath. Once J.P. was in clean pajamas, Daniels let his son play while he started a load of laundry and dinner. When it was ready, he set J.P. in his high-chair and cut him some chicken and gave him some rice mixed with asparagus. While J.P. ate, Daniels set the table, opened a bottle of white wine, and called Marjorie downstairs.

She came down a few minutes later, her hair damp and wearing a bathrobe. Stifling a yawn, she sat at the table. "This looks great. Thanks."

Daniels sat beside her and wiped J.P.'s face, which was already messy. "Eat up, hon. Then you can go back upstairs and rest if you want."

She cut her chicken. "I'm okay. I can clean up since you did the cooking."

"I appreciate it, but I want you to take it easy."

"You mean I better enjoy it because tomorrow, it's back to the usual?"

Daniels poured her some wine. "That's not what I meant, but unfortunately, that's probably true. Our killer may strike again, and if he does..."

She sighed. "Yeah. I know."

"Once we catch him though, we'll get back to our normal routine and my hours will improve."

Nodding, she ate a bite of chicken and took a sip of wine. "I'm sorry I've been so difficult. It's just...I don't know...been a difficult week. You've been gone. Moira's gone."

"You saw her yesterday, though." Daniels ate some asparagus.

"It's not the same. You know what it's like with a new baby. Moira's exhausted and breast feeding has been hard. You think I'm moody, you should see her."

"Poor Todd."

"At least he works from home."

Daniels shot her a sideways glance. "I'd drive you nuts if I worked from home."

"Why? I wouldn't be here. I'd be at school."

"And the minute you came home, I'd pester you to death. I'd want to get out of the house, and you'd want to stay in it. You'd pay me to leave you alone. Admit it. You like your solitude once in a while. Having me underfoot could be just as bad as having me work late."

"I guess there are trade-offs no matter what we do."

Happy to see his wife looking at ease and more of herself, he smiled and ate some chicken, then wiped the rice off of J.P.'s fingers. "Can you imagine going through this week if we had a newborn?" He snorted. "What a nightmare."

She stilled. "What does that mean?"

Daniels picked up his wine, realizing his mistake. He should have not brought up the subject of another child. "It doesn't mean anything other than it would have been rough."

"Are you trying to prove your point that we shouldn't have another baby?"

He sipped his wine and cursed inwardly.

"Because if you don't want more children, just tell me and stop beating around the bush."

He set his wine down. "What I want to do is enjoy dinner and do what we promised. Talk about it when J.P. turns two."

Marjorie wiped her hands on her napkin, and he could see the tension in her shoulders. "You're not going to give in, are you?"

Daniels set his fork down. "I never said no. All I said was I wanted to wait. What's wrong with that?"

"I just..." She set her napkin down. "...I don't know." She closed her eyes and shook her head. "You're right. I'm not myself."

Daniels put his silverware down and faced her. His worry bloomed. "Are you sure everything is okay at work? Is there something I should know?"

"Like what? You want me to tell you about my kids and their various issues, or their parents? I can if you want."

"No. Not that. I mean anything suspicious or out of the ordinary?"

She straightened. "Why? Are you worried about something?"

Daniels placed his napkin on the table. "I want to be sure you're okay." He considered another explanation. "Could you be sick? Should you see a doctor?"

"I'm not sick, Gordon. I'm tired." She narrowed her eyes. "What's this all about?"

Daniels dropped more pieces of cut chicken onto J.P.'s plate and J.P. happily grabbed one and stuffed it in his mouth. "It's this case," said Daniels. "It's just got me on edge."

"Why? Because of Margaret?"

The smug look on Allison's face flickered in Daniels' mind. "Yes. That's part of it." He paused. "I wanted to ask if you'd feel comfortable staying at your mom's for a few days." She widened her eyes, and he raised a hand. "Just until we get this case sorted out."

"I can't keep going to my mother's every time you have to catch a killer. Do you know how many times this is? I have a house to run, a child to raise and work to do."

"It might be a good thing. Your mom could help with J.P. while I'm not here."

Her eyes flared. "Is that what this is about? Is this your attempt to soothe your guilt of not being around by pawning me and J.P. off on my mother?"

"That's not what I meant at all."

She tossed her napkin down. "Yes, it is." She paused. "Is this because of what happened with J.P. when I fell asleep? Do you not trust me to be alone with our son?"

Daniels stifled a groan. "Of course not. I was only thinking it could be a temporary solution until you feel better." He offered J.P. his sippy cup. J.P. drank some water and it dribbled down his lip. "I could finish this case, you would have help, and then we can get back to our routine." He dabbed J.P.'s mouth and chin with his bib.

"I don't believe this." She crossed her arms.

"What's so hard to believe?" asked Daniels. "It's been tough for both of us the last few days. You're tired. Margaret's out there running around."

"Margaret's been out there for several months now. You didn't seem to care before. What's got you on edge, other than me?"

Daniels took a healthy gulp of his wine. He set the glass down and sighed. "I spoke to Allison Albright today."

Marjorie widened her eyes. "What? I thought you and Rem weren't supposed to talk to her."

"Rem didn't go for obvious reasons. But we needed to ask her questions about these murders. The killer is connected to Margaret and Victor, which makes Allison a possible lead."

"Did you go by yourself?"

"God, no. I went with Kate."

"Kate?"

"The prosecuting attorney. Kate Schultz."

She set her jaw. "Oh, her."

Daniels noticed Marjorie's change in tone. "Something wrong?"

Marjorie shifted in her seat. "I'm not a fan. I'm sure she's an excellent attorney, but she's a little too chummy with you."

Daniels dropped his jaw. "We were friends when we were kids. I told you that."

"Oh, she wants more than friendship. If you weren't married—"

Daniels scoffed. "That's silly. She is, or was, with Allen."

"Was?"

"They broke up last month. He cheated on her."

Her brow rose. "You sure it wasn't the other way around?"

He stared in surprise. "What does it matter? I don't care about Kate so she can do whatever she wants. Can we get back to Allison?"

She slumped in her seat. "Fine. What happened with Allison?"

Daniels gave her a quick recap of the meeting. "Then when she was about to leave, she suggested she might know who's responsible for these attacks, but she would only tell Rem."

Marjorie snorted. "God. She's a piece of work. You told her no, didn't you?"

Daniels picked at the edge of his napkin, his mind warring over whether he should tell her the rest. "I didn't say anything. I was too shocked."

"It's obvious what she's doing. She's bribing you. She pretends to have valuable information to get what she wants. Rem's not going, is he?"

"I haven't told him. Lozano was going to." He put an elbow on the table. "I just can't help but think, though, that if she does know something, it could prevent another murder."

"You think Rem should go?"

He straightened. "No, but..."

"But what?"

"Someone's in danger. Don't I have a responsibility to help them?"

"You have a responsibility to Rem, too, but I see your point. It's a difficult spot to be in."

"I guess that's why I'm jumpy. The whole thing makes me uncomfortable. That's when I had the thought that I'd feel better knowing you're safe when I'm not around."

"You can't put me in a safe and lock me up. You're always going to have bad guys to deal with. I can't go into hiding every time you get nervous. Besides, Allison's in jail and Margaret is more concerned with Victor and his frenemies. I think you're overreacting."

Daniels picked at his rice with his fork. "What would you do if someone else dies tomorrow? Would you change your mind?"

"No. I don't think so." She put her napkin back in her lap. "Rem seeing Allison would do a number on his mental state, which is shaky at best, but it could also jeopardize the State's case against her. Personally, I'd tell her to go..." she eyed J.P. "...well, you know."

Daniels' stomach churned and, wanting to tell her everything, he turned to face Marjorie. "Actually, there's—"

J.P. shrieked and smacked at his sippy cup. The lid flew off and the cup shot across the table, spraying Marjorie and Daniels with water. Marjorie stood and wiped at her robe and shook out her hands. "J.P."

Daniels stood, too, and wiped at the drips of water running down his legs. "I'll get it."

"Thankfully, it's just water." Marjorie picked up her napkin to dab at her clothes. "I'll get some paper towels." She walked to the counter and grabbed a roll of them.

Daniels attempted to clean the mess, but his doubts ate at him. He had to tell Marjorie the truth. "Listen, Marjorie—"

Her cell rang, and she groaned. "Hold on." She reached for it and sighed. "It's Moira's sub. I should take it. I told him to call me if he had any questions." She handed Daniels the roll of paper towels, answered the phone, and left the kitchen, leaving Daniels with a wet table, a messy son, and a guilty conscience.

Chapter Nineteen

SITTING AT HIS DESK, Rem studied the file in front of him and reviewed the evidence from Stella's and Reynaldo's murders. He'd been staring at the same page for several minutes. Frustrated, he blinked his eyes and closed the file.

"Nothing new?" asked Daniels, who was studying the evidence as well.

Rem shook his head. "Nothing."

Daniels leaned back in his seat. "Me, either."

After staying late the previous evening, Rem had gone home and tried to sleep, but he'd tossed and turned, replaying the conversation with Mikey in his mind. In addition, Lozano had informed him of what had happened at the meeting between Allison and Daniels. Conflicted, he'd been debating about what to do and how to handle it. Lozano had told him the decision had already been made. Rem would stay put, and if Allison had anything useful, she'd have to prove it. Rem hadn't said much, mainly because he wasn't sure what to say. He'd expected this, but now that it had happened, it bothered him.

Unable to sleep, he'd come in early to try and search for any new leads. This was day two since Reynaldo's death, and he was acutely aware that a new target was at risk. Because of that, Allison's offer flickered through his mind.

Daniels had arrived not long after Rem but had said little about Allison or his previous evening. Rem, caught up in his own thoughts, hadn't said much either. He'd buried himself in work in an attempt to distract himself. Now on his third cup of coffee, he needed a break. Turning in his chair, he saw the nearly empty coffee pot and decided to make some more. He stood and reached for the grounds.

Daniels spoke from behind him. "How late were you here yesterday?"

Rem grabbed a filter. "I left around nine."

"Lozano said you and Mel followed up on some new leads."

Rem nodded. "Garcia located a couple of followers willing to talk as long as they remained anonymous. Mel and I spoke to them, but they didn't have anything new to offer. Then we went back to the neighboring shops around Reynaldo's, hoping someone had a camera that caught something. No luck there, either." He wiped at his tired eyes. "We did get some interesting information, though. Garcia talked to Stella's sister. Apparently, Stella wore a silver bracelet that she rarely took off, but it wasn't on Stella's body."

Daniels sat forward. "Really?"

"That made me curious. I called Reynaldo's father and apparently, Reynaldo always wore a gold pinky ring. That wasn't on Reynaldo's body, either."

Daniels shoulders fell. "Our killer's taking trophies."

"Seems so." Rem reached for the coffeepot. "How did your evening go? Was Marjorie pleased you got home early?" He filled the pot with water from the dispenser.

"I think she was. It's hard to know."

"What does that mean?"

"She was sound asleep when I got home. J.P. was standing on the edge of the kitchen counter with a steaming pot beside him. He was going for the cookie jar."

"The kid's Spider-Man." The pot filled and Rem added the water to the machine, returned the pot and flipped it on.

"Yeah, well, Spider-Man almost got hurt. Marjorie slept through the whole thing."

"He's okay, isn't he?"

"He's fine. It just scared me. What if I hadn't come home?"

"But you did. What did Marjorie do?"

"I woke her up. She was mortified and blamed herself, then went upstairs to rest. I took care of J.P. and made dinner. Marjorie came down but she was still moody, and we bickered a little. We talked through it though, and I thought the evening would improve, but she got a work call and thirty minutes later, she went to bed. Said she was tired, and another headache was coming on." He sighed. "I have to admit, I'm a little worried."

Waiting while the coffee percolated, Rem leaned against the wall and crossed his arms. "You think she should see a doctor?"

"I mentioned that, but she said no. She's attributing it to her friend being unavailable, her workload, and me working late, which is understandable."

"So maybe give it a week. Let's see where we are with this case and how she's feeling. If it doesn't get better, maybe she'll reconsider the doctor."

Daniels picked at the seam in his jeans. "Yeah, maybe." He looked up at Rem. "Did Lozano talk to you yesterday? About what happened with Allison?"

Rem nodded. "He did."

"You're uncharacteristically quiet about it."

Rem pushed off the wall. "You've been a little quiet yourself this morning." He eyed the coffee machine.

Daniels picked up a bottled water from his desk. "I guess between Marjorie, Allison, and this case, I've been preoccupied."

Rem thought of Mikey. "Me, too."

Daniels cracked his water open. "What do you think about what Allison said?"

Rem picked up his new insulated coffee mug. "It's hard to know what to think. I'm not surprised, though. I expected something like this from

her. The question is, does she really know something or is she bluffing?"
He added sugar and creamer to his mug.

"That's the tricky part."

Waiting for the coffee to finish, Rem resumed his position on the wall.
"You think I should go? It could save somebody's life."

"Kate says we can't let Allison dictate our actions and she's right. For all
we know, Alison will give us a name of some random follower who knows
as much about the killer as we do. And you'll end up having to deal with
whatever crap she throws at you three months before you're supposed to
testify against her."

"I would go with Kate, like you did."

Daniels shook his head. "It wouldn't matter. You know Allison will plan
for that."

The thought of talking to Allison again made Rem break out in a sweat.
"I'll admit, I don't relish the thought." He leaned his head back against the
wall. "Dealing with her at the trial is going to be hard enough, but I'd do it
if I had to."

Daniels held his water bottle, but still hadn't drunk from it. He stared
off. "Let's just see what the next day or two brings."

Rem studied his partner, surprised at his response. Normally, he'd have
left no room for argument.

Daniels roused himself and eyed Rem. "There is some good news
though. I don't know if Lozano mentioned it, but I asked Allison about
what Dexter told Mel and Garcia about Victor wanting child's blood. She
looked as disgusted as you did."

Feeling a small measure of relief, Rem nodded. "Lozano told me. You
sure Allison was sincere?"

"As shocking as it sounds, yes. I think she was being honest. My gut tells
me Victor was either messing with Dexter, or Victor came to realize that
his idea would not be well accepted by his followers, and he dropped it."

Rem crossed his arms. "Let's hope so."

"I think that particular rumor has been laid to rest, so try and take that worry off your plate." He paused. "How was your talk with Mikey?"

Rem pulled out the partially filled coffee pot and filled his mug. He didn't want to talk about Mikey but knew Daniels would expect an answer. "It... didn't go well."

"Did you discuss Allison and the baby?"

Rem stirred his coffee, put the lid on his cup and sat at his desk. "We did. She handled it okay."

"You don't seem too thrilled. Is there something else? Is it about what happened with Margaret?"

Still seeing the tears swirling in Mikey's eyes, Rem reminded himself that his decision was for the best. "It came up. I...uh... mentioned why I went to Merrimac and how I'd planned to tell her how I felt about her when I got back."

Daniels widened his eyes. "Really? What did she say?"

Rem sighed at the memory. "It's not what she said; it's what I said. I told her that despite whatever feelings I have for her, it's better she be with Kyle. The two of them are good for each other and she'll be safe with him. She can't have that with me." His stomach clenched and he stared at his coffee.

Daniels was quiet. "What was her response?"

Rem's throat tightened. "She disagreed." Mikey's words echoed in his mind. While he hated the thought of her being with someone else, he couldn't stomach her getting hurt.

"Rem—"

"Before you lecture me, I know what I'm doing. This is for the best, for both of us. She'll understand. She and Kyle will be happy."

"Would you listen to yourself? You've already decided her future."

Rem shot a look at Daniels. "That's because I already know her future if she chooses me."

"No, you don't."

"Yes, I do. You know what I've been through. Don't tell me you wouldn't go to the ends of the earth to protect your loved ones." He gripped his coffee mug, thinking of what it would be like if things were different. "I can't be what she wants me to be."

Daniels dropped his head. "Hell."

Rem stared at the file in front of him. "Can we talk about something else?" He checked the time. "We could get the phone call that this guy struck again at any time. Let's just focus on trying to find something that might lead us to him, other than Allison." He opened the folder and tapped on his keyboard. His monitor flickered to life.

Daniels lifted his head but didn't say anything. Rem glanced at him and noted his partner's weary features. They obviously had a lot on their minds. "Since you're not arguing with me, I'm going to revel in my small victory." Rem sipped his coffee. "How about you go over Stella's crime scene again and I'll go over Reynaldo's? Maybe something will stand out."

Daniels held his water, pulled his chair closer to the desk and sighed. "Okay."

Questioning his partner's emotional state and his own, Rem stifled a yawn and got back to work.

Mikey sat at SCOPE and stared at her laptop screen, accomplishing little. Mason had been there earlier but had left after lunch to meet a potential client. Trick sat at his desk, and with her peripheral vision, Mikey had caught him several times peering over at her. She'd ignored it and had tried to focus, but her conversations with Rem and Mason the previous day kept interfering. She told herself to concentrate on the information in front of her. Trying to complete that month's billing, she blinked at the screen when she caught Trick looking at her again.

She kept her gaze forward. "Are you going to come out and ask me what's on your mind, or just keep staring at me?"

He chuckled. "Am I that obvious?"

"I think a monkey climbing the shelves would be less noticeable." Giving up on trying to finish anything, she closed her laptop. "I'm guessing Mason told you what happened?"

Trick grimaced. "Don't be mad. I knew something was up, and I asked him about it. He told me this morning."

Mikey nodded. "It's okay. It's not like you wouldn't have found out anyway."

"I figured something was wrong when you didn't return yesterday and went straight home."

"It was a rough afternoon."

Trick sat back in his seat and propped his ankle on the desk. "I wouldn't worry too much. Rem will come around."

"Mason said the same thing." She eyed the uneaten sandwich on her desk. She'd had little appetite since her discussion with Rem. "But I'm not so sure."

Trick watched her. "I've seen him with you. I know you two are friends, but it's more than that. I can tell the difference between friendship and attraction. He wants you, he's just not ready to act on it."

"Rem is stubborn. He could hold out for a while."

"Stubborn has no clout when it comes to love."

Mikey scoffed. "Maybe you should write for *Hallmark*."

"I've got more. They'd be lucky to have me."

Mikey glanced over at him. "I'm not sure Rem feels anything close to love."

Trick smiled softly. "He does. Trust me."

Mikey pushed away from the desk. "Well, I'm glad you and Mason are so confident." She stood and went to the couch, where she sat. "Mason told me to take it slow and just be a friend for now. I'm wondering if Rem even wants that much."

"Did he tell you he didn't?"

"No."

"There you go. He left the door open."

Mikey grabbed a throw pillow and held it in her lap. "Maybe Rem's right. Kyle is a good guy." She rested her head back. "Maybe I should give him a chance."

Trick stood with a sigh and joined her on the couch. "That's just what every guy hopes to hear. That he's nice and, since the man you want is unavailable, you're going to give him a shot." He rolled his eyes. "Let me speak for all men, including Kyle, that none of them want a woman to be with him because he's a safe bet. Kyle wants you to feel for him what you're feeling for Rem right now. Don't make Kyle jump through hoops just to prove Rem right or wrong. Be honest with him. Kyle deserves that, and he'll understand."

Mikey's emotions surfaced again. "I know. I wouldn't do that to him. My mind is just all over the place. I think I have my crap under control and then it all spins out again."

"Get used to it. That will be the norm for a while. My advice? Take time for yourself but stay in touch with Rem. He's probably spinning, too."

"I will, but I think I need a few days."

"Be careful it's not too long, or those days become weeks or months."

Mikey raised her head. "Knowing you and Mason, you won't let that happen. You'll be inviting Rem over for tacos in no time."

Trick smirked. "Believe me, Mason and I will be in the background, but we won't be casual onlookers. If we have to ask Rem to a few casual dinners or ask for his help on a case, we will. I'm sure Daniels will be doing his part, too."

"Which means you'll all be sticking your noses into this."

"You bet." He paused. "It's worth a few dinners to encourage Rem to see that what he's looking for is right in front of him. He's a smart man. It won't take long."

If Mikey had felt better, she might've argued, but she didn't have the energy. "Thanks. I'm sorry I'm such a downer."

"Don't worry about it." He patted her knee. "You've been in worse situations, and you've handled it. You'll do the same here."

Mikey thought back. "I guess that's true." She recalled some difficult times when she was with Victor. "I remember, back when I was still in the cult, I'd take long walks or go for a swim in the ocean. Mason had been trying to get through to me and Victor and Margaret were fighting to convince me otherwise. Although I knew in my heart that Mason was right, I still needed time."

"It kind of sounds like what Rem is going through."

Mikey fiddled with the frayed edges of the pillow. "Mason waited me out and I eventually caved. But it wasn't easy. It took a lot of reflection for me to finally take action." A memory flickered and she smiled. "I remember Gina and I would play board games to get our mind off things. At the time, she wanted out, too." Mikey paused as more memories surfaced. "We'd play cards and talk. Victor would see us and want to join in. He wasn't much for cards, though. When he wanted to settle his mind, he'd do..." A new memory surfaced, and she sat up, her heart thumping. "Oh, hell."

Trick stilled. "What is it?"

Mikey held her head as more memories swirled. "He liked puzzles. He had different types. Some easy and some hard." She gaped at Trick. "I'd get bored, but Gina enjoyed them. Victor's favorite was this huge one. It was like a thousand pieces and all sky with some clouds. He and Gina worked on it for weeks." She tossed the pillow aside. "That's what the puzzle piece is..." She sucked in a breath, "It's about Gina." Jumping up, she scanned the room for her phone. "I've got to call Rem."

Furrowing his brow, Trick stared as Mikey ran for her cell. "Good for you. Like I always say, there's no time like the present."

Chapter Twenty

DANIELS HUNG UP THE phone with a fatigued groan. He sat back and stretched his shoulders. Despite their review of the crime scenes, they hadn't discovered any new clues, and Daniels couldn't stop thinking about his problem. Although he kept telling himself that Allison was playing him, he couldn't help but worry he was making the wrong decision and endangering Marjorie. But asking Rem to talk to Allison seemed just as dangerous.

Weary, he yawned and jumped when Rem walked up from behind, holding drinks and a bag.

"Here you go," he said. "An apple juice and some trail mix, per your request." He set the juice down and dug in the bag and pulled out the small bag of trail mix.

Daniels took it and, not having much appetite, he tossed it in his top drawer. He reached for the juice and opened it. "Thanks."

Rem went to his desk. "I thought you were hungry. You didn't eat much for lunch." He set a cup of coffee down and pulled a chocolate muffin out of the bag.

"I'll eat it later."

Rem gave him a look and sipped his drink. "Did you talk to Reynaldo's brother?"

"I did. He's not happy about our lack of leads."

"Are you surprised?"

"No, I'm not. I tried to assure him that it's going to take time, but we'll catch the person who killed his brother." He paused. "I don't think it helped much, though."

"He's lost a loved one. He wants answers."

Not wanting to think about losing loved ones, Daniels took a drink of his juice and recapped it. "I told him I'd call him as soon as we knew anything."

"Let's hope that's sooner rather than later."

"Let's hope." Daniels eyed the time. "So far, we haven't heard about any deaths. Maybe that's good news."

"There's still time," said Rem. "Our killer struck Reynaldo in the afternoon." He glanced at the clock. "Probably right around now, as a matter of fact."

Daniels thought about Marjorie. Would she still be at work, or heading home? He debated calling her when Rem's phone rang.

Rem pulled it out of his pocket and his face fell.

"Who is it?"

He set the phone on his desk. "It's Mikey."

"Aren't you going to answer it?"

Rem stared as it rang again. "I don't know." He sighed. "Yesterday is still...fresh. I'm not sure what to say."

"It's hard to know what to say until you actually answer." Daniels watched his partner's internal debate flash across his face. "You don't pick up and it's only going to get harder the next time she calls." The phone rang again. "You're still friends, right?"

"Yes. At least I think so."

"Then answer the phone. Don't ignore her, or six months will go by before you talk to her again."

Rem flashed Daniels an annoyed glance. "Fine." He picked up the phone and answered. "Hello?"

Daniels watched as Rem listened and frowned. He sat up. "Wait. What? Slow down," said Rem. "What about Gina?"

Daniels straightened in his chair.

Rem's eyes widened. "The puzzle piece? It's about Gina?" He eyed Daniels, who stood.

Rem stood, too. "You're sure?"

Daniels ran to Lozano's office to give him the update.

"No," said Rem. "You stay put. Don't move. I'll call you as soon as I know something." He hung up as Daniels returned. "Mikey says the puzzle piece is about Gina. She and Victor worked on a puzzle of a sky for weeks." He grabbed his jacket. "Gina's the next victim."

Daniels grabbed his jacket, too. "I told Lozano. He'll pull Gina's info and call her and he's sending back-up. They'll probably get there before us."

They ran for the door. "Let's hope," said Rem.

Daniels pulled into the parking lot where two police cars sat outside Gina's apartment building. With blue and red lights swirling around them, Rem and Daniels jumped out of the car and ran up the stairs. Gina's door stood open, and Daniels ran up to it, seeing an officer just inside the door and another inside. "What happened?" he asked.

The officer pointed. "The door was partially ajar when we got here. We went in and found the place like this." He waved a hand and Daniels looked to see Gina's previously neat apartment was a mess. Overturned furniture, broken glass, and remnants of broken items from her bookshelf littered the floor.

"We checked the place and found her in her room. Pemberton and Overly are with her now. We're waiting for the ambulance."

"Ambulance?" asked Rem. "Is she alive?"

The officer nodded. "She was still breathing, yes, but barely."

Daniels headed toward the bedroom, and Rem followed as the distant sound of sirens grew louder. Turning the corner, he saw an officer giving Gina mouth to mouth while another officer squatted beside him.

Gina was clothed, but her shirt was ripped, and her neck bruised. An infinity sign was drawn in black marker on her forearm, although it was smeared and not as neat as the others.

The other officer squatting beside Gina looked up as Rem and Daniels entered. "We found her like this. She had a weak pulse but wasn't breathing. Pemberton started mouth-to-mouth."

Daniels eyed Gina's pale face and took her wrist. He felt the slight beat of her pulse against his fingers. "You're doing great, Pemberton. Ambulance is almost here."

Pemberton glanced up between breaths. He looked as pale as Gina. "I've never done this before."

"She's still alive," said Daniels. "You're doing it right. Can you keep going?"

Pemberton nodded. "Yes." He leaned and gave her another breath.

The officer from the front door popped his head in. "The ambulance is here. They're coming up the stairs."

"Show them in," said Rem. "Then secure the area. This guy probably left right before you got here. Call it in and start checking with neighbors, the manager, and nearby apartments. We need to talk to everyone and grab every possible video footage we can find. You got that?"

The officer nodded. "I got it."

"And don't touch anything in here," added Rem, "and whatever you did touch when you entered, we need to know."

"Okay." The officer disappeared around the corner just as Rem heard a commotion out front. Two paramedics with a stretcher entered the room. They took Pemberton's place and started to treat Gina. Within minutes, they were giving her oxygen, had her secured on a stretcher and were wheeling her out.

Daniels patted Pemberton on the back. "Go take a break. You need it." Pemberton appeared winded and flushed and his partner didn't look much better. "Go with him, Overly. Rem and I will search the apartment."

Both officers nodded and walked out. Rem and Daniels followed and entered the living room. "Damn it," said Rem. "We just missed him."

"She put up a fight, though. Maybe she got some DNA off of him." He eyed the strewn glass from a broken bowl. "He must have left in a hurry."

"You see the infinity sign on her arm?" asked Rem. "It looks like he scribbled it as an afterthought." He walked to the bookshelf, where most of the items had been knocked off.

"You think she knew him?" asked Daniels.

"Maybe." Rem squatted, seeing the board games he'd noticed from his first visit knocked from their space on a shelf. Two puzzle boxes had also fallen from their perch. "Ah, hell."

Daniels looked over. "What is it?"

Rem pointed. "You see that?"

Daniels moved closer.

"If I'd noticed she liked puzzles before..." He sighed.

"We didn't know about the puzzle piece at the time, and we weren't here to peruse her belongings," said Daniels. "Besides, those were beneath the board games. How were you supposed to see them?"

"I should have been more observant. Instead, I was annoyed with her, and didn't pay attention."

"Sorry, partner. If anyone should take the blame, it's me. I called her but never followed up about the puzzle piece after Reynaldo's death."

Rem looked over. "We both called. She never called us back." He stood. "But if I'd noticed the puzzles earlier..."

"And we could have returned and talked to her in person, but we didn't. We made assumptions we shouldn't have. But sitting here blaming ourselves isn't going to help. She's still alive, so we got here before he could finish the job."

"We've got Mikey to thank for that."

"Maybe Gina, too," said Daniels, looking around. "That's probably why this place is a mess. It looks like she used her PK on our killer."

Rem turned from the bookshelf. "Maybe we'll get lucky and she injured him."

"What about the note? Do you see one?"

Rem turned toward the kitchen. "I'll look in here."

Daniels eyed the rest of the room but didn't see a paper or photo.

"Nothing," said Rem.

"Let's check the bedroom." Daniels headed toward the back and entered Gina's room. Other than the unmade bed and trash discarded by the paramedics, the room appeared undisturbed, other than a messy desk with a laptop and piles of loose papers and notebooks.

Rem walked over to it and stopped. "Here." He pointed.

Daniels stopped beside him, seeing a ripped piece of spiral-bound paper with words written in black marker. He read it.

For Margaret. Two days. Beside it was a red plastic whistle. The letters were in a scrawl as if written hastily.

"Definitely in a hurry," said Daniels. "Looks like he ripped the paper out of one of the notebooks." Frustrated, he massaged his tight neck. "We almost had him."

Rem grabbed a tissue from a box on the desk to slide a paper aside. "There's the photo." They looked closer. It was a picture of Gina and Victor sitting at a table in a restaurant. He had his arm around her, and they were smiling.

"I don't see an envelope," said Daniels. "Did he mail the picture or bring it with him?"

"Maybe when Crime Scene gets here, they'll find something." Rem crumpled the tissue. "Why Gina?" he asked. "It can't be because she shared a puzzle with Victor."

Daniels studied the laptop. He touched the mouse with a nail and the screen saver faded and a password request appeared. Below it were the words *Incorrect password. Please try again.* "Looks like someone was curious."

"Was he trying to access it?" asked Rem.

Daniels grabbed another tissue and opened one of the spiral notebooks on the desk. Seeing the notes written inside, he began to read. Getting through the first few sentences, he narrowed his eyes and kept reading. "Hell. Is she...?"

"What?" asked Rem.

Surprised at what he was seeing, Daniels looked up. "This is about her time with Victor." He flipped through more pages and scanned the notes. He saw chapter headings and names, including Allison's, Margaret's, and Mikey's.

Rem used his tissue to open another notebook, his eyes widening as he read.

Daniels closed his book and eyed Rem, who appeared just as surprised. "Looks like Gina is writing her memoirs." Daniels paused. "I'd wager a guess she almost died because of it."

Chapter Twenty-One

OSWALD FRY ENTERED HIS bathroom and stared at himself, replaying his altercation with Gina Rodriguez in his mind.

It had not gone as he'd planned. After leaving work, he'd stopped at a gas station restroom to change. While Stella and Reynaldo had minimal security to worry about, Gina's apartment complex had a camera system he would not be able to avoid.

He'd removed his work clothes and thrown on some baggy sweats and a hoodie to disguise his build and had added some sunglasses, a wig, and a fake nose. Since he had to consider that Gina might be suspicious now that the detectives had spoken with her, and that a camera would catch him approaching her apartment, he had to take precautions.

He'd studied the area well enough to know that if he parked and walked, he'd bypass the parking lot cameras, and no one would see his car. Her neighbors would be at work until after five p.m. so the timing would be perfect. No one would see him until he approached her apartment.

After leaving his car on a side road off a busy commercial street, he'd put on his glasses and had walked down the path he'd already designated as the safest. It took him down back alleys and behind shops where he wouldn't be noticed by passersby or picked up on camera, and when he needed to, he'd returned to the street where he'd blended in with bystanders. After crossing a busy intersection, he'd pulled his hoodie up and casually strode to her front door. Listening, he'd heard nothing from inside and had rested his hand on her doorknob. Although it was not his strength, with enough concentration, he could access locks and open them. It required him to use some of his prized energy, but it wasn't enough to drain him. Once he was past the lock, alarm systems were easy. He merely had to hold his hand over the panel, sense the feel of each button, and he would intuitively know the code. It was a skill he'd honed over the years. At first, he couldn't do it fast enough, and the alarm would sound. But now, it took him mere seconds to silence it. Then he could walk through a home at his leisure.

Sometimes, when he was bored, he'd do it just for fun. He'd wait for someone to leave their home, and then he'd enter their house and look around, just to see how they lived. It was an insightful exercise, and he'd learned a lot about people and their secrets. Most of them weren't good.

The benefit of breaking into a house while someone was home was that few people set their alarms while they were inside, so Oswald could walk right in. Some people did have an alert when a door opened but many didn't, and Gina was one of the latter. He'd surprised Stella that way and Gina would be next.

Knowing of Gina's PK abilities, though, he'd had to be cautious. If she managed to throw or shove him, she could escape, so the element of surprise was key.

It hadn't taken Oswald long to unlock Gina's door, widen it and slip inside. It had been the riskiest moment. If Gina had seen him enter, she would have run, so he didn't delay. Once inside, he was relieved when he didn't see her, but he heard what sounded like a sink running. It turned off and Oswald stood to the side of the wall outside the hallway and waited. A few seconds later, Gina had walked past him, and he'd grabbed her from behind. She'd shrieked, but he'd immediately closed his arm around her throat and squeezed. She'd flailed and pulled on his forearm, struggling to free herself and he'd squeezed harder, feeling the thrill of her animated spirit and his excitement that it would soon join his. His heart racing, he couldn't wait to breathe in her last breath.

But then her belongings around the apartment began to fly off their shelves, hit the walls, and crash to the floor. He'd pulled her back to avoid the flying objects, but one had hit him in the head, and he'd loosened his hold.

Gina had sensed the opportunity, and he'd felt a strange pull on his stomach, and then he was flung against her bookshelf. Everything on it toppled and he heard another crash when something else fell. She ran into the bedroom, but he caught up with her and knocked her to the ground, where he'd sat on top of her and wrapped his fingers around her neck. Her strength waning, he'd waited for her to weaken further, eager to absorb her remaining life force when he'd heard the distant sound of a siren.

Gina had gone limp and, disappointed he couldn't remain during her last moments, he stood. Pulling the pen and whistle from his pocket, he walked to her desk which held the notebooks he'd read through on his first visit. He ripped a piece of blank paper from one of them, wrote his message and left the paper and the whistle on her desk. Then he took the photo from his pocket and left it, too. He hadn't mailed it because he didn't want to warn Gina that she would be next. Seeing her laptop, he'd punched a key. The familiar password request had appeared. He'd tried to access her computer on his initial visit but had failed. Feeling a little daring, he tried another password, just to see if he was correct, but got the same message. Out of time and with the sirens growing louder, he'd stepped over Gina, drawn the symbol on her skin, and returned the pen to his pocket.

Satisfied, but angry he had to hurry, he left the bedroom and picked up a fallen arrowhead from her floor. He slipped it into his pocket and went out her back door to her small patio. He left out a side gate, crossed an alley and returned to the same sidewalk he'd just left as a police car raced into the lot. Two policemen emerged just as another patrol car joined them.

Ignoring the activity, Oswald had returned to his car and driven home.

Still staring at himself, he looked for any signs of injury, but didn't see any. Whatever had hit him in the head had likely left a bruise, but after removing his wig, he saw his hair covered it and it wouldn't be a concern. He took off his sweats and fake nose and tossed them in a plastic bag along with the wig. After dropping the bag at his feet, he noted his trembling fingers. He clenched and opened them. Focusing on drawing in the energy he'd received from Gina, he removed the rest of his clothes, turned on his shower and stepped into it.

Letting the warm water cascade down his skin, he was grateful he'd allowed only two days before his next victim. His original plan had been three, but since he hadn't benefited from Gina's death as he'd expected, he'd need to strike again soon.

After shampooing and cleaning his body, he felt better. He stepped from the shower, dried off and got dressed. Thinking again of Gina and his hands around her throat, he smiled and picked up the bag. He dug through it and pulled out the arrowhead. Studying it, he took a deep breath and recalled the thrill of feeling Gina succumb. Wishing again he'd had more time, he slid a drawer open beside his bed, placed the arrowhead beside the silver bracelet and the gold ring, and closed the drawer. Holding his bag of discarded items, he left his bedroom to toss it into the trash.

"We've got one day," said Daniels, leaning back in his seat, "and almost nothing to go on." Frustrated, he tossed his pen onto his desk.

Rem looked up from studying one of Gina's notebooks. "That's not entirely true. We got a video this time." He closed the notebook.

Daniels snorted. "Of a man in an oversized hoodie, sunglasses and a lot of hair."

Rem picked up his coffee. "They didn't have much else on the Unabomber except a sketch, but they still caught him." He took a sip.

Daniels stared at his partner. "It took seventeen years to catch the Unabomber."

Rem stared back, his face weary. "They still caught him."

Daniels didn't bother to argue. "If you're trying to be positive, you're failing."

"Sorry." He made a face at his drink and set his cup down. "I'm out of practice."

Daniels scooted his chair up to his desk, wondering what to do next. Other than the video from the apartment complex, nobody had seen anything. Gina was in ICU and the doctors couldn't be sure if she'd ever wake up. Nobody knew what the whistle meant, and although they had found fibers from a wig and a similar sweatshirt from Stella's crime scene, there were no fingerprints or DNA left behind despite Gina's resistance. They'd read through Gina's notebooks and had learned plenty about Gina's escapades as a member of Victor's cult, and how much she'd resented anyone who'd drawn Victor's attention away from her, but they'd provided no clues as to who'd attacked her, or anyone else.

They'd spent the previous evening reviewing everything they knew. Everyone was on high alert to move fast since they had such a short period of time before their killer would strike again. Daniels had gotten home late, but Marjorie had already been in bed asleep. J.P., too. He'd kissed J.P., and had checked on his wife, but she hadn't stirred when he'd pulled her covers up. He didn't know if she was faking her sleep or not, but he'd figured it would at least mean she wouldn't argue with him for coming home late. Exhausted, he'd showered and gone to bed, and he'd left early the next morning. Marjorie had been cordial, but quiet. Daniels had taken J.P. to daycare and returned to work. Marjorie had still not been her usual self, but there had been no indication of any danger to her either at work or at home, so his decision to not tell her or Rem about Allison's threat seemed sound, although it still weighed on him. He debated talking to Marjorie again about going to stay with her mom until this case ended.

Rem blew out a loud sigh. "That whistle means something. What are we missing?" He typed on his keyboard. "I've even Googled the word. I know its definition, how to make one and where it appears in the Bible, but even Google can't figure out who our next victim is."

"You should file a complaint."

"If I thought it would help, I would." Rem pushed away from his desk and swiveled in his chair. "You think the color matters? Is it a kid's whistle?"

"It's plastic, so it's possible." Daniels thought of J.P., but neither he nor Marjorie were dumb enough to give their kid a whistle. "Anyone you can think of who has a history with Victor and has a child who might play with a whistle?"

"None." Rem stifled a yawn. "I asked Mikey, but she doesn't know either."

"Well, at least you're talking to her."

Rem glanced at him. "I told her we could still be friends."

"That was nice of you."

Rem smirked at him. "How's Marj doing? Any better?"

"She was asleep when I got home, so no chance for an argument. Tonight could be different, though. We'll find out soon enough."

Rem stood and stretched his arms out to his sides. "Rate we're going, we might as well both go home early."

Daniels rubbed his face, trying to wake himself up. "Tell me about it."

Rem raised his arms over his head and leaned sideways. "We've talked to Penny and Dexter. No luck there. And we talked to Ronald, Gina's brother. No luck there, either."

"The man's distraught. He's on the verge of losing another sister."

Rem leaned to the other side. "Yeah. I know."

"My question is where did he go?"

"Who?" asked Rem. "Ronald?" He stretched up to the ceiling and did a few jumping jacks.

"No, Richard Simmons," Daniels rolled his eyes. "Our killer. He walked away from Gina's apartment and disappeared. Did he walk home? Take a bus? Get in a car?"

Rem stopped jumping. "If I don't move, I'm going to fall asleep." He did some high knee raises. "Mel and Garcia checked bus routes and ride shares. Nothing. He must have gotten in his own car. He probably parked on the street somewhere."

Daniels pointed. "What about checking cameras along the roads leading to the complex? There are shops, restaurants, and apartments around. Maybe their cameras caught this guy walking down the street."

"They canvassed the area. Nobody mentioned seeing anything." Rem twisted from side to side.

"They canvassed the surrounding area, but they didn't go beyond that. I say we go talk to anyone we can find who has a camera along an entry point and look at the footage."

Rem stopped his exercises. "Do you know how many places we'd have to check? We don't even know what direction he went in."

Daniels stood. "You got any better ideas?" He grabbed his jacket. "If nothing else, it will keep you moving."

Rem put his hands on his hips and hesitated. "I guess it's better than nothing." He walked to his chair and picked up his jacket. "Can we stop for a coffee?"

Daniels shook his head. "Does a certain partner drive another partner nuts?"

Rem half-smiled. "You don't bug me that much." He followed Daniels out of the squad room.

Twenty-four hours later, they still had nothing. Rem followed Daniels back into the station after a long day of stopping at businesses they'd missed the previous day and asking to check their video footage, with no luck.

Rem fell into his seat. "If I see one more grainy video of cars driving down the street and pedestrians looking bored, I'm going to scream."

Daniels dropped into his own seat. "I almost did scream at that last place. I can't believe that owner wanted us to buy something before letting us look at his footage."

"I think the snarl you made when he showed you that pink tie finally convinced him to help."

"I glared and bared my teeth, too."

Rem smiled. "It sure as hell scared me."

Daniels put his head in his hands. "A lot of good it did us, though." He looked up. "How did this guy avoid all the cameras?"

Rem rested his head back on his chair. "He either blended in and we didn't see him, or he changed before he returned to his car. And a lot of those places had cameras that only captured their front entrance and not the road. There's no way to know." He blinked his tired eyes. "At least we tried." Rem checked the clock. "It's already after five." He sighed, sat up, and put his elbows on his desk. "I hate to say it, but whoever the next target is may already be dead."

Daniels looked at the clock on the wall. "I know." He fell back in his chair. "Shit."

Rem swallowed, gathering his thoughts. "There's one other thing we can do."

Daniels raised his brow, but then frowned. "No way."

"If she knows—"

"Allison doesn't know anything. Don't go there."

Anxious, Rem scratched his head. "Fine."

"I know it's tempting, but we have to play it by the book."

"I hate this." Rem bounced his knee. "Someone's out there, maybe dead or dying right now, and we can't do a damn thing."

Daniels nodded. "I know."

They sat quietly for a moment. Daniels fiddled with some papers on his desk and Rem checked his email, then eyed his partner. "Why don't you go home? It's stupid to stay here and wait for bad news."

"Why? So I can wait for bad news in my living room?"

"No. Because the last two nights you've barely spoken to your wife or seen J.P."

Daniels hesitated. "Yeah. You're probably right." He squeezed his temples.

"I know I am. Go home. I'll call you if anything happens. I'll let Lozano know what's up."

Daniels raised his head. "You're sure? Maybe we should keep it quiet. He's as much on edge as we are."

Rem shrugged. "He won't know anyway. I have it on good authority he's got another commitment tonight. His stepdaughter has a piano recital, and Cap promised his wife he'd go."

"You sure he won't break that promise?"

Rem narrowed his eyes. "You've heard about Sheila and her temper. I doubt he'll back out. He'll leave soon and you'll be fine." He looked around the squad room. "Unless someone around here tells him, but I'll put the word out. Someone squeals, they'll deal with me."

Daniels eyed the other detectives in the room. "I'm not worried about it. We don't have whistleblowers around—" He stilled.

Rem heard what he said and froze. His mind raced and he tensed. "Whistleblowers?"

Daniels dropped his jaw. "You don't think..."

Rem tried to do just that. "...that our whistle refers to a whistleblower?" He stared off. "Who knows Victor and is a whistlebl—" An answer hit him, and he stood at the same time as Daniels. "Oh, shit."

His face taut, Daniels pointed. "Penny Bartolo or Dexter Fallon." He paused. "One of them is the next victim."

Rem grabbed the phone, and Daniels darted away from his desk to tell Lozano.

Chapter Twenty-Two

REM PULLED UP IN front of Dexter Fallon's home and squealed to a stop. On their way to Dexter's, Lozano had contacted them, saying they'd reached Penny and she was at her mother's, but that a patrol would check her home anyway. Dexter had still not been reached.

He and Daniels jumped out the car, their guns drawn, and raced to the door. Rem ran up to one side and Daniels ran up to the other. A siren blared and a police car pulled up. Two officers jumped out, ran across the yard, and Daniels directed them to go around the back.

Rem had pounded on the door and called for Dexter, but there was no answer. Daniels identified themselves as police and had tried the knob. It turned, and Daniels opened the door.

Rem went first and swiveled, aiming his gun into the front room. It was quiet. "Dexter Fallon?" he yelled. "Police. Are you in here?"

Daniels came in behind him. They walked slowly into the house. "He's got a roommate, doesn't he?" asked Rem.

"I think so," said Daniels. "Don't know the name, though." He stepped into the living area. "Anybody here?" he yelled.

Rem turned to the right and peered around a door. "The kitchen's clear." He joined Daniels again and they headed toward a hallway. Rem spotted one of the officers on the back porch through a window. The officer saw him and opened a sliding door.

"Nothing out back," said the officer. "There's a car in the garage, though."

Rem nodded. "Is there an alley?"

"Yeah."

"Go check it," said Rem. "And be careful."

The officer closed the back door and joined his partner on the steps. They ran through the backyard toward a fence.

"Dexter?" called Daniels, stepping into the hall.

Rem aimed his weapon forward and swiveled into a doorway. It was a small room with a made bed. He quickly ran in and opened the closet. "It's clear," he said, rejoining Daniels.

Daniels checked a small bathroom off the hall. "Clear here, too."

They continued their careful approach until they neared the main bedroom. Daniels nodded at Rem and Rem swiveled right while Daniels went left.

Rem saw a window and a treadmill and Daniels cursed. Rem turned to see Dexter Fallon lying on his back on the carpet, his arms and legs straight, staring blankly at the ceiling. He wore a t-shirt and blue-jean shorts, and purple splotches marred his neck.

Daniels ran over and squatted next to Dexter, and Rem checked the main bathroom and closet. They were empty, but beside the sink was a piece of paper. A photo was tucked into the side of the mirror. Rem walked over and eyed both. The photo was a picture of several people on and behind a couch. Victor sat in the middle of the couch and right behind him was Dexter. The paper had the familiar words written on it in black marker. *Two more days. For Margaret.* Beside it was a necklace with a small bluebird pendant.

Fighting the urge to pick up the paper and crumple it, Rem returned to the bedroom, where Daniels took his fingers from Dexter's neck.

Rem holstered his weapon and watched as Daniels' shoulders slumped. "We're too late." Daniels dropped his hand and looked up at Rem. "Dexter's dead."

Disheartened, Rem sat on the front steps outside Dexter Fallon's house as an officer rolled crime scene tape around the property. The Coroner and Forensic teams had arrived, and they were inside with Daniels. Neighbors had gathered on the corner to watch the activity, and Rem groaned when a news van pulled up.

They'd learned after calling in Fallon's murder that Fallon's roommate had been at work and had spoken with Dexter earlier in the day. Dexter had been fine and there had been no indication of any threat. Officers had since been dispatched to do a canvas of the area, but Rem had no illusions they would learn anything of value.

He thought of the necklace with the bird pendant and wondered who was next. They had two days to find out. Without more evidence to go on, though, the likelihood of finding the killer was still slim to none.

He thought again of Allison. The pressure to see her was mounting, but he understood the danger. She could be bluffing just to get him to see her. The question was, at what point was it worth the risk?

"Penny for your thoughts?"

Rem looked up to see Daniels standing beside him. He scooted to the side of the step and Daniels sat. "Learn anything new?" asked Rem.

Daniels set his elbows on his knees. "Let's see. Dexter was strangled. Been dead around two hours. No sign of forced entry. You saw the note and photo, plus the necklace. They'll do the usual and check for fingerprints and DNA."

"So, no. Nothing new."

"I'm afraid not."

"Other than we've lost a witness for Allison's trial." Rem's stomach fell. "Kate will be thrilled."

Daniels studied the group of neighbors on the street. "It's worse than that."

Rem frowned at him. "What could be worse than this whole mess?"

Daniels sighed. "I talked to Lozano to give him an update. He told me he talked to Penny Bartolo and she's freaking out. She may not testify after what happened to Dexter."

Rem dropped his head. "This just keeps getting better and better."

"I suspect that was the killer's plan. Kill one witness to scare the other off."

"Maybe." Rem looked up. "We should still protect Penny. Any chance that necklace has anything to do with her?"

"Lozano is going to ask about it once she calms down a little. We have a couple of days so..."

"A whole forty-eight hours," said Rem. He glanced at his watch. "Make that forty-six."

Daniels interlaced his fingers and was quiet. "Where do you want to start?"

Rem blinked his weary eyes, thinking of the trial and Allison, and wondering if the State's odds of convicting her were rapidly dwindling. "I think we have to reconsider Allison's offer."

"Rem—"

"Hear me out." Rem shifted to face him. "Dexter's dead and Penny is scared. This looks like an orchestrated attack against them. That could mean Allison's involved, or at the very least, knows who this is."

"You don't know that."

"The only way to know is to go talk to her."

Daniels raised a hand. "Have you considered that she could be part of whatever this is? First knock out the two witnesses, then get you to talk to her, and effectively knock you out, too? Then the next thing is she walks free." He shook his head. "We don't know what any of this means. Allison had no reason to hurt Stella or Reynaldo. Granted, she didn't care for Gina, but my gut tells me she doesn't know what's happening here anymore than we do. She just got lucky that Dexter was targeted."

Annoyed, Rem gripped the edge of the stair. "We have to do something. We can't just keep twiddling our thumbs, waiting for this guy to screw up." He nodded toward the press van. A reporter stood at the curb while her cameraman aimed a video camera at her. "Now the press has the scent. This whole thing is going to blow up in our faces if we don't make some progress soon." He ran a hand over his head. "I'm not that fragile, am I? Is my mental state so weak that I can't handle Allison?"

Daniels set his jaw. "You're the strongest person I know, but it doesn't change the fact that this woman tortured and almost murdered you. The first time you visited her, you took off and disappeared, and you had to hide your gun in your trunk to prevent yourself from doing something stupid." He paused and Rem studied his sneakers. "Why don't we give it a day? Then decide," said Daniels. "If we don't have anything by this time tomorrow, we'll talk to Kate and Lozano, and go from there."

Rem debated arguing, but deep in his gut, he knew Daniels was right. Although Rem felt stronger, he didn't have any doubts about Allison's motives. She would use any means at her disposal to prevent going to prison, including using their child, to do it. He watched the reporter speak into her microphone while her cameraman filmed. "Okay. We'll wait." He glanced at Daniels. "For now."

Chapter Twenty-Three

DANIELS ENTERED HIS HOUSE and closed the door behind him. Eyeing the time, he saw it was after nine o'clock. He'd hoped to be home sooner, but after Dexter's murder and the short time period before the next assault, they'd needed every set of eyeballs and hands on deck to try and find anything that might lead to the killer. They'd reread Gina's notebooks, reviewed all their notes, and sent more officers to reinterview business owners and neighbors and review video footage again in case anything had been missed. It had been exhausting and the next day didn't look much better.

Thinking of Marjorie and J.P., he took the stairs two at a time to the second floor. He entered J.P.'s room and saw him sleeping, his soft breathing making Daniels smile, but feel sad at the same time. He hated missing dinner, bath, and bedtime. Leaning over, he smoothed his son's hair and then kissed his forehead. He stared at him for a second before quietly leaving the room and closing the door.

He entered his own room, seeing Marjorie in bed. She was awake, although her lids were heavy. Seeing him, she pushed up to her elbows. "Hey," she whispered.

"Hey." He sat on the edge of the bed beside her. "How are you?"

She sighed and rubbed her eyes. "Exhausted." An open book was on her lap, and she closed it. "I'm trying to read but keep dozing off."

Daniels took the book and set it on the nightstand beside the bed. He couldn't help but notice the dark circles beneath his wife's eyes. His concern edged up. "How was your day?"

"Typical." She stifled a yawn. "How was yours? Any progress?"

He'd texted her earlier to tell her of Dexter Fallon's murder. "None. And worse, Penny Bartolo is threatening to not testify."

"I can't say I'm surprised." She leaned back onto the pillow. "She's likely next."

"We put her into protective custody, but it's not helping her mental state. She has no idea what the necklace means, so we can't be sure if she's a target or not."

Marjorie adjusted the strap on her nightgown. "How's Rem?"

"As frustrated as I am."

"Mmm." She closed her eyes and opened them. "I bet."

"Sorry I'm so late. How was J.P.?"

"He did okay tonight. He missed you."

"I missed him, too."

"Maybe one of these days we'll see you again."

Daniels pulled the covers up. "Go to sleep. You need it."

She settled her head against the pillow. "There's dinner in the fridge. Just toss it in the microwave. Oh, and there's a package for you."

Daniels kissed her cheek and stood. "Thanks. Love you."

Sighing with her eyes closed, she turned on her side. "Love you, too." She hugged the pillow, and Daniels wondered if she'd already fallen asleep.

Sliding off his jacket, he quietly left the room. He headed down the stairs, tossed his jacket on a kitchen chair and opened the fridge. Spotting the prepared plate, he didn't even bother to look at what it was. He removed the covering and popped it in the microwave.

Yawning, he went to the front table and saw the mail. A small manilla package, addressed to him, sat beside other envelopes. He picked it up, ripped it open and returned to the kitchen for some water. Pulling down a glass from the cabinet, he peered inside the package, seeing a piece of paper and some bubble wrap. Curious, he set the glass down and pulled out the paper. He opened it and saw handwriting in black marker. *A Blast from the Past* was all it said.

His heart began to thump, and he pulled out the bubble wrap. It wasn't much bigger than his hand and he unwrapped it. A small stone fell into his palm and his whole body went ice cold and chill bumps raised on his skin. It was an exact replica of the stone that had been sent to him not long after being assigned to Victor D'Mato's case, only this one was much smaller. The carved-out eyes stared back at him, and he dropped it onto the counter, remembering the mental torture the first one had caused him. It had wreaked havoc on Daniels' relationship with his wife, partner and career, and Daniels had even come close to shooting Rem and himself. The memories rushed back, and Daniels grasped the edge of the counter when his knees almost buckled. Breaking into a cold sweat, he told himself to calm down. This wasn't the same statue, and he could tell by the feel of it that it didn't have the same evil mojo that the first one did. This one was meant to scare and intimidate.

Feeling the familiar fear, he backed away from it but never took his eyes off of it. Trying to collect himself, he took several deep breaths, the way Rem did when he had a flashback. Daniels now understood the intensity of Rem's episodes. Daniels had had occasional bouts of unpleasant memories and regrets, but nothing like this. Just seeing the small statue had transported him right back to the past and he could feel the ugly thoughts and almost hear the voices in his head.

Telling himself over and over again that he was safe and so was his family, he began to calm, and his breathing slowed. He returned to the edge of the counter, now angry with whoever had done this. Was it Margaret? Was she messing with him the way she'd messed with Rem in the warehouse?

The microwave dinged but he ignored it. He reached for the stone and then froze when a horrifying realization occurred to him. What if

Marjorie's fatigue and mood swings were due to something more sinister? Could she have been sent one of these smaller statues at work? Was it sitting at her desk right now, messing with her mind and body? The shock of that terrified him and he jolted into action. He pulled an oven mitt out of a drawer, picked up the statue with it and dropped it back into the package. He did the same with the note. Debating what to do, he decided to hide it for now, and went to the front closet and stuck the package up on a high shelf.

Glad it was out of sight, he ran up the stairs and returned to the bedroom. He shook Marjorie's shoulder until she woke. "Marjorie? I have to talk to you."

She moaned and blinked her eyes. "What? Is it J.P.?"

"No. J.P.'s fine. I have to ask you something."

"Gordon. I'm tired." She closed her eyes.

His concern growing, he shook her shoulder to keep her awake. "Was anything sent to you at work? Anything weird?"

She groaned in annoyance and opened her eyes. "What are you talking about?"

Daniels bit his lip, trying to think of what to say. "Remember when I got that statue? From Victor?"

Her eyes opened wide. "Of course. I'll never forget it." She pushed up on her elbow. "What is this about?"

"I...uh...I just had a scary thought that maybe someone sent you something like that at work? And maybe that's why you're so tired."

She squinted at him. "Seriously?"

He nodded. "Yes. I'm serious."

"You think something is wrong with me? So much so that you think I'm going crazy?"

"You have to admit. You've been a little off. You even said so yourself."

Her face furrowed. "Maybe that has something to do with my husband barely being home. And after demanding days at work, I have to handle an eighteen-month-old with no help from you."

"Are you sure that's it?" Daniels could see she was angry and that waking her may have been a poor choice, but he had to know. "We've dealt with tough times before, and you've been..." He wasn't sure what to say.

"I've been what?" she asked, her voice clipped.

"Been...less confrontational." It was the only thing he could think to say.

She tossed the covers back and sat up. "What is going on here?"

He sat back. "I'm just worried. With this case—"

"Stop. Despite all your difficult cases, you've never had to wake me to ask inane questions."

He stood. "Marjorie, I can see you haven't been well."

She raised one of her eyebrows. "I haven't been well? Is that what you said?"

He put a hand on his head and paced. "Listen—

"No. You listen. I'm sick of this crap. You've come home late the last three nights and I have been doing my damnedest to stay cool because I know what you have to do. I work hard at my job, and I work hard at home, and I work hard as a mother. And you have the nerve to stand there and say I'm not well?" She slid to the side of the bed. "You know what it takes to take care of J.P. It's hard enough when the two of us are here. And now you want to blame some crazy statue because I'm not acting like your sweet little wife when you come home after a long day?"

Realizing he was screwing this up big time, he tried to find the right words. He stopped pacing and sat beside her. "I'm sorry. I'm...I'm...not handling this well."

"Why don't you try and fix it before I knock you into the wall." She scowled. "What is going on?"

Daniels, realizing he was going to have to come clean, took a deep breath. "I'm scared because when I went to see Allison, she said something. Something I should have told you."

She squared her shoulders. "What did she say?"

"After Allison said she'd only tell Rem the name of the supposed killer, she...she added that the killer was targeting people who'd betrayed Victor and Margaret, and...and that I fall into that category." Daniels paused. "And that I...and my wife...should be careful."

Marjorie's jaw fell open.

Chapter Twenty-Four

SITTING AT HIS DESK, Rem checked the clock and went back to his file. Daniels had texted earlier telling Rem he would be late that morning, to tell Lozano, and he'd explain when he got in. That was an hour ago. Rem wondered what was going on and was about to call Daniels when the squad door opened, and Daniels strode in. His rumpled hair, puffy eyes and serious stare told Rem something was off. Daniels carried a small manila envelope and he walked up to Rem's desk.

"Everything okay?" asked Rem.

"We need to talk." He glanced at Lozano's office. "Right now."

Rem looked over and, through the glass, saw Lozano working at his desk. Their captain seemed to feel their gazes on him, and he made eye contact.

Rem stood as Daniels turned and headed toward Lozano's office. "Okay," he said to Daniels' back. Wondering what was going on, he set his pen down and followed Daniels.

Daniels opened Lozano's door and walked in. "Captain."

"Daniels," said Lozano. "I heard you needed some extra time this morning. Everything okay?"

"No. It's not." Daniels set the envelope on the edge of Lozano's desk.

Rem shut the door. "What's wrong?"

Daniels put his hands on his hips and seemed to collect himself. "I got this in the mail." He picked up the envelope and dumped the contents on the desk.

Rem leaned close and saw the statue. A shiver ran through him when he recalled the bigger one just like it. "Oh, hell."

Daniels opened the note by grasping the edges. Rem read it and checked the envelope. There was no return address. Lozano stood, eyed the statue, and saw the note. He grunted.

"I received it yesterday and opened it when I got home." Daniels started to pace.

"Did Marjorie see it?" asked Rem.

"No. Thank God." Daniels closed his eyes. "But it scared the hell out of me."

"I'm not surprised," said Rem. "It's scaring the hell out of me."

"Margaret's messing with you, too," said Lozano.

Rem recalled the hood over his face and took a calming breath. "These are her tactics. It's got Margaret written all over it."

Daniels continued to pace. "It's not just the statue. The minute I saw it, I had this awful thought." He stopped. "Marjorie's moods have been all over the place this week. Combined with her fatigue and headaches, I wondered if...if..."

Rem held his stomach. "That she was sent something like this?"

"Exactly." Daniels resumed his pacing. "I ran upstairs to wake her and ask her. I had to know. She thought I was crazy, but I had to tell her..." he glanced at Lozano. "...what happened with Allison."

Lozano frowned and looked at Rem, then back at Daniels.

"I thought you already told her," said Rem.

"Not everything." He and Lozano kept staring at each other. "She needed to know," said Daniels.

"Daniels, you know our thoughts on this," said Lozano.

Rem could see the unspoken communication between his captain and partner. "What am I missing here?"

"Captain," said Daniels, "I can't keep this to myself. Marjorie was furious with me and rightly so. I slept in the guest room last night and took her to her mother's this morning where she'll stay until this case is over."

Lozano barked back. "You have no reason to believe she's a target."

Daniels grabbed the envelope and shook it. "What the hell is this, then? A notification from *Publisher's Clearing House*?"

Lozano lowered his voice. "You know what to expect if you say more. And I still stand by the belief that Allison is bluffing." He waved toward the package. "And that is nothing more than another intimidation tactic. Just like Rem and the hood. Don't let these people manipulate you."

Rem tried to keep up but was failing. "Is someone going to tell me what the hell is going on here?"

Daniels smacked his hand against his chest. "We're talking about my wife."

Lozano yelled back. "And your partner."

Daniels cursed and turned away from the desk.

Rem waited, hearing Daniels' heavy breathing and seeing Lozano's angry stare. He made the obvious deduction that he'd been left out of some critical decision. "You two plan to keep yelling at each other or is one of you going to have the guts to tell me what I'm guessing I should have been told sooner."

Daniels turned to face him. "When I went to the jail and talked to Allison, she made a threat. Against me...and Marjorie."

Rem's gut twisted and he didn't move.

Daniels raised a hand. "We didn't say anything to you because we knew that would persuade you to visit Allison, and I thought, along with Lozano and Kate, that Allison was bluffing, and using that threat against me to convince you to see her."

His emotions swirling, Rem bit back an angry retort.

Daniels dropped his head. "I tried to tell myself I was doing the right thing." He raised his head and spoke to Rem. "But the worry wore me down. I told myself I was protecting you and that Marjorie was safe. That her unusual behavior was due to plain old family problems, and nothing else. But then I got that..." He pointed at the statue. "And it changed everything. I had to tell her, and you." He sighed. "I should have told you from the start, but I didn't...I wasn't..." He blew out a breath.

"You'd thought I'd rush out of here to confront Allison." Rem kept his tone even, but inside he was furious. He glanced at Lozano. "All of you thought that."

"We did it with good intentions," said Lozano.

Daniels took a step toward Rem. "I'm sorry. I shouldn't have kept it from you."

Rem set his jaw. "You're damn right you shouldn't have." He looked between the two of them. "None of you expected for one second that I could handle it? You couldn't include me because you thought I'd be irrational?"

"You have to admit, Remalla," said Lozano. "You've been known to be a little impulsive."

"Rem," said Daniels, "this is on me. I went along with it. I thought it was the right thing to do. And I still think Allison is playing with us. I don't know if this statue has anything to do with her threat. It's probably all Margaret's doing. But it sure as hell made me realize that I can't assume anything. I can't assume Marjorie is safe even if there's no evidence that she isn't, and I can't assume what you would do either."

"How kind of you," said Rem. He turned toward the door. "Anything else you've been keeping from me?"

"Rem...," said Daniels. "Listen—"

"I think you've said enough." Rem grabbed the knob. "Am I excused?"

Lozano glared. "Don't take that tone. You know why we made this decision. It was in your best interest."

Rem shot back. "My best interest? Whether I'm impulsive or not, how about you let me decide what's in my best interest? You two are no better than the damned DA." He scowled at Daniels. "And you should have told Marjorie from day one. She should be pissed at you."

"Well, that's not an issue." Daniels ran a hand over his haggard face. "She barely spoke to me this morning."

"You'll be lucky if I speak to you." Rem fought to decide what to do. They had one day to find a killer with nothing to go on. His partner had lied to him with his captain's and Kate's consent. His anger growing, he opened the door.

"Where are you going?" asked Lozano. "We've got to move past this. You've got a bruised ego. I understand. But we have to figure out what's next with this case."

Rem stilled. "Bruised ego?"

"We were doing what we felt was best," said Lozano, his voice rising.

Rem had had enough. "Well, now it's my turn." Holding the door, he faced Lozano. "You think I make rash decisions and can't be trusted? Fine. Then I'll do exactly what you expect. I'm going to see Allison. Right now."

Lozano glowered. "Remalla. You step out that door and I'll suspend you."

Rem erupted. "Then do it. But I'm going."

"Rem," Daniels walked over. "Think this through. You can't go by yourself. I'll go with you."

"You've done enough," Rem said flatly. "You stay here and work the case. If I get a name, I'll call you."

"Damn it, Remalla," said Lozano. "You're doing exactly what she wants."

"I know that," said Rem. "But I'm doing it anyway." He started to leave.

"Then wait for Kate," said Daniels. "Don't go alone."

"He's right," said Lozano. "Wait for Kate."

Angry, Rem glared. "Then you better call her because I'm not waiting around. Either way, Allison and I are going to talk." He yanked the door wide and stomped out of the office.

Chapter Twenty-Five

REM SAT IN THE plastic chair, bouncing his knee. He checked his watch and saw he'd been waiting for almost an hour. Since he'd arrived at the jail and signed in, he'd been replaying the argument in Lozano's office in his mind and some of his anger had abated. Realizing what he was about to do, his anxiety had ramped up. Were Lozano and Daniels right? Was he walking into an ambush? Was he too impulsive, and would he be able to handle Allison without going off the deep end?

His thoughts warred in his head and self-doubt crept in. But then he remembered what was at stake. Someone else was due to die the next day, and whether anyone wanted to admit it or not, Allison's threat should be taken seriously. If Marjorie or Daniels was at risk, they had to learn more.

Nervous, but determined, Rem reflected on his last visit with Allison, when she'd told him she was pregnant. That tidbit of info had sent him reeling. How much worse could it get? Besides, he told himself, a few months had passed, and he was better. Allison was in jail and wasn't going anywhere. He steeled himself for the conversation, telling himself he could handle this. He'd dealt with worse criminals than her.

His phone buzzed, and he saw it was Daniels. He'd already called once, and Kate had called twice. He hadn't answered because he was too pissed to talk. All he wanted to do was get in there and get this over with, but it was taking forever.

He stood and went to the front desk. The woman at the counter was reading. "Angela?" he asked, reading her name tag. "Any idea how much longer this is going to take? I've been here a while."

Angela didn't look up from her book. "It takes as long as it takes, Detective." She flipped to another page.

"What's going on back there? Everybody getting an early lunch and watching soap operas?"

She looked up, her face expressionless. "It takes as long as it takes."

Rem got the message and nodded.

A door opened and closed, and Rem turned to see Kate enter the facility, carrying her jacket and briefcase. She approached the counter, giving Rem a snarky look. "Hey, Angela."

Angela smiled. "Hey, girl. How are you?"

"I am much better now." She signed in. "Thanks for delaying."

"You got it." Angela smirked at Rem. "Happy to help."

Rem glared. "I see I've been played."

Kate set the pen down. "I know a few people around here and called in a favor." She spoke to Angela. "I owe you lunch."

"Just let me know when and where." Angela took the sign-in sheet. She glanced at Rem again. "I'll let them know you're here."

"We're waiting for Counselor Measy, too," said Kate. "He should be here soon."

Rem cursed.

"Language, Detective," said Angela, typing into her computer.

Rem narrowed his eyes at her and turned from the counter. "Pretty slick, Kate. You got me to wait. But I'm still talking to Allison." He sat in his seat.

Kate sat beside him and put her things in the chair next to her. "Can we at least discuss it?"

"There's nothing to discuss, other than the three of you lied to me."

"Please. Let's not play the victim. You know why we did it. To prevent this very thing."

"Maybe stop treating me like the victim, then."

She paused. "You've been through a lot. I think you can understand Daniels' need to protect you."

Rem chuckled. "Boy. You're good. Maybe almost as good as Allison. Now who's manipulating who?"

She scowled and faced him. "Think this through, Detective. I know you're not stupid. To the contrary, you're smarter than most and you've held up better than others would have under difficult circumstances, but everyone has their limits."

"I'm—"

"Let me finish. I've just lost one witness and I'm on the verge of losing another, and you want to walk into the lion's den? You're going to testify against this woman in three months. Did you forget what happened the last time you did this?"

"What's she going to do? Tell me she's having twins?"

"Don't make jokes, Detective."

Rem, his anger returning, swiveled to face her. "Believe me, I'm not laughing. You think I want to be here? I'd rather be getting my face tattooed with a picture of Margaret's crazy eyes. I don't want to talk to Allison, and I know she's ready for me. But I don't have a choice."

"Yes. You do."

"Some guy out there has killed three people, almost a fourth with Gina barely hanging on, and he'll kill again tomorrow. All the victims knew D'Mato and have some connection to Margaret. Our best lead is sitting behind these bars and you, Daniels and Lozano know it. But nobody wants to upset me, so you decide not to pursue it. I get it that I haven't exactly been the Mr. Rogers of stability. But this woman threatened Marjorie? Daniels' wife?"

"Mrs. Daniels is in no danger. Allison just wants you to think she is."

Rem tried to curtail his rising disgust. "You don't know who, or who isn't, in any danger, Kate. You're an attorney, not a mind reader."

"The fact remains that—"

"The only fact I care about is preventing the next murder. I have to talk to Allison."

The door opened again, and Rem spotted Measy enter the building. He looked tired and his clothes were rumpled. He passed them and frowned. "Never a dull moment, is there?" He walked to the counter and signed in.

"You can thank your client for that," said Rem.

He smiled. "Believe me, Detective. I know all about my client." He set the pen down. "I just hope you're prepared." He smiled wider and before he could sit, a door beside the front counter clanged and opened. A guard stepped out. "Albright?" he said.

Measy walked toward the guard.

Kate grabbed Rem's arm. "You sure about this?"

Rem stood and his heart rate picked up speed. "I am."

She stood with him. "Then you follow my lead. Any smart-ass tactics and I'll pull the plug." She walked to the door.

Rem didn't respond. They followed the guard down a corridor. They took a turn and stopped at another door. The guard opened it, and Rem saw a table with four chairs. Measy entered and turned back. "Give me a few minutes with my client." He closed the door. The guard remained in the hall.

Starting to sweat, Rem paced, trying to work off his anxious energy.

"I'm serious," said Kate. "This goes wrong and we're both leaving. You don't say one word about Victor, the trial or what happened to you."

"I'm not the one you have to worry about."

"She goes there, and pushes your buttons, we're done."

He stopped pacing. "Maybe we just see what happens first. I may have to sing a show tune or two to get her to talk."

"Rem, don't get cocky. Play it by the book. One wrong move and it could come back to haunt you."

"I'm aware. Thanks for the advice." He swiped at a bead of sweat on his forehead, told himself to relax and took a long breath, trying to slow his pounding heart.

She watched him. "You look pale."

"Sorry. I didn't have time to put on my foundation and blush." He shook out his hands.

"Please reconsider. We can leave right now."

"I'm not leaving. I'll be fine when I walk in there, no matter how I'm feeling right now."

"She can sense weakness. Do not let her get to you."

"I'll be—"

Measy opened the door, and Rem could see Allison in an orange jump-suit, sitting at the table. Her long wavy hair ran past her shoulders, and she smiled at him. "You two can come in," said Measy. He widened the door.

Mustering as much confidence as he could, Rem walked into the room.

Daniels watched the slow-moving clock tick away the seconds and he wondered again what was happening with Allison. He'd tried to call Rem twice to tell him Kate was on her way and to wait, but his partner hadn't answered. Kate had assured Lozano that Rem would not go anywhere near Allison until she arrived. Daniels hadn't heard a thing since.

Thinking of Marjorie, he wondered if he should try her again. He'd called her, but she hadn't answered either. He replayed their argument in his mind and cringed. She'd been furious that he hadn't told her about Allison's threat and no amount of explanation from him had helped. She'd accused him of worrying more about Rem's safety than her own and he'd attempted to justify his actions, but she wasn't listening to any of it. In some part of his brain, he had to wonder if she was right. Had he put Rem first? He didn't question that if there'd been the slightest evidence that Marjorie was in danger, he'd have thrown both himself and Rem to the wolves, but nothing had triggered his alarm bells until he'd received the package with the statue. That had changed everything.

Marjorie had agreed to pack a bag for her and J.P. in the morning and had informed Daniels that he would be sleeping in the guest room. He hadn't argued and figured they could use the distance.

He looked at the clock again. Certainly by now, Rem and Kate were talking to Allison. He wondered how it was going.

Tired, frustrated, and impatient, he picked up the phone and tried Marjorie again, hoping to catch her in a free moment. The line rang three times and she picked up. "Yes, Gordon?" she asked, sounding exasperated. "What do you want?"

Glad he could talk to her, he sighed in relief. "I...uh...wanted to check in on you. See if you're okay."

"Now you're worried about me?"

He sunk into his seat, thinking he deserved that. "I know I screwed up."

She sighed into the phone, and he heard the rustle of papers. "Now is not the time to talk about this."

"I realize that, but I just needed to hear your voice. You're pissed and I get it, but I still plan to check in."

She didn't speak for a second. "Did you tell Rem what Allison said?"

"I did." He paused and picked at the edge of a piece of paper on his desk. "He took off to see Allison. He's probably talking to her right now."

"Sounds like he's more worried about me than you were."

Daniels closed his eyes. "Marjorie—"

"Listen, Gordon. I'm at work and it's going to take more time to get anywhere in this conversation than you or I have right now. Plus, I'm being snide because I'm angry and not in the mood to be nice. So, do yourself and me a favor and give me some space." She paused. "Maybe catch your killer first and when you have some time for your wife and son, let me know."

Opening his eyes, Daniels bit back a groan. "You're good at snide. You know that?"

"I'm just getting started."

He poked at his armrest. "Despite the mess I've made, I want you to know I love you very much."

"The mess you've made doesn't change the fact that I love you, too, but we've got some issues to work through."

"I'm more than willing to work through all of it." He heard muffled voices in the background.

"I appreciate that." She spoke to someone else and came back on the line. "Listen. I've got to go. I'm doing the early lunch with Oswald and Loretta and they're waiting."

Daniels recognized Loretta's name but not Oswald's. "Who's Oswald?"

"Moira's sub."

Daniels nodded. "Okay. Enjoy your lunch. Can I call you later?"

"Call me after work. I'll have more time."

Glad she was at least communicating with him, Daniels relaxed. "Thanks. I miss you."

"You be careful, and I'll talk to you later."

"Bye."

"Bye."

He hung up, glad she wasn't furious anymore and was willing to talk. Eyeing the time, he set his phone down and wondered again what was happening with Rem.

Rem walked into the small room and sat in the chair across from Allison. Kate sat beside him and Measy sat next to Allison. Rem took a second to adjust to being so close to the woman who'd almost killed him. In their first meeting, they were separated by glass and talked through a phone. This time around, he could reach out and touch her. It unnerved him.

Kate set her jacket and briefcase on the table. "Let me reiterate as I did before that we are only here to discuss the case Detective Remalla is currently working on, and nothing else."

"I think my client is okay with that," said Measy.

Rem stared and Allison stared back. "Hello, Rem. It's good to see you," she said.

Rem didn't bother with small talk. "I heard about your conversation with Daniels."

"You should have joined us. It would have saved you some time." She smiled and put her forearms on the table.

He resisted the urge to lean back. "I hear you have a name. Of someone who may be committing these murders."

She shrugged. "Maybe. Who knows? But based on your partner's questions, the person I know is definitely worth considering."

"Who is he?"

Allison smirked. "How's Daniels doing? He and his wife all right?"'

Rem's annoyance spiked. "They're both fine."

"Good. Glad to hear it." She scooted back in her chair and rubbed her round stomach.

Rem swallowed. Seeing her pregnant threw him and he forced himself to focus. "The name?" he asked.

She set her elbows on the armrests. "Chloe."

Confused, Rem sat up. "Chloe? We're looking for a man."

"Not the killer, silly. Our daughter. I want to name her Chloe. It's pretty, don't you think?"

Kate put a hand on the table. "We are not here to discuss Allison's child."

"And Rem's," said Allison.

"Or whoever the father is," said Kate. "Tell your client to stick with the subject we're here for."

Measy looked bored. "Stick to the subject, Allison."

"I just thought he'd like to know, in case he has a different name in mind." Allison held Rem's gaze. "Have you thought about what you'd like to name her?"

Rem's heart thumped. He'd settled himself down well enough when he'd entered the room, but he had no desire to talk about their possible child. "Like Kate said, let's stick to the case."

"Okay, then. Chloe it is. Don't say I didn't ask." She rubbed her stomach again.

Rem grit his teeth. He took a deep breath and tried to gather his thoughts. "Listen, Allison. I'm under no illusions as to why I'm here. You're trying to get under my skin. I get it. I'm about to testify against you and tell a jury about your monstrous acts and you're scared shitless."

Measy perked up and looked at Kate. "Counselor—" said Measy.

Rem ignored him. "But let's get one thing straight. I'm not here to talk about that, or Chloe, or whatever messed up crap is swirling through your head. I'm hunting a killer, and either you know something, or you don't, so stop wasting my time, because I've got things to do."

Allison's smug look fell, and he detected a hint of anger.

"Tell Detective Remalla to back off," said Measy.

"Detective Remalla is doing just fine," said Kate. "Is there anything you can offer Remalla that might benefit him, Allison? Because if not, we need to go."

Allison sat up, her confidence slightly diminished. "I heard you lost a witness, and might lose another? Maybe you two shouldn't be so smug." She eyed Rem. "You can talk big all you want, but if I take that stand, you're going to regret not speaking to me sooner."

"I regret speaking to you period," said Rem. "Since the day we met."

She scoffed and aimed a satisfied look at him. "Not the night we created Chloe. As I recall, I believe you screamed my name."

Kate stood. "That's enough. This meeting is over." She grabbed her briefcase.

Rem felt the bile rise in the back of his throat. "I'm with you, Kate." He stood. "Let's go."

Allison stared. "Fine. You want the killer's name?"

Rem hesitated.

Kate picked up her jacket. "Forget it, Rem. She's bluffing. She has been from the start."

Rem debated what to do, then turned to leave. "See you at trial."

"Detective Daniels mentioned the infinity sign," said Allison, sitting up, her eyes flaring. "This man has a tattoo of one running down his spine. He has a weird affinity for it."

Rem looked back, hesitating again. "You could have made that up."

"But I'm not," said Allison. "He strangles them, doesn't he?"

Rem glanced at Kate, wondering how Allison would know that. Had Daniels mentioned it?

Allison smiled. "No. Your partner didn't bring that up. I know because the man you're looking for almost strangled someone at a party. Someone had bothered Margaret and demeaned Victor. I saw the whole thing. Your killer was almost peaceful while doing it, like it was as simple as getting dressed in the morning. People pulled him off and the victim was fine but strangely detached and could barely walk. Others attributed it to the attack, but I was fascinated. I talked to the man who'd done it and asked him about it. He confessed how he could pull the energy from people. He'd literally been absorbing the life force from the person he was strangling. He said he could do it with anyone and didn't have to strangle them to do it. He wasn't lying. I could feel him doing it to me. I had to tell him to back off." She leaned back, looking relaxed. "I suspect that's exactly what he's doing to your victims when he kills them. He's getting off on it."

Rem's conflict grew and he had the sudden insight that Allison knew exactly who their killer was and was just having fun drawing out the reveal. "Who is he?"

Kate pulled on his arm. "Let's go, Rem. She doesn't know anything."

Rem waited and Allison smirked. "Five minutes," she said.

"Five minutes what?" asked Rem.

"I want five minutes with you. Alone. Just you and me." Allison crossed her legs and put a hand on her knee.

Kate chuckled. "Out of the question."

"I agree, Allison," said Measy. "Counsel needs to be present."

Allison rolled her eyes. "No, you don't."

"I can't do that," said Rem.

"You can if you want the name," replied Allison.

"C'mon, Rem," said Kate. "Let's go."

Unsure, Rem watched Allison, trying to judge what she was up to.

"It's just five minutes," said Allison. "What are you so afraid of?"

"Rem. Let's go. Now," said Kate.

Rem raised his hand. "Hold up."

Kate moved closer and spoke into his ear. "Don't you dare do this."

Allison held Rem's gaze. Measy went over to talk to her, but she shoved his shoulder. "I know what I'm doing," she said.

Measy sighed and straightened. "Fine. It's your future."

Kate stood in front of Rem. "You can't do this. We need to go."

"You want the name or not?" asked Allison. "We are talking about saving someone's life, aren't we?"

Rem made up his mind. "Go wait outside, Kate."

"Damn it, Rem...," said Kate.

Rem returned to his seat. "I'll be out in five minutes." He prepared, telling himself he could handle whatever Allison was about to throw at him.

Measy walked around the desk. "C'mon, Counselor. It appears they've made up their minds."

Kate glared. "Whatever happens in here—"

"Is between him and me," said Allison. "And no one else." She waved. "Bye-bye."

Rem turned toward Kate. "Go. I'll be fine."

Kate's look shot daggers at him. "I can't save you from this."

"Nobody's asking you to save me," answered Rem. "I'm doing this of my own free will."

Kate shook her head, turned, and walked out of the room.

Furious, Kate leaned against the wall while Measy took a phone call. Her mind raced with what Allison would do or say, and would Remalla even tell Kate what they'd discussed? How could she be expected to try a case against this woman when the main witness pulled a stunt like this? She huffed and wished she had a cigarette. She'd given them up two years earlier, but when the stress got to her, she always craved one.

Measy hung up and leaned against the wall next to her. "Relax. Anything they say is one's word against the other." He chuckled. "You ask me, those two deserve each other." He pulled on his tie and loosened it. "Personally, I think he's always had a thing for her. Don't you?"

Disgusted, Kate moved to another wall. "Shut up, Measy."

Measy chuckled again. He pulled out a piece of hard candy, unwrapped it and popped it in his mouth. "Bad habit," he said. "I love sweets." He pulled out another candy. "You want one?"

Kate checked the time. "Please stop talking to me."

Measy shrugged. "Suit yourself." He put the candy back in his pocket and sucked on the one in his mouth.

The five minutes felt like five hours, and Kate was about to enter the room when the door opened, and Rem walked out. His face was pale, and he looked like he'd been speaking to a zombie Victor D'Mato.

Kate pushed off the wall. "What happened?"

Rem didn't waste time. He strode down the hall. "I got a name."

Chapter Twenty-Six

DANIELS SAT IN LOZANO's office, reviewing the progress on the case, but both were anxious. Each of them watched the time.

"We should know something soon," said Lozano.

"What's taking so long? We should have heard something by now." Daniels thought of Rem and wondered how he was holding up.

"Let's get back to the case. I'm sure we'll hear from them soon."

Frustrated, Daniels scoffed. "What case? We don't have anything worth mentioning. You know as much as I do."

"That photo left at Dexter's. There were several people in it other than Dexter and D'Mato. Have you tracked any of them down?"

"We don't know who they are. We showed the photo to Mikey Redstone, but she's been away from the group for a while now and none of the people were familiar to her. We tried Penny Bartolo, but she's too scared to say anything. All she said was that the other people were followers at the time but didn't want to elaborate." Daniels shook his head. "My gut tells me it doesn't matter, though. The killer needed a picture of Dexter and D'Mato together and that's the one he had. The other people in the picture, just like the other guy in Stella's photo, don't matter."

Lozano rocked back in his seat. "Still, any of them could provide a lead."

"We have to find them first," said Daniels, raising his voice. He sighed. "Sorry. I'm just worried. Where the hell is Rem?"

On cue, his phone rang. Daniels saw Rem's name on the display. "It's him." He quickly answered. "Rem?"

Rem's voice traveled over the line. "I got a name."

Daniels heard a car door slam. "Who?"

"Oswald Fry."

Daniels gripped the phone, recalling his conversation with Marjorie.

"He's a follower. Devoted to Margaret and Victor. Has the ability to suck the life out of people whether he's strangling or just hanging out with them. Has an infinity tattoo on his back." The sound of his car starting and tires squealing traveled through the phone. "I'm on my way—"

"Wait. Stop." Daniels' heart slammed into his chest and his adrenaline surged. Lozano furrowed his brow.

"What's wrong?" asked Rem.

Daniels broke out in a sweat. "I...I just talked to Marjorie. She said she was having lunch with Moira, her friend's, sub. His name is Oswald."

There was a brief pause. "That's a hell of a coincidence."

Fear sliced through Daniels. "It's not a coincidence. Get to the school. Right now."

"I'm on my way. Meet you there." Rem hung up.

Frozen to his spot, Daniels lowered his phone.

"What's going on?" asked Lozano.

"The name Allison gave Rem is Oswald Fry, and I think he's currently working alongside my wife at her school."

Lozano stood and grabbed his phone. "I'll call it in. Put the school on lock down."

Breaking free from his shock, Daniels ran out of the office.

Daniels drove like a madman, running lights and stop signs, and got to Marjorie's high school in record time. Patrol cars were out front with their lights swirling. Daniels parked next to them and jumped out of his vehicle. Realizing he couldn't get in, he found the officer in charge who was talking to another officer inside the school with the principal, Jeanette Brotherman, who Daniels had met at various school functions. Daniels got on the phone, explained the situation and asked for someone to meet him at the door. He ran to the entrance where he spoke to Jeanette's assistant. He showed his badge and entered the building. Jeanette was in the front office speaking to an officer, who looked anxious.

"Jeanette," said Daniels.

She looked over. "Gordon. What is going on?"

He ran behind the desk. "The school's completely locked down?"

"Yes, it is, but no one can give me a straight answer." She nodded at the patrolman. "He seems to think there's someone dangerous in the building."

"There is," said Daniels. "His name is Oswald Fry. You know him?"

Her eyes widened. "Oswald? Are you serious?"

"Very serious. We have reason to believe he's killed people. Where's Marjorie?" His heart skipped and he knew he wouldn't calm down until he saw his wife.

"Marjorie?" she asked. "I assume she's hunkered down in her office or in a classroom like she's trained to do in these situations."

"And where is Fry?" asked Daniels.

"I assume he's doing the same thing," said Jeanette.

"He's not," said the assistant. Daniels couldn't remember her name. "He left."

Daniels fought the urge to grab the woman by the shoulders. "What do you mean, he left?"

Her face, already pale, went white. "Right before the police called, he walked out. Said he had an emergency. I was trying to find someone to cover his last two classes." She wrung her hands.

Stressed, Daniels tried to think. "I need any information you have on him right now." His phone buzzed and he saw a text from Rem. "Plus, my partner's here and he needs access. His name is Detective Remalla." He texted Rem and told him to come to the door. He spoke to Jeanette. "And I need to see Marjorie."

The assistant went to the front and let Rem in. He flashed his badge, saw them, and ran over. "What's the status? Where's Oswald?"

Daniels gave him a quick update. Rem agreed to take over getting the school cleared and contacting Lozano with Oswald's information while Daniels went to search for his wife. He realized the classrooms would be closed and locked and the kids would be scared but he had to find Marjorie. She'd had lunch with a damn murderer and if Daniels hadn't been so stupid, he could have protected her from that.

His first stop was her office. It was locked and he banged on the door. "Marjorie? Are you in there?" He'd tried to call her on her cell, but she hadn't answered. He banged again. "Marjorie? It's Gordon. Open the door." He considered she wasn't inside, and he identified himself as a police officer, said he had his badge, and it was okay to let him in.

The lock clicked and the door opened. Daniels recognized Shonda, the assistant school counselor. He held out his badge and stepped inside. "Shonda? Where's Marjorie?"

"Detective Daniels? Is everything okay? Why are we on lockdown?"

Daniels realized how nervous she was. "It's okay. There was a suspicious person in the building, but we believe he left. We still need to check the classrooms, though, and be sure everyone is okay. You should be able to leave soon. Where's Marjorie?"

Looking calmer, she rubbed her shoulders. "She went to the nurse's office. Said she wasn't feeling well. The alarms went off not long after that."

"Where's the nurse's office?"

Shonda told him where to go and he told her to stay put until someone came for her. He left and headed down the hall. He found the sign for the nurse and knocked on the door. "Police," he said. "I need to find someone." He knocked again. "Marjorie? It's me, Gordon. Open the door."

A quiet second passed when he heard the lock turn. The door opened and a woman poked her head out.

He assumed it was the nurse and he held out his badge. "I'm Detective Gordon Daniels. Marjorie's husband. I need to see her."

The woman pulled the door wider, and he saw Marjorie. Her eyes were red and the dark circles beneath them were darker. "Gordon?" she asked.

He pushed inside past the nurse. "Marjorie." He hugged her. "Are you okay?"

She held him for a second and then looked up. "What are you doing here?"

"Is this about the lockdown?" asked the nurse. "Has there been a shooting?"

Needing to talk to his wife alone, he let go of Marjorie. "There's no shooting, but there was a suspicious person. We're just being cautious." He walked to the door and looked down the hall. He saw a police officer and waved at him. The officer jogged over.

"I need you to escort the nurse out." Daniels stepped aside, took the woman's arm, and spoke to her. "Marjorie and I will be right behind you."

The nurse eyed the officer. "It's safe?"

"Yes, ma'am. Come with me and we'll get you out of here." The officer took her elbow, and the nurse went with him.

Daniels closed the door.

Rem set up a perimeter around the campus grounds to prevent anyone else from leaving or entering the property and instructed officers to check each classroom, get a headcount, ensure everyone was safe, and then get them out. Parents had been contacted as to where they could pick up their children. After talking to the assistant, he'd gotten Oswald's name, address, and photo id. He'd sent it all to Lozano, who was sending officers to the address. According to the assistant, Oswald didn't drive, so Rem had someone check bus routes and ride share services to see who might have picked up a man matching Oswald's description.

He'd studied Oswald's school id. He had shoulder-length shaggy dark hair, brown eyes, a trimmed beard and mustache, bushy eyebrows, and a wide nose. He wore wire-rimmed glasses and looked like any other intellectual, but slightly nerdy, high school teacher.

Angry they'd missed him, he wondered who'd tipped Oswald off. He'd left the campus right before the school had been locked down, so someone must have warned him. Had Margaret somehow known Allison was talking? Had Measy been the informant?

Thinking of his visit with Allison, he kicked at a chair. He'd endured five minutes of hell with that woman, who'd made a disgusting threat and more disgusting offer, only for him to find Oswald and then lose him again. Fed up and disheartened, he considered punching the wall.

Knowing he needed to settle down, he thought of Daniels and Marjorie. Neither had returned and Rem wondered where they were. The school was slowly being evacuated and he'd expected Daniels to have been back by now.

He spoke to the principal's assistant, who was on the phone talking to nervous parents. She'd pointed out Shonda, who was the assistant counselor who worked with Marjorie. Shonda had been evacuated and was standing out in the front drive, helping as kids and staff left the building.

Rem ran over and after talking to her, he headed back inside to look for the nurse's office, He found it and was about to knock when he heard raised voices. Daniels and Marjorie were arguing.

Rem held off but since they were yelling, he couldn't help overhearing. Marjorie was shouting about Oswald and Daniels was trying to explain. The voices grew louder, and Rem considered walking away when he heard Marjorie call Daniels a name and blame him for everything. Frowning and knowing that wasn't her, he braced himself and knocked.

It went quiet and the door opened. Rem saw Daniels' worried face. "Can I come in?" Rem asked.

"Now's not a great time," said Daniels.

"What?" said Marjorie. She appeared behind Daniels. "You've never denied him before. Why start now?"

Rem eyed Daniels and entered. He spoke to Marjorie, who gripped her head. "Can I talk to you for a second?"

She laughed and whirled on him. "You want to talk about the killer I've been working with for the past week? A man I've been speaking to and sharing lunch with who's strangled people? Who has not only put me at risk but children, too, and other staff? While my husband went about his day, disregarding every warning bell and protecting you instead of me?" She put her hands on her hips. "By all means. Let's talk about that. Please tell me how you can explain any of this before I kick you into the brick wall the way I want to with my husband." Breathing hard, she turned and put her hand on a file cabinet.

"Marjorie—" said Daniels.

"Stop talking to me," she yelled. "I'm just so...so..." She held her chest and took a shaky breath.

"Tired?" asked Rem. "Worn out? Can't think straight? Confused and unfocused?" He stepped closer. "Like you just want to lie down and sleep forever?" He took another step. "Probably have a lousy headache, too."

Her face furrowed and she glanced back at him.

"Is that why you came to the nurse's office?" asked Rem. "Because you felt bad?"

She turned toward him, her eyes narrowed. "I've felt bad all week, but I'm sure Gordon told you that. Probably told you I was a terrible mother, too."

Daniels glowered. "I would never—"

Rem chuckled softly. "Daniels has never spoken a mean word about you for as long as you two have known each other. You're the best thing that's happened to him since me, and that's saying a lot."

Marjorie looked between the two of them. "I am a bad mother. I...I've been so short-tempered and...and..."

"That's not your fault," said Rem. "It's Oswald Fry's."

Daniels stepped up next to him. "What do you mean?"

"I told you," said Rem, recalling his conversation with Allison. She'd told him more about Oswald's abilities during their five minutes. "Oswald can suck the life out of people. He does it when he kills people, but he can also do it just by standing next to someone. He has the rare ability to pull energy from anybody, like some sort of energy vampire." He looked at Marjorie. "I suspect he's been doing it to you all week, and the more time you spent with him, the worse it got." He paused while Marjorie's expression shifted as his information penetrated. "I bet you'd start to feel better after you got some sleep, but it returned after you saw him again."

Marjorie ran a shaky hand through her hair. "I didn't know what was wrong with me." Her posture slumped and she sat on the nurse's chair. "Oh my God."

"There are plenty of reasons to be mad at Daniels," said Rem, softly, "but keep in mind that a lot of your fury and fatigue comes from being around Oswald, and now that he's been found and you won't see him again, you're going to start to feel better."

She leaned over, put her face in her hands and sighed. A second passed and he heard her take a heavier breath. Her shoulders shook and he could tell she'd started to cry.

"Honey." Daniels walked over and squatted beside her.

Hoping he'd helped, Rem walked to the door. "I'll go check in with Jeanette and Lozano. Give you two some space," he said, and left the office.

Chapter Twenty-Seven

REM ENTERED THE SQUAD room, tired but glad the school had been cleared and everyone was okay. Daniels had taken Marjorie back to her mother's and had picked up J.P. along the way while Rem had stayed to finish at the school. Lozano had called to tell him that officers had gone to Oswald's address, but the only person at the home had been Oswald's father. They'd learned that Oswald had not been there for several months, and they were bringing the father in for questioning.

Rem approached his desk, saw the full coffeepot, but was too worn out to get any coffee. He sat in his chair with a plop and rested his forehead in his palm. The morning's events replayed in his mind. He recalled what Allison had said and felt physically ill. Now that he had some distance from it, he found himself considering her offer and if he was willing to do it. He thought of his daughter, Chloe. What was best for her?

"Remalla?"

He sat up, seeing Lozano standing beside his desk. "Captain."

"How you holding up?"

Rem almost chuckled. "I've had better days."

"How's Daniels?"

"I'm sure he's had better days, too. He's getting Marjorie and J.P. situated but he should be back soon."

Lozano nodded. "I'm glad Marjorie's okay."

"Me, too."

"Mr. Fry arrived about ten minutes ago. I want you and Daniels to question him. He's in room two. We set him up with a soda and some chips and told him to wait."

Rem wondered what Mr. Fry would have to say about his son. "Okay." He fiddled with the edge of his daily calendar that sat on his desk. Thinking of the argument in Lozano's office that morning, he wasn't sure what else to do or say. He swiveled in his seat.

Lozano stood still for a moment, and Rem felt his gaze on him. A second passed and Lozano picked up Rem's empty travel mug. Rem heard him slide the pot out and fill the mug. Then he heard the sugar and creamer packets opening. A few seconds later, Lozano set the mug in front of Rem. "I think you need it."

Rem half-smiled. "That's a first. You've never gotten me coffee before." He took a sip. "Thanks."

Lozano grabbed Daniels' chair, rolled it over and sat next to Rem's desk. "I think we need to have a conversation."

Rem sighed. "It's all right, Cap."

"How about you let me decide that."

Rem studied his coffee mug.

"I realize after what happened this morning, that I owe you an apology. We all made assumptions about things we shouldn't have, and it put Marjorie at risk."

Rem nodded.

"So, I apologize I doubted you. I should have been up front, but nobody believed Allison. Daniels didn't like not telling you, but Kate and I put the pressure on. I realize he's a big boy and can make up his own mind, but we didn't make it easy."

"Captain—"

"That being said, if I had to do it again, I don't know if I'd make a different decision."

Surprised, Rem narrowed his eyes. "What do you mean? We got Oswald's name and protected Marjorie."

"At what cost though?"

Rem didn't understand.

Lozano leaned in. "What happened during those five minutes?"

Rem deflated and looked back at his mug.

"Kate told me about the meeting. That you ignored her advice and spent time with Allison alone. And you haven't told her what you and Allison discussed."

"I've been a little busy, Cap."

"Do you plan on telling her?"

Rem picked at the lid on his mug.

"You plan on telling anyone?"

Rem shrugged. "Not sure."

Lozano sat back. "You're a big boy, just like Daniels. But this woman can pull your strings."

"I can handle it, Cap."

"Can you?"

"I'm a cop. It's what I signed up for."

Lozano put a hand firmly on Rem's desk. "Nobody signs up for what you've been through. You've endured more than most could possibly bear. That's why I didn't want you to see Allison. I didn't want you to bear more."

Rem gripped his mug. His chest tightened and his throat constricted. "I had to go. Despite the risks."

"And that's why you're damned good at what you do. You put everyone else's safety before your own. That's why Daniels didn't want you to go either. Whether you agree with it or not, he was trying to shield you."

"I get it." Rem paused. "But if we're at a point where you think I'm too fragile to handle the truth, then maybe I shouldn't be doing this job anymore." He glanced at his captain.

"I'm not worried about telling you the truth. I'm worried about what you'll do after you hear it."

"I admit. I act first and think later. I did the very thing nobody wanted me to do. But it worked."

Lozano expelled a long breath. "Sure. We got Oswald's name. And Marjorie is safe. All bonus points. If you want me to say you were right and we were wrong, I'll say it."

"That's not what I want."

"You want me to be honest, don't you? Well, I'm being honest. But I'll add this." He took a second and tapped on Rem's desk. "I know whatever was said between you and Allison has got you on edge. Kate said as much. Allison claims she's carrying your child, and if she's using that to manipulate you, then don't do it."

Rem set his jaw.

"Because if getting Oswald's name and protecting Marjorie means I lose a good detective to a bad decision, and Allison walks free..." he lowered his voice, but sharpened his tone, "...then no. Nothing you did today was worth it."

Rem met his captain's gaze but didn't answer.

Lozano stared back. "How's that for honesty?" He stood and returned Daniels' chair then headed toward his office. "When your partner gets here, go question Mr. Fry."

Daniels took the stairs to the second floor and entered the squad room. Seeing Rem sitting at his desk and sipping coffee from his mug, he went to his own desk and sat.

"Hey," said Rem. "How's Marjorie?"

Frazzled, Daniels ran a hand through his hair and let out a ragged breath. "She's better. I got her to her Mom's, and she went to bed. I suspect she'll sleep the rest of the day. Her mom's watching J.P. and Lozano said he'll add a patrol to watch the house."

"You think Oswald would go that far?"

Thinking of his wife and her anger with him, Daniels shook his head. It had been a stressful day. "I don't think so, but I was wrong before. I can't take the chance I'm wrong again." He paused. "I'm still in shock that he targeted her. Why?"

"To get to you."

Daniels closed his eyes. "What would he have done if we hadn't found him?" He opened his eyes. "I can't stop thinking about that."

"Well, do your best." He set his coffee down. "Because we've got work to do." He stood. "Mr. Fry, Oswald's dad, is here, and Lozano wants us to question him."

"I heard." Daniels tried to put Marjorie out of his mind. "I heard a few other things, too."

Rem stilled and made a face. "Don't tell me. You talked to Kate."

"She called me on the way over."

"She's persistent. I'll give her that."

"She's got a case to win, and she doesn't want any unexpected curve-balls."

Rem shifted on his feet. "She's got nothing to worry about. C'mon. We've still got a murderer on the loose who's due to strike again tomorrow. Let's go talk to Fry."

Daniels stood. "What happened in that room, Rem? What did Allison say to you?"

Rem headed to the doors. "None of your business." He pulled on the door and walked out.

Daniels cursed. Not only did he have a wife on the verge of losing it, but his partner didn't seem much better. "Rem. Wait." He slid his jacket off, tossed it over his chair, and jogged out of the squad room.

Rem stood outside one of the interview rooms. "You ready?"

"We need to talk."

"Nothing to talk about."

"What happened this morning...in Lozano's office."

Rem held up a hand. "Lozano and I talked. We're good."

"I'm happy for you and Lozano, but you and I need to discuss some things."

"Later." Rem opened the door and entered the room.

Muttering another curse, Daniels took a second to focus on questioning Mr. Fry and followed Rem inside.

A thin, balding man with narrow eyes and a wrinkled face sat at the table with a can of soda and a bag of chips. "It's about time," he said.

"Sorry about the wait, Mr. Fry," said Rem. He introduced himself and Daniels and they sat at the two chairs on the other side of the table. "We'd like to ask you about your son, Oswald."

"I already answered a bunch of questions when your people barged into my house." He wore a stained white t-shirt, and he wiped his hand on it. "And call me Winston."

"We understand, Winston, but we need to follow up," said Daniels. "We'll try not to take up much of your time."

"I hope not. I got things to do." Winston dug into his chip bag. "You got any more chips?"

"We'll get you some in a minute," said Rem. "Can you tell us when you last saw Oswald?"

"Like I said, I ain't seen him in months."

"You have any idea where he is?" asked Daniels.

Winston shrugged. "Hell if I know. He hangs with a weird crowd."

"What kind of crowd?" asked Rem.

"I don't know. Weirdos." Winston sipped from his can. "Can I get another soda?"

"Sure," said Daniels. "In a second. What kind of weirdos?"

Winston rolled his eyes. "You know. Like hippies. Long hair. Smokin' weed. Tattoos. Doing crap like meditating and thinking they're creating world peace. All that horseshit."

"Do you know any of these friends of Oswald's?" asked Daniels.

"No way. I kicked 'em out and told Oswald not to invite 'em back. A waste of space if you ask me. But I guess I shouldn't be surprised." He pulled out a chip and popped it in his mouth. He raised the bag. "That's the last one."

Daniels sighed and stood. He went to the door and stuck his head out. He saw an officer he knew walk past. "Hey, Mulson. Can you get us a bag of chips and a soda, please? I'll pay you back."

Mulson nodded. "Sure."

"Thanks." Daniels closed the door. "They're on their way." He sat again.

"So why weren't you surprised?" asked Rem.

Winston smirked. "Oswald has always been a joiner. Never been one to pave his own way. He shirks from tough decisions and is scared of his own shadow. His mother babied him. I tried to toughen him up. He got bullied in school and I told him to face the bastards down and fight back, but he'd come home crying. It didn't help that he was into that sissy theatre stuff. I told him if he'd stop pretending to be someone else, he might get left alone, but he didn't listen to me. After a while, I gave up. If you can't face your demons, you better figure out how to live with them. He learned that the hard way." He smiled.

Rem shifted in his seat. "When did he join up with these weirdos?"

"I don't know. Couple years ago, I think?"

"Has Oswald always lived with you?" asked Daniels. Despite Oswald's actions, he was beginning to feel some empathy toward him.

"Nah. When his mom moved out he lived with her until she got re-married. Then her husband kicked Oswald out and she moved to the east coast."

"Do they stay in touch?" asked Rem.

"They talk. Oswald's always been a momma's boy."

Daniels thought of his own father, and he gave thanks he'd gone in a different direction than Oswald. "What happened the last time you saw Oswald?" asked Daniels.

Winston chuckled. "You really want to know?"

"We really want to know," said Rem.

"Hell. I'd had a few drinks." He drained his soda.

"Try," said Rem, his face taut.

Winston gave Rem a look, and Rem stared back.

"We'd appreciate anything you can remember. Any little detail might help," said Daniels. The last thing they needed was to piss off Winston and have him clam up.

Winston glanced at Daniels. "You two honestly think Oswald's killed people?"

"We won't know for sure until we find him," said Daniels. "But he is a suspect."

Winston scoffed. "Oswald had some brains, but no brawn and he certainly never had the guts to stick up for himself. Not until his junior year in high school, at least. Then he showed some promise."

Rem straightened. "What happened?"

"Some kid was messing with Oswald. Taking his lunch and embarrassing him in the gym and in front of girls. Typical kid stuff."

Daniels clenched his hands together.

"Anyway," said Winston, "one day, I get a call from the school. Some kid who'd bullied Oswald was in the hospital and they said Oswald put him there. I called them liars 'cause my kid didn't have the balls." He snorted. "We ended up going to the school, meeting the principal and school counselors. Blah, blah, blah. Ultimately, the kid was fine, and he and Oswald returned to school."

"Oswald returned too?" asked Daniels.

"He got suspended." Winston crumpled his chip bag. "Life went on."

"What happened after that?" asked Rem. "Any more bullying?"

"Come to think of it, no," said Winston. "At least not that Oswald mentioned. He'd come home and head to his room. Didn't see him much and he talked even less."

"Did the school say what happened?" asked Daniels.

"Something about Oswald knocking the kid down, then trying to strangle him. The other kids pulled him off, but the other kid stayed down, like he was sick or something. It took him a while to recover."

Rem flicked a glance at Daniels. "Oswald ever do that to anyone else?" asked Rem.

"If he did, I never heard about it. I figured it was a one-time thing. He finally took out his anger on someone. It was about time. I'd hoped that would be a turning point, but he just got moodier. Then his mom and I divorced, and Oswald stayed with her until she married and moved away. Then he came to stay with me. Kid could never hold a job for long. He'd always get fired. Then he started hooking up with the weirdos." He eyed the door. "Where the hell are my chips and soda?"

"You mentioned tattoos," said Rem. "Did Oswald have any?"

Winston pursed his lips. "Come to think of it, yeah. He got one on his back. Some stupid symbol. Probably some weirdo made him do it."

"Was it the infinity sign?" asked Rem.

"I guess," said Winston.

Daniels tensed. "Any idea why he chose that?"

"How the hell should I know?" said Winston. "As long as I didn't fork over the money for it, I didn't ask questions."

"What happened the day you last saw Oswald?" asked Rem.

Winston fiddled with his empty chip bag and shot a look at Rem.

"Your chips and soda will be here soon," said Daniels.

Winston set the bag aside. "We'd been fighting a lot. And my health hadn't been great, so my patience was thin at best."

Daniels ticked up a brow. "What kind of health problems?"

Winston tapped his empty soda can on the table. "Aches and pains. Not getting enough sleep. Brain fog. Couldn't pull it together. Doctors told me there was nothing wrong with me, which just made me crankier."

Daniels eyed Rem. There was a knock on the door and Rem stood.

"About time," said Winston.

Rem walked over and opened the door. "Thanks," he said and closed it. He returned and dropped the soda and chips in front of Winston. "Dig in."

Winston pulled open the chips and popped the soda. "That last day, Oswald brought some lady over. Pretty but the weirdest yet. Had spooky blue eyes that followed me around the room."

Daniels heard Rem's intake of breath.

"I didn't like her and told her so." Winston bit into a chip. "Oswald took exception. Got in my face. Told me to respect her."

"Did you listen?" asked Daniels.

"Hell, no. By then, my usual exhaustion had set in, and between that and the beers I'd had, I lit into him. Told him to get out and when he got rid of his kooky friends, maybe I'd be nice enough to consider letting him back in the house. He sneered, grabbed some of his stuff, called me an ugly name, and left with his weirdo girlfriend. I expected him back in a few days with his tail tucked between his legs, but to his credit, he hasn't returned." He chuckled. "Good riddance if you ask me." He took a sip of his soda. "Funny thing is, ever since that day, I feel way better. It's like him being gone healed me." He set his soda down. "Personally, fellas..." he leaned toward them and whispered, "...I hope he never comes back." He relaxed back in his chair and ate his chips.

Chapter Twenty-Eight

MIKEY ENTERED SCOPE AND saw Mason on the sofa reading a magazine and Trick at his desk, talking to Kyle, who'd pulled up a chair and was sitting beside him.

Mikey set her purse on the front desk. "Looks like a full house."

Mason tossed his magazine on the coffee table. "I just got back from the Kleinmans. You can send them an invoice when you're ready."

"Okay." Mikey opened the top desk drawer and looked through it. "Hey, Trick. Hi, Kyle."

Trick sat up. "Kyle and I are going over his latest case."

"Hi, Mikey," said Kyle. His long braid ran down his back and he wore a blue t-shirt with jeans. Both emphasized his lean, but muscular physique. "I've got some research to do and Trick's giving me some tips."

"That's great," said Mikey. She glanced up. "Trick's good at research." Not finding what she wanted, she closed the top drawer and opened another.

"Looking for something?" asked Mason.

Mikey tried not to yawn but failed. "Mom's bracelet. I was going to wear it this morning but couldn't find it." She shut the other drawer. "It must be at my apartment, although I swear I brought it with me to the house."

"I'm sure it will turn up. It's probably at your place. How's Gina doing?" asked Mason. "Any better?"

Mikey shrugged, recalling her visit to the hospital. "Not much change. The doctors say there's been some improvement, so I guess that's good news. Poor Ronald's a wreck though." She checked one more drawer, but not seeing the bracelet, she closed it and went to sit next to Mason on the couch.

"Poor man lost his sister Lenora and may lose his other sister," said Trick. "I can imagine he's having a hard time."

Mikey sighed. "I was worried after Gina and I argued that he wouldn't want me there, but he couldn't have been nicer." She leaned back against the cushions. "I feel terrible about the whole thing."

"None of this is your fault," said Mason. "You're lucky you remembered the puzzle piece at all. The whole reason she's alive is because of you."

"If I'd remembered sooner though…" She shook her head.

"You can't hold on to regrets, Mikey," said Kyle. "It's a battle you won't win, and it will weigh your energy down. Just trust that you remembered when you were supposed to, and if Gina is meant to pull through, she will."

"Kyle's right," said Mason. "You can't blame yourself. You've got enough to deal with."

"And now there's a necklace clue left behind," said Mikey. "I wish I knew what that meant."

"Maybe you should take some pressure off of yourself," said Trick. "I'm sure Daniels and Remalla will find this guy."

"Before or after someone else dies?" asked Mikey with frustration.

Mason studied her. "I think someone needs some sleep."

"Sorry," said Mikey. "I guess I am a little tired." She hadn't slept well since her conversation with Rem. "You're right. I'm sure they'll catch him soon."

Kyle stood. "Thanks, Trick. I appreciate your help."

"You got it. You have any questions, you let me know." Trick sipped from a mug on his desk.

Kyle walked to the couch. "I've got to head out, but I wanted to ask, Mikey, if you'd like to meet for coffee tomorrow morning? We haven't done it in a while, and I thought you might want to get away from the office for a bit and talk."

Mikey looked over at him, wondering if she was stupid not to want him and want Rem instead. Should she reconsider? Feeling Mason's and Trick's gazes on her, Mikey nodded. "Sure, Kyle. That would be nice."

Kyle smiled. "Great. How about I meet you here at nine o'clock? Then we'll walk down to the place on the corner."

"Okay. Sounds good," said Mikey.

Kyle grabbed his blue-jean jacket that hung on a hook beside the door. "See you tomorrow then."

"Yeah," said Mikey, feeling weary. "See you tomorrow."

Kyle said his goodbyes to Trick and Mason and left. Trick stood and sat in the chair across from the sofa. "Dare I ask?"

"It's none of our business, Trick," said Mason. He glanced at Mikey. "But I have to admit, I'm curious, too."

Mikey swiped at a speck of dirt on her jeans. "Despite my continual doubts about my decision, nothing's changed. As wonderful and great as Kyle is, he's still not the one I'm meant to be with. And I should tell him that." She rested her head back on the couch cushion. "Might as well break it to him now and get it over with. Then I can resume my unrequited love for Remalla with no interruptions."

"We keep telling you," said Trick, "it's not unrequited."

"That's not the way it feels," said Mikey.

"You two have talked since his revelations to you," said Mason.

"And it's been purely professional. All business," said Mikey.

"He has been a little busy," said Trick. "Let him get through this case, then he might start to come around."

Mikey groaned and put a hand over her eyes. "God, I hate myself right now. All torn up over a boy. It's so pathetic."

Mason patted her knee. "You'll be fine. And you're not pathetic. It might be rough for a while but you two will figure it out."

She dropped her hand. "The bigger question is can you two put up with me while I'm in this funk? I know how I am around people like me. I can barely tolerate them."

"I've considered leaving SCOPE," said Trick, "but Red threatened me and said not to leave him alone with you, so I guess I'm stuck."

Mason raised a hand. "Guilty as charged."

Mikey couldn't help but smile. "I promise. I'll get better. I won't torture you forever."

"Promises, promises," said Trick.

Mason widened his eyes and pointed toward her. "You know what you need? A little social interaction, some laughter, and a good margarita."

"I'm all ears," said Trick.

"Any ideas where I'm going to get that?" asked Mikey.

"At the house," said Mason. "Tomorrow night. It's Valerie's birthday. I was going to take her out for dinner, but I can do that this weekend instead. I'll make dinner myself." He spoke to Trick. "Can you be in charge of the drinks?"

Trick shrugged. "Is Rem brooding and conflicted? Hell, yes. I can do drinks."

"Valerie's birthday? Are you sure?" asked Mikey.

"She'd love it," said Mason. "You want to make the cake?"

"Me?" asked Mikey.

"You do like to bake when you're stressed. Seems like a win-win," said Trick.

Mikey thought about it. "What flavor?"

"Nothing crazy. Just a yellow cake with chocolate icing," said Mason. "We'll eat, drink, relax, play some music and a few games. It will be good for all of us."

"You sure Val won't mind?" asked Mikey.

"Not at all. In fact, I think she'll be mad she didn't think of it herself."
Mason grinned. "You in?"

Mikey had to admit she could use a little fun, and after her conversation
with Kyle the next morning, she was going to need a drink or two. Plus,
it might help get her mind off Remalla for at least an hour. Feeling a little
better and excited to have something to look forward to, she smiled. "I'm
in."

Daniels followed Rem back into the squad room. Lozano stood near
their desks, speaking to Mel and Garcia. Seeing them enter, he thanked Mel
and Garcia, who returned to their desks. Lozano crossed his arms as Rem
and Daniels approached. "How'd it go with Fry?" he asked.

"He's a regular ray of sunshine," said Rem with a scowl. "I'm surprised
Oswald's left him alive."

"Did he offer anything useful?" asked Lozano.

Rem went to his desk and Daniels gave Lozano a quick summary of Fry's
interview. "We did manage to get Oswald's mother's information. We'll
call her but she's currently out of town on business, so we might not hear
back today."

"Well, give it a shot. You might get lucky." Lozano pointed toward Mel
and Garcia. "I was telling them that Oswald's picture is hitting the early
news. We're setting up a tip line, so things are about to start moving."

"Oh, man," said Rem. "Here come the crazies."

"I know what it means," said Lozano. "So, if you've got things to do, do
it now, because in less than two hours, you're going to be wishing you'd
taken the chance when you had it."

Daniels glanced at Rem, who'd sat at his desk. "Okay, Cap." He wondered if Rem had any plans to talk to him about their argument or what had happened with Allison.

Lozano looked between the two of them. "When's the last time you two ate anything?"

Daniels recalled his granola bar breakfast as he got J.P. packed and Marjorie out of the house that morning. "A while."

Holding his mug, Rem leaned back in his chair. "Food? What's food?"

"Go on, then." Lozano waved. "You've both had rough mornings. Take thirty minutes and get a bite downstairs because once the phones start ringing, who knows when you'll get a chance to eat again."

Rem sat up. "It's fine, Cap. I can wait."

Lozano glared at him. "It wasn't a request. I can't have you two dead on your feet when you're needed the most. So get your ass up and go get some food. And while you're down there, talk to your partner. I don't need you both in a snit when you're supposed to be working together to find Oswald Fry. It's a perfect storm for making a mistake."

Daniels made eye contact with Rem. "You heard him," said Daniels. He was grateful Lozano was giving them some time to talk, whether Rem wanted it or not. He spoke to Rem. "You ready?" He checked the time. "We go now, you might get lucky and snag their last jelly donut."

Rem perked up at that. "You got a point." He stood and pushed his chair in. "Might as well eat before the zoo releases the monkeys."

"Thirty minutes," said Lozano. "Not thirty-five."

"You're all heart, Cap," said Rem. He followed Daniels out of the squad room.

A few minutes later, Daniels sat at a table with a turkey sandwich, an apple, and his water. He'd called Oswald's mother on the way down, but she hadn't answered, and he'd left a message. Rem doctored a fresh coffee and, carrying a tray with a hamburger, chips, and the last jelly donut, he walked toward the table and sat.

"Congrats on capturing the last donut," said Daniels.

"At least something is going my way." He sat and ate a chip. "Cap was right. I'm starving."

They ate and Daniels started to feel better. He hadn't realized how hungry he'd been. Seeing Rem's mood improve, he decided to dive in. "We should talk," he said.

"I know." Rem ate another chip.

"You want to go first?"

Rem sipped some coffee. "Not really."

"Lucky me." Daniels finished his apple and tossed it in a nearby trash can. "First of all, I wanted to thank you for talking to Marjorie at the school. It helped." Daniels held his water bottle. "She's still mad, but at least she understands what was wrong and knows she'll start to feel better."

"Yeah, well, I heard some of your argument. I figured I'd better say something before I ended up investigating your death, too."

Daniels recalled Marjorie yelling at him. "I'm pretty sure you saved me, or at least gave me a reprieve."

"Once she feels better, you guys can talk. You'll work it out." Rem poked at his chips but didn't eat one.

Daniels hoped Rem was right. "And about Allison," he paused, "I should have told you what she said to me about Marjorie. I just...I don't know...thought I was helping by preventing you from seeing her. It's the last thing I wanted for you and it's exactly what happened anyway."

Rem snapped a chip in half. "I understand why you did it."

"We all believed Allison was manipulating me."

"She was," said Rem, "but that's not the point." He dropped the piece of chip onto his plate. "You lied by not telling me."

Daniels opened his mouth, but Rem cut him off.

"We're partners, Daniels," said Rem. "You have to tell me the good, bad and the ugly, no matter how you think it will affect me."

Daniels rested his elbows on the table. "And if the situation were reversed, what would you have done?"

Rem wiped his fingers on a napkin. "I don't know, and I don't want to know."

"Why not?"

"Because I don't want to imagine you going through what I went through with Allison."

Daniels picked at the label on his water bottle and nodded. "Then you can understand why I didn't want to tell you." He drank some water.

Rem sighed. "Let's just call it a mistake. I know you meant well, but I hate knowing that everybody's talking about me behind my back and making decisions for me like I'm some preschooler. Please don't hold back again, even if you think I'll run into a pit of vipers to save you or anyone else." He put his napkin on the table. "At least give me the opportunity to discuss it."

"I hear you." Finished with his sandwich, Daniels pushed his plate back. "But you're not always great with discussion, especially when you're pissed."

"Neither are you."

Daniels couldn't disagree. "How about this then? Either of us gets ahold of information we think the other might not handle well, we both agree to sit down and talk first before telling anyone else and taking any action." He raised a finger. "And that doesn't mean an argument. That means a solid discussion of the pros and cons until we agree on what to do."

Rem stared at his plate. "I can live with that."

"Good."

"The only exception being if life or limb is immediately threatened, then we trust each other to do the right thing."

"I agree." Daniels narrowed his eyes. "But life and limb does not extend to you dying from a lack of Taco del Fuegos."

Rem frowned. "You always were a stickler for details."

"I know you too well."

Rem pulled his jelly donut over. "That you do." He picked at the edge of the donut and ate a crumb.

"So, spill it," said Daniels.

Rem looked over. "Spill what?"

Daniels leaned back and hooked an elbow over the back of the chair. "We just agreed to talk to each other before making any rash decisions. What happened between you and Allison at the jail?"

Rem's face fell and he pushed the donut away. "We didn't say when it would take effect."

"It was implied that the agreement was immediate."

"Says who?"

Daniels grunted. "Rem, what did she say to you?" He unhooked his arm from the chair. "I can tell it's not good because you're looking at your jelly donut like it's broccoli."

Rem eyed his donut. "I'll get a to-go box."

Seeing his partner's reluctance, Daniels told himself to go slow. "Kate told me how Allison named the baby Chloe." He paused. "Was that what the conversation was about?"

Rem's face lost some color. "I don't really want to talk about it."

Feeling his frustration rise, but understanding Rem's unease, Daniels guessed the obvious. "She's using that baby to manipulate you, isn't she?"

Rem played with his napkin. "I think you mean my baby."

"I keep reminding you…you don't know that it's yours."

Rem set the napkin down. "I think it is, and that means I have to consider Chloe's safety."

Daniels bit back his automatic reply that Rem should wait and see first but Allison had obviously made headway into the battlefield of his partner's mind. Thinking about how to push Allison back into the trenches, he faced Rem. "I see you're calling her Chloe, too."

"That's her name."

Daniels nodded. "What does Allison want from you?"

Rem interlaced his fingers and set his hands on the table. He studied them.

"You might as well tell me. We'll honor the agreement and have an honest discussion. The kicker is going to be agreeing to a course of action."

"I don't think you're going to like what I'm thinking."

"Then this will be our first test. To see if it can withstand some tough choices and disagreements." He eyed the time, aware of Lozano's thirty-minute warning. "So?"

Rem paused, closed his eyes, and opened them. "Allison told me she wanted to make a deal."

"What deal?"

"About Chloe." He clenched his fingers together and paled some more. "I agree not to testify against Allison, and she'll sign all her parental rights over to me."

Daniels couldn't prevent his intake of breath. "Rem, I hope—"

"She said if I testify, Chloe will never be safe. If Allison's convicted, she'll make sure that her loyal followers stay in touch with me and Chloe, and she can't be responsible for what they might do. And if she's acquitted, she'll take Chloe and raise her on her own. And if I fight for custody, she'll either disappear or find ways to keep Chloe from me, and she'll tell Chloe things about me that won't exactly portray me as an upstanding dad."

Getting a better idea of what Rem was dealing with, Daniels slumped into his seat. "I get the picture."

"If I back off and get Allison released, she'll leave Chloe with me, sign over custody and I'll never have to see her again. Said she's really not the mom type anyway."

Daniels stifled a curse. Allison had indeed had a plan. She'd used Oswald's name to dig her claws further into Rem. "If you don't testify, Kate will subpoena you."

"Just because I'm on the stand doesn't mean I have to say anything."

Daniels set his jaw. His partner was seriously considering not prosecuting Allison. "You do that, you'll ruin your reputation and risk your career."

"If I raise Chloe, I'd have to leave the force anyway."

Stunned, Daniels took a steady breath, but his heart thumped. "I can tell you've thought this through."

"All day, outside of our talk with Fry."

Daniels' mind raced. "Would you at least give it more than a few hours? There's no rush to make this decision."

Rem put his head in his hands.

"And you have to consider the possibility that Chloe isn't yours. What happens then?"

Rem ran his hands through his hair and sat up. "Then I guess I'm out of a job, raising somebody else's kid." He chuckled sadly. "Hell. I don't know."

Daniels took a second to think. After a pause, he took a deep breath. "Can I ask you something?"

"I'm surprised you think I could stop you."

Daniels debated how to word his question. "I can see you're attached to this child, but I'm worried you're in too deep. I understand you think she's yours but if you're wrong, you're setting yourself up for big disappointment. Don't you think you should hold off on any decisions until you know for sure?"

Rem stared for a second and then sighed. "My cousin Selma and her husband Serge...they've been trying for years to have a kid. They've tried everything. She's gotten pregnant a few times but has never made it to term." He eyed the table. "I told you my mom had the same issue. She miscarried twice before me and three times after. I was the lucky one that made it."

"I remember." Daniels waited to hear more.

Rem shrugged. "I don't know. I guess in my addled brain, after Jennie and, well, everything else, I'm…I can't help but wonder if this is my only shot."

Surprised, Daniels raised a brow. "You think you can't have kids with anyone else?"

"I'm thinking the odds may be slim." He raised a hand when Daniels opened his mouth to argue. "And I know what you're going to say. That I'm overthinking, but I'm not sure I am. If Margaret isn't caught, I don't think I'm willing to take the risk. If this kid is mine, I have to take care of her. And by not fighting for her now, I feel I'm not doing my job. And I realize she may not be mine, but if that turns out to be true, then I think I can handle that better than if I stay detached and then discover she is mine and I didn't do enough to protect her."

Daniels marveled at Rem's capacity for compassion under such difficult circumstances. "You never cease to amaze me, partner."

"I don't know that I'm doing anything special. It's just none of this is Chloe's fault. Someone needs to look after her and right now the only person doing that is me."

"I can appreciate that." Daniels paused. "Can I at least offer a counter argument to this situation?"

"Based on our agreement, I don't have a choice."

Daniels was thankful for that much. "What if Allison's lying about her offer? What if, after all you've suffered, you refuse to testify and she's freed, but then she doesn't turn over her parental rights. What then?"

Rem pushed the remaining chips around on his plate. "I hunt her down and kill her. Is that an option?"

"Not if you want to raise Chloe."

"What if…uh…I ask Kate to delay? Make the trial happen after the baby's born?"

"Considering how these things go, it's likely to get delayed anyway. But DNA tests take time and Allison will still have to give her consent. And you know how well that's gone so far."

"If she's claiming I'm the father, she'll have to consent eventually."

"She will, but you know she'll make it as difficult as possible."

Looking defeated, Rem crumpled his napkin. "I doubt Allison will go for me stalling anyway." He shook his head. "Delaying will only make it worse."

"You can't trust her, Rem."

Rem shot out a hand. "What choice do I have? What happens when I testify, and she's convicted? Do I go on the run with Chloe to protect her from Allison's goons? Or if Allison's acquitted? Do I have to fight to see my kid if I even see her at all? And deal with Allison's lies about me?"

Daniels took a second to collect himself. "Listen to me. You are getting way ahead of yourself. You just spoke to Allison this morning and the trial is three months away. When we go upstairs, you're going to have to flip back to cop mode and pick up the hunt for Oswald who will likely kill again tomorrow. Give yourself some time to figure this out. Allison's not going anywhere, and neither is Chloe. Let's catch Oswald first and then discuss what's next."

Rem swallowed and stared at the tabletop. "I've been in a state of shock ever since I left the jail. I have no idea what to do but I'm coming to the uncomfortable conclusion that Allison's going to win this war."

"She's not winning anything. Not yet at least." Daniels hardened his tone. "She's won some battles, but we're not done fighting. I don't care what it takes, but that lady is not going to get away with her crimes. No matter what she threatens." Rem didn't look convinced. "Just hang in there. Focus on Oswald Fry. That should help take your mind off Allison. Once we get through the next few days, we'll talk again." He paused. "We can take it to Kate, too. Maybe this little stunt will sink Allison even deeper into the pit."

"There were no recording devices in that room. And she told me that if I tell anyone, she'll deny it. It's her word against mine."

"That may not be as easy as she thinks, but we'll ask Kate."

Rem groaned. "Can we hold off on telling anyone else? At least for now?"

Daniels nodded. "Of course. We'll wait until we catch Oswald, and then go from there." He checked his watch. "We have to go or Lozano's going to come looking for us."

Still pale, but looking more at ease, Rem nodded. "Yeah. I know." He swept some crumbs into his palm and dropped them onto his plate. "I guess the good news is that our agreement passed its first test."

"So far, so good." Daniels wondered how well the agreement would hold up if Rem chose to free Allison to protect Chloe, because Daniels damn sure wasn't going to agree to that.

Rem stood, grabbed his plate, and put it in the trash. He held his donut. "I'm going to grab a to-go container."

"At least you plan to eat it. That's a good sign." He stood and threw his own plate into the trash.

"Considering we're going to have another late night, it will probably be dinner." He turned.

"Hey," said Daniels.

Rem looked back.

"We're going to figure this out."

Rem hesitated, then nodded. "Yeah. Sure." He turned and headed toward the counter.

Wishing he could return to the jail and tell Allison exactly what he thought about her and her heinous offer, Daniels headed toward the stairs to wait for his partner.

Chapter Twenty-Nine

PHYSICALLY AND MENTALLY EXHAUSTED, Rem entered his house. He shut off the alarm, closed the door and reset it. Moving on autopilot, he dropped his keys onto the front table. Trying to make himself move after a crazy afternoon and night of following up on leads that led nowhere, his plan was to get a quick bite of food and go to bed.

Thinking that the only good thing about the tip line was it effectively took his mind off of Allison, he headed into his kitchen. He opened his fridge and stared. Several seconds passed before he realized he wasn't doing anything, and he shut the fridge. Then he stood for a second, thinking. Should he eat or sleep? Sack out in front of the TV? Checking his watch, he noted he had to be back at work in nine hours. Tomorrow would be another long day, especially if Oswald struck again.

Knowing he needed food, he turned to get a glass of water and stopped when he saw his coffee pot in his sink. Confused, he walked over to it and picked it up. While Rem tended to be a slob in most areas, when it came to his coffee machine, he was fastidious about keeping it clean. After he had his morning coffee, he'd clean out the filter and rinse the pot. He liked having it ready to go when he wanted to make more. He'd cleaned it that morning and returned the pot to its base. Or had he?

He tried to think, but it was all a blur. Assuming he must have left it in the sink after rinsing it, he returned it to the machine, but sat and stared at it. Something nudged at him, and a chill traveled up his spine. He walked to the counter, trying to put together whatever was trying to take shape in his weary brain when his doorbell rang.

Startled out of his thoughts, he told himself he was just tired and over-thinking everything. He went to the door and looked out the peephole. Kevin, his neighbor, stood on the porch, holding a bag.

Rem turned off the alarm and opened the door.

"Hey," said Kevin. "I saw you drive up. Obviously, you've had a long day."

Rem ran a hand over his face. "It's been a rough one."

"I won't take much time then, but I thought I'd bring you some of these." He held up the bag.

"I hope to God that's food."

Kevin smiled. "Mrs. Wilson paid me a visit this afternoon. This time she brought me blueberry muffins. I guess I'm ranking higher on the charts. Or the more likely scenario is she saw the argument between me and Nancy the other night, and she just needed a reason to get the scoop."

"My guess is it's the latter. Told you she was nosy."

"She gave me a dozen. There's no way I'm going to eat a dozen, and Nancy won't touch them. They're carbs which are the devil's food." He shook his head. "I remember you said these were your favorite, so I brought you some." He raised the bag.

Rem almost burst into tears. "Kevin, you're my new best friend. Don't tell Daniels." He took the bag, imagining digging into a muffin with a glass of milk and then going to bed. "Thank you."

"I thought you might appreciate it."

Rem noted the car in Kevin's driveway. "Nancy back from her trip?"

Kevin glanced behind him. "Yeah. She got home a couple of hours ago. We've actually been civil to each other."

"That's good."

Kevin put his hands in his jacket pockets. "I've been thinking about what you said the other night about your partner's advice. About being happy?"

Rem nodded, wondering again about his own decision regarding Allison. "Any help?"

Kevin shuffled his feet. "I'm going to talk to Nancy. Tell her that unless we get counseling, I think we should separate."

Rem put his hand on the doorframe. "That's a big decision."

"I know. But it's the right one."

"What do you think she'll say?"

Kevin shrugged. "Guess we'll find out. You hear another screaming match out on the lawn, you'll know how it went."

Rem recalled his talk with Daniels. "Maybe you two should agree on some ground rules before you talk. Agree to discuss it with calm heads before making any decisions."

Kevin pursed his lips. "It's a good idea. We could use a good adult conversation." He chuckled. "Maybe you should give relationship advice."

Rem couldn't help but laugh. "Believe me, Kevin. I'm the last person who should be giving any advice. If you knew the shit I was dealing with..." he scoffed, "...I suspect you'd ignore me completely."

Kevin sighed. "I guess we all have our issues, don't we?"

"I guess so."

Kevin half-smiled. "I'll spare us both from any philosophical discussions then. We'll save them for when we have time. You enjoy the muffins."

"They may all be gone by morning. Thanks again."

"You bet. Have a nice night."

"And good luck with your talk with Nancy."

Kevin looked back and headed down the stairs. "Thanks. I'm going to need it. Good night."

"Night."

Desperate for a muffin and sleep, Rem shut the door.

The next day was a whirlwind of activity. Rem and Daniels and anyone else Lozano could pull in helped to work through the leads that had been generated after the news had aired Oswald's photo. Although the incoming tips had slowed from the original onslaught the previous day, there were still plenty to follow up on.

Tired and anxious, Daniels noted the time. "This day is rushing by. Oswald is due to strike again."

"Maybe. Maybe not." Rem sat back in his seat after hanging up with a woman who'd sworn she'd seen a man matching Oswald's description at her daughter's school. Only problem was the man was pushing sixty and overweight. Rem had thanked her, hung up, and crossed her name off the list. "Keep in mind, Oswald's jobless now. He had to strike in the afternoons because he had to teach during the day."

"So, you think he may have already killed his next victim?" asked Daniels.

"Don't know. Or he'll strike this evening."

"Anybody hear from Penny Bartolo?"

"She's holed up with a family member and Lozano put a patrol car outside her house for today. I'd say she's safe, which means someone else isn't."

Daniels closed a folder. "This is ridiculous. We're not getting anywhere. Nobody's seen a thing."

Rem propped his foot on his desk. "I think he's disguising himself. His school ID and driver's license photo don't match the guy in the video at Gina's apartment."

"He had to disguise himself at Gina's," said Daniels. "He knew there'd be cameras."

"If he could do it then, then he could still be doing it, which is why no one's seen him."

"What about his car? Nobody's seen it either."

Rem fiddled with a pencil. "He didn't drive to the school. Why?"

"I don't know." Exasperated, Daniels stood and picked up his mug. "I'm going to grab some coffee. You want a warmup?"

"Sure. Thanks." Rem stared off. "Maybe he didn't want anyone at the school to see his car."

Daniels filled his cup. "Why not?"

"Maybe someone might recognize it?"

"Who?"

Rem swiveled in his seat toward Daniels. "Maybe Marjorie?"

Daniels raised a brow. "You think Marjorie saw his car at some point? Away from the school?" He set his cup down and picked up Rem's.

"It's possible."

Daniels added more coffee to Rem's mug. "So, Oswald's been hanging out with either Moira or her husband, or the daycare teachers?"

"Are any of them dangerous?"

"Not particularly, although Mandy at the daycare can make J.P. eat his carrots. She's kinda scary."

"It's worth considering."

Daniels added cream and sugar. "I'll send Marjorie a pic of the car. See if she knows it from somewhere." He handed Rem his mug.

"Thanks." Rem took the coffee from Daniels and swiveled back to face his desk. He took a sip. "What about looking for whoever tipped Oswald off at the school? Someone told him we were coming."

Daniels sat. "Any idea who?"

Rem groaned. "Let's think about it. Who knew Allison was planning to tell me Oswald's name?"

Daniels put his coffee down. "There's the obvious. You, me, Lozano, Kate and Measy."

"You think it could be Measy?" asked Rem.

"That would mean he knows Oswald, which means Allison put him in touch with Oswald. And there lies our problem."

"Which is?"

"If Allison told Measy, she could have told anyone. A guard. Another inmate. Someone on a phone call. Our snitch could be anybody, and if they were watching you and knew you were on your way to see Allison, there's no telling who it could be, never mind proving it."

Rem huffed. "Well, it was worth a thought." He leaned back in his chair. "Nothing from Oswald's mom?"

"Nothing. I'll call her again." Daniels flipped through some papers. "What do you think about Gina's memoirs? Should we force ourselves to go through her notebooks one more time?"

Rem made a face. "We've been tortured enough. I thought it would be hard enough reading about D'Mato, but the level of minutiae Gina goes into, I think I'd rather read about Victor." He sat forward. "Did she really need to tell us when she got up in the morning, what she bought when she went to the grocery store and how the gas station attendant flirted with her? It was like reading a Lewis and Clark inventory list for their expedition across the country."

"Don't remind me," said Daniels with a sigh. "It was more a Gina autobiography instead of a secret look into the mind of a dangerous cult and its leader."

"And there was no mention of a bluebird necklace, so I say no. We're done with the notebooks."

"Agreed." Daniels yawned and sipped his coffee. "But you know what that means."

Rem yawned, too. "Yeah. I know. Back to the list of leads."

Blinking to stay awake, Daniels picked up his cell to text Marjorie at the same time as Rem picked up his desk phone to make another call.

Mikey entered Mason's house, turned off the alarm, waved at Mason as he drove off, and closed and locked the door. She dropped her purse onto the couch, slid her jacket off and tossed it next to her purse.

She headed into the kitchen and opened the pantry door. Seeing the cake mix and icing, she pulled it out and set it on the counter. She'd planned to make Valerie's birthday cake the day before, but she and Mason had stayed at SCOPE longer than expected and by the time they'd come home, she didn't want to bake, and he didn't want to shop. So, they'd decided to leave work a little early today. Mason had dropped her at the house to start baking and he'd headed to the grocery store to pick up what he needed for dinner. Trick would be there in a couple of hours with the drinks and Valerie was expected to arrive not long after that.

Looking forward to a night where she could get her mind off Rem and Kyle, she found the mixer, pulled it out of the cabinet and set it on the counter. Recalling her morning coffee with Kyle, she stopped and sighed. It had been a difficult conversation, but she'd been honest with him, and had told him about her feelings for Remalla. To his credit, he'd been kind and understanding although hopeful she'd feel differently one day. He didn't push it though, agreed to remain friends, and they'd left the shop on good terms. Mikey had hoped he would continue to work at SCOPE, and he had no plans to stop, which pleased her and certainly pleased Mason.

Glad the talk had gone well, the rest of the day had passed uneventfully, and they'd all left a little early as planned to prepare for the birthday party.

Mikey read the back of the box. As much as making the cake from scratch appealed to her, she didn't have the energy and Mason had said a box cake would be fine. Valerie would be happy no matter what Mikey made.

Feeling a little tired and wanting to clean up before everyone arrived, she eyed the time and determined she had a few minutes to rinse off in the shower, change clothes and then make the cake. She set the oven to preheat and headed to her bedroom.

After getting cleaned up and dressed, she eyed herself in the mirror. She ran her hands through her hair to smooth it and noted her jeans were a little looser. It didn't surprise her because her appetite hadn't been its usual robust strength, but she planned to make up for that tonight. Mason was making his famous chicken tortilla soup with guacamole and queso and Trick was making the margaritas. Her stomach rumbled.

Guessing she looked good enough, she thought of Rem and wondered what he was doing, although it wasn't a difficult guess. He was looking for Oswald Fry. She'd seen the photo on the news, and had studied it, ensuring she didn't know the man, but he didn't ring any bells. Hopefully, someone out there knew something and would contact the police. She had to wonder if capturing Oswald would lead to Margaret's capture as well, since it seemed they knew each other.

Saying a small prayer that it would, Mikey left her bedroom and returned to the kitchen. She grabbed the cake box and read the back of it. A movement in the living room caught her eye, and she leaned to look and stopped cold. Terror sliced through her, and she dropped the box. A man was standing in the living room, and he matched the description of Oswald Fry.

Rem hung up on another pointless phone call. "How hard is this? This guy wanted to report about his missing dog and since no one would help him, he called the tip line instead."

Daniels looked up from his notes. "The bigger question is who forwarded that lead? They should have directed him to animal control."

Rem leaned his head against the back of the chair. "Probably someone as tired as me."

"The good news is the leads are slowing."

"They'll pick up when they run the picture again on the news." Rem checked his watch. "Which will be soon."

"Yeah. I know." Daniels rubbed his eyes. "One of them is bound to come through. Titus and Georgios left to follow up on a possible sighting."

"Mel and Garcia are checking out a few, too. I guess we'll cross our fingers and toes." He massaged his pounding head.

The squad doors opened, and a tall man with dark hair and dark eyes walked in. "Hey," said Rem. "Isn't that Ronald Rodriguez, Gina's brother?"

Daniels turned in his seat. "It is." He stood. "Ronald?"

Rem stood, too.

Ronald saw them and came over. "Hey. Sorry to bother you." He held out a hand.

Daniels shook it, along with Rem. "It's no bother at all," said Daniels.

"How's Gina doing?" asked Rem.

Ronald shook his head. "Not great. I haven't seen much progress, but the doctors seem hopeful. She's still alive, at least."

"The doctors know what they're doing. She's in good hands," said Rem. "Hopefully, she'll come around soon."

"I hope." He stared off and looked a little lost. "I don't mean to bother you, but I saw the news, and I was wondering if you'd made any progress finding Gina's attacker?"

Daniels' face fell. "We're working on it, but there's nothing to report right now."

"We've got plenty of leads, though," said Rem. "We're expecting one of them to pan out. They'll run the photo on the news again, so the pressure is on the man who did this. We'll find him."

"You...uh...you don't think he'll come after Gina again, do you?" asked Ronald. "In the hospital?"

"No," said Daniels. "We don't expect that. Why? Have you seen anything suspicious?"

He shook his head. "No. I haven't. I just want to be sure."

"Oswald Fry stays in the shadows, and he certainly isn't about to walk through a hospital with his face all over the news." Rem tipped his head. "But if you see something or are worried, let us know. We may be able to assign someone outside her door."

Ronald nodded. "Yeah. Okay. I'm sure you're right." He paused. "I guess she's not much of a threat to him anyway, if she's unconscious."

Rem had thought the same but hadn't voiced it.

"As soon as we know something, we'll tell you," said Daniels. "I'm sorry we don't know more. It's hardest on the family members, I think, who have to wait and see."

"You can feel pretty helpless," said Rem.

"You sure can." Ronald put his hands on his hips and studied the ground. A few seconds passed and he popped his head up. "I'll get out of here and let you get back to work. I'm sure you have a lot to do."

"It's fine," said Daniels. "Can we get you a water or some coffee?" He gestured toward the machine.

Ronald waved. "No. I'm good. Thanks. I should go."

"Feel free to call us if you have any questions," said Rem. "We're happy to help in any way we can." He felt for Gina's brother, knowing how hard it was to lose someone you loved. He hoped Gina would pull through for Ronald's sake.

"I appreciate that." Ronald turned to go but stopped. "I almost forgot." He reached into his inner jacket pocket and pulled out a folded spiral notebook. "I wanted to bring this to you in case it might help." He held it out. "It's one of Gina's notebooks for a supposed book she was writing. She wanted me to read it."

Rem groaned in his head. Not another notebook. "That's great. Thanks."

Daniels took it from Ronald. "We'll read through it."

"I don't know if it will tell you anything," said Ronald. "To be honest, it's pretty dull, but I got through it. I kept my opinion to myself though." He chuckled softly. "Gina would have had my head if I'd told her the truth."

Daniels chuckled, too. "We get it."

Rem smiled softly. "I don't suppose it mentions a bluebird necklace?"

Ronald's face tensed and he frowned. "As a matter of fact, it does."

Rem stilled, unsure he'd heard right.

"Gina talks about a bluebird necklace in here?" Daniels waved the notebook.

Ronald nodded. "Yes. Is that important?"

"It is." Rem made eye contact with Daniels. "You remember what Gina said about it?" His heart rate picked up.

Daniels started to flip through the pages.

"Uhm..." Ronald stared off. "It belonged to that Victor guy. Gina took it from him."

Rem looked over Daniels' shoulders as he looked through the notebook. "Why'd she take it from Victor?" asked Rem.

Ronald scoffed. "She was jealous, as usual. Victor was going to give it as a gift, and it pissed Gina off."

"Gift to who?" asked Rem. His hope rose that they were about to learn the next victim's name.

"Who do you think?" said Ronald. "Gina's rival. Mikey Redstone."

Chapter Thirty

MIKEY DIDN'T MOVE, BUT her mind raced. Within a split second, she determined that her escape paths were cut off. Oswald blocked the front door, and he could get to her before she reached the side or garage door. The guest bathroom was her safest option and her best chance at survival. Her heart and adrenaline racing, she fought the urge to scream and told herself to wait and see what he would do.

He stood there watching her, and she stared back. He looked much like the photo they'd shared on TV except he didn't have glasses. He had unkempt, wavy hair down to his shoulders, a beard and mustache, bushy eyebrows, and a hoodie. The gloves he wore scared her the most.

"Mikey Redstone," he said. "I've heard a lot about you."

Struggling to remain calm, she spoke. "You're Oswald." Despite his relaxed demeanor, something about him seemed off, which Mikey figured had something to do with him being a murderer.

"I know your sister," he said.

Rigid, Mikey eyed her path to the bathroom. "How is she?"

"She's angry."

"Obviously. What's she angry about?"

"A lot of things."

Mikey took a small step toward the living room, which got her closer to her destination. Needing to keep him talking, she tried to keep her voice even, but it still shook. "Why is she angry at me?"

"Family stuff. Victor stuff."

"Is that why those other people died? Because Marge is mad?" She took another sidestep.

"Yes. I'm mad, too. Those people betrayed her and Victor. They deserved to die."

"What did they do to you?"

"It's not about me. Stella told Victor his future was bright, and he was dead a month later. If that stupid woman had known what she was doing, Victor might still be alive. And Reynaldo. Took money from Victor and then betrayed him. Looked the other away when Victor needed him. And Gina was writing lies about Margaret and Victor. And you know what Dexter was going to do. Betray those who took care of him."

"Dexter was testifying against Allison. She killed Victor."

"There are other ways to deal with Allison."

Scared enough for tears to fill her eyes, Mikey continued to talk. "Killing people serves no purpose. It doesn't bring Victor back."

He smiled. "It does serve a purpose. They helped me, just like you will."

Her hands began to tremble, and she clenched her fingers together. "How do I help you?"

"You'll sustain me. I just need a few more days, and then I'll be done." He opened and closed his fingers, and Mikey could see his hands shaking, too. "This will all be over," he added. "And your sister will be happy."

Mikey blinked back her tears. "You're going to kill me, like the others?" She took another step.

"I asked Margaret for her permission, and she said yes." His posture shifted. "I asked about your brother, too, but she has other plans for him. Especially since he'll be vulnerable from grieving you."

Mikey swallowed. She had to survive this. "And what happens in the next few days?"

Oswald narrowed his eyes. "I've made my own plans out of necessity. Your sister won't be happy about my choice, but it's personal. The police are getting close so after you, I'll take care of my last victim, and then I can leave with no regrets."

Mikey, fighting not to panic, took another step. "Who's your next victim?"

He didn't answer.

Her body trembling, Mikey prayed she'd escape. "How did you meet my sister?"

Oswald moved for the first time. He took his own step toward Mikey. "She befriended me. She was nice to me. When no one else was. She took me in and introduced me to Victor, who valued my gifts."

"What are your gifts?" A tear escaped and slipped down her cheek.

He grinned. "You're about to find out."

"Oswald, think about what you're doing. Please." The last word came out as a whisper.

"I promise. It will be fast. I'll take from you quickly. You probably won't even feel it when I put my hands around your neck. Then I'll mark you with my sign and place you comfortably on the ground. It's my way of recognizing your offering and thanking you for your sacrifice."

Mikey sucked in a constricted breath. She had to move and move fast. If she could somehow surprise him and get a slight head start, maybe she could get to the bathroom before he touched her.

They stared a moment longer and Mikey's phone rang from her purse on the couch. Oswald glanced at it and Mikey ran.

Daniels ran out of Lozano's office as Rem slammed his phone down with a curse. "No answer."

"I told Lozano. He's sending people. Let's go." Daniels ran out of the squad room with Rem. They raced down the stairs and out of the building to Rem's car. They jumped in and Rem started the car and squealed out of the parking lot.

"I'm calling Mason." Daniels typed a number while Rem drove at high speeds, his siren and lights on. Cars honked and skidded to a stop as they passed.

Rem whispered something behind the wheel as Mason answered and Daniels asked about Mikey and told him what was going on.

Another car braked hard and honked as Rem raced through a red light. Daniels hung up and put his hand on the armrest. "Careful, partner. We don't want to get dead before we make it there."

"What did Mason say?"

"He's at the grocery. He dropped Mikey at home. He's on his way back to the house." He glanced at his pale partner.

"Try Mikey again." Rem turned onto a side street.

Daniels called her. It rang several times. "No answer."

"Shit."

"Patrols are on their way. They may already be there."

Rem picked up his whispering, and Daniels listened, finally hearing his partner's quiet mantra.

"Please don't be dead. Please don't be dead. Please don't be dead."

Daniels said a quiet prayer that they'd get to Mikey in time to save not only her, but his partner, too. He gripped the armrest again as his partner took another squealing turn.

Mikey raced across the living room as Oswald broke from his stance and charged her. She almost made it, but his hand caught her waist. She stumbled and he held on and threw her against the mantel. The pictures toppled and fell, and Mikey fought to escape. Her self-defense training course from a few months prior came back to her, and as Oswald shoved her back and lifted his arms to her neck, she raised hers and brought her elbow down, knocking his hands away. She swiveled out of his grasp, then brought her palm forward and smashed it into Oswald's face. Falling back, Oswald cried out and blood gushed from his nose. He blocked her route to the bathroom, though, and before he could come at her again, Mikey kicked him in the midsection. He tripped over a cord and fell into the side table. The lamp fell and crashed to the floor, and Mikey darted for the bathroom, but Oswald was quick, and he reached for her foot and tripped her.

She fell to the floor and hit her knee. Pain rippled up her leg, but she kept moving. Oswald tried to drag her, but she kicked out at him, and he let her go. After getting to her feet, she raced into the bathroom, slammed the door shut on him and turned all three locks. Mason and Trick's secret project from the previous week had been to install a fortified door and locks to create a panic room. Mikey had scoffed when she'd learned about it, but now sobbed with gratitude.

Breathing fast, she slumped to the floor as Oswald screamed at her from the other side of the door. He banged on it, and she shrieked and opened the cabinet beneath the sink. Seeing the gun and the phone, she pulled them both out and scooted backwards into the bathtub, while Oswald yelled obscenities from the other side of the door.

Trying to think straight, she gripped the phone, but she shook so hard, she could barely dial nine-one-one. Oswald banged on the door and Mikey shouted at him that she was calling the police and had a gun. The operator answered and Mikey, trying to speak coherently, told her what was happening and to send help.

Failing to calm herself, Mikey shook as tears slid down her face and her heart pounded. It had gone quiet on the other side of the door and Mikey prayed Oswald had given up and left. The operator had told her to remain on the line and Mikey wished she could call Mason or Rem. Terrified, she sat in the tub and listened to the silence.

Then one of the locks began to turn.

Still whispering his prayer that Mikey was alive, Rem turned onto a residential street. He blew through a stop sign and raced to the next turn. His tires spun and caught as he took it and driving down the street, he could see swirling lights. He squealed to a stop outside Mason's house. He and Daniels jumped out of the car and seeing the front door open, Rem rushed inside.

He saw Mikey's purse on the couch, the broken lamp and fallen pictures. An officer stood outside the bathroom door.

"Ma'am? It's the police," he said.

Rem raced over. "Where is she?"

Daniels talked to the other officer in the house. "What happened?" he asked.

The first officer pointed at the bathroom. "I think she's in there."

Rem banged on the door. "Mikey? It's Rem. Are you there?"

The second officer answered Daniels. "We just got here. The front door was unlocked, and we made entry. We found the place like this."

Rem knocked again, praying desperately that Mikey was inside and alive. "Mikey? Can you hear me? Open the door."

He waited, his heart pounding against his chest, and he had the awful image that they'd get the door open, and Mikey would be dead inside with the killer's note and a photo beside her body. Trying to keep his fear under control, he reached for the knob when he heard a lock turn, and then another.

The door opened and Mikey, her face white and tear-stained, flew into his arms. Relief coursed through him, and he held her tight. "It's okay," he said, his own emotions rising. "You're safe. I've got you." He felt her body tremble against his. "Are you hurt?"

Her breath caught but she shook her head. Her fingers dug into his shirt, and she spoke into his shoulder. "Oswald. It was...was him." A sob broke free and she buried her face in his neck.

Daniels walked over. "I'll take the scene."

Grateful, Rem nodded, and he whispered to Mikey. "C'mon. Let's get you out of here." His arms around her, he guided her out of the house. Her legs were wobbly and he half-way had to hold her up. After getting her outside, he looked for a place for her to sit when another car screeched to a stop outside the house.

Mason jumped out. "Mikey," he yelled, running over. He raced up the front walk and Mikey lifted her head. Tears spilled over her lashes, and she let go of Rem and grabbed onto her brother. Mason closed his eyes and held her. "Are you okay?" he asked.

Her head bobbed up and down, and her arms went around him.

"Thank God," said Mason. He eyed Rem. "Thank God."

His own gut-twisting terror lifting, Rem whispered his own prayer of gratitude.

Chapter Thirty-One

OSWALD FRY PULLED OFF his bloody shirt. Studying himself in the mirror, he looked for any other injuries beyond his damaged nose. Satisfied his nose had taken the worst of it, he turned on the water and splashed his face, cleaning the blood from his cheeks and neck. After toweling dry, he checked his injury. His nose was not broken but he worried he'd have bruising around his eyes. If he did, he'd have to apply makeup but hoped, with his dwindling amount of time, that it wouldn't be needed. His fingers shook and his body ached. Without the energy he'd anticipated from Mikey's death, his body was weakening. He'd expected to have enough strength for three more days, but now he'd have to shorten his timetable.

Digging into his other pocket, he muttered a curse when he didn't find his paper and pen, or the flower, but then realized it didn't matter. The photo remained, and he pulled it out, seeing the picture of Mikey and Victor on the beach, beside a bonfire. No longer needing it, he threw it in the trash.

A sliver of pain moved through him, and he gasped. His doctors had given him less than a year, and that had been sixteen months earlier. He'd survived this long without treatment, just on his own ability to fuel himself with the energy of others. The need had increased over the last few months and last week's accomplishments had provided him with enough strength to bring Margaret's wishes to fruition before he took his final breath.

There was one more job to complete, though, and it had nothing to do with Margaret. After losing his battle with Mikey Redstone, his plan to take his last victim in three days wouldn't work. With his declining physical state, his final task would have to be done tomorrow. Shirtless, he wrapped his bloody clothes into a ball and walked into his bedroom. He opened the drawer beside the bed and admired Stella's bracelet, Reynaldo's ring, Gina's arrowhead, and the seashell he'd taken from Dexter's shelf. Mikey's mother's bracelet lay beside it. He picked it up and held it.

Thinking of his final victim, and perhaps the most important one, he returned the bracelet and closed the drawer. With a shaky hand, he picked up the phone to make his call.

Daniels drank the rest of his water and set the cup in Rem's sink. Rem entered the kitchen, holding an empty glass. He set it in the sink beside Daniels' cup.

"How's Mikey?" asked Daniels.

"Doing better," said Rem. "Mason is with her, trying to get her to relax so she'll sleep."

Daniels nodded. "How's Mason?"

"I think he's more shook up than Mikey."

"It was a close call."

Rem released a deep breath. The color had returned to his face and his tension had eased. "Don't remind me."

"How are you holding up?" asked Daniels.

"A little shaky myself. But better knowing she's okay." He leaned against the kitchen counter. "What'd Lozano say?"

"They've checked the area, but no Oswald. There's blood at the scene, though, so Mikey got a few blows in. That, along with the black marker we found, means we have his fingerprints and DNA."

"What about that dried sunflower?"

Daniels recalled seeing it on the floor at the crime scene. Obviously, in Oswald's scuffle with Mikey, his paper and pen, along with the flower, had fallen out of his pocket. "My guess is it's the clue he planned to leave behind to point to the next victim."

"So he's going after someone else, but we don't have a timeline on this one."

"Nope. He never got a chance to leave his note."

"Thank God."

"Mikey said he told her he had one more victim and then he'd be done."

Rem cursed. "Which means if we don't find him before he kills again, he'll disappear, and we may never catch him."

Daniels stretched his tight neck. "It's possible."

"Plus, he's been working with Margaret."

"To fulfill her wishes."

Rem glanced over at him. "He told Mikey that Margaret wouldn't approve of the next one. That it was personal. What do you think that means?"

Daniels tried to think, but his mind was fuzzy with fatigue. "I don't know, but I'm glad you're all three in the same house tonight."

"You want to stay? I can make up the couch. It's more comfortable than it looks."

"Thanks, but I'm going to head over to see Marjorie at her mom's and hopefully catch J.P. before bedtime." He checked his watch. "So, I should go."

"What time is it?"

"Almost eight-thirty."

Rem groaned. "It feels like it's midnight."

"It's been a long day."

Hearing footsteps on the stairs, Daniels looked to see Mason coming down them. He still wore his clothes, but he'd removed his boots and his shirt buttons were undone to reveal a white t-shirt beneath. He entered the kitchen, holding a crumb-laden plate.

"How's Mikey?" asked Rem.

"I think she's finally asleep," said Mason. He set the plate down. "I got her to eat the toast, so that's something."

"You should get some rest yourself," said Daniels.

Mason nodded. "I know, but I need to call Val. She didn't get much of a birthday and she's worried about me and Mikey."

"I think she'll be happy to celebrate later," said Daniels.

Mason closed his eyes. "I just can't stop thinking about how close it came with Mikey." He opened his eyes. "If we hadn't made those changes to the bathroom..."

"That was smart," said Rem. "And so was Mikey. She got Oswald talking and stalled for time. Plus, she got a few hits in herself before escaping into the bathroom. She's resourceful."

Mason crossed his arms and leaned against the fridge. "That she is. I sometimes wonder if she should have joined the Rangers."

"They would have been lucky to have her," said Daniels.

"I'm glad she's not hurt," said Rem. "Physically, at least."

"Her knee's banged up and bruised, but thankfully, that's it," said Mason.

Rem gestured toward the stairs. "I put fresh towels in the bathroom and fresh sheets on the beds, so you two should be comfortable."

"Thank you," said Mason. "We're fine. And thank you for letting us stay here."

"It's better than a hotel or a safe house or sleeping on Trick's floor," said Rem. "Plus, there's safety in numbers. You're helping me, too."

"Until Oswald's found, we have to assume none of us is safe," said Daniels.

"I realize we took the upstairs bedrooms," said Mason to Daniels. "Are you comfortable going home?"

Daniels nodded. "I'm going to see Marjorie and J.P. I'll stay with them tonight."

"Good," said Mason. "We should all have someone looking out for us after today." He shook his head. "Trick offered to stay outside in his car and watch Rem's house. I told him to go home and get some rest. We can talk tomorrow about what to do next."

"What happened tonight scared him, too," said Rem. "It's terrifying knowing your loved ones are in danger and there's little you can do about it." He put his hands in his pockets and studied the floor.

Daniels glanced at Mason who raised a brow. "That's true, Detective," said Mason. He sighed and rubbed his eyes. "I should call Val before I fall asleep myself."

"There's coffee and bread, and some peanut butter, but not much else in the house," said Rem, "if you get up first."

"Maybe I'll surprise you all in the morning, and bring bagels," said Daniels.

Rem perked up. "Don't forget the cream cheese."

"Perish the thought," said Daniels.

"Drive safe, Detective. And be careful," said Mason. "I'm going to head up and call my girlfriend."

"Tell her happy birthday," said Rem.

"I will." Mason left the kitchen. "Good night."

"Night," said Rem.

Mason walked up the stairs and disappeared into his room.

"I'm going to go," said Daniels.

"You sure you don't want to stay? Maybe have a night cap?"

Daniels noted Rem's worried tone. "I'm fine. Oswald isn't going to come after me."

"You sure? After what happened with Marjorie?"

Daniels hesitated.

"See?" said Rem, pointing. "It's possible."

Daniels found his jacket and slid it on. "I can't exclude the possibility but it's unlikely. I don't have the connection to Victor and Margaret that the other victims did. If anything, I should stay here to protect all of you."

Rem raised his brows. "The couch beckons."

Daniels checked that his phone was in his jacket pocket. "And he won't strike tonight. Not after what happened. He's licking his wounds. Besides, I won't be alone, and neither will you. And we know Oswald likes his solitude. Plus, I want to see my wife and kid."

Rem slumped. "Okay. You win. But call me when you get there." He walked to the door.

"I will." He joined Rem, but movement caught his eye and he spotted someone on the stairs. "But if you want to have that nightcap, you still can." He nodded to his right.

Rem turned to look. Mikey was at the top of the stairs with a blanket wrapped around her shoulders.

"I can't sleep," she said, pulling the blanket closer. "Did Mason go to bed?"

"He went to call Valerie," said Rem. "You want me to get him?"

"No." Mikey shook her head as she came down the stairs. "He's been attached to me since we left his place. And he needs to talk to Val."

Daniels looked between Rem and Mikey. "I'm heading out. I'll see you two tomorrow." He opened the door. "Good night, Mikey. Glad you're okay."

"Thanks. Me, too," said Mikey. "Good night."

"Uh...Uhm..." Rem stammered. "Just hold on a sec."

"What is it?" asked Daniels.

Rem glanced at Mikey. "You sure you don't want to try and sleep?"

Mikey, favoring her bad knee, made it down the stairs. "I can't relax. I just keep seeing him."

Rem paused. "Then have a seat on the couch. I'll get you some fresh ice for your knee. I'm just going to walk Daniels out first."

Mikey stared for a second before she nodded. "Okay."

Daniels stepped out with a nudge from Rem, and Rem closed the door.

Daniels shot a look at Rem. "You know I'm perfectly capable of walking to my car, although I appreciate the gesture."

"What am I supposed to do?" Rem looked back at the house.

"About what?"

"About Mikey?"

Daniels wondered if his partner had suffered a head injury at some point during the day. "Go get her an icepack."

"No, stupid. She's sitting on my couch. It's late and...and..."

"And what?"

Rem threw out a hand. "What am I supposed to say?"

"How about you open your mouth and let words come out."

"You know what I mean."

Daniels didn't understand. "Since when do you have a problem talking to women?"

"This isn't a woman. This is Mikey."

"Uh...I hate to break it to you, but Mikey is very much a woman."

"I know that." Rem snorted with impatience.

Daniels narrowed his eyes at his partner. "Am I supposed to know what you're trying to tell me?"

Rem whispered. "I just had a conversation with her about staying friends and not letting it go beyond that."

Daniels frowned. "What? Are you afraid she's going to jump your bones?"

Rem ran a hand through his hair. "No, you idiot."

"You're afraid you'll want her to jump your bones? Or do you want to make the first move?"

Rem blew out an impatient breath. "Why do I talk to you? No. I don't want that. I mean, certainly not now. Not after today. But I...I...just don't want it to seem like..."

"Like you want to jump her bones but not really? Or maybe sometime in the future when you get your shit together?"

Rem dropped his shoulders. "Forget it."

Daniels almost chuckled. "You're overthinking, as usual. I understand that after the conversation you had with her, you don't want to send mixed signals, but she's still your friend."

Rem nodded.

"And your friend has just had a hellish day. Oswald almost killed her. You know how that feels. So go talk to your friend, like you've done a million times before you ever had that silly conversation."

"It wasn't silly."

"Then we'll have to agree to disagree."

Rem hesitated. "You're right. I'm overthinking."

Daniels considered something else. "You could talk to her about Allison. Get Mikey's take on things."

Rem widened his eyes. "That's the last thing she'll want to talk about."

"How do you know? She's trying to get her mind off Oswald. That should do it."

"And give her another reason not to sleep?"

Daniels gestured toward the house. "She's your friend too, you know? She'd want you to confide in her. And it might help to discuss it with someone other than me."

"The last thing Mikey wants to hear about is Allison and the baby."

"Why?" asked Daniels. "You've already told Mikey you can't move beyond friendship, so what does Mikey care? It's not like the two of you have a future together. At least not a romantic one."

Rem stilled and held Daniels' look. His face fell. "Okay. I'll consider it."

"Good. Can I go now?"

Rem grunted. "Sure."

"Thank you." Daniels stepped off the porch and shot out a thumb. "Go be a friend."

Rem scowled at him. "Text me when you get there."

"Will do." Smiling to himself, Daniels got in his car and closed the door. *He is so going to lose this battle*, he muttered, before starting the car and driving away.

Chapter Thirty-Two

AFTER DANIELS DROVE OFF, Rem entered his house and closed and locked the door behind him. He set the alarm and saw Mikey sitting on his couch. The blanket was wrapped around her, and she held the remote, but the TV wasn't on. He walked over. "How's your knee?"

She put her sock-covered foot up on the coffee table and carefully stretched out her leg. "It hurts."

"I'll get your ice. You want some water?"

"Sure. And maybe something a little stronger from that stash beneath your sink."

He watched her fiddle with the remote. "Be right back." He went into the kitchen and put some ice in a plastic bag, then filled a glass with water. After finding two shot glasses, he opened his cabinet, pulled out a bottle of vodka and filled both. He set the bottle down and picked up the shot glasses along with the bag and water. He paused. *Just be her friend*, he thought, and carefully carried the items into the living room. He set it all on the coffee table.

"You missed your calling," said Mikey. "You should have been a server at a restaurant."

"It was my second choice after police officer. I probably should have stuck with server 'cause I think it pays better." He picked up the bag of ice and set it on her pajama-covered knee.

Mikey adjusted it. "Thanks."

Rem handed her a shot glass and sat beside her. She took it and he picked up his own. "To better days ahead," he said.

"We can only hope."

She clinked her glass to his and downed the vodka. Rem did the same. They both grimaced and set their glasses down.

"That should help us relax," said Rem, lying back against the cushions.

She resumed her fiddling with the TV remote.

"It actually works better if you hit the 'on' button," said Rem.

"Yeah. I know." She spoke softly. Rem had left a lamp on, and soft light reflected off her face.

"You want to talk about it?" asked Rem. He recalled his own reaction after being rescued and how off balance he'd felt afterward.

She gripped the remote. "I keep seeing him, you know? Standing there in the room, talking to me." Her knuckles turned white as she clenched the remote tighter. "He seemed almost normal, like what he was doing was no big deal." She paused. "I sensed his sadness and pain, though. He's messed up and doesn't even know how much."

Rem stayed quiet, letting her talk.

"I almost thought I could get through to him. That maybe he'd back off, and he'd...he'd leave. But then...his face changed, and I knew...I thought...I was going to die." She bit her lip. "That's when I ran, and he chased me." She sucked in a breath. "I was so scared." Her eyes filled and she sniffed.

Feeling his own angst and recalling his terror when he'd thought she was dead, Rem moved closer and put his arm around her. "You got away, though. You fought him off and survived."

Her head fell into the curve of his neck. "I...I just went on autopilot. Something else took over."

Rem rubbed her shoulder and rested his jaw on her head. "It's the survival instinct. You do what you have to do to stay alive."

Her voice caught. "I...I don't even recall getting into the bathroom. I just remember slamming the door and turning the locks, and him banging on the door, screaming at me."

Rem closed his eyes, wishing he'd been there to stop Oswald. He felt her pull on his shirt to dab her eyes. "You have a tenacious spirit," he said. "Your experience with Victor made you strong. Oswald had no idea what he was up against."

Mikey's shoulders shook and she cried against him. "I didn't want to die."

Rem sat with her while her emotions spilled over. A minute passed and she calmed. She fiddled with a button on his shirt. "I was sitting in the tub and talking to nine-one-one, and I thought of Mason...and you."

Rem's heart thumped. "You did?"

"I didn't want either of you to find me dead." She swiped at her cheek. "And I...I...wished I'd told you...that...that..."

Rem swallowed and pulled her closer. "What?"

She rolled her face into his shoulder. "That you're stupid."

Rem frowned. "I'm what?"

Mikey pushed back and looked up with her tear-stained face. "How could you say those things to me? At the station? You can't tell me that despite whatever feelings we have for each other that I should go off with Kyle. That's just stupid. And after what happened tonight, don't tell me that us staying away from each other is the answer. I was staying with Mason, for God's sake, and avoiding you, because that's what you wanted, and look what happened, you big oaf." She smacked him in the chest. "Your brilliant plan failed. I'm no safer either way." She used his shirt to wipe her nose. "Don't you see that?"

Rem tried to keep up with her argument. "Are you trying to tell me that since you almost died, that justifies us being together?"

"I'm trying to tell you that us staying away from each other makes no difference." She pushed the blanket off her shoulders.

"So, you think we should start seeing each other? With everything going on? With Allison and the baby? And Margaret?" He leaned to the side and grabbed a tissue from a box on an end table. "Here. In lieu of my shirt."

She took it and blew her nose. "I'm saying straight out that you and I like each other. We've both considered taking this beyond friendship, right?"

Not expecting her to take the conversation in this direction, Rem hesitated.

She smacked him again. "Would you stop avoiding this? I know the timing sucks and I know what we're both dealing with, but we should still discuss it."

"Mikey..." He sighed heavily. "I said what I said for a reason. And I stand by it. I still think it's better if we stay friends."

"Why?"

"Why?" His stomach twisted. "Look what happened to you today. I can't keep my head on straight and try and catch Oswald and Margaret and deal with Allison and a possible child if I'm constantly worried about you."

"You're already worried about me."

"Yes...I suppose...but..." Rem struggled with what to say. "but there's another layer when it comes to romance or...or..." He couldn't muster the courage to say *love*.

Mikey wiped her nose with the tissue. "You should know I told Kyle I don't have feelings for him. So you can stop telling me to go have a life with him."

"You did?"

"Of course, I did. As great as Kyle is, I don't want to be with him. He needed to know that so there wouldn't be any confusion."

Rem shook his head and eyed the ceiling, trying to sort through his own emotions. He thought of his discussion with Allison and its potential repercussions. "Mikey, I...I don't know if I can give you what you want."

She sat back against the couch. "Are you telling me you don't want to be with me?"

Rem set his jaw. Seeing her face in the lamplight, her eyes puffy and her cheeks red, he fought the urge to kiss her senseless. "No. I'm not saying that. But there are things I'm going to have to deal with that you shouldn't have to. I can't ask you to go where I may end up."

"You're talking about Allison, aren't you?"

He nodded.

"Can't you let me decide what I want to deal with?"

Rem cleared his throat and heard Daniels' voice in his head. *Tell her. Be honest.* He forced himself to speak. "I saw Allison yesterday."

She dropped her jaw. "You did? Why?"

He took a deep breath and told Mikey everything about his visit to the jail. "That's how I got Oswald's name. And why Marjorie is staying at her mom's."

Mikey studied her fingers. After a pause, she spoke. "Are you considering it? Allison's offer?"

"I'd be stupid not to."

"But Rem—"

"I know. I know. Daniels and I have already talked about this. I understand the consequences."

Mikey studied him and put an elbow on the back of the couch. "Have you already made up your mind?"

Rem shifted on the couch. "Daniels and I agreed to discuss it later, after we catch Oswald."

"That's not what I asked."

He looked away.

"You're going to do it, aren't you? You're going to do what she wants and not testify."

Rem sighed and closed his eyes. "I don't know what else to do."

Mikey didn't say a word.

His eyes still shut, Rem put an arm up on the couch and rested his forehead in his hand. "That's why I have even more reasons to be careful with you. I don't want to hurt you."

It was quiet and he felt her shift on the couch, then she resumed her position and came up close to him. She put her arms around him and returned her head to the hollow of his neck.

Surprised, and his throat tightening, he put his arms around her and hugged her back, wishing with all his heart that he didn't have this looming uncertainty and fragile future hanging over his head. "I'm sorry," he whispered. "I'd kiss you right now if it was the right thing to do."

Mikey squeezed him harder and turned her face into his neck. "You'll know when the time is right."

He felt her hot breath against his skin and almost moaned.

"This is all going to be okay," she said. "You'll see."

He ran a hand up her back and another to her head, where he pressed her closer. His body warmed with her against him, and he imagined running his fingers to her jaw and tipping her head back. Her lips would be so close to his.

Groaning, he gently pushed her shoulders back instead. "We're going to have to talk about something else or this is going to head in the wrong direction."

She pulled away and her hand grazed across his stomach. More heat sizzled through him, and he wondered if her touch was deliberate. "What do you want to talk about?" she asked.

"Let's talk about Oswald. That should ruin the mood." He shifted uncomfortably on the couch. "Anything else you remember?"

Her face pensive, she studied him, and he half wondered if she'd ignore his advice and do what Daniels had suggested. Jump his bones. Her expression changed though, and she sighed. "What Allison told you about him made sense." She sat back against the couch and pulled the bag of melting ice off her knee. "He had a weird vibe. I remember feeling a strange tingling sensation when I was sitting in that tub. Like slightly numb and strangely weak."

Grateful there was some distance between them, and he could breathe easier, he sat up. "You think that was because of his gifts?"

"Definitely. If he can do what Allison says, it makes sense. He was pulling energy out of me and into him. He would have taken all of it if he'd managed to finish the job."

A chill ran through Rem. "He obviously did it to the rest of his victims."

Mikey's eyes widened. "The lock. Did I tell you about the lock? He opened it."

"What lock?"

She turned toward him. "Mason and Trick put three locks on that door. I turned all of them. But when I was on the phone, one of them opened." She put a hand on her stomach. "Oswald somehow opened it." Her face paled. "That's how he got in the house. The doors were locked but he got inside."

Rem recalled Daniels telling him there were no signs of forced entry. "What are you saying? He can unlock doors?"

"I saw him do it."

Rem thought about it. "That would explain how he got into the other victim's houses."

"It was terrifying. I thought he was going to get into the bathroom. But then he stopped. He must have heard the police coming."

Rem sighed with frustration. "Great. Now we know he can get through locked doors. That's comforting." He found the remote that Mikey had placed on the couch cushion and needing some distraction, he flipped on the TV. He debated contacting Daniels now or waiting until the morning.

The TV came on and the light flickered in the room. A news anchor spoke about the national events of the day.

Mikey glanced at the TV. "Since when do you watch the news?"

"Since never. That's the second time it's done that." He flipped to another station and a movie played. "I get enough reality during the day. I was watching *The Birds* last night."

"Me, too." She rubbed her knee. "Doesn't it stay on the same channel, even if you turn it off?"

"It does, or it did. Maybe they made a—" An uncomfortable thought occurred to him. Recalling the coffee pot in his sink, he turned off the TV and turned it back on. The movie returned. Rem changed the channel and saw black and white footage of a plane, turned the TV off again and turned it back on.

"What are you doing?" asked Mikey.

The black and white footage flickered to life on the screen. Feeling a little sick, Rem had a visual of Oswald walking through his living room, turning on the TV and watching the news. "I...uh...nothing."

Mikey narrowed her eyes. "No. It's something."

His mind whirled, coming to potentially terrifying deductions. He set the remote down. "I know you and Mason have encountered some strange things. You think Oswald's weird energy ability could get him past an alarm system?" He thought back, recalling the picture of him and Jennie being on the wrong side of the lamp. Then he thought of his missing travel mug and the moved snow globe at work.

"What are you saying?" asked Mikey.

"Have you had anything weird happen at Mason's? Items being out of place? Or missing things?"

Mikey paused, stared off and nodded. "Yes, actually. I can't find my mom's bracelet. And I swear I brought it from my apartment. And Mason's blanket that he keeps on the edge of his bed. That's moved, too." She furrowed her brow. "And the damn flowers keep getting trampled. I think it's the neighbor's dog, but I never see him." She shook her head. "And the weirdest thing happened. I went out the other day to replant the flowers and there was a single yellow rose in the flower bed. It made no sense. I have no idea where it came from."

Rem froze, recalling the yellow rose on Jennie's grave. More pieces clicked into place. "Holy hell." He sat up, his stomach churning. "It's Oswald, and maybe Margaret, too." He eyed Mikey. "They've been in our homes."

Chapter Thirty-Three

DANIELS MUNCHED ON A chip and sipped some water. "I still don't think I buy it."

Rem picked up a french fry. "What's so hard to understand? You said you had stuff move, too."

Daniels shook his head, trying to wrap his head around Rem's theory, but it had been another long day, and his doubts swirled.

Since Marjorie had taken the rest of the week off after the school lock-down, Daniels wanted to spend time with her and J.P., so he'd left the morning bagel run to Trick. Rem had met Daniels at the station and Rem had told Daniels his wild theory about Oswald getting into their houses. Daniels had been skeptical, but they'd had little time to discuss it after spending the day writing reports, reviewing the evidence found at Mason's home, updating Lozano to determine their next steps, and following up on more leads.

Worried about Oswald, Rem didn't want Mason and Mikey to leave his house. Knowing the situation, Lozano had agreed to let Rem and Daniels take dinner to them since Rem didn't have much food in his house. With Mason and Mikey out of the office, Trick and Kyle were handling the business at SCOPE and Trick had agreed to stop by later with some groceries.

Mikey sipped on her soda and set her cup down. "I think it's plausible."

Rem pointed at Daniels. "You had that picture on the fridge move and also J.P.'s blanket." He picked up his burger, took a bite and spoke through a mouthful of food. "And don't forget the snow globe on your desk."

"I remember the wooden box was moved too, at SCOPE," said Mikey.

Mason stopped in mid-chew of his turkey burger. "You didn't tell me that."

"I didn't think it was a big deal," said Mikey.

"That's exactly it," said Daniels. "None of these things are big. All of them can be easily explained."

"Not the yellow rose," said Rem.

Daniels wiped his fingers on a napkin. "A friend of Jennie's could have left it there."

"What about the one I found in Mason's flower bed?" asked Mikey.

"Maybe it got mixed up with the other plants you bought," said Daniels.

Rem rolled his eyes. "Maybe if it was just one of us, but both of us?"

"But why a yellow rose?" asked Daniels.

Mason swallowed his bite. "I'll tell you why. Ever heard of the Yellow Rose of Texas?"

Mikey stopped chewing. "That's exactly something Margaret would use as a sign to us."

Rem gripped his soda can.

Daniels had to admit the rose was odd. "What about the doorbell cameras?"

"If he can get past an alarm, he may be able to get past those, too," said Mikey.

"My garage door doesn't close properly," said Rem. "If they got under it, they could have gotten in through the garage entry to the house."

Mikey widened her eyes. "When I was in the cult, there were some members who robbed houses by waiting for owners to leave. The owner would hit the garage door button and drive away before it fully closed. Whoever was waiting would slide something under the door to trigger it to open again. Then they'd get in through the back instead of the front. It worked pretty well."

"I bet," said Mason. "Especially since most people don't lock the door into their house from the garage."

"I do," said Daniels.

"Me, too, but that wouldn't stop Oswald," said Rem.

"This is still hard to believe," said Daniels. "Especially bypassing our alarms."

Mason held his turkey burger. "When Trick and I were Rangers, there was a thief stealing from wealthy people's safes across the state. He did it for months and we could never catch him, and nobody could figure out how he was doing it. One day he screwed up though, and the owner of the house's dogs cornered him. He was captured and Trick and I interrogated him. We wanted to know how he was opening the safes and he kept telling us it was easy. That he'd always had a knack for it. Told us he could 'see' the numbers in his head. We didn't believe him, but we never found a tool on him or anyone who'd ever seen him crack a safe open. He ended up getting twenty years."

Rem sipped his soda. "He still around? Maybe we can talk to this guy."

Daniels snorted. "You planning on flying to Texas?"

"Doesn't matter," said Mason. "He stole from the wrong guy. Guards found our thief in his cell with broken fingers and broken other things. His talking days are over."

Rem paled. "Never mind then. But at least it proves my point. Oswald may be able to do the same thing."

"What are we supposed to do then?" asked Mikey. "Stay together and not leave the house until he's caught?"

"That's exactly what we're going to do," said Rem.

"We can't expect to hole up in our homes forever," said Mikey. "Trick's bringing some basics, but we still need to go to the grocery store. You've got no food."

"We can figure that part out," said Rem. "And hopefully, we'll have some movement with Oswald soon. Daniels and I talked with Lozano, and we considered something we think may have to do with why no one has seen him."

"What's that?" asked Mason. He ate a piece of strawberry from a fruit bowl.

"Oswald disguised himself when he went to Gina's," said Daniels, "so we had to wonder if he disguised himself for that driver's license photo and when he was working at the school."

Rem dunked a fry in ketchup. "Lozano contacted our tech guys to see if they could alter Oswald's picture. Take away the beard and mustache. Shorten his hair and get rid of those crazy eyebrows and the glasses. Give him a clean-cut look. Maybe then, somebody will recognize him."

"That's a great idea," said Mikey.

"We're hoping to have something before the early news. Then we can show both photos," said Daniels. "Lozano's going to send us a copy when he gets it."

"I hope it works," said Mason. "What about the dried sunflower? Anything on that?"

"Nothing," said Daniels. "So far, it's a dead end."

"We're hoping Oswald keeps to his two-day timeframe, because if he doesn't..." Rem eyed the time. "He may have already struck again."

"Considering the way he looked and felt, I'd say he's not going to wait long," said Mikey. She pushed her half-eaten sandwich away. "He didn't seem well, and I don't just mean mentally."

"You're not hungry?" asked Rem.

Mikey crossed her arms. "I'll save the rest for later." She held Rem's look. "I'm guessing you two are headed back after you eat?"

"Once the new photo hits the airways, we'll have to be ready," said Daniels. "Lozano told us to hang tight for now, but we're on call in case we're needed."

"I give us maybe thirty more minutes," said Rem.

"You're being unusually optimistic," said Daniels.

"Enjoy it while you can," answered Rem.

Daniels' phone rang, and he picked it up. "Hey." He smacked Rem's arm. "It's Oswald's mom."

"It's about time." Rem wiped his mouth with a napkin.

Daniels answered. "Hello? Mrs. Fry?"

"It's Mrs. Perkins now," she answered.

They spoke for a few minutes while Oswald's mother discussed her work and why she hadn't called sooner. Managing to steer her back on the subject of her son, he put the phone on speaker and set it on the table. "What can you tell us about Oswald, Mrs. Perkins?" he asked.

"Oswald?" she asked. "He's a good boy. He can't possibly be guilty of the crimes you suspect him of."

"When's the last time you spoke with him?" asked Rem.

There was a pause. "Last month? Maybe three weeks ago?"

"You have any idea where he's staying?" asked Daniels.

She made a huff over the phone. "I thought he was with his father."

"He left your ex-husband's place months ago," said Daniels.

"That man," said Mrs. Perkins with distaste. "Such a waste. He never did know how to parent. I'd hoped that if they'd spent more time together, they might forge a bond. Obviously, I was wrong."

"Does Oswald have friends he might stay with?" asked Rem.

"I think so. I believe he was seeing someone. I wondered if it was serious, but he'd never say much other than she was a friend."

"Do you know who she is?" asked Daniels, sitting up in his seat.

"I'm sorry but I don't. He would never tell me." She paused. "I know a while back he had a friend named Victor. Perhaps if you find him, he could be of more help."

Rem sighed.

"Anybody else he might be staying with?" asked Daniels.

Rem's phone buzzed and he picked it up. "It's Lozano," he whispered. "He's texting Oswald's altered photo."

"Nobody that I can think of," said Mrs. Perkins. "Listen. I know Oswald has his moments. He was bullied as a child and saw a therapist for a while. I thought it helped a little. At least he seemed better."

"We can appreciate that, Mrs. Perkins," said Daniels. "But we still need to find him and talk to him."

"Picture's coming through," said Rem.

"I mean," Mrs. Perkins continued, "he was a good son. At least to me. He actually taught school for a while, contrary to his father's opinion that he couldn't hold a job. Oswald was good at it, too. And at home he kept his room fastidiously clean. I never had to ask him once to make his bed or do his laundry. He was particular about everything."

Rem furrowed his brow, sucked in a breath, and gripped his phone.

"What is it?" asked Mikey.

"I mean, even his diet was strict," said Mrs. Perkins. "I remember when the whole high protein thing started. That boy wouldn't touch a carb. He's so disciplined."

Rem turned white and set his jaw.

"What's wrong?" asked Daniels.

"Rem?" asked Mason.

"Mrs. Perkins?" asked Rem, his voice unsteady.

"Yes?" she replied.

Rem, still staring at the picture, spoke softly. "Was Oswald a fan of nature shows?"

Confused, Daniels waited for her to answer.

"Nature shows? I suppose. He did enjoy the *National Geographic* channel," she said.

Rem kept staring at his cell. "When Oswald was younger, did you live in a haunted house, where there'd been a murder-suicide?"

There was a brief silence. "How on earth did you know that?"

Rem's face lost the last of its color. "Thank you, Mrs. Perkins."

Mrs. Perkins kept going. "What does that—"

Rem leaned over and hung up on her. Then he stood, knocking his chair back and put his hand on the wall for support.

"What is it?" Daniels leaned to look over at Rem's phone. The picture of a clean-cut Oswald stared back at him. "Do you know him?"

Rem pointed. "That's my neighbor, Kevin Chapman."

Shocked, Daniels picked up Rem's phone and studied the photo.

Rem grabbed the back of the chair beside him. "Oswald Fry, and his supposed wife, are living across the street from me."

Rem tried to stay on his feet, but his shock and horror almost made his legs buckle. He thought of Kevin knocking on his door to look for Chester, and the two of them going in Rem's backyard, while Rem's house was empty. He recalled sitting in Kevin's house and sharing a beer and Kevin sharing some of the muffins Mrs. Wilson had made. His stomach turned and he thought of Kevin's wife, Nancy. Was she in on everything? He had a sickening thought that she'd been in his house while he and Kevin had searched for Chester.

Daniels stood. "Are you sure?"

Mikey grabbed Rem's phone. "This man? He's across the street?"

Rem pulled it together and shoved a chair aside. He went to the window, trying to think. "I'm sure. The nose is a little off, the eye color is wrong, and his mouth isn't quite right, but that's him. I swear it on Jennie's grave." Feeling ill that Oswald and likely Margaret, had been to see Jennie, he pulled his weapon. "He's got a wife, too, or at least he says it's his wife. Her name's Nancy."

Mikey gasped and eyed Mason, who stood from the table.

"What is it?" asked Daniels.

"Nancy is Margaret's middle name," said Mikey.

The ground beneath Rem's feet seemed to move. He caught the wall, trying to deal with the knowledge that Margaret and Oswald had been living across the street from him.

Daniels spoke to Rem. "Did you ever see Nancy?"

Rem thought back. "A couple of times, but only as she was leaving. The first time she wore some long jacket, a hat, and sunglasses. The second time it was dark, and I couldn't see her face." He recalled the fight between Kevin and Nancy in their front yard. Had it been a ruse to get Rem's attention? He took a heavy breath and told himself to calm down. "Hell. She's been over there this whole time." A chill ran through him. "And she's been in my house. How could I be so stupid?"

"Sure." Daniels scoffed at Rem. "Oswald and Margaret living across the street is such an obvious conclusion. How could you have possibly missed it?"

Rem checked his weapon, returned it to its holster and walked to the door.

Daniels followed. "Hold up. Before you barge in there, guns blazing, we need back-up."

"They are over there right now," said Rem, his fury rising.

"You don't know that," said Daniels.

Rem opened his front door. "Their car is in the driveway." He pointed and Daniels looked. "That's Nancy's car."

"Where's Oswald's?" asked Daniels.

"I don't know. I've never seen it. It's probably in the garage." He took a step.

Daniels took his arm. "Let's call Lozano. We need to tell him first."

Mason came up behind them. "Don't go in on your own. If I know Margaret, she'll be ready." He stared at the house and Rem suspected he'd be more than happy to join them in storming Kevin's home.

"You stay here with Mikey," said Rem.

"I plan to," said Mason.

Mikey walked up beside Mason and peered out the front door. "Daniels is right, Rem. Don't do something stupid."

Rem bit back his impatience. "Mikey, I'm not going to sit here and—"

"Wait. The door opened," said Daniels, staring across the street.

Rem turned to see Kevin, or rather Oswald, step out onto his porch. He had a backpack on, and he pulled it up. He stopped suddenly and looked in their direction.

Rem froze as they made eye contact.

"That's him," said Daniels.

"I know," said Rem.

"Get back, Mikey," said Mason.

"I'm not going anywhere," said Mikey, but she moved closer to Mason.

Oswald stared, then swiveled and returned to his house. He closed the door.

"He's on the move," said Rem, pulling his weapon again.

Daniels pulled his, too. "Mason, call nine-one-one."

Rem turned to Mikey. "Call Lozano. Tell him what's going on."

Mikey, her face reflecting her worry, stared back. "Wait for back-up. Don't go in there."

"There's no way I'm letting him, or Margaret get away again." Rem eyed Daniels. "You ready?"

"As ever." Daniels held his weapon. "Let's go."

"Be careful," said Mason.

"Don't leave this house," said Rem. He noted Mikey's expression and understood her fear. "I'll be okay."

"You better be," she said.

Mason closed the door and locked it.

Chapter Thirty-Four

REM RAN UP THE porch to one side of the door, and Daniels ran up to the other side. Their guns drawn and aimed toward the ground, they nodded at each other, and Daniels banged on the door. "Oswald Fry? Police. Open the door."

Rem listened but heard nothing. The house was quiet.

Starting to sweat, Rem imagined Oswald and Margaret running out the back.

Daniels tried the door, and it was unlocked. He pushed it open, and Rem swiveled around the door frame, his gun raised. He saw no one and stepped inside. Daniels followed.

"Oswald?" yelled Rem. He aimed upstairs.

"In here, Detective."

Rem whirled to his right and headed toward the kitchen, his gun still aimed. Rounding the corner, he saw Oswald standing in front of the sink with a gun in his hand. He was pointing it toward his head.

Rem stopped at the counter and Daniels came up beside him. They both trained their guns on Oswald.

"Put it down," said Rem. He could hear Daniels' rapid breathing, but he kept his eyes on Oswald.

Oswald appeared calm. "Hello, Rem." He kept the gun against his skull. "Surprised? I was wondering when you'd realize it was me. My disguise worked pretty well, didn't it?"

The bile rose in the back of Rem's throat. "I know who you are now."

Oswald gripped his gun. "I thought we got along well. The catnip I put under your porch worked beautifully. Chester went right for it."

Rem swallowed.

"Where's Margaret?" asked Daniels.

Oswald flicked his gaze to Daniels. "She's not here. She took Chester and left. It's just us. It's nice to finally meet you, Detective Daniels." He smiled. "Your partner spoke highly of you, and your wife is very nice. I enjoyed working with her."

Daniels stepped closer, and Rem could see his partner's glare. "Leave my wife out of this," said Daniels, his voice low.

"I did," said Oswald. "Believe me. If I'd wanted her dead, she would be."

Rem fought to think. They needed to get the gun from Oswald. Their back-up would arrive soon. Would that scare him? Would he pull the trigger if he felt cornered? "Why'd you target Marjorie?" Rem asked, hoping if Oswald kept talking, they'd find an opening.

Oswald glanced back at Rem. "Nancy always taught me to know my enemies, and their weaknesses. When I saw that Marjorie's school needed a substitute teacher, I thought I'd offer to help. Not only would I be close to Mrs. Daniels, but there would be an easy supply of energy. Kids have loads of it." He looked back at Daniels. "How is Marjorie feeling? Better, I hope?"

Daniels set his jaw. "Put the gun down, Oswald."

"You're upset," said Oswald. "I can tell, but that was kinda the point."

"Why'd you move in here?" asked Rem. He felt he knew the answer, but he needed to get Oswald off the subject of Marjorie before Daniels shot him.

"For the same reason," said Oswald. "Nancy..." he paused. "I started calling her that when we moved in, and it stuck." He chuckled. "And we're not actually married but we thought it would be fun for you to think we were." He paused again. "Nancy wanted me to get to know you. So, I did.

I can see why she likes you." He furrowed his face. "Sorry about the hood thing. That was her idea." He glanced back at Daniels. "The statue, too. Nancy likes her mind games."

Rem kept his gun trained on Oswald but forced himself to relax and soften his voice. "Listen, Oswald. Just put the gun down. Then we can talk, and you can tell us your side."

Oswald grinned. "You're lucky I'm not taking from you. I could, you know. Pull the strength right out of you. But my time is short, my reserves are low, and Nancy wouldn't like it. I promised her I'd leave you alone." His grip on the gun eased. "I suspect she wants your energy all to herself."

Rem didn't want to think about that. "We'll catch her eventually."

"You want to know where she is, don't you?" Oswald sighed, "I can't help you. I don't know where she went. We parted ways after I told her my plans and she got angry."

"What plans?" asked Daniels.

"I had to move things along after I messed up with Mikey. I didn't expect her to be so spry." Oswald's expression tensed. "She and her brother were smart to create that room, but Margaret will finish what I couldn't so it will all work out."

Rem took a step.

Oswald pushed the tip of his gun harder against his head. "Stay where you are. I have no fear of death, Detective. In fact, I'm expecting it."

Worried that meant he planned to pull the trigger, Rem recalled what Mikey had said about seeing the lock slide open and he kept talking. "Did you get into our homes?"

Oswald's tension eased. "I did. It's a talent of mine. Nancy always encouraged me to use my gifts and I hated to disappoint her. I taught her a few tricks, too. She's getting better with locks but she's lousy with alarms. No matter how much we've practiced."

Rem wanted to throw up. "You both went into my house and visited Jennie's grave?"

"We went to your place, too," Oswald said to Daniels. "And Mason's. We even dressed as part of the cleaning crew and walked through your squad room after hours. It was fun. We moved small things, just to mess with you." He smiled at Daniels. "I even played with some of J.P.'s toys. Reminded me of my youth."

Daniel shoulders bunched and he scowled. "Just put the gun down."

"C'mon, Oswald," said Rem. "You've had your fun, but it's over now. Nobody has to die today."

"Oh, but they do," said Oswald. "In fact, I know somebody already has, and it won't stop with them. Today is a day for dying."

Rem feared Oswald was referring to his final victim. "Does this have to do with the sunflower you left behind?"

"It does." Oswald's demeanor shifted. "I didn't like my final task, but it had to be done." His expression changed and he glowered. "She used me." He paused. "So, I used her. That's why Nancy is angry with me."

"Angry about what?" asked Daniels. "Who used you?"

Oswald held his gun tighter. "Nancy was always kind to me. She introduced me to Victor. He was kind to me, too. They both appreciated my abilities and what I could offer. They didn't want to hurt me."

"Did somebody try to hurt you, Oswald?" asked Rem. He could hear the distant sound of sirens.

Oswald stared off, and Rem wondered if the sirens would bother him, but then he kept talking. "I met someone else. Someone who I thought would appreciate me, too. And she did. But not in the way I thought. She smiled and laughed with me. Told me I was handsome. Nancy warned me against her, but I was smitten and didn't listen. One night, Victor's house was empty except for her. I brought her a sunflower because I knew she liked them. She took it and started talking to me like I was important. Asked me about my gifts and what I could do. She flattered me and gave me something to drink. I was thrilled she liked me." He stopped and his face hardened. "But I started to feel funny. I couldn't think straight, and then she seduced me. I didn't understand at first. I wanted her but then I didn't. I tried to leave but failed, and then I couldn't stop." He paused and sneered. "She was on top of me, and I realized what she was doing. She was trying to take from me like I could take from others. She was stealing from me. Using me."

Rem's belly flipped. Oswald was describing something eerily similar to what had happened between him and Allison. Had the same happened to Oswald? "What did you do?" he asked, his voice uneven.

"I woke up, confused and alone." Oswald moved the gun to the base of his skull and Rem prayed he wouldn't fire. "The sunflower was in the trash. I knew then what she'd done. She didn't want me, she wanted what I could give her." His voice trailed off and then he seemed to return to the present. He looked back at Rem. "A week later, Victor was dead." He narrowed his eyes. "And I think she used whatever she got from me to do it. I knew then that I would kill her."

A spike of dread ran up Rem's spine. He heard Daniels' intake of breath.

"You're talking about Allison," said Rem.

"She's your last victim," said Daniels.

Rem's heart thudded faster, and the sirens blared outside the house. "What have you done?" asked Rem. There was no way Oswald could have gotten to Allison in jail.

Oswald's face relaxed. "Exactly what I had to."

"She's pregnant," said Daniels.

"She is or was," said Oswald. He eyed Rem. "And it's either yours or mine." He lowered his gun and pointed it toward the ground. "But it doesn't matter anymore."

His mind racing with Oswald's revelations, Rem approached Oswald. "Drop it."

Oswald let go of the gun and it clattered to the ground. He got on his knees. "It's for the best, Detective." He put his arms above his head. "No child should come into this world with Allison as its mother."

Rem put his gun away and pulled out his handcuffs. He made eye contact with Daniels.

Daniels lowered his gun. "I'll call Lozano." He ran out of the house.

Rem handcuffed Oswald, thinking of Allison and the baby. *Chloe.* He prayed they were okay. "If you've hurt them…" He didn't know what else to say.

"I did you a favor. She was using you, too. You couldn't take care of it, so I did."

"You're going to prison." He grabbed Oswald's shoulder.

"No. Actually, I'm not." Oswald moved his jaw. "I'm not long for this world and I'm leaving on my own terms." He bit down on something, and Rem heard a crunch. "Good luck with Nancy, Rem. I may be finished, but she isn't."

Rem pulled on his arm. "What are you doing?" Oswald tensed and his face turned red. "Oswald?"

Two police officers ran in as Oswald gasped, his eyes bulged, and he went rigid and fell to the floor.

"Get an ambulance," yelled Rem. Oswald began to seize, and Rem got to his knees and held him as Oswald jerked and spasmed. One of the officers ran out and the other squatted beside Oswald and tried to hold him as foam began to form and drip from Oswald's lips.

Helpless, Rem could only watch as Oswald's face turned purple and he grunted and grimaced and finally went still. His body still rigid, he stopped breathing.

Rem shook him. "Oswald?" He turned Oswald onto his back. "Oswald?" He slapped his cheek, but Oswald, his eyes open, had gone limp. His hands trembling, Rem put his fingers on Oswald's neck. Feeling nothing for several seconds, Rem realized what Oswald had done. Shocked, he fell back and tried to catch his breath. "He's dead."

The other officer looked stunned, and Rem figured he didn't look much better. Unsteady, he tried to stand but had to use the banister at the end of the stairs to pull himself up. He leaned over and held on to his knees. "Get the coroner," he told the officer. "And cancel the ambulance."

More uniformed police entered and Rem, thinking of Daniels, managed to straighten on wobbly legs and leave the house. Seeing Daniels standing on the lawn and talking on his phone, Rem ran over to him.

Daniels lowered the phone.

"He's dead," said Rem, breathless. "Oswald is dead. He took something." He ran a hand through his hair, still in disbelief.

"Rem...," said Daniels.

Rem noted Daniels' pale pallor and somber expression. "What? What is it?" He thought of Allison and Chloe and his stomach dropped. "Oh, God."

Daniels hesitated before he spoke. "I...I talked to Lozano. Allison collapsed at the jail about an hour ago. They rushed her to the hospital, but she was DOA."

Fear bubbled up in Rem's chest and it hurt to breathe. He held his stomach. "Chloe?" he whispered, barely able to speak.

Daniels shook his head, his face grim. "I'm so sorry, partner. They tried, but she was too little."

Spots formed in Rem's vision, and he struggled to draw in air. "No," he said. "No, no, no." He doubled over. "Not Chloe."

"Rem." Daniels put a hand on Rem's shoulder.

"Not Chloe." He clenched his eyes shut. "Please."

"Take it easy." Daniels squeezed Rem's arm.

"No. Don't." Rem straightened and pushed Daniels' arm away. "I can't. This can't...I just...not this."

"They tried, Rem," said Daniels, crestfallen. "I'm so, so sorry."

Confused about how to feel, Rem fought to control his emotions. Heartbroken over the loss of a child he'd never met, he bit his lip and, fighting the urge to be sick, he clutched at his stomach. Despite all of Allison's games, the risks involved, and the changes he would have had to make, he'd secretly almost hoped to become a dad. And now that had been ripped from him, too.

Daniels tried again and put a hand on Rem's back. "You need to sit down."

Rem stepped away. "I don't want to sit down." The area had quickly filled with patrol cars and officers were running across the lawn, but Rem barely noticed. "I have...I have to get out of here." His breathing came is short spurts, and he couldn't seem to control it. He realized then how much Chloe had meant to him, regardless of Allison.

"We'll go to your place."

Rem didn't want to go anywhere, and he didn't want to talk to anyone. "I have to leave." His anguish rising, he turned and walked away.

"Where are you going?"

Barely able to see straight, Rem didn't bother to answer.

Chapter Thirty-Five

Daniels sat in Lozano's office, bouncing his knee up and down.

Lozano sat at his desk. "You haven't talked to him?"

"Not since yesterday," said Daniels. "I texted with him last night, but all I got were basic answers. 'I'm fine', or 'don't worry'. But he wouldn't tell me where he was." He couldn't stop thinking about the shock of the previous afternoon and the look on Rem's face when he'd told him about Allison and her baby.

"What about Mason or Mikey? Have they spoken to him?"

Daniels shook his head. "No. I don't think so. Mikey's been trying but he won't talk to her either." He rubbed his head. "She and Mason went back to Mason's after what happened yesterday. Once I finished up at the scene, I went to see Marjorie. Rem may have gone home but I'm not sure."

"I left him a message," added Lozano. "Told him to take the morning. But he'll need to come in and finish the reports. I'm fine if you both leave early today. You two need it."

Daniels rubbed his neck. "Any idea how Oswald got to Allison?"

"The warden is investigating. My guess is Oswald, through his own connections, or possibly Margaret's, got to somebody on the inside. They arranged to poison Allison's food."

"Hell." Daniels dropped his head. He didn't mourn Allison, but her baby was innocent. He wondered if Margaret had thought the same, which is why she hadn't approved and had left Oswald. He looked up. "Any word on Margaret?"

"Nothing," said Lozano. "Neighbors don't know anything. They found Oswald's car in his garage and the other victims' personal items in a drawer in the bedroom, including Mikey's bracelet. They found Remalla's coffee mug in the kitchen. Plus, they discovered another ID under Kevin Chapman's name in his backpack. And they found wigs and various other makeup and prosthetics."

"He knew what he was doing when he disguised himself." Daniels compared Kevin's clean-cut look to Oswald's driver's license photo. "He did a hell of a job going to school looking one way and living across from Rem looking another." He had no doubt that Rem was beating himself up over not catching that Oswald and Margaret were his neighbors.

"I can see how people would have missed it," said Lozano. "Comparing Kevin Chapman to Oswald Fry, I doubt I would have noticed either." He scratched his jaw. "How did people not see Kevin's car, though?"

"If he kept it in the garage, he would have left out the alley. Not many would have paid any attention." Daniels thought about Mrs. Wilson, Rem's next-door neighbor. She would not have missed Kevin leaving his house, especially looking like someone else. "My guess is that Oswald left home looking like Kevin in case someone saw him, stopped at a public restroom near the school, changed, and walked to work." He made another deduction. "He likely didn't take his car to the school on the off-chance Marjorie saw it. If she'd gone to Rem's, it risked her seeing and recognizing it."

"Neighbors mentioned a second car. We're trying to run it down, but no one got a license plate."

"My guess is it belonged to Margaret. God knows where she and her car are now." Daniels rested his elbow on the armrest. "Either Oswald had this whole thing planned, or Margaret played a big role and got Oswald to do her bidding." He cursed. "She was watching Rem and probably cackling her ass off at the same time."

Lozano leaned back in his seat. "Oswald had more to deal with than just Margaret. They found medical files in the house. I called and talked to Oswald's doctor this morning. Get this. Oswald had an inoperable brain tumor. The doctor didn't know how he was still walking around."

Daniels studied his hands, thinking of Rem. "I think I have an idea." He raised his head. "We need to get a DNA test on Chloe. We have to find out if Rem's the father. He needs to know."

"Already requested it." Lozano sat up. "We have to get some approvals, but even after that, it's going to take some time to get the results."

"Yeah. I know."

"You think Oswald could be the father?"

"If what he said was true, he could be."

Lozano sighed. "I hope he was, for your partner's sake."

Daniels nodded. "That's what's really tearing Rem up. Even though he hoped Allison was lying, and it wasn't his child, he'd adapted to the idea of being a dad and was preparing himself to take care of Chloe." He paused, wishing he could talk to Rem. "If he was going to be a dad, he was going to be a good one, no matter what it cost him."

"He'll be okay. He just needs some time."

Daniels hoped Lozano was right.

"How's Marjorie?"

Daniels tried to pull himself out of his well of worry. "She's okay. When I leave here, I'm going to pick her and J.P. up and take them home." He sighed. "I can't wait to have us all back under the same roof."

"Good." Lozano nodded. "Then go finish your reports and get out of here. And let me know if you hear from your partner."

Weary, Daniels stood. "I will. Hopefully, I'll talk to him soon." He left Lozano's office and returned to his desk. He eyed his computer and thought of Rem again. Seeing the snow globe with the hot dog inside, he picked it up and shook it. Memories surfaced of Daniels giving Jennie the snow globe for her birthday as a joke. He'd told her she could put it on her desk and think of Rem. He'd been dating Marjorie for only a couple of months at the time, but she'd already hit it off with Rem and Jennie. Marjorie had been amused by the gift and told Jennie she could shake it whenever Rem got on her nerves.

Rem had given Jennie a pair of red lollipop earrings. She'd opened them and had given him a look. He'd shrugged and told her he'd tried to get Elton John tickets, but they'd sold out. He'd seen the earrings at a gift shop and thought she'd love them.

To Jennie's credit, she'd smiled and put on the earrings, and he and Marjorie had gushed over them. After dinner and cake, Rem gave Jennie a card. She'd opened it and broke out into a grin when she'd spotted the two tickets to Elton John. Then she'd read the card, and her eyes shining, she'd kissed Rem and had told him she loved him. Daniels had already bought two tickets of his own and a month later, all four of them had gone to the concert, sung at the top of their lungs, and had had a blast. Recalling that night, Daniels smiled. The yellow flakes swirling and settling, Daniels debated calling Rem again, when his phone rang.

Hoping it was his partner, he picked it up and saw it was Marjorie. He sat and answered. "Hey, honey."

"Hey," said Marjorie. Her voice was quiet, and he heard her sniff.

"What's the matter? You all right?"

She sniffed again. "Gordon. We need to talk." Her voice was thick.

Daniels sat up. "What is it? Is J.P. okay?"

"He's fine. It's not about him." Her voice caught. "I've been doing a lot of thinking...about everything." She paused and took a breath.

Daniels tensed in his seat. "That's understandable. You've been through a lot."

"So much has happened."

"It has, but Oswald's dead. He can't hurt you or anyone else anymore."

She paused. "It's more than that."

"What's more than that?" Daniels gripped the phone. "Honey, I know what he did, and I can imagine how you feel. We can talk about it, or you mentioned talking to someone else if it helps."

"Gordon..." She made a groaning sound. "This is not going to be solved by talking. At least not in the short term. Everything that man did. To you. To me. He was in our house." She let go of a sob. "And he wasn't the first."

"Marjorie..." he stammered. "I know it was scary, but it's safe now."

"Is it? For how long?"

"What are you saying?"

"I...I don't know. I...I just think I need some time. I'm...I can't..."

"You can't what?" His chest tightening, Daniels squeezed the snow globe.

She moaned. "I can't come home, Gordon. Not right now. I need to think."

Daniels dropped his jaw. "What do you mean you're not coming home? Marjorie...we're a family."

"There's too much to deal with." She sniffed again and he heard the rustling of what sounded like a tissue. "I have to figure out what's best for me...and for J.P."

Daniels went still, trying to comprehend what she was telling him. "I would never let anything happen to you or J.P."

"I know that. You're a good husband and father and I love you. And I would never keep J.P. from you."

His breath caught. "What are you trying to tell me?" His mind raced. "Are you leaving me?"

He heard her breath catch and another sob. "I'm sorry. I need some space, Gordon. I'm not sure what to do. After all that's happened. Between Oswald, and Rudy and Ginger, and even Rutger and what he did. I can't ignore the past."

Daniels tried to keep his fear at bay. "Marjorie. You knew who I was and what I did for a living when you married me."

"I know. And...and I thought I could handle it. But now..."

"Marjorie. I love you."

"And I love you." She paused and moaned. "But I don't know if it's enough."

"Marjorie. Please..." He closed his eyes.

"I'm sorry. I've been thinking about this since I left, and I have to honor how I feel and take it seriously."

"What about how I feel?"

"Gordon, please..."

"No. You're thinking about leaving me. How am I supposed to take that?" He heard J.P. screech and wail in the background.

"I'm sorry, Gordon. But this is for both of us. I need to do this." She took a shaky breath and J.P. screeched again. "I have to go. J.P.'s crying and he's probably hungry." She made a strangled sound and sobbed again. "We'll talk more, but...but don't...don't pick us up today."

"Marjorie, please don't do this. Think this through."

"It's all I've done, and this is the decision I make every time. I can't go home with you. Not now." She sucked in a breath. "I have to go."

"Marjorie, wait."

"Bye, Gordon." He heard another muffled sob and she hung up.

"Marjorie," he said, but he spoke to dead air. She was gone. Speechless and stunned, he stared at the phone, not believing what had just happened. Had Marjorie just broken up with him?

Trying to comprehend it all, he set the phone down and stared off. His body shaking, he shook the globe with nervous energy. Determined to get through to his wife, he picked up the phone to call Marjorie back when the squad doors opened. He turned to see Rem enter.

His hair disheveled and his eyes red and puffy, Rem strode in, still wearing the clothes he'd been wearing the day before.

"Rem?" asked Daniels, standing.

"Hey," said Rem, softly. He marched past Daniels with barely a glance and walked into Lozano's office. He closed the door, and Daniels watched through the glass. Rem spoke first and then Lozano. Rem pulled something out of his pocket. It was a piece of paper and he handed it to Lozano. Lozano took it, read it and glared, then he yelled, and Rem yelled back.

Lozano went quiet and folded the paper. Rem said something, then pulled out his gun and what appeared to be his badge and set them on Lozano's desk. Then he turned and walked out. He passed Daniels, hesitated, and stopped.

Daniels didn't know what to say and Rem glanced at him. "I'm sorry, partner," he said.

"What is going on?" asked Daniels. "Where have you been?"

Looking lost, Rem blinked and shook his head. His gaze traveled to behind Daniels and Daniels saw Lozano leave his office.

"I have to go." Rem turned, headed toward the doors, and left.

"What the..." Daniels stared at the exit. "Wait a minute. Rem?"

Lozano walked up. He held out the paper to Daniels, who opened and read it. It was Rem's resignation.

"Your partner just quit," said Lozano. "Said he's done and doesn't plan to come back."

Unsteady, Daniels sat in his chair. Still holding the snow globe, he watched the flakes flutter and settle, and the liquid clear. Daniels reread the note, not believing his eyes. In the span of two minutes, he'd lost both his wife and his partner. Thinking again of happier days, Daniels leaned over, held his head and for the first time, wondered if things would ever be the same again.

∞∞∞

Want more from J. T. Bishop? Sign up at jtbishopauthor.com to subscribe to her newsletter. Get the Daniels and Remalla prequel novella, *The Girl and the Gunshot* for **free**, in addition to extra content, plus opportunities for more free books. Follow J.T. on her Amazon Author page to be notified when new books are released.

I hope you enjoyed *Of Power and Pain* but get ready for the next installment with *Of Love and Loss*. Daniels and Rem are both coping with their losses and Margaret uses their struggles against them with a shocking attack. Will she finally win or face retribution? There's only one way to find out. Preorder *Of Love and Loss* to be the first to know. Enjoy an excerpt below.

In the meantime, get ready for the next installment of *The Redstone Chronicles* with *Lost Hope*. Margaret isn't letting her brother and sister off the hook, and when Mason and Mikey's estranged father shows up, his presence is just the start of some tumultuous and jaw-dropping revelations. Enjoy an excerpt below.

If you liked *Of Power and Pain* and this is your first foray into the world of J.T. Bishop and her paranormal thrillers, then you're in luck. Check out the four-book *Family or Foe* saga, which introduces Detectives Daniels and Remalla. A killer with powerful abilities is out for revenge against those he believes wronged him. Can he be caught before he kills again? This series includes *First Cut, Second Slice, Third Blow* and *Fourth Strike*. Or grab all four in *The Family or Foe Saga Boxed Set*.

Or if you haven't already, jump straight into Daniels' and Remalla's own series, starting with *Haunted River*. The ghost of a woman whose murder remains unsolved haunts a small town with secrets. When another woman turns up dead years later, are Daniels and Remalla next? This book is followed by *Of Breath and Blood* where our detectives investigate a cult leader and will have to rely on each other to survive. In *Of Body and Bone*, they'll hunt for a kidnapper whose unique abilities make him impossible to catch, but his connections to a dangerous foe creates a greater threat. *Of Mind and Madness* continues the story line.

And if you like Mason and Mikey Redstone and their paranormal exploits, introduced in *Of Breath and Blood*, then grab *Lost Souls*, the first book in *The Redstone Chronicles*, a crossover series with Daniels and Remalla.

Chronologically, *Lost Souls* follows *Of Breath and Blood*, but can be read on its own. In this book, Mason's estranged partner returns and asks for Mason's help to solve a murder, but can he be trusted? This is followed by *Lost Dreams* where Mason battles his inner demons while he and Mikey attempt to exonerate their brother after he's framed for murder. And in *Lost Chances*, book three in the series, Mason gets the help he needs but finds himself caught up in a deadly web of deceit and makes a dangerous enemy. *Lost Hope* continues the series.

Note: Because the Daniels and Remalla books and The Redstone Chronicles are a spinoff and crossover series, they share an overarching story, and the characters from each are mentioned or appear in all the books, so reading both is ideal. The books published alternate between both series. A list of books in chronological order follows below.

Or, if you like light sci-fi with urban fantasy and a delicious romance thrown in, then check out Bishop's first series, *The Red-Line Trilogy*. One woman holds the key to unlocking a secret that will ensure the existence of a secret community. One man, assigned to protect her, will risk everything to keep her alive, but when he falls for her, will their destiny be enough to save them both?

And the Red-Line series continues with the sister series to the trilogy, *The Fletcher Family Saga*. A distant but deadly threat risks the lives of three unique siblings, but life can't stop because of who they are. They'll endure love, loss and a dangerous enemy determined to destroy them.

Either the trilogy or sister series can be read first. Take your pick. Boxed sets are available, too!

A Note from J.T.

I LOVE TO HEAR from my fans about my books and I hope you enjoyed *Of Power and Pain*. If you've been keeping up with Daniels and Rem and the Redstones, then you can see where I'm heading. There's definitely a reckoning coming between Margaret, her family, and Daniels and Rem. This will be further addressed in the next Redstone book, *Lost Hope*. Before that reckoning, though, I needed to deal with the Allison situation and that's what *Of Power and Pain* is about. I wanted to explore the parental side of Remalla and how he would handle becoming a father. I knew from the beginning that he would take care of his child no matter what it cost him. Plus, he's also still dealing with the trauma of Allison's attack, a potential relationship with Mikey he won't allow himself to have, and Margaret's escapades. It's a lot to handle and with the death of Chloe, it's the last straw.

I couldn't let Daniels off the hook either. I wondered how he'd handle relationship issues with Marjorie since it can't be easy being married to him. This story allowed me to delve deeper into his loyalties to both his wife and partner. How would he handle it if one of his loved one's safety was pitted against the other? And we touch on how he feels about having more kids.

While I love the mystery thriller side of my books, I think what I enjoy most is the emotional aspect. Fatherhood, marriage, friendship, love, fear, trauma, and loss are themes that are immensely gratifying to walk my characters through and see how they emerge on the other end. The mental aspects of survival are great fodder for a good story, and I hope you agree.

I'm still determining how the Margaret story arc will end. I'm not exactly sure yet, but now that I have *Lost Hope* written, it's starting to become clearer. In *Lost Hope*, Mikey and Mason will have to deal with their estranged father and psychotic sister, which will lead us into *Of Love and Loss*, We'll answer some big questions about Rem and Mikey and Daniels and Marjorie. *Of Love and Loss* is going to be fun to write. I hope it will be as much fun to read.

Reviews are a huge plus and big help for an author and potential readers. I would love it if you could please take a couple of minutes to leave a quick review for *Of Power and Pain*. And if you'd like, please leave a few comments, too.

As always, thank you for your time and readership. It is deeply valued and appreciated.

Now, on to the next book!

Books in Chronological Order

Lost Chances
Of Power and Pain
Lost Hope
Of Love and Loss

Acknowledgements

ANOTHER BOOK IS COMPLETE, and again, I have many to thank. This doesn't happen alone, and I am indebted to family and friends for their help, support and encouragement. It is truly appreciated.

I also want to thank my Beta and ARC teams. You guys keep me on my toes, ensure I write a great story, and help with early reviews. Thank you for being honest and offering your guidance.

I love writing about the bonds between loving family, deep friendships and the ties that hold them together. Plus, my fascination with the unknown thrown into the mix makes for a satisfying story and hopefully, adds a little more thrill for my readers.

I especially want to thank my fans. Hearing from you and knowing that you're enjoying my books makes all the hard work worthwhile. None of this would matter without your tremendous support. If I can help you escape from this crazy world for a short period each day, then I've done my job.

Here's to more stories, more fun, and more time for yourself. If you can have a little of that each day, you're on the right track.

Enjoy an excerpt from Lost Hope, Book Four in The Redstone Chronicles

THE CRICKETS CHIRPED, A soft, cool breeze blew, and the city lights twinkled in the distance. Appreciating the view, Jag sat by himself on a bench at the overlook. After leaving work at two a.m., he'd come here because he knew he'd have the place to himself. As a bartender, he could sleep in, and he liked the quiet of the early morning hours. Needing to decompress before returning home, he would frequently come to this spot in the hills, where he could look down on humanity and feel some distance from it. His job, while entertaining, also exposed him to the seedier side of life, and not wanting to take it home with him, he'd stop at the overlook, where he'd go quiet, relax, and focus on the positive. That wasn't always easy since he was broke, his girlfriend had broken up with him, and his attempts at making it big as a singer had so far failed. He'd left L.A. because he couldn't take the rejection anymore and his friend had offered him a job. It had seemed like a reasonable alternative at the time, but now he wondered if he needed to return to L.A. and try again. Maybe he'd licked his wounds long enough. And after tonight, maybe the universe was giving him the signs that his luck was turning.

He eyed the time and wondered if his new friend would show. Thinking back on his shift, Jag smiled. He'd met a woman at the bar, which wasn't unusual. Women gave him their numbers all the time. It was his job to schmooze and flirt to get them to buy more drinks, and he was good at it.

Listening and smiling were attributes that served him well. He rarely acted on any of the interest though, mainly because he'd had a girlfriend and also knew the women were drunk and would likely forget about him the next day. Tonight, though, had been different.

A woman had arrived around midnight, had sat at the bar, and ordered a gin and tonic. He'd made her drink and they'd started talking. The bar had been slower than usual, and he'd had more opportunity to talk. She'd introduced herself as Eleanor and had an easy laugh and a pretty smile. Her hair was up in a bun and loose tendrils framed her face. She'd told him how she'd left her boyfriend and family in Ohio six months earlier and had come to San Diego to start a new life. Jag had told his story, too. They had an easy camaraderie, and she had a charisma he rarely found in other patrons. Since breaking up with his girlfriend, he hadn't made much of an effort to date, but Eleanor made his stomach flutter, and he'd found himself telling her about his spot where he'd come at night to overlook the city. When the bar closed, he'd invited her to meet him out here. She'd hesitated, and he'd promised he wasn't a stalker or serial killer. After a thoughtful moment, she'd told him a firm maybe, and she'd left.

Jag didn't know whether she'd join him or not and she hadn't given him her number, so if she didn't show, he might never see her again. He understood. Not many great romances were born in bars between a bartender and a customer, although it would be a cool story if they did.

Deciding he'd wait a few more minutes, he settled back on the bench and enjoyed the peaceful panorama, telling himself that no matter what happened, it would be for the best. Thinking about L.A. and what was next for him, he contemplated his future when he heard the sound of a car approaching. He turned and squinted at headlights that turned off the road and saw a car pull into a rocky space and stop.

His heart thumping, he waited. The car turned off, the door opened, and he grinned when he saw her step out. She smiled and closed the door.

Jag stood from the bench. "Glad you could make it."

Taking a deep breath and blowing it out, Eleanor walked over to him and widened her eyes at the view. "You weren't kidding. It's beautiful."

"It's one of my favorite places," he said. "Most people hang out here during the day or evening, but I like it when it's just me."

She set her purse down on the bench. "I can see why." The breeze blew and the tendrils around her face fluttered.

"What made you decide to come?"

She shrugged. "I knew I wouldn't be able to sleep. And you seemed like a nice guy, and I haven't met many of those." She glanced sideways at him. "And you're cute."

Jag felt his cheeks warm. "You're pretty cute yourself."

She sat on the bench. "Thank you."

"You're welcome." He sat beside her.

They didn't talk for a minute and Jag enjoyed the moment. He pondered whether his great love story would start with serving a pretty lady in a bar.

"How long do you normally stay out here?" she asked, draping an arm over the back of the bench.

"I don't know. Depends on the night. Thirty minutes? By then, the fatigue sets in and I go home to sleep."

"You ever bring your ex here?"

He shook his head. "No. She's in L.A. Had no interest in coming to San Diego. She's still hoping to hit it big as an actress."

"Good for her. That's a tough gig."

"It is, especially since she's terrible at acting. Can't remember lines to save her life. She got fired from her waitress gig because she couldn't remember the menu."

Eleanor giggled. "Oh, dear."

Jag shifted to face her. "I know."

Eleanor crossed her legs. "Maybe she'll get lucky. Some do, you know."

He nodded. "Some do."

They stared for a moment, and she turned slightly toward him. "You hoping you might get lucky, too?"

Jag chuckled. "It crossed my mind."

She smiled and scooted closer. "It crossed my mind, too. I just don't want you to think I'm the kind of person that meets and makes out with strangers every night."

"Definitely not." His heart thumped faster. "Maybe just once a week."

Her smile grew. "More like once a month."

Jag moved closer. "I can live with that." He looked into her eyes and saw her gaze travel to his mouth. He lowered his head and let his lips graze over hers. The sensation was electric, and he heard her take a breath. "I really like you," he whispered.

"I really like you, too," she whispered back. She pressed her lips against his and the kiss deepened.

He felt her hand on his thigh and he brought his to her cheek, where he cupped her jaw and moved his lips over hers, slow at first, but then the pace picked up. He opened his mouth and their tongues touched. His whole body tingled, and he told himself to go slow, but Eleanor was picking up speed. She slid her hand up his leg and nipped her teeth against his lips. She moved her body closer, and her other hand slid into his hair.

Trying to catch his breath, Jag slid his lips from her mouth and trailed a path to her jaw. He heard her moan and his body responded to the sound. He moved his hand down to her shoulder and then cupped her breast. She gasped and gripped his hip, pulling him close.

She dropped her head back, and he nibbled her ear and kissed her soft skin. "You taste so good," he said between kisses.

Eleanor grasped his hair and pulled him away. She raised her head and stared into his eyes. "I bet you do, too." She kissed him hard, swiveled, and slid her leg over his until she straddled him on the bench. The move thrilled him, and he put his hands on her thighs.

She moaned and rocked her body against his, dragging her mouth from his lips to his throat, where she teased him with her tongue. His heart was thudding so fast, he hoped it wouldn't stop from shock. She ran her hands over his chest, and up to his neck, where she nibbled him. "I want you," she said against his skin.

"I want you, too," he said, although he could barely speak. Everything was happening so fast. He cupped her buttocks with his hands, wanting to yank her clothes off, when she abruptly shot away from him just as he heard an ear-splitting shriek from behind. It penetrated his hazy senses and frightened, Jag stood as she jumped up. A man, bellowing and holding a wicked knife, had swung at them, the blade barely missing Eleanor's head and Jag's face.

Terrified and shocked by the unexpected attack, Jag froze, realizing how close he'd come to dying, and realizing he still might.

The man stood beside the bench in jeans and a dirty t-shirt, holding his long knife and glaring. His muscled shoulders and arms bunched beneath the fabric and his dark and menacing eyes bore into Jag's. Jag didn't know what to do. He was too scared to move. Eleanor stood still and didn't speak or scream. She simply glared back.

Jag raised a hand. "Lis...listen. We don't want any trouble. Ju...Just leave us alone." His breath came in short gasps.

The man took a step closer, and Jag stepped away. Eleanor didn't move. "Go," said the man, in a gravelly voice.

Jag assumed he spoke to Eleanor. "Run to the trees. I'll try and fight him off while you get help." He didn't think for a second he could defeat this man, but he wouldn't sacrifice Eleanor to save himself.

"He's not talking to me," said Eleanor.

The man waved his free hand toward Jag. "Go. Now. And don't return."

Jag looked between the man and Eleanor, not understanding. "What?"

"I said go," screamed the man, his face stern.

His tone and volume broke through Jag's fear, and since Eleanor made no effort to do anything but glare, Jag ran.

His adrenaline propelled him down the dusty road. On his right was the steep embankment and on his left was the pebbled road that led from the street, where he'd parked, down to the overlook. If he could get up it and back to his car, he could call for help if he could stop shaking long enough to use his phone. Running as fast as he could, he debated going back. He'd left Eleanor alone with a crazy man and his knife. She would be murdered, and Jag would be the loser who'd let it happen. For a second, he almost slowed and turned around, when he heard a guttural yell which morphed into a shriek, and then a terrible gut-wrenching wail that abruptly stopped.

His terror ramping up further, Jag forced himself to run faster. The loose rocks made his feet skip and slide and he almost fell. Gasping for air, he could see his car and raced toward it.

Hearing a scraping sound and what sounded like rapid footsteps behind him, he had the horrifying feeling he was being followed. Something was chasing him. Too terrified to look behind him, he scrambled up the small hill, praying to get to his vehicle in time. His feet slid and he fell forward but righted himself. Desperate, he heard whimpering and realized it was him.

Reaching his car, he felt a small kernel of hope that he might survive this, when something slammed against him from behind. His body was thrown into his car with a hard thump and another blow sent him over the hood. His mind and body went numb. After hitting the pavement, his vision spun. His legs wouldn't move and although he wanted to scream, nothing emerged. And then it was on him, and helpless to stop it, he was dragged into the brush.

Enjoy an excerpt from Of Love and Loss, Book Six in the Detectives Daniels and Remalla Series

"ARE YOU SERIOUS?" ASKED Harry. A thin oily strand of hair fell in his face, and he brushed it back. "You're talking about a cop and a former cop. You want the entire force after you?"

Margaret Redstone smiled, her intense blue eyes twinkling in the light of the room. "The whole force is already after me. What's the difference?"

Frank Winston Monk observed the exchange and eyed the sniveling man sitting across from him. Two other men sat at the table, but neither of them said a word. Perhaps because they knew who they were dealing with and how pointless objecting would be.

"The difference is things have settled down." Harry pointed a finger and Monk almost smiled at the show of rebellion. "Staying out of sight keeps you under the radar. Something like this..." he waved a hand, "it's suicide."

Margaret stared, her eyes unblinking and Monk sensed her underlying tension. He almost felt sorry for Harry. "Are you saying you won't do it?" asked Monk.

Harry went quiet but then looked at his buddies. "C'mon, guys. You seriously think this is a good idea?" He interlaced his fingers and his knuckles turned white with his grip.

Terence, a black man with short cut hair and pearly white teeth, shrugged. "If she says do it, then we do it."

Curtis, his jaw unshaved, frowned and the scar across his right cheek deepened. "What's the big deal, man?" He scratched at one of his bulging shoulders that stretched the fabric of his t-shirt. "These guys have it coming."

Harry scoffed. "Are you crazy?"

Margaret glanced at Monk. "Winnie?" she asked. She'd called him Winnie since the first night they'd met, and he'd told her his middle name. "Thoughts?"

Monk sighed. "It's a solid plan." He tipped his head at Harry. "I like it, but if you think you can't handle it..." he gestured toward the door "...feel free to leave."

Harry, whose forehead began to shine with sweat, hesitated. "I just don't see the point. These guys are old news. You've left them alone this long, so why not longer?" He spoke to Margaret. "Hell, you could go anywhere. Why not disappear? Lay low. Take it easy. You've already scared the shit out of them once, plus what you did to your brother and sister. You ended up back in the news for a while, but now it's calming down again." He shook his head. "And you want to do this?"

Margaret didn't answer but her look spoke volumes.

"You'll have every man in a uniform out looking for blood. And not just for you." Harry patted himself in the chest. "Us, too."

"The boss says we do it, so we do it," said Terrance.

"And we ain't going to get caught," said Curtis. "Stop being such a pussy."

"Watch the name calling, Curtis," said Margaret. "Harry is allowed to express his opinion. I can respect that." She aimed her gaze at Harry. "You've understood my motives from the start. This is not news to you. I will follow through whether you agree with the plan nor not." She paused. "Everyone here is on board except you. Like Winnie said, either jump on or get off. It's up to you."

Harry's gaze darted among the group at the table. The sheen of sweat on his brow shined brighter. "When would we do this?"

"I'm not sure," said Margaret. "But when the time is right, I'll be in touch, and it will be imperative that you act quickly and do exactly what I ask. After today, there are no more questions. Either do as I say or suffer the ramifications."

Watching her, Monk admired Margaret's ability to say so little but yet communicate so much. Her body language had remained relaxed but the energy exuding from her had intensified. It filled the room and was probably why Harry was sweating so much.

"Well, Harry?" asked Margaret.

"Are you even capable of this?" asked Monk. "You came recommended but I'm wondering if you're up for the job."

Harry's face tightened. "I can do it. I just wasn't expecting the cop part." He set his jaw and glared at Monk. "If you think it's so easy, why don't you do it?"

Monk held Harry's look. "You think I haven't before?" He leaned in and lowered his voice. "Watch your assumptions, Harry."

Margaret narrowed her eyes. "Winnie has his own responsibilities, which are not your concern."

Harry broke his gaze with Monk and leaned back in his seat. "We do this and we get out of town?"

"With a handsome payday," said Margaret. "I reward those who are loyal to me."

"Did that include Oswald?" asked Harry.

Monk marveled at Harry's stupidity. "Watch it, Harry."

Margaret's only reaction was to raise the side of her lip. "Oswald was dying anyway, and he acted against my wishes. He chose his own demise." She paused. "You're welcome to do the same, Harry. Would you like to choose your own demise?" Her tone suggested she was done arguing.

Harry was smart enough to sense the same. "I was just messing around." He made a snort. "Someone needs to lighten the mood."

Terrence shook his head. "Put up or shut up, man. What's it going to be?"

"I say he's out," said Curtis. "The guy's stalling too much."

Harry held up a hand. "Just hold your horses." He put his hand down. "Jeez. Everybody's so uptight." He sighed. "Fine. I'm in."

Monk focused in on the man across from him, sensing his honesty.

"You're sure?" asked Margaret. "You'll do exactly as I ask, without questioning or second guessing? You'll act when I say?"

Harry hesitated, but then smiled. "Whatever you say goes, boss." He tapped a finger on the table. "You can count on me."

Monk studied him and knew the truth. He sat back, leaned close to Margaret, and whispered in her ear. "He's lying."

Margaret offered a small grin but didn't respond to Monk. "Terrence. Curtis. I need to talk to you about what's next. Harry. You're free to go. Just stay by the phone. When I need you, I'll call."

"You sure?" asked Harry. He waved a hand toward Terrence and Curtis. "I can help these guys out with whatever you need."

Margaret shook her head. "Your presence is no longer required, You've committed. Now all I want you to do is wait, so go do that." She paused. "Now."

Harry dragged a long-sleeved arm across his forehead, wiping the sweat from his brow. "I hope you didn't take offense to my—"

"Are you deaf?" asked Monk. "Get the hell out of here."

Harry stiffened but then grabbed his Raiders baseball cap off the back of the chair and put it on his head. He slid out of his seat and stood. "I'll be waiting for your call."

"Good," said Margaret. "I hope you're a patient man."

Harry opened his mouth but then seemed to think twice about whatever he was going to say. "I am."

"Glad to hear it," said Margaret.

Monk leaned and whispered to her again. "He's still lying."

"I know," she said.

Harry said his goodbyes, walked to the front door, and left the house.

"That guy's a loser," said Curtis.

"You sure about him?" asked Terrence. "I know he's helped you out in the past, but—"

"He's lying to us," repeated Monk. "He can't be trusted."

"I knew it," said Curtis. "Guy's probably on his way to the airport, or worse."

Margaret tilted her head. "Maybe, but not yet. He's thinking about it though." She reached over and put her hand over Terrence's. "It's a good thing I have you two to help me out though."

She glanced at Curtis, who grinned back. Terrence smiled, too.

"Can I count on you to take care of it?" asked Margaret.

"With pleasure," said Curtis.

"Happy to help," said Terrence. "I never liked that guy anyway."

"You sure about this?" asked Monk. "This could attract the wrong attention."

"Winnie," said Margaret. "You worry too much." She sat back in her seat with a satisfied look on her face. "This might even work in our favor." She glanced out the window. "That tends to happen a lot with me."

"I've noticed," said Monk. It amazed him how many lives the woman had. No matter what risks she took, she always came out on top. She'd been free after an escape from a psychiatric unit for almost eight months without even a suspicious glance or a report to the police.

An orange cat jumped up on the table and nuzzled Margaret's arm. "Hello, Chester," said Margaret, petting the animal's head.

"I hate cats," said Curtis with a scowl. He swiped a hand across the table. "They get hair on everything."

Margaret displayed the first sign of obvious irritation. "Would you like to take Harry's place, Curtis? I can arrange that."

Curtis straightened and paled. "Just ignore me, boss. Sometimes I speak first and think later."

Terrence made a disgusted face at Curtis and shook his head.

Margaret rubbed Chester's ears. "Sounds like someone else I know." She sighed. "I'm looking forward to getting reacquainted."

Monk knew exactly who she was referring to. He couldn't help but wonder why she had a thing for the former detective. Monk found him irritating and would have killed him at the first opportunity, but he kept his opinion to himself.

The three men stared while the cat purred and leaned into Margaret's hand. "Why are you still sitting here?" she asked Curtis and Terrence. "You have a job to do."

Curtis and Terrence glanced at each other and stood. "Any particular way you want it done?" asked Terrence.

Margaret smiled. "Surprise me."

Curtis nodded. "You got it." He smacked Terrence on the back. "Let's go."

"When you're done with that," said Monk, "lay low and wait for the next assignment." He fiddled with the edge of his sleeve. "And I'll be in touch with the money."

"Anything else?" asked Terrence.

"Just have fun," said Margaret. "There's no need to be so glum."

Monk chuckled. "You heard the lady."

Curtis and Terrence slid their chairs in, said their goodbyes and left.

Monk watched them leave. "You sure that's the best way to handle Harry?"

Margaret picked up Chester. "It's the only way to handle Harry. He's served his purpose. It's time to cut him loose."

Monk scratched one of Chester's ears. "He's cute."

"He's a she."

Monk frowned but didn't ask the obvious. "Somehow, I'm not surprised." He eyed the kitchen and considered a shot of something strong. "What do you want me to do?"

"What you do best. Tell me what I need to know."

Monk nodded. "I can do that."

"Curtis and Terrence," she said. "You still sense their honesty?"

"I do. They'll do exactly what you want. They'll go down with the ship if they have to."

Margaret smiled. "Good." She held Chester against her chest. "When they're done with Harry, we'll discuss when to make the first move."

"Have you decided what that is?"

The cat purred and jumped out of Margaret's arms. "I have." She leaned forward, wiped some cat hair from her shirt, and rested her elbows on the table. "We'll start where he works...at the zoo."

Made in the USA
Monee, IL
18 March 2023